By Steven Gore

FINAL TARGET
ABSOLUTE RISK

D0019171

ABSOLUTE
RISK

STEVEN
GORE

HARPER

An Imprint of HarperCollins*Publishers*

HARPER

An Imprint of HarperCollins*Publishers*
10 East 53rd Street
New York, New York 10022-5299

Copyright © 2010 by Steven Gore
ISBN 978-0-06-178220-6

First Harper paperback printing: November 2010

HarperCollins® and Harper® are registered trademarks of Harper-Collins Publishers.

Printed in the United States of America

Visit Harper paperbacks on the World Wide Web at
www.harpercollins.com

10 9 8 7 6 5 4 3 2 1

For my dad,
Victor M. Gore.
He was a sweetheart of a man.

ABSOLUTE
RISK

tonement.

Michael Hennessy felt the shadow of the Basilique Notre Dame de la Garde enfold him like the unadorned robe of a novice monk, a fortress against evil and a refuge against sin. He stood behind the parapet of the neo-Byzantine church and stared down at Marseilles, its brick and stone, its white walls and terracotta rooftops, its chaos of steep steps and angled streets, all softening and fading to gray in the dying light of the winter evening.

As he gazed over the city, the variegated blue Mediterranean darkened to cobalt and the streetlights brightened, restoring solidity to the apartments and offices and monuments that spread out from the limestone hill beneath him toward the distant port.

He blinked hard against the breeze tearing his eyes, and then glanced at his watch: fifty-five minutes left. And his mind spoke again.

Atonement.

But this time the word resonated and he wondered why it came to him now and what it meant.

Then his mind asked, *Can there be atonement without confession and redemption without forgiveness?*

He twisted his head upward toward the golden statue of the Virgin Mary atop the bell tower, but then realized that it wasn't a religious question, for no saint could grant the absolution he sought, nor could there be reconciliation by proxy. It had to be done face-to-face, hand-to-hand, and man-to-man.

But where was that man?

Nausea waved through him. His muscles tensed. His jaw clenched. It was less a question than an accusation, one that over the years had left gouges in him like self-inflicted wounds that never healed, but only bled and bled into a vast emptiness.

Where ... was ... that ... man?

Hennessy's vision blurred. He saw the face of Professor Hani Ibrahim hovering before him, the same wide and disbelieving eyes as when he'd first displayed his FBI identification at the door of Ibrahim's MIT office, snapped on the handcuffs, booked him into the detention center, and then walked him past news cameras into federal court for his arraignment.

As Hennessy watched what he knew was nothing but the projected face of his own guilt, the economist's brows furrowed, and his pupils contracted into a stare, and then into a glare of accusation.

The image perished in a mortar burst of floodlights that exploded around him, turning night into artificial noon. Stripped of the shadow's protection, Hennessy imagined crosshairs marking the front of his trench coat and a distant figure steadying a barrel and squeezing a trigger.

He bolted down the zigzagging marble steps and

ducked under the pedestrian bridge. But even as he bent over to catch his breath, with blood hammering at his temples and the frozen air biting at his throat, he cringed at his paranoia: Not everything worth dying for is worth killing for.

Hennessy crept to the shadow's edge, where he obtained a view of the Vieux Port, fifteen hundred yards away. The building façades glowed yellow, orange, and purple in the lights reflecting off the water. He pulled binoculars from his coat pocket and scanned the bordering streets, his shoulder braced against a granite wall, afraid to blink, taking long, slow breaths to keep the lenses steady.

One minute passed, then two or five. The time seemed discontinuous, measured not by the watch on his wrist, but by a mental clock that pulsated with fear, guilt, and shame, and with the hope that the man he came to meet would find a way to meet him.

Hennessy wondered what excuse Federal Reserve Chairman Milton Abrams would give for his late arrival at the French president's dinner, and whether it would be inert enough that it wouldn't draw to him the intelligence services that enveloped the International Economic Forum like an invisible chemical cloud.

A procession of limousines emerged from the gap-toothed head of the port, down from the four-lane La Canebiere and from the direction of the Old Stock Exchange a block away that had hosted the Forum.

No. Not a procession. Just two. He'd seen more than what was there: If there were two, then there had to be—there had to be—twelve or twenty following behind, and one of those would be Abrams's.

But there wasn't.

Chance had once again imposed an order that didn't exist, and self-doubt vibrated through him, for it had been this same trick of mind that made him see a crime nine years earlier where one hadn't occurred and made him accuse an innocent man.

Where . . . was . . . that . . . man?

What had the secretary of defense called it in his speech to him and the other members of the FBI Antiterrorism Task Force?

"The prism of 9/11."

Except Hennessy had realized too late that it hadn't been a prism, it had been a mirror, or maybe a kaleidoscope in which every turn displayed the same pattern to men predisposed to see it.

He'd been one of those men, and now he trusted no one, not even himself.

As he stared out at the brilliant city, he wondered whether what he really wanted from Abrams wasn't help in righting a wrong and in averting a disaster, but only someone to bear witness to his sanity.

Another minute. Or three. Or six.

Moving black specks slid across the unified frame of his binoculars' lenses. More limousines. They headed west toward the water, then swung south along the Quai, a gravitational force seeming to link them in position, invisible strings, mysterious and unbreakable, threading through the chaos of traffic and beyond the reach of his tightening hands.

The last nine years of his life condensed into this instant. His breathing stopped. He felt his eyes turn catlike, lids tensed open, surfaces drying in the wind.

One of the limousines spun away, north into the woven

alleys of La Panier, the Basket—Abrams had broken free.

Hennessy's eyelids shut and his held breath exploded. He pushed up his sleeve and looked down. The glowing face of his watch marked the remaining time: forty minutes to drive across town to the North African restaurant where the chairman would be waiting.

Hennessy slid along the foundation wall behind him until he could look down the dark hillside. Gray-scaled shadows between the trees and bushes tunneled toward streetlights below and marked the path toward his car.

A medieval gloom met him as he left the concrete curtilage of the church and descended into the obscurity of the forest. He sidestepped down into the blackness, reaching for branches and boulders, counting his steps, trying to impose a rhythm on his staccatoed pace.

His right shoe lost purchase. His spine wrenched as he jerked backward. Arms flailing, body twisting, tumbling through shrubs, sliding—sliding—sliding, and thudding against a tree trunk.

And silence.

Wings fluttered. A dog barked. Car tires squealed below.

Pain in his hip overwhelmed feeling in his arms and legs. Then hot panic. A terror of paralysis. Pinned to the earth and condemned to watch the hourglass of his hope for redemption drain away.

He clenched his teeth and hardened his body against the throbbing, and then rolled onto his stomach.

An image displayed itself on the screen of darkness: him walking vagrantlike, scraped and soiled, through the restaurant entrance. The chairman gazing up at him in disgust and in self-reproach for having agreed to meet with a lunatic, then pushing back from the table and striding out through the door and escaping back into his limousine.

Hennessy felt for his notebook and cell phone, his palm resting for a moment on each as if over his heart. He then struggled to his knees and fingered the wet ground around him to discern whether anything had fallen from his pockets. After finding nothing, he rose and leaned against a pine and wiped his hands on its needles. He couldn't risk another fall, so he covered his eyes with his palms and tried to force them to adjust to the dark.

His heavy breath drew in the smell of resin, bringing back memories of where his journey had begun almost a decade earlier, hiding in the Fisher Hill woods in Brookline, Massachusetts, watching his target and the men gathering around him, the professor's house seeming more like a mosque than a home, and the special agent in charge encouraging him, pressuring him, whispering in his ear, "Get this guy. It'll make your career."

When Hennessy opened his eyes again, the blackness around him had grayed and a route reappeared.

A rush of vertigo shook him as he looked down. He grabbed the pine again to steady himself. When it passed, he descended, hoping to arrive on the street below near where he'd parked his car.

Twenty yards farther down, he emerged into a meadow. He covered one eye to protect its night vision, and looked over his shoulder at the glowing Madonna statue. He used it to approximate a path and then angled to his left until he reached the edge of the pavement. He crouched behind a bush and peeked out; first left, then right. A cat hissed at the darkness between him and his car twenty yards away. His body realized his miscalculation before his mind, and it pulled him back.

Someone was lying in wait.

Hennessy scanned the rooftop at the near end of the three-story apartment building across the road. A light blinked. Movement against the bright city. He made out the silhouette of a raised head. It rotated like a periscope and then lowered.

The hourglass again began to drain. Thirty minutes left. It was a twenty-five-minute drive and now no car to take him. The nearest taxi would be on Boulevard Notre Dame, two blocks away, but the shortest route wasn't a straight line. Instead, it was a looping route through woods that would take him only to a connecting street.

Rushed and panicked by the clash of time and distance, he stripped off his trench coat, balled it up, and jammed it into a shrub. Even if it wasn't muddy, it would've served as a bull's-eye, for it had been his uniform during the last frozen weeks.

He paralleled the curving street, then slipped into the trees on the opposite side and followed a path behind the buildings. Lights cast from the windows above him made a twisted chessboard of the uneven trail. His ankles wobbled and his wrenched back ached. He steadied himself for a few seconds against a stucco wall, then pushed himself forward.

Against the background of kitchen noises and televisions and the distant rumble of traffic, Hennessy heard a couple arguing in Arabic. It seemed to echo, not off other buildings, but rather from across the reflecting surface of the Mediterranean, from Algiers, where he'd spent ten days looking for Ibrahim.

The voices jerked his thoughts out of the present, and for a moment he felt the vertigo of waking up in a hotel room and not knowing what country he was in. Then the mirrored images of the two cities triangulated his position; not fixed, but seeming to move in pace with a receding mirage.

He paused and listened for footsteps behind him, thinking how close he thought he'd come to finding Ibrahim in Algiers, only to discover that he'd followed a false scent, one that had taken him through merchant-mobbed streets and burrowlike alleys, and finally out to the universities in Ben Aknoun, El-Biar, and Bouzareah. Days spent watching the entrances to the faculties of economics, only to be met with the emptiness of failure.

Even now, as he readied himself to emerge from the shadows, he didn't know who'd dragged that scent through that city, only that it had vanished like wind-blown smoke.

He glanced at his watch and then shielded his eyes as he stepped into the glare of the light-polished street to hail a cab. A quivering in his chest upwelled into a surge of self-doubt, and with it the dread that the scent he'd followed had been of his own manufacture and that it would now lead him, if not into the crosshairs of an unknown enemy, into an abyss of his own design.

CHAPTER 1

San Francisco private investigator Graham Gage handed his Rollaboard to the chauffeur, and then climbed into the backseat of the Town Car stopped at the slick and frozen curb in front of terminal one at John F. Kennedy Airport.

"Thanks for coming out," Federal Reserve Chairman Milton Abrams said, the words emerging as a sigh. "Sorry I was so cryptic on the phone. The flight must've felt like a red-eye into the unknown." Abrams made a show of surveying the solid shoulders on Gage's six-foot-two frame. "And a cramped one at that."

Gage inspected Abrams's face. He found it difficult to make out beneath the lined and sagging flesh the academic who'd first sought him out two decades earlier. Back then, as an assistant professor of finance at MIT, Abrams had viewed economics as a form of play, mathematics as a form of poetry, and algorithms as a form of magic. While his days had been spent in intellectual combat and in a struggle for mainframe time, he celebrated his nights in a dream world of weightless possibilities and of ambition without responsibility.

But that game had come to an end six months earlier, with his appointment by the president and his confirmation by the Senate. Now he resided in a nightless world of twenty-four-hour securities markets and currency speculation, of war and terrorism, of human-made and natural disasters, all of which bore down on him at sub-atomic speed and seemed to have etched away his youth.

As the car accelerated away from the curb, Gage glanced out of the window at the line of just-arrived passengers standing in the taxi queue, shielding their eyes against the rising sun, stark and brilliant in a blue sky that had been unmasked by the overnight passing of a January blizzard.

"I shouldn't be doing this," Abrams said. "If the press finds out, I'll look like an utter lunatic."

"I'm not sure they're paying attention to Michael Hennessy anymore," Gage said, looking over. "He was at the center of only a single news cycle. It was pretty small in diameter and it's already a week old."

The only coverage of Hennessy's death that Gage had found was a local story in *Metro Marseilles* and in Hennessy's hometown paper: Former FBI agent found dead. Suicide suspected.

In the *Albany Times Union*, the special agent in charge had referred to Hennessy's life as a train wreck that they'd been helpless to stop. It seemed to Gage that he wasn't at all grief-stricken by the tragedy. His tone had suggested a kind of relief, as though a disturbing episode for Hennessy, for the Bureau, and perhaps for Hennessy's family, had come to an end.

Abrams mumbled what sounded to Gage like lines from a poem as they drove from the airport grounds and onto the Van Wyck Expressway toward Manhattan.

"Was that intended for me?" Gage asked.

Abrams half smiled and repeated the words. Gage recognized their source in the Old Testament:

"*I know that for my sake this great tempest is upon you . . . So they took up Jonah, and cast him forth into the sea.*"

"Which means that you don't believe Michael Hennessy killed himself," Gage said.

Abrams shook his head. "No one works as hard as he did to convince me to meet with him, only to devise a creative way to do himself in."

Gage had seen too many people flinch or pivot or self-destruct just short of their goal to find the argument convincing. Humans didn't run on a track like the Staten Island Railway. Decades as a police officer and as a private investigator had taught him that humans were a maze of intersecting thoughts, motives, and fears, any one of which could lead them into the abyss of a life not worth living and then over the edge toward homicide or suicide.

"After Hennessy first contacted me," Abrams said. "I called the deputy director of the FBI. He told me that Hennessy had been fired because they considered him obsessed and delusional."

"Then why'd you agree to meet with him?"

"It was something my assistant said. She has an undergraduate degree in psychology and did her economics dissertation on Adam Smith's *Theory of Moral Sentiments.* She told me that delusional people chase phantoms around inside their own heads or within their own neighborhoods, they don't pursue them overseas. And the first time Hennessy called he said he was in China."

Gage shrugged. "Unless believing he was there was part of his delusion."

Abrams shook his head. "Evidence showed up on my cell phone bill as an incoming call from a local Shanghai number. And the second time it was from Dubai, and the third from Algeria. And he never sounded nuts. Not paranoid. Not thinking that people were out to get him—"

"Or at least shrewd enough not to say it aloud."

"I don't think that's it," Abrams said. "He just sounded guilty, genuinely ashamed of himself. Desperate for my help in making up for what he'd done to Hani Ibrahim."

Although Gage hadn't remembered Michael Hennessy's name when Abrams called the day before, he did recall the FBI's arrest of Ibrahim for a terrorist financing conspiracy. Ibrahim had been a financial mathematician who'd come to MIT a few years before Abrams had moved on to Harvard. He masterminded a scheme for funneling money from within the U.S. to foreign terrorist groups by using offshore trusts and charities. No criminal case was ever proven, but he was nonetheless deported.

"At some point," Abrams said, "when, I don't know—how, I don't know—and why, I don't know, Hennessy began to suspect that Ibrahim had been framed."

"You mean that Hennessy participated in framing him."

Abrams nodded. "But not knowingly. Or at least that was Hennessy's claim."

Gage thought back to the few years after 9/11, and asked, "Was Ibrahim simply deported, or was he flown to a country where a stronger case against him could be developed through torture?"

"I don't know, but I got the sense that the rendition possibility figured into Hennessy's desperation. The first time I spoke to him, he seemed to be at the opposite end of the exhilaration he'd displayed after Ibrahim's arrest. I remember the photo. Him standing behind the director at a press conference in Washington, basking in the glory. It was his career case. He got a promotion to senior special agent and was made second in command of the FBI's Anti-terrorism Task Force."

"Where was he on the arc the last time you spoke to him?"

"More toward the bottom, but with a feeling of hope. He told me that he had reason to think that Ibrahim was still alive."

Abrams fell silent. Gage watched his eyes narrow as though he was looking into the tunnel of the past.

"I don't know about the present condition of Ibrahim's mind or body," Abrams finally said, "but his reputation hasn't suffered much in the long run. I imagine that if the Swedes could find him now, they'd probably give him the Nobel Prize in economics."

Even though Gage's practice focused on finance from the perspective of fraud and money laundering, he was familiar with Ibrahim's work. And in the years since his disappearance, Ibrahim and his quantum theory of finance had achieved mythological, Janus-faced status, with his name either issued as an epithet or whispered in awe. His fame rested on a few papers he'd published twenty years earlier, when he was in his thirties, and on claims by a few large hedge funds, known as chaos funds, that they invested and traded based on his theories.

"I suspect that if he'd stayed in physics rather than moving into finance," Abrams said, "he would've gotten the Nobel in that and he'd still be puttering away at MIT instead of . . ."

"Instead of what?"

Abrams shrugged and stared at the road ahead. "I don't have a clue. Maybe Hennessy knew."

Gage circled back to the call from Abrams that brought him from San Francisco to New York.

"I don't see what any of this has to do with you," Gage said. "I haven't read your job description, but I'm sure it doesn't include rectifying nine-year-old presumed wrongs committed by the Justice Department."

"That assumes that I was Hennessy's first choice." Abrams glanced back at Gage. "I wasn't. He'd already tried the CIA and the head of the European Central Bank and who knows who else. They all turned him away after recommending that he have his head examined. That's why he wanted to meet with me. He wanted to prove by his manner and his presentation that he wasn't crazy. He saw on the news that I'd be in Marseilles for a central bankers' meeting, and called me at home one night and—"

"How did he get your number?"

Abrams shrugged again. "I don't know. Other than my assistant, only the secretary of the treasury and the president were supposed to have it. That's part of the reason I called the FBI. They promised to do an investigation, but never followed through, or at least didn't give me the results. In any case, Hennessy said he'd be somewhere along the Mediterranean at the same time as the conference. The deal was that I would give him fifteen minutes in person at a restaurant in the Oliviers District—"

"That's crazy. It's a drug-infested—"

"But not a place where anyone would recognize the Federal Reserve chairman."

Gage shook his head. "It was just substituting one danger for another."

Abrams dismissed the thought with a wave of his hand. "No damage done. He promised to lay out his case and then leave it to me whether I wanted to pursue it."

"But he didn't show up. Instead he jumped off a cliff."

"Or was spit out."

Gage turned toward Abrams. "I don't understand why you think he's a modern-day Jonah. He could've just as easily decided that he'd made a fool of himself, or that he'd deluded himself for a second time, and couldn't face going home."

"That was the theory of the local police, that he'd come to the end of his rope. Encouraged no doubt in that conclusion by the FBI's claim that he was crazy and by the fact that diving headfirst onto the rocks along the Côte d'Azur isn't an unusual way to do yourself in. The area is Marseilles' version of the Golden Gate Bridge."

Gage recognized that the logic also worked the opposite way: What better way to disguise a murder than as a suicide, but there was still the question of motive and whether it had anything to do with Abrams.

"Did the Marseilles police know that he was there to meet you?" Gage asked.

Abrams shook his head. "I couldn't take the risk—the U.S. couldn't take the risk—of having my name connected with Hennessy's, at least until I knew whether he had told me the truth." Abrams spread his hands. "What do you think would happen in the markets if the press put out a story that I had engaged in some sort of mind-meld with a lunatic?"

Gage looked up to see that they were now heading due west, the midtown skyline and Manhattan rising in the distance against the now graying sky, the city seeming less like a destination than a way station, for he knew that Abrams hadn't asked him to come to New York just for a talk.

"Did you contact the FBI again after his body was discovered," Gage asked, "and try to find out the backstory?"

"I left a vague message for the deputy director." Abrams paused, and then glanced over at Gage. "But it was the director himself who returned my call."

CHAPTER 2

He didn't get on a flight," the caller spoke into his cell phone. "Just picked up a tall, middle-aged guy near the taxi stand outside of terminal one. I'm about a hundred yards behind him on the Long Island Expressway heading toward the city."

Kenyon Arndt hunched over his desk in the fifty-sixth-floor office of Shadden Phillips & Wycovsky. It was an involuntary motion, like his whole being, mind and body, had cringed at the thought of what he was doing. He whispered his response, even though his door was closed.

"Did you get a photo?"

"We're not amateurs, Mr. Arndt. I'll e-mail them to you when they get wherever they're going. Maybe you'll recognize him."

Arndt felt as though he was standing in quicksand just deep enough to trap him, but not deep enough to suck him under. He didn't know who their client was or why he wanted the chairman of the Federal Reserve followed. And in a sleepless week of nightmares and night sweats, he'd thought of lots of reasons a client might want it done, but none that was legitimate for a law firm to pursue.

If Abrams had committed a crime, then the FBI should be doing it.

If Abrams had leaked insider Fed information about interest adjustments or corporate bailouts to the financial community, then the FBI and the SEC should be doing it.

If he had sold out the country to foreign interests, then the FBI and the CIA and the NSA should be doing it—not Shadden Phillips & Wycovsky. Not three floors of the whitest of white collars and the blackest of three-button suits.

What Arndt did think of were all the nauseating consequences of public exposure: disbarment, embarrassment, maybe even federal prison. He'd even be disavowed by the rest of the members of his Yale Law School graduating class—not for doing it, he knew, but for getting caught.

"Are you sure you won't lose him?" Arndt asked.

"No chance. We have, shall we say, an electronic means of tracking his car."

"Isn't that—"

The man laughed. "Creative?"

"I was going to say illegal."

"Seems to me that you're getting paid a bundle to find a way to argue it isn't. *Capisci?*"

Arndt felt his palm perspiring against the receiver. He'd known only one other person who'd used the correct Italian for "you understand." He had been a mafioso who'd lived across the street when Arndt was growing up on Long Island—that is, until the gangster was found sitting in the driver's seat of his car in his garage with a bullet hole in the back of his head.

"Yes," Arndt said. "I understand."

Arndt set down the receiver, and then wiped his hands on his pants in what felt like a gesture of cleansing. He leaned forward to rise from his chair, but his childhood nightmare of the neighbor's chunks of exploded skull and brain crusted on the dashboard rose up in his mind. A wave of nausea rolled his body forward. He rested his forehead on his folded arms, sweat beading and his mouth watering.

After it passed, he straightened up and wiped his face with his shirt sleeve. He then pushed himself to his feet, shrugged on his suit jacket, and made the long walk down the wood-paneled hallway toward the office of Edward Wycovsky, the senior partner in the thirty-two-attorney firm, who was awaiting his report.

Arndt's hands dampened again before he reached Wycovsky's door. They began to vibrate, not just in fear, but in frustration and anger. A cold shockwave shot up his arms and into his chest. He felt his fingers tightening into fists and imagined himself walking around Wycovsky's desk and flattening the man's angular nose into his pockmarked face.

But not yet, Arndt told himself. He needed to stay with the firm and with this assignment long enough to discover what they were up to, and then turn them in.

A glance at the distant reception station at the center of the two wings of the floor restarted the drama in his mind. Him standing there watching the FBI lead Wycovsky and the others toward the elevators and then down to the lobby where news video cameras would seek out their pale rat faces. He'd follow them and watch them duck their heads behind their cuffed hands and he'd watch people crowded on the sidewalk leaning hard against the police lines and shaking their fists and screaming out their outrage and—

But he knew these fantasies were nothing but imaginary flight, relative to nothing and anchored to air—for that was his character: honest enough to recognize his self-deceptions, but too weak to act on the knowledge. That's why his wife had once told him that the law was the perfect profession for him. It was all form, and no substance; all talk, and no responsibility. And she was right. Even the bar's code of ethics had read to him like a permission slip to do evil without shame or guilt.

As he approached Wycovsky's office, Arndt steeled himself against the reality of his role and the roles of the other Ivy League graduates with whom Wycovsky had jeweled the firm: They were nothing but gemmed pendants hanging from a whore's neck.

Wycovsky raised a forefinger as Arndt entered the office, holding him at attention while he completed his telephone call with a cryptic "Then we understand each other." He lowered his right hand as he hung up the phone with his left and looked over at Arndt.

"We don't accuse the private investigators we retain to assist us of engaging in criminality," Wycovsky said.

Arndt reddened.

"We only hire professionals and we rely on them to act within the law—and we don't second-guess them."

"I didn't think we'd want to risk—" Arndt caught himself, for he realized that this was exactly the risk Wycovsky had been willing to take.

Wycovsky didn't respond, his silence pressuring Arndt to finish the sentence.

"I mean, I thought we should make sure we were on solid legal ground."

Wycovsky waved the argument away. "Do you ask Acme Plumbing whether their corporate filings are in order before you hire them to fix a leak? Do you ask to look at your bank's cash reserves before you write a check?"

Arndt clenched his jaw and shook his head.

Wycovsky never argued facts or law; he crushed his opponents by analogy. It was a form of argumentation ridiculed at Yale, but encouraged at the street fighters' law school that Wycovsky had attended at night forty years earlier.

"Don't question the surveillance people," Wycovsky said. "Just write down what they tell you and report to me." He pointed at Arndt's face. "I don't want to receive another call like this again."

Arndt's emotions battered at him as he walked back to his office. Anger. Fear. Self-reproach. And him defenseless, straitjacketed by the life he'd chosen. Twenty-eight years old and confined to the debtors prison of Shadden Phillips & Wycovsky by mortgage and credit card balances that he was permitted by his bank to carry only because greed had made him accept the most lucrative offer after law school, not the best.

And what tore at him most of all as he paused in the doorway to his office was why it hadn't crossed his mind why Wycovsky had been willing to pay partners' wages for associates' work—

Until right then.

was so preoccupied that I forgot to ask about your wife," Abrams said, sitting across from Gage at the breakfast table in his Central Park West apartment.

"Faith is fine. She took a team of students to Sichuan Province to work on an archeological dig."

Abrams frowned. "Isn't that a little dangerous? We're getting reports of labor riots from Guangzhou all the way up to Mongolia."

"They're in a village way out in the countryside. They only stopped in Shanghai to change planes and in Chengdu just long enough to get on a chartered bus." Gage tapped the cell phone in his shirt pocket. "She calls every few days."

Abrams reached over to the kitchen counter, spread out a stack of Federal Reserve finance and economic discussion papers, and handed one of them to Gage titled "Human Capital in China."

"There are a hundred million migrant laborers over there," Abrams said. "Another ten million added in the last year. Fleeing farms that can't produce even enough to support the villages around them. An average wage of fifty cents a day, and their life expectancy is dropping as though the Chinese economy was collapsing instead of expanding." He pointed at the cover. "If all the little wildfires come together, there'll be a conflagration. I'd hate to see her caught in the middle of it."

"Given the places I've spent my career," Gage said, "I'm not in a position to issue warnings." Even though he knew that there were many times when he wished he was. But that was between him and Faith alone.

Abrams rose and retrieved the coffeepot and refilled their cups.

"You're a tougher man than me." Abrams paused and gazed out of the window down toward Central Park. "I was afraid even to let Jeanine jog around the reservoir." He shrugged and offered a weak smile. "Maybe that's why she ran away altogether."

"Have you heard from her lately?"

"Not since I was appointed chairman. Not even an e-mail after I was confirmed."

Gage didn't have to ask why. He knew Jeanine well enough to understand that for her it was like Abrams had become the high priest of a materialistic religion that, in words she'd written to Faith, reduced hope and fear to matters of cash value. And it wasn't that Jeanine had become a new age mystic. It was that she could no longer see the man she'd married under the vestments of his office or hear the voice that had once known how to speak in words other than data.

"Has she filed for a divorce?" Gage asked.

Abrams shook his head. "And I haven't either."

Gage wondered whether Abrams's anxiety over the

twisted life of Michael Hennessy was an unconscious attempt to prove to himself he wasn't the man his wife believed he'd become.

Abrams sat down again and slid a file folder across the table.

"This is all I've been able to gather up about the Ibrahim case," Abrams said. "And there was something screwy about it. If the case was as real as the FBI said it was, he'd be doing life in Leavenworth." His voice trailed away and his eyebrows furrowed as he stared down at the file. "I don't get it."

"Was Hennessy still trying to figure out whether Ibrahim was guilty of something," Gage said, "or was he certain that Ibrahim had been framed and decided to go looking for him?"

"For what?" Abrams spread his hands. "To ask forgiveness? The facts are the facts. Hennessy could've just written a blog and posted it for the world to see: Dear Professor Ibrahim. So sorry. Give me a call and we'll do lunch."

Gage imagined Abrams's wife cringing at Abrams's drift into sarcasm, his method of protecting himself from experiencing Hennessy's guilt and Ibrahim's terror, but Gage chose neither to confront Abrams nor to participate.

"Maybe Hennessy was the kind of man who needed to do it face-to-face," Gage said, trying to imagine the strivings of a human being he didn't yet understand. "A message in a bottle won't do for some people, they need to touch the hand of the person they've wronged."

Abrams smiled. "You're the only investigator in the world who thinks like that." His smile faded and he squinted at Gage. "Doesn't that get to you after a while?"

"What get to me?"

"Climbing inside other people's minds."

"That's what you do, but inside hundreds of millions of them at once, instead of one at a time."

"Not quite. I mostly see people once removed, out of a limousine window or through economic data." Abrams's face reddened. "Except it's really a kind of self-created distortion. Economics isn't a science, it's fantasy adorned in jargon."

Gage drew back, stunned and puzzled by the seeming non sequitur, the leap from Hennessy to Abrams's professional self-doubt. Somehow everything had become wrapped together into a personal crisis, and Gage wasn't sure why.

"Even behavioral finance," Abrams said, "to which I devoted the best part of my life, is just a form of modern voodoo, a collection of anecdotes shrouded in mathematical equations."

"I'm not sure what—"

Abrams elbowed his way past Gage's attempt to return him to the problem that had brought them together.

"I'll tell you what I've really learned and what no one wants to hear." Abrams pounded the table with his forefinger. "No one. The markets are nothing but a form of gambling driven by fear and greed. And all of the world's mainframes linked together couldn't predict when one or the other will lead the charge."

Abrams's voice hardened as if he was arguing with a naïve colleague, or with himself.

"A science that can't predict anything isn't a science. They shouldn't give a Nobel Prize in economics. They should just make it a subcategory of literature."

Abrams's breath came hard as he ended his unintended speech. He stared at Gage, eyes blank, as if he was looking through him at something in the distance.

"I don't understand what this has to do with Ibrahim," Gage said.

Abrams didn't answer for a moment, then blinked and shook his head.

"It's just that I feel like I'm trapped in a labyrinth with no way out. People like me oversold ourselves to the public, and now I'm their poster boy even though I stopped selling the fantasy fifteen years ago." Abrams tapped the folder. "And despite what happened to Ibrahim, I'm pissed at him because he was just another in an endless line of mathematicians and physicists who claimed that they could not only make economics into a hard science, but design real-world models to guide real investments for people to rely on for their retirements."

"And you're certain that he can't."

"When I went up to MIT for a symposium a few months ago, no one in the economics department—not even the ones who recruited him—could tell me what he'd been doing at the time of his arrest, or even for the five years before that. A quarter of a million dollars a year, and for all anyone knew, he could've spent the whole time meditating in his office."

"Didn't they examine his work afterward?"

"Everyone did. FBI. CIA. NSA. The department head told me that his equations read more like poetry than science."

Gage flipped open the folder and turned the pages, skimming through a printout of Ibrahim's old MIT faculty Web page from the Institute of Financial Engineering, his curriculum vitae, and news articles about his terrorist financing arrest and deportation.

"I don't see anything here suggesting that he had an academic interest in structuring offshore transactions," Gage said. "It's all string theory and entanglements and quantum mechanics. I'm not sure what esoteric route takes a person from MIT, through the space-time continuum, and to the Cayman Islands. It strikes me that they're in different dimensions."

"That was one of the reasons his arrest was so shocking," Abrams said. "The other was that he was completely apolitical. He was born in Saudi Arabia, but for him it wasn't a country to which he bore any allegiance, only a position in space defined by latitude and longitude and time, and of no more significance than any other place."

Abrams paused, and then smiled and said, "I once ran into Ibrahim at Shaw's Market in Boston right after he came to MIT. He pointed at a picture of the globe on the side of a crate of fruit from Chile. He said that if there's no real north and south in the universe, then why don't we start making maps with what we call north at the bottom, or even lay the globe sideways."

"And giving the Middle East the top position?"

"That was the implication."

"That could've been religious rather than political," Gage said. "Islam is transnational."

"Except that Mecca is Mecca, the center of the Islamic solar system." Abrams paused again and then shrugged. "There's no way of knowing. Later he asked me why the Middle East is called the Middle East. Middle of what? East of what? Why not west? If anywhere can be the center of the universe, there's no scientific reason why it should've been England that made itself the reference point and then named the parts of the world. He seemed to be saying that the West's deciding on what the regions of the earth were called was a form of cultural imperialism."

"Somehow I don't expect to see that argument on a jihadist Web site," Gage said, "along with a map on which north is west and east is south."

"And he was in no way anti-Semitic. I would've known it, felt it. To him, no one in the economics department was anything more than a brain on legs. Smart or dumb, not Jewish or Muslim."

Gage searched through the folder until he found Ibrahim's indictment and read over the "overt acts" section.

"This is pretty vague," Gage said. "It doesn't detail exactly what he did."

Abrams pointed at a tab in the middle of the folder. "You'll find an excerpt from a congressional hearing in which the U.S. Attorney said that disclosing the details of the scheme would endanger national security because others would be able to imitate it."

"That's silly," Gage looked up at Abrams. "Anybody who participated in setting it up would know how to replicate it. It's only the American public that was denied the information."

"That embargo may be the reason Hennessy didn't go to the press or spill everything in a blog. He would've had to ask the FBI for permission, they'd have refused and threatened him with jail. Maybe they would've even held him incommunicado like they did with that spy Aldridge Ames."

"If it was important enough," Gage said, "he could've taken the risk, published it, and hoped a jury would see it his way. He wouldn't be the first whistle-blower that went that route."

Gage closed the folder and then asked, "Did you talk to him on the day you were supposed to meet?"

Abrams shook his head. "Those conferences are mobbed with intelligence agents, both government and private. He didn't want to take a chance of the call being intercepted or of either of us being spotted."

"Then how did you confirm the meeting?"

"He said that he would put himself in a position to watch the procession of limousines traveling from the Old Stock Exchange to the French president's dinner. I told him that if I could get away, I'd break off at the meridian at the east end of the Vieux Port. I assume he was posted there watching, waiting for me to drive by, planning to grab a taxi and follow me to the restaurant."

Abrams paused and his eyes clouded with distant thoughts. Finally, he said, "I know it sounds melodramatic—maybe spawned by the mystery of his death—but I have a really creepy feeling that if Hennessy had lived long enough to meet me, I'd now be dead, too."

CHAPTER 4

Faith Gage awoke in darkness to Mount Qingcheng quaking beneath her. Dishes shattered against the kitchen linoleum. Bottles exploded against bathroom tile. The metal lamp on the nightstand next to her thunked as it rocked. She grabbed for it, but it spun off and crashed on the floor.

Her mental Richter scale told her that the earthquake was in the sevens or eights, and exponentially higher than anything she'd felt at home in California. A hundred times, maybe two hundred.

A distant rumble grew into an avalanche of sound. She imagined the muddy hillside behind her three-room bungalow sliding down and submerging the village around her, and then the distant dam cracking and rupturing under the pressure of the reservoir's water and sweeping the three thousand villagers down into the farms and fields of the Chengdu valley.

She rolled to the floor and felt around for her cell phone. Her fingers bumped against it. She gripped it in her hand and then pressed herself against the cinder-block wall and edged her way toward the front door.

Another ground shake jolted the house. She heard the

pop of mortar bursting from between the brick and the wood-framed windows. She reached for the doorknob and turned and pulled, but the door was stuck, jammed in place by the fractured walls. Another shake and a twisting window shattered to her right. She reached for a broom and knocked out the remaining glass, then climbed onto a chair and out into the moonlit night.

Swirling smoke and dust and screams in Mandarin met her on the packed dirt front yard. She ran past the collapsed fish and vegetable markets toward the students' bungalow down the road. She imagined carp gasping and thrashing on concrete floors that were now barbed with the glass of their shattered tanks. She cringed as she approached the house. The clay-tiled roof had fractured and angled down into the living room to the right of the front door.

The earth shook again. An exploding flash of yellow and orange lit the far end of the street, rising upward like an erupting volcano. Then a bang. Sight before sound. Another flash, then another bang.

Flash, then bang, bang, bang.

It took her a moment to realize that they were propane tanks igniting, the town's gas supply shop now transformed into a weapons dump. She could see figures running toward her in the distance, backlit by flames rising in a firestorm.

She pushed on the door of the students' house, now strobe lit by the distant explosions, then kicked at it until it gave an inch. Someone pulled from the other side and it scraped open. She called out the students' names as she entered, taking attendance of the living.

A flashlight beam shot through the dust from the left bedroom, then swept side to side in the hallway.

A male voice yelled Faith's name, then said, "In here. We're in here," followed by coughing and stumbling and moaning.

Another explosion outside lit up the room long enough for her to push aside an upended chair and to skirt around the dining table. As she felt her way toward the bedroom door, shafts of light appeared from behind her and boots sounded on the concrete floor.

A soldier from the garrison who'd been assigned to watch them since their arrival came up behind her and shined his lantern into the bedroom. They stepped inside, then helped a student to his feet and lifted the top bunk off the bottom one on which it had collapsed. A male student lay there, blood oozing from a gash in his forehead. He reached out so Faith could help him up, but she lowered his hand and held him down. Shock had concealed from him that his shinbone had been broken by the falling bed frame.

"Don't move," Faith said to him, and then to the soldier in Mandarin, "We'll use the bunk as a stretcher to carry him outside."

The three women staggered out of the other bedroom and Faith guided them to the front door. A second soldier followed her back inside. As Faith cleared a path, he helped the first ease the narrow bed through the doorway, and then out the front door and away from the house.

Under the light of flames rising at the end of the street, the pavement looked to Faith like a dry riverbed, winding through stone and rubble, with the collapsed houses and stores along its banks defining its course.

Faith heard villagers' wails rise up around her, some in pain, others in grief. The flattened warehouse across the street opened a view of fires burning in Chengdu City, spreading to the east from the base of the mountain. With eleven million victims on the plain below, she knew that her village would be the last to receive help. They might be on their own not just for days, but for weeks.

Only then did Faith feel the subfreezing cold and she turned back toward her house. The motion of an elderly neighbor crawling through the dust caught her eye as she approached. She ran over and helped her up, and then steadied her with an arm around her shoulders.

The woman gazed through the swirling dust at the shambles of brick and board that used to be her house and then shook her head and whispered, *"Tian ming. Tian ming."*

The mandate of heaven.

Faith felt a chill shudder through the old woman's body. She sat the woman down on a low wall and ran back inside her own house and put on a coat. She pulled the blanket from her bed and grabbed sheepskin slippers, then returned to the woman, wrapped the blanket around her shoulders, and slid the slippers onto her feet.

By the time Faith returned to the students' bungalow, they had bandaged the injured boy's head and stabilized his leg.

Faith turned away and pressed a button on her mobile phone. The screen lit up. She saw there was a faint signal, and redialed the last call.

Gage smiled when he saw the number appear on his ringing cell phone, and then calculated the time difference. His smile died. It was long past midnight in China.

He connected and asked, "Are you all right?"

Milton Abrams looked over at Gage from across the kitchen table.

"Fine. The kids, too. There was an earthquake. Just a few minutes ago. What phone circuits are left will be jammed in a few minutes, so I thought I better call."

Gage pointed at Abrams, then at the television on the counter.

"How bad?" Gage asked.

Abrams grabbed the remote and turned it on. It was tuned to CNBC.

"Huge. The worst I've ever seen. I can see fires spreading in Chengdu valley. But I think we can hold out for a while. There's an army garrison nearby."

"I'll contact the consulate in Chengdu and let them know you're all right," Gage said, "and see what they can do about getting you out of there."

"I doubt that they'd be able help, at least for a while."

Gage noticed the worry on Abrams's face as he looked back from the television.

"She's fine," Gage said, and then circled his finger to tell him to scan the channels. Abrams paused when he arrived at CNN, the screen flashing red with breaking news.

"It just came on TV," Gage told her. "Looks like it was an eight-point-one. Centered in the mountains west of you."

Gage heard her sigh. "What?"

"I'm glad it wasn't to the east."

Neither had to supply a place name. She meant the six fault lines near the Three Gorges Dam. Had the quake been centered there, fifteen million people would've drowned and their bodies swept down the Yangtze River from Yichang to Wuhan to Shanghai and finally into the East China Sea.

Abrams's cell phone rang. His mouth twisted into a smirk when he looked at the screen, and then he shook his head. He glanced at Gage and said, "It's God's representative in D.C." He turned away and connected the call as he headed down the hallway toward the living room: "Yes, Mr. Vice President."

"What was that?" Faith asked.

"I'm with Milton Abrams in New York. He may be getting some more information about the earthquake. Maybe I can leverage his connections to get you out of there."

"Let's wait and see. There are people who need the help more than we do."

"If I can get through, I'll call you back in an hour and let you know what I find out. Be careful."

Gage stared at the phone for a moment after he disconnected, trying to retain Faith's image in his mind, then walked to the living room. He found Abrams still on the phone, standing at the window and looking out over a snow-covered Central Park. He glanced back as Gage entered, then pointed toward the sofa, indicating that he didn't mind Gage overhearing the conversation.

"At this point, I don't know enough to make any kind of assessment," Abrams said. He then blocked the microphone and again looked back at Gage. "How could the president have picked this lunatic as his running mate? And make the same mistake twice."

Abrams listened for thirty seconds, then said, "Yes, Mr. Vice President. I'm in a meeting in New York right now and can't make it down to Washington, but I'll get my staff looking into it. We'll have something for you by 11 A.M."

Abrams disconnected.

"You have any idea how many calls I get from him? He seems to think that a butterfly flapping its wings somewhere in the galaxy will not only cause a tornado in his neighborhood, but that some crook will use it as a diversion to pick his pocket."

Gage raised his eyebrows. "So chaos theory really does explain an irrational universe."

Abrams shook his head, mouth sour. "He's not that sophisticated. He just likes butterflies, and says he's a firm believer in Einstein's opinion that God doesn't play dice. Of course, he's never read Einstein."

"What's he going to make of the earthquake?"

Abrams bit his lip, thinking. Then he nodded and said, "I think he'll make it into a lesson in faith-based economics. Somehow he'll construe it as God's punishment for something the Chinese did, maybe for inventing Confucianism. If he could construe the Holocaust into a divine hint that the Jews of Europe should create the state of Israel in order to set the stage for the Second Coming, his mind is elastic enough to wrap any tragedy inside a theory about God's purpose."

Abrams looked down at the phone in his hand. "I hate this thing." Then back up at Gage. "Just say the word if you need help getting Faith out of there. It can be used for good as well as for nonsense."

Distant thumping drums drew them both to the bay window overlooking Central Park West. The sound was approaching them from the north.

"If the antiglobalization groups are marching," Abrams said, "it must be World Trade Organization Friday." He chanted along, "No. No. WTO," and then said, "I wish they'd go back to rioting down on Wall Street instead of up here. You'd think they're trying to interfere with my work."

"Do they pass by or stop out front?"

"Pass by"—Abrams tilted his head in the other direction—"on their way to Columbus Circle so they can jump onto the subway after the march and get to class or to the Starbucks where they work."

"Then I guess they don't know you live here."

Abrams shrugged and smiled. "Not yet, but they will, and the dictators on the co-op board will not be pleased to pay for all of the windows they'll break."

CHAPTER 6

H ell, I even called the CIA."

Vice President Cooper Wallace glared at his chief of staff sitting across the desk from him in his ceremonial office in the Eisenhower Executive Office Building.

Paul Nichols knew the outburst wasn't meant for him, but for a world that was resisting Wallace's will. It had been that way during the ten years that Wallace served as the CEO and Nichols had been the CFO of Spectrum, the world's largest multilevel marketing company. Wallace's father had started it in the family garage to sell Christian products, and after it mainstreamed into foods, vitamins, and nutritional supplements, the son used it as a springboard into politics. And this was one of those times that Nichols wished he hadn't.

Wallace pulled the phone away from his ear and turned it toward Nichols.

"A billion-dollar investment," the sharp but distant voice said, "and you're telling me you don't even know whether the goddamn building is still standing?"

The caller was the CFO of RAID Technologies, a U.S.-based microchip manufacturer, and corporate backer of Wallace's elevation from business executive to senator, to presidential candidate, and finally to vice president.

Turning the phone back toward his ear, Wallace said, "Half of Chengdu is on fire. For all I know even the Spectrum distribution center has already burned. It's not the fault of the United States government if your people over there are too busy to pick up the telephone to report to you." He listened for a moment, then said, "I'll have Paul contact you as soon as we have some information," and disconnected.

"Why is he so worried?" Nichols asked. "They built the RAID plant to resist the largest earthquakes."

Wallace shook his head. "They *designed* it to resist. Whether the Chinese construction company built it to those specifications is a different thing." He spread his hands. "And at what magnitude? Even the Three Gorges Dam was built only to withstand a seven-point-zero, not an eight-point-one. At least that's what I was told years ago by the staff of the Commerce Committee."

Wallace rose and gazed down on Seventeenth Street, already closed to traffic in anticipation of Saturday's anti–World Bank and International Monetary Fund demonstration. He hummed Buffalo Springfield's "For What It's Worth" as he surveyed the flak-jacketed D.C. police officers posted at the corners.

Nichols heard the music in his head and recognized that neither of them knew what was really happening outside and what it meant for them or the country. He watched Wallace's head nod in rhythm as he looked out, as if the images were melding with the words: guns, signs, and songs embodying divisions deeper than mere political disagreement.

He remembered the first time—the exact day—he'd heard the song in 1967. He'd gone to a friend's house after school where they'd played the record on the stereo over and over, memorizing the words. His father, a police captain who was home on his day off, rose from his chair and glared at Nichols as he walked in through the front door singing:

> *Paranoia strikes deep*
> *Into your life it will creep*
> *It starts when you're always afraid*
> *You step out of line, the man come and take you away—*

Then the man stepped out of the song, walked across the living room, and slapped his son across the face.

Nichols blinked away memory and focused again on Wallace.

"I was right when I warned RAID not to build over there," Wallace said, then held up his hands. "*So Jeshurun waxed fat and spurned the Rock of his salvation.*" He lowered them again and turned back toward Nichols. "I guarantee you that Spectrum won't call today. They couldn't wait for me to be gone so they could go into China, and now look how they've been punished for it."

Nichols cocked his head toward the reception area where the president and executive officers of the Baptist Missionary Convention waited.

Wallace smiled. "Don't worry. I won't say that in front of the cameras. The public isn't quite ready to face the truth without blinders on. When the time comes, they'll rip them off themselves." He paused in thought, then snapped his fingers. "This may be a chance for BMC to send some missionaries into China, maybe as relief workers. We should encourage RAID to take a few along when they go over to assess the damage."

"There's no way they'll get visas."

"We'll make it a human rights issue. That way—"

"And I'm not sure we should put kids at risk. Things are only going to get worse."

"Then that's exactly where they need to be to do the most good. What do the Chinese say about crises creating opportunities? This is one of those times."

Nichols tensed. Wallace's central weakness was that he was impulsive. It was a defect Nichols had long ago discovered in the character of boys with strong but loving fathers, like Wallace's, who forgave mistakes too easily.

"You'll need to run it by the president's people before you start down that road," Nichols said, but knew Wallace wouldn't.

The last time Wallace had shoved the president in the direction of religious freedom in China, the Chinese maneuvered him into a position where he either had to speak out in support of the anti-Christian Falun Gong or step back. He retreated and was weakened when he went to Beijing to negotiate the terms of a revised trade agreement.

"The president shouldn't have chickened out last time," Wallace said. "Anything that encourages instability in China helps us. Combine a hundred million landless laborers rioting in the streets and fifty million Falun Gong members lotusing in the intersections and a bunch of Tibetans and separatist Muslims bombing the power stations, and the whole government will collapse and we'll get the kind of revolution that should've happened the first time."

Wallace stepped toward the door.

"Anyway," Wallace said, reaching for the knob, "I'm not going to push the president to do the right thing — these people are."

CHAPTER 7

D riving north through a snowstorm from New York toward Albany, Gage felt the uncertainty of Faith's situation, but resisted calling again for fear of turning his worry into interference.

At the same time, he felt as though Milton Abrams had sent him walking on a trampoline.

"Are you asking me to find out whether Hennessy was murdered," Gage had asked as he rose from the living room couch, "or whether Ibrahim was framed?"

"Neither, exactly. I want you to find out why the possible framing of Ibrahim became a matter of life or death for Hennessy."

"It didn't seem all that important to Ibrahim. He's had nine years to proclaim his innocence, but he's remained silent and out of sight."

"Then maybe that's the answer I'm looking for—assuming that he's still alive. But I don't think it's the one we'll discover."

Gage found it hard to make out the Hudson River to his right as he looped over the thruway and headed west toward downtown. The Dunn Memorial Bridge reached into the gray nothingness, looking more like a pier than a span. Only the creeping headlights emerging from the swirling fog confirmed that it was attached to the opposite bank. From there on he let the rental car's GPS guide him through the blurred intersections to the Adirondack Plaza Hotel along State Street, a few blocks from the capitol.

After checking in, he called his assistant, Alex Z, at the firm's office in San Francisco. He smiled to himself as he pictured the wild-haired, multitattooed Alex Z perched at his cockpit of a desk, surrounded by computers and monitors, trolling cyberspace for information that allowed Gage and the twenty other investigators in his firm to triangulate their position inside the cases they worked.

"Court records in Albany show that Elaine divorced Hennessy five years ago," Alex Z said. "She got the house and half his retirement. He got joint custody of the kids, but I don't think that meant that much in the long run because they were already in their mid-teens."

"Was it contested?"

"At the start, but he caved in before they got into the juicy details of exactly what their differences were and what made them irreconcilable."

"How about making a pretext call to the house to see if she's there. Pretend to be a pollster. Run it through a New York number so she'll think it's local."

"No problem and I'll hit you with an e-mail of everything I've found out about them."

During the following hour, Gage tried to construct a living human out of the papier-mâché of Alex Z's research, then drove west and walked up the concrete steps to a century-old brick Craftsman two blocks from the frozen Washington Park Lake in the center of town. He was wearing a suit, but left his overcoat in the car, playing the odds that she might let him into the house if only to get him out of the cold—but first he'd have to get past a young woman peeking out from the near edge of the living room drapes as he raised his hand to knock on the door.

She swung it open, but before Gage had a chance to identify himself, she said, "My mother doesn't want to talk to anybody."

Her features were too soft for the hard look she tried to use to wall Gage off, but he didn't try to break through it with a smile, for it seemed to be part of an honest attempt to protect her mother.

Reaching out with his business card, Gage said, "I'm a private investigator—"

"For who?" Her voice went from protective to demanding. "Who sent you?"

"Someone who was worried about your father before he died."

She didn't accept the card. He lowered it. Her knuckles whitened as she tightened her grip on the door.

"You mean, before he was murdered."

Gage didn't yet know whether that was true, but he neither wanted to challenge her nor agree with her and thereby set up a future betrayal if it wasn't.

"That's what the man who hired me suspected," Gage said, "and asked me to find out."

An older female voice called out from the interior: "Who's at the door?"

The young woman glanced behind her and said, "A man."

The voice rose, the tone of an exasperated mother. "What man?"

Footsteps thumped on the hardwood floor, becoming louder as they approached.

The woman who appeared at the door matched the school librarian that Alex Z had described in his e-mail. Slim. Short. Red hair tied back. She looked at Gage, then at her daughter.

"You're right, Vicky. It's a man."

Vicky reddened. "I was just trying to—"

"And she did it very well," Gage said. He smiled and handed her his card. "I may want to hire her to protect me."

Elaine examined it as her daughter backed away.

"You came all the way out here from California to talk to me?"

"Actually, I came all the way out here to talk to someone who wanted me to talk to you."

"Who was that?"

"I'd rather not say right away."

Reaching out to return the card, she said, "I've had enough mysteries already."

Gage held up his hands. "How about this? I'll explain to you why I'm here, and then you decide whether it makes any difference who hired me."

Elaine stared up at him for a few moments, and then turned away from the door and said, "Come on in."

As Gage stamped his feet to knock off the snow that

had collected on his shoes as he walked from his car, she looked back and smiled and said, "Nice try with shivering-in-the-cold gimmick. My husband used to use that one, too. He knew all of the tricks." Her smiled died. "A lot of good it did him in the end."

only divorced him so he couldn't spend all of our savings trying to find Ibrahim," Elaine said, as they sat across the kitchen table from each other. She gestured toward the 1950s knotty-pine cabinets, the Formica countertops, and the lime green refrigerator. "He spent our kitchen remodeling money chasing him across Eastern Europe." She exhaled, shaking her head. "Assuming Ibrahim was even in Eastern Europe."

Lying between them were online newspaper articles about Gage that Vicky had printed out. He was sure that she'd searched for them hoping to find something that would convince her mother not to talk to him. But they had the opposite effect, and he respected her courage in bringing them down to her mother anyway.

Elaine spun one around and faced it toward Gage. It was about Gage's capture of a fugitive in Budapest who'd stolen five hundred million dollars from a Russian-U.S. oil production joint venture.

"Since you found this guy," Elaine said, "maybe you can locate Ibrahim and figure out what happened to Michael. And why." Her gaze settled on the article. "I suspect that if Michael had been worth half a billion dollars, too, there'd have been more people interested in finding out."

Elaine's hands shook as she took a sip of tea. Gage wasn't sure whether it was from anger or fatigue. Her gray-framed eyes and errant strands of hair suggested the latter.

"What was driving him?" Gage asked.

"You mean, why was he obsessed?"

Gage shook his head. "I don't know enough about him or what happened to say that." He smiled. "It may be that after a few weeks working on this, people will say the same thing about me."

She stared at him for a moment, and then smiled back.

"I think I like you," she said. "Most investigators I've met, especially FBI, have been assholes. Pricks with badges." She flushed. "Sorry for the body part analogies. I learned them from my kids." She pointed at the church events calendar held to the refrigerator by an apple-shaped magnet. "It's hard for a preacher's daughter to admit, but 'asshole' is the most exquisite and versatile word in the English language."

Elaine's eyes went vacant as though images of those to whom the word applied were passing through her mind, then she blinked and said, "It really wasn't an obsession. People who collect stamps and who pull slot machine handles in twelve-hour shifts are obsessed. For Michael it was a moral crusade, one that I'm afraid I didn't understand. And because I didn't understand it, I didn't support it." She raised her teacup to take another sip, but then set it back down. "That's not right. I couldn't find a way to support it. And I tried. I really did."

"You mean you don't think Ibrahim was framed?"

"I never saw anything that showed he wasn't guilty." She glanced upward. "I even searched Michael's office when he wasn't home, trying to find out. All I ever got from him was, 'You don't understand,' and 'It's too dangerous for you to know,' or 'I can't violate Bureau policy. I know they'll take me back once I prove I'm right.'"

"You mean he was concerned that he might violate FBI policy by disclosing what he'd learned when he was an agent?"

Elaine nodded.

"Which means that whatever he learned, he learned while he was still with the agency."

She nodded again.

"Did he leave anything behind?"

She hesitated for a moment, and then said, "The FBI came and took everything, including his safe, which they weren't able to open while they were here."

"Did they have a search warrant?"

"You mean, did they see him as a suspect, rather than as a victim?"

Gage shrugged. "I guess you could say that's the flip side of the question."

"They said they needed it in order to investigate his death, so I signed a consent form. They may have had a search warrant with them just in case, but they didn't show it. They said they'd send me a receipt once they had inventoried everything."

"Have they?"

"No. And it's been a week." She sighed. "I wonder if I made a mistake by making it so easy for them."

"If they hadn't brought a warrant, they could've easily gotten one just based on the suspicion that he took FBI records with him when he left the Bureau."

She shook her head. "I think it was less a theft and more that he failed to return the files. He'd started on his crusade about eight years ago and when he wouldn't let it go, they fired him."

Elaine paused, the memory seeming to well up in her. "Devastating. It was devastating. For the first few months he sat in his office just staring out of the window, then something happened, I don't know what, and he went manic over the thing again."

Gage pointed up toward her husband's office. "You mind if I look at what's left? Maybe it'll help me understand him."

"Then you'll know a lot more than I did, and I was married to him for almost twenty years."

Elaine led him up the oak staircase they'd passed on the way to the kitchen, then down a carpeted hallway to a converted bedroom.

"Before he lost his sense of humor," she said, as she gestured him inside, "he used to invite people in here by saying, 'Welcome to the scene of the crime.'"

Elaine's face reddened as her eyes traveled from the desk to the battered file cabinet and paper shredder and past the sagging bookcases toward a framed FBI shield on the wall.

"And the agents who came here sure as hell treated it that way."

Gage walked over and scanned the titles of the books. He noticed a few that were also on his own shelves: manuals on securities fraud, money laundering, and financial investigation, along with a shelf devoted to stock and bond trading, technical analysis, and principles of finance.

"Did he do day trading?" Gage asked, flipping through

a twelve-hundred-page volume on financial modeling. He turned toward her. "This is pretty sophisticated material. Graduate-level math."

Elaine shook her head. "He barely passed algebra in high school. I know. I sat behind him and fed him the answers."

She reached past Gage and pulled out a volume titled *The Fractal Analysis of Finance.*

"Look at this thing," she said, opening it near the middle. "He highlighted almost every sentence and I'm not sure whether he understood any of it."

Gage recognized the book. It was an attack on the theories of finance that had guided the actions of the central banks in both the U.S. and Europe for two generations, and on the models used for risk assessment by corporations, investment houses, mutual funds, and currency traders. He wasn't sure whether anyone other than the author of the book understood the argument, or if anyone did, whether he'd found a way to make use of it, except—according to legend and the prospectus of the offshore Relative Growth hedge fund—Hani Ibrahim.

"Did he study Ibrahim's journal articles?" Gage asked, glancing over at her.

Elaine nodded. "But the FBI took the whole lot because he'd written notes on them."

Gage's mind looped back and he repeated her earlier words, "'Treated the place like a crime scene.' What did you mean?"

"They even dusted for fingerprints."

Elaine stepped toward the desk and pointed to the floor next to one of the legs.

"And they cut out a sliver of the carpet where they found blood. I told them it was Michael's from when he sliced himself moving the file cabinet, but they didn't believe me."

Or they had a theory, Gage suspected, about how it got there, one in which Hennessy's blood was evidence as much as anyone else's.

Gage bent down to separate the wool pile to examine the surrounding backing. If there had been a fight, there would've been surrounding spatter.

He felt Elaine staring at him as he straightened up.

"One of the news articles said that you were once a homicide detective," she said, "so I know what you're thinking. The FBI thinks that Michael fought with someone in here."

"Was there more blood?"

She nodded and indicated a path toward the door with a wave of her hand.

Gage surveyed the room. Every dent in the file cabinet, every scuff on the wall, every missing chip of paint on the windowsill now seemed to speak of violence instead of wear.

"And they think it was Ibrahim?" he asked.

She shrugged. "They didn't say. But I have no reason to think he was here. If he had been, Michael wouldn't have raced off to Europe looking for him."

That pursuit would've explained why Hennessy was in France, Gage thought, but maybe not why he was in Marseilles, or at least not the only reason he was there.

Gage felt the crime scene shift back to the Mediterranean.

"Do you think Ibrahim might have killed your husband, maybe out of revenge?"

Elaine's eyes narrowed and her body stiffened.

"I'm not going to answer that until I know who hired

you." She folded her arms across her chest. "I don't want to end up like Michael."

"The problem is that the person who brought me into this is afraid if it becomes public that he's interested, the press will portray him in the same way your husband was described by the FBI."

"You mean, as a raving lunatic."

Gage nodded. "But I can tell you this. He's the person Michael went to Marseilles to meet."

Elaine's face flushed again. "You're just like my husband. You're asking me to trust you, but you're not willing to trust me."

"It's more complicated than that."

Elaine threw up her hands. "Now you're quoting him. Everything was always too complicated for my little brain." Her voice rose. "What now? Are you going to pat me on the head, tell me to go bake some cookies like a good little girl?"

Tears appeared in her eyes and streamed down her cheeks. She dropped into the desk chair, then leaned over and covered her face, her body heaving with sobs.

Gage knelt down next to her. "I didn't mean it that way. I only meant that I have to trust the person who hired me just as much as I'm asking you to trust me."

Footsteps pounded in the hallway. Vicky ran into the room.

"What the fuck did you do to her?" she yelled, then pushed Gage away and wrapped her arms around her mother.

Gage regained his balance, but didn't rise.

Elaine straightened in her chair, then took in a long breath and exhaled as she wiped her eyes. She gazed up at Vicky.

"He didn't do anything to me. Life did something to me."

Elaine looked over at Gage. "I'm just so angry," she said. "At myself for divorcing him. At him for abandoning us."

Vicky pulled away, her face reddening, clenching her fists. "He didn't abandon us. Stop saying that. He didn't."

"Then why isn't he here?" Elaine said, opening her hands toward her daughter. "Why isn't he still alive?"

Vicky glared at her mother, mouth open, but no answer emerged. She then turned and stared out through the window at the blizzard that had walled off their world.

Gage could see that every time she'd reached out to protect her mother, she found herself handcuffed and speechless, paralyzed by conflicting emotions and loyalties and unanswered questions.

"I can't dissolve the cloud he left behind," Gage said, rising to his feet. "But at least let me try to take some of the mystery out of how his life ended."

Gage looked at Vicky.

"The man who asked me to do this believes that your father died for something important."

And then at Elaine. "And after my meeting you two, I wonder if maybe his search was really an attempt to find a way to come back home as a man you could be proud of."

CHAPTER 9

Two years ago," the president of International Society for Econometrics said, "the Federal Reserve was in disarray, having been managed by a succession of chairmen who spent their days testing the political winds, instead of interrogating the hard economic data."

Harold Lasker scanned the upturned faces of the twelve hundred conference attendees in the ballroom of the Grand Hyatt in midtown Manhattan. To Milton Abrams, sitting to his left on the raised dais, they looked like refugees huddled in the safety of a school gymnasium after fleeing a war zone.

Antiglobalization demonstrators had gathered for a second time that day, blocking the hotel entrance, forcing the attendees to sneak in by way of Grand Central Station, their underground route fortified by police and private security guards against the surging protestors.

"What changed?"

Lasker shifted his gaze to Abrams, who felt himself

recoil as twenty-four hundred eyes fell on him. He felt less like an honored keynote speaker and more like a burglar caught in a patrol officer's high beams. The sudden attention caused him to cease his fidgeting that had accelerated during Lasker's introduction. He withdrew his hand from the sweating water glass and the tracks its erratic movements traced on the starched white tablecloth, then dried his fingers on his napkin and dropped his hands to his lap.

"I'll tell you what changed," Lasker said. "We finally have a chairman who has refused to play politics with the economy by pursuing policies that brought a series of booms and busts because of the central bank's unwillingness to control the expansion of credit."

Lasker held up a copy of the society's latest journal. Everyone in the room knew the single topic to which it was devoted: the coming collapse.

"The question is whether it's too late." Lasker paused, and then said, "I believe that it isn't. If . . . if . . . we're tough-minded enough."

Easy for him to say, Abrams thought—for all of them to say. He knew that to the tenured academics in the room, "tough-minded" meant nothing more than standing firm in their demand for a new photocopier for the economics department or for an extra teaching assistant to whom they could shift more of their work. And to the corporate executives, it meant nothing more than holding their ground with the homeowners' association design review board or two-putting a par three, or fighting with the company's compensation committee over an additional million dollars in salary or an additional ten million in stock options.

None of them, Abrams knew, possessed the kind of toughness required to bring the financial life of the country to a standstill in order to break the cycles of inflation and deflation that were eroding the foundation of the economy.

And Abrams wondered whether he himself possessed it. Even the fact of his presidential appointment to be Fed chairman hadn't done much to dampen his self-doubt.

"And the first place to draw the line is with China."

Abrams's jaw tightened. He felt like grabbing Lasker's jacket collar and tossing him backward off the dais.

Lasker had promised not to raise the issue of China's currency policies—and the whole world was watching. Even worse, Lasker had just criticized the previous chairmen's testing of the political winds, only to throw Abrams into the storm.

Abrams knew that as far as the international financial community was concerned, a nonresponse to Lasker's claim by the chairman of the Federal Reserve would be viewed as a response and would move the markets. Abrams therefore put on what he called the Bernanke Face, the dull-eyed expression of a goat oblivious to the slaughterhouse into which it was being led.

Staring ahead, Abrams noticed motion at the back of the ballroom. A CNBC producer he recognized was walking out to the foyer, and he grasped what she was doing: alerting the studio that a story was about to break.

Abrams glanced at his watch. The markets would close in forty minutes. He decided that he would find a way to stretch his speech and wait until question time to respond to the China issue, and let the mass of overnight news dissipate the impact of his reaction.

"China's currency policies," Lasker continued, "have destabilized the capital flows throughout the world."

Idiot. Abrams thought. *Id-i-ot.* The esteemed president of the society was one of those who'd demanded for decades that the Chinese let their currency float instead of keeping it fixed unreasonably low against the dollar. Finally they did, and as predicted by its advocates, the price of their products on the international market increased, costing them some of their competitive advantage.

But as Lasker and others hadn't predicted, it also sucked into China a trillion dollars a year of foreign investment. Investors, who'd once received only seven hundred thousand Chinese yuan for a million dollars, now received one point four million yuan.

If it had made economic sense ten years earlier to invest a billion dollars in China, it was insanity not to invest two billion today, for the dollars now bought fifty percent more of the country.

"The PRC's dual exchange rate policy," Lasker said, "one for domestic transactions and one for foreign investment, creates exactly the kind of unfair subsidy prohibited by the WTO."

Id-i-ot. What pisses you off is that they outsmarted you. Did you really think they'd follow your advice like it was a doctor's prescription: Drink liquids, get lots of rest, take one of these tablets twice a day?

Lasker and his followers had learned the lesson too late: Chinese economics was like Chinese medicine: counterintuitive and impossible to swallow.

Lasker paused, and then sniffed the air. Seconds later, members of the audience were coughing and wiping their eyes. Those at the back of the room ran toward the exits, the ones in front bunched up behind them.

Abrams clasped his hands together under the table.

Thank God for tear gas.

CHAPTER 10

How does your wife feel about the work you do?"
Elaine asked Gage.

She stood with her back to the fireplace in the
den, warming her hands. Observing her from the couch,
Gage wondered whether the chill she was fighting was
internal or external.

"Those news articles made it seem like you never
sleep in your own bed."

Gage glanced at his watch. It was mid-morning in
Asia.

She caught the motion, and asked with an edge in her
voice, "You need to be somewhere?"

"No. I'm worried about my wife. She's in China."

Elaine's eyes widened. "Not near the earthquake, I
hope."

"Too near, but she's okay."

"Why is she there?" She stiffened and cocked her
head as if there was another question concealed behind
the one she'd asked.

"She's an anthropologist. She teaches at UC Berkeley."

"Oh, I see." Elaine's body relaxed again. "I wondered

whether she was working on this, too. Michael thought Ibrahim's wife might be living over there. Not in the earthquake area. In an autonomous zone called Xinjiang."

Gage now understood Hennessy's call from China to Abrams. He must've been thinking that he could get to Ibrahim through his wife. The fact that he'd kept traveling suggested that he hadn't.

"She's a Muslim, too," Elaine said. "They met in Boston when he was in graduate school."

"How did you . . ."

She pointed upstairs. "I said I didn't find anything that exonerated Ibrahim, but I once found some bits and pieces about her." She smiled. "I spent a lunch hour or two at work trying to fit shredded pieces of paper back together."

She lowered her voice as though not wanting Vicky to overhear.

"That's the reason I let him keep using the bedroom as his office even after he moved out. So I could spy on him. I felt a little guilty about it because the kids thought I did it so he could spend more time with them."

"Do you know whether he found her?" Gage asked.

"I don't think so, but that part of the story didn't make it into the shredder."

"Did you save the material you rescued?"

Elaine smiled and said, "Like a squirrel preparing for winter, I folded them up and tucked them away."

She walked over to the entertainment center, selected a DVD from the shelf, and handed it to Gage.

He flipped it open and turned it toward her. Her mouth gaped. It was empty. No papers inside. She grabbed a second one from the stack and opened it. Then a third.

She ran to the doorway and yelled toward the stairs, "Vicky. Come down here."

Her daughter entered half a minute later and Elaine displayed an empty case toward her.

"Did you or your friends—"

"*Chitty Chitty Bang Bang?*" Vicky smirked as she looked at the title. "You've got to be kidding, Mother. I haven't watched that since I was ten years old."

Elaine bit her bottom lip and lowered her hands, then said to herself, "I was in here when the FBI searched. I would've noticed. I'm sure I would've."

"Not the whole time," Vicky said, looking at her mother as though she was a grandparent edging toward Alzheimer's. "Remember, they took us into the garage to point out which boxes were Daddy's."

Elaine's head drifted down, "I guess that's it."

"Why's that movie suddenly so important?" Vicky asked.

"No reason," Elaine said. "You know how I am about keeping things in order, that's all."

Vicky glanced at Gage, then back at her mother as if trying to divine what course of events could've led to the opening of a child's DVD. She scanned the shelf holding the others, then shook her head, and left the room.

Gage rose and led Elaine to the couch and took a notebook out of his suit pocket.

"Tell me what you remember about what was on those pages."

Elaine leaned back and stared at the ceiling as though her husband's notes were written there in invisible ink. She exhaled and closed her eyes.

"Ibrahim's wife's name is Ibadat. I looked it up. It means 'devotion.'" She looked over at Gage. "It's ironic because she stayed in the U.S. for a year or so after he was deported, then did kind of a European tour before she finally settled in China."

"Do you know where in Xinjiang she's from?"

"It was unpronounceable. Kizl-something. It's hard enough to piece together shreds of handwritten English, much less in transliterated Uyghur."

"Children?"

"I didn't see anything about kids, or parents for that matter. There were a few words that suggested that she may have been a hydrologist or an agronomist or something like that."

Elaine thought for a moment, and then said. "I think Michael had written out the notes in order to figure out a route to travel in searching for Ibrahim. One scrap I found had Algiers, Marseilles, and Dublin listed, in that order."

"And when he died in Marseilles?"

"I thought that Ibrahim or terrorists working with him had led Michael into a trap."

Gage looked out through the French doors toward the backyard. The fog had finally reached in from the river, but the snowfall had stopped, leaving mounds on top of the woodpile, the toolshed, the rusted swing set, and the brick barbecue. He imagined that it hadn't been too many years earlier that young families had gathered out there for children's birthdays and Easter egg hunts.

Elaine sighed. "I'm bushed. Or maybe just beaten down by all of this."

Gage turned toward her. "I didn't mean to—"

"It's not you. It's the mess everything has become."

Her brows furrowed and she shook her head. "It wasn't supposed to turn out this way. Everything was once so perfect. It really was morning in America for us when Michael and I met in high school in the eighties, now it's all a nightmare."

Elaine closed her eyes again. Gage could see her pupils moving under her lids like she was searching through pictures of the past.

"The Tupperware Family. That's what my mother called us."

She paused, then looked at Gage.

"When she was growing up, Tupperware and Corning glassware and color television and KitchenAid all meant progress, people on the go, on the way up. The American dream. She saw us as an updated version of her generation. Earnest FBI agent, fresh-faced school librarian, kids, a house, two cars." She pressed her lips tight for a few seconds, then said, "I'm glad she didn't live to see what it turned into."

Gage didn't respond. He still didn't know whether her life could've come out otherwise. But he did know that pretending that her life was different than it was would destroy the trust they'd developed.

And they both knew that their conversation had come to an end.

As he walked down the front steps a few minutes later, Gage's peripheral vision caught a break in the pattern of snowbound cars parked along the street. The windshield of one had been wiped during the last few minutes of the blizzard. The passenger side was misted, the driver's side clear, but there were no fresh tire tracks in the slush or fresh footsteps in the snow on the street or on the sidewalk bordering the car.

Gage came to a stop near his rental car, patted the breast pocket of his suit, then frowned and turned back toward the house.

When Elaine answered the door, he said, "Don't look past me, but I think someone has your house under surveillance."

"That's ridiculous. Only the FBI would still be interested and they got everything."

"Trust me on this one. I have thirty years in this business. I've learned to read the signs." Gage pointed toward the interior. "Go back inside and bring me an envelope."

Elaine kept her eyes fixed on his and said, "I don't think you're right, but I'll play along."

She returned a minute later and handed him a soiled letter-sized envelope. "These are my Price Chopper coupons." She smiled. "They're having a two-for-one special on crescent rolls and canned yams."

"I'll make up for your loss," Gage said, sliding it into his jacket pocket, "and take you out to dinner."

"You mean you want to use me as a decoy to see whether they're watching me or following you?"

Gage nodded, and then smiled back. "I think I like you, too."

CHAPTER 11

I t's me. I'm outside Hennessy's house," private investigator Tony Gilbert said in a call to Kenyon Arndt as he watched Gage walk back down the steps.

Gilbert was annoyed at having to report in to a lawyer as naïve as Arndt, whom he pictured as a clueless Ivy League grad who'd probably spent his weekends playing squash or lacrosse or maybe field hockey with the girls. Wycovsky was a different story. That was a guy he wouldn't mind sharing a Humvee or a beer with.

"Have you figured out who the man is?" Arndt asked.

"Not yet. We'll probably know by tonight. But that's not why I called—hold on."

Gilbert reached for another cell phone and switched to direct connect mode.

"Get ready," Gilbert told the two men parked a few blocks away. "He's getting into his car. He'll be coming your way. Four-door. Dark blue. Headlights on."

Then back to Arndt.

"Hennessy's wife gave him something. Looked like an envelope. Maybe it's something we missed."

"What do you mean missed?"

"Hold on."

"He's almost to the corner," Gilbert told the surveillance team. "He's got his left turn signal on, so he's probably heading back toward downtown.

"You still there?" he asked Arndt.

"Yes."

"We searched the place after the FBI got done."

Gilbert smiled to himself. *Let's see if Mr. Ivy League learned a lesson from having his hand slapped by Wycovsky after objecting to the tracking device they'd placed on Milton Abrams's Town Car.*

After a long silence, Arndt said, "I see."

Putz. He should've accused us of incompetence for missing whatever it was that Elaine Hennessy had put into the envelope.

"Does that mean you have to go in again?" Arndt asked.

"It's probably too late. But we'll find out where he works or lays his head and take back whatever it is."

"You don't mean—"

"What do you care what I mean." *You fucking punk asshole.* "I mean what I mean. *Capisci?*"

Gilbert didn't wait for an answer. He just disconnected and tossed the phone onto the seat next to him.

Mystery Man may be our only lead to Ibrahim, and Ivy League thinks we're gonna kill him? What kind of shit has this guy been watching on TV?

Gilbert watched the car turn onto Madison Avenue two blocks away and head downtown. He then turned his ignition and pulled away from the curb.

"What's he doing?" Gilbert said into the other cell phone.

The man on the other end laughed. "Driving like an old lady."

"He's an amateur, that's for sure. He didn't check the

street when he came out of the house." A laugh. "And kind of a doofus. He even forgot the papers he came for and had to go back to get them."

"How do you want to handle it?"

"I don't know yet. Let's give him some rope and maybe he'll trip on it all on his own." Gilbert paused as a sliver of a memory gave him an idea. "You still in contact with . . . with . . . what's that guy's name, the one who did time for that two-bit robbery by the statehouse?"

"Strubb."

"Yeah, Strubb. Is he out?"

"I'll check."

The other man called back a few minutes later. "He's back in town. Working for a bail bondsman as a sort of unlicensed bounty hunter."

"Give him my number and have him call me."

"Why are we looking for this Ibrahim guy anyway?"

"Why do you think? So I can make the payments on my ocean-view condo in Mazatlan."

The other man laughed. "Which means you don't know either."

"Don't know. Don't care—just show . . . me . . . the money."

CHAPTER 12

Nothing like tear gas to change the subject, Milton Abrams thought after the attendees gathered again in the ballroom and after the Econometrics Society president completed the introduction he was supposed to make instead of reaching for the political hammer that Abrams now wanted to ram down his throat.

Thinking about Lasker's criticism of China's currency regime, Abrams wondered whether Lasker had shorted the market, knowing that forcing the Fed chairman to admit the helplessness of the U.S. in the face of Chinese economic expansion would drive down the exchanges by a couple of percentage points the following day. Abrams had seen others do it before and he considered it to be the niftiest, and scummiest, form of insider trading ever invented.

As he approached the podium, Abrams wondered whether anyone else in the room recalled that Lasker was the inventor of ETIFs, exchange traded index funds, that allowed investors to bet on the movement of the entire market at once instead of just one stock or mutual fund at a time, and recalled Lasker's onetime slogan: Whoever moves the market, rules the world.

Abrams thanked the president for the introduction, made the obligatory how-many-economists-does-it-take-to-screw-in-a-light-bulb joke, and then moved into the substance of his speech.

"What I want to address today," Abrams said, "is the fact that the economic models that have guided the central banks of both the U.S. and Europe and the risk assessment analyses of financial institutions throughout the world have failed. They have provided us with a picture of the economy that is simply mistaken. It has been . . ." Abrams felt like he was raising a sword to strike down and split the society in two, and then swung. "It has been nothing more than the imposition of mathematical fantasy over reality."

The audience fragmented into groups of nodding and shaking heads, and then coalesced into what seemed to Abrams like bands of guerrilla fighters poised for battle in an academic jungle.

The Nobel Prize winners, who'd built their careers designing those models, had taken up defensive positions among their sycophants. Arms folded across their chests, heads fixed forward like obstinate children refusing to wash their hands before dinner.

Young professors of finance and physics and mathematics sat on the fringes, looking up at Abrams as though waiting for the order to fire.

"All of these laissez-faire models rest on the assumption that there's an invisible hand that brings the market to equilibrium if left unfettered by government interference. It looks at economic history through the distorted lens of this model, and views the boom and bust cycles of the last hundred years merely as aberrations, when—in fact—they are the norm."

Abrams thought of Hani Ibrahim, that puzzling little man whose office at MIT was the gravitational center of those rebellious youngsters, and of Michael Hennessy who'd driven him not only out of the country, but into hiding.

"What would the public think if it knew that the entire edifice—the . . . entire . . . edifice—of economic theory on which the hopes and dreams of two generations has been built rests on nothing—nothing—but on centuries-old analogies with the way particles of pollen drift around in space and with the way gas distributes itself in a container and with observations of water seeking its natural level."

An image of a basement filled with putrid water flashed through Abrams's mind and a wave of nausea wrenched his insides. Maybe Ibrahim was dead, had reached a final place of rest. Maybe Gage's speculation was right: He'd not simply been deported, but sent somewhere to be tortured. And torture was no more of a science than economics. It was trial and error, and the extreme limit of that kind of error was death.

"Any plumber could've explained to the good men— and they're all men—of economic science that water reaches its natural level in a man-made world only when the plumbing has failed."

And maybe for all those years Hennessy had been searching for a ghost, a creature that persisted in existence only in his guilt.

"Let's think back a few years, to the beginning of the mortgage crisis. Former chairman Greenspan testified before Congress and admitted—in his words—that 'there was a flaw in the model that defines how the world works' and that 'we obviously are viewing an economy that does not resemble our textbook models.'"

Abrams raised both his eyebrows and his finger like a teacher who'd led students into an intellectual trap.

"Except the second comment was made in 1994, not in 2008—and in private, rather than in public, where it deserved to be heard. Which means that the Federal Reserve chairman knowingly encouraged the public in a delusion that he himself recognized as such."

The youngsters in the audience sat up, puppylike, as if their owner was about to toss them a treat.

"And the country went more into debt and more into debt and the bubble grew and exploded and grew and exploded and wealth became more and more concentrated at the top and economic insecurity became concentrated at the bottom. And as sure as a syllogism, it has only gotten worse."

The puppies began panting.

"It's time to start with a new model. One that begins with the supposition that equilibrium is not the natural state of the market, and it's not like water reaching its own level. A model that understands that the market's natural tendency is to seek the extremes of expansion and contraction." Abrams raised his finger again. "Once we begin from that assumption, the aim of the central banks ceases to be one of maintaining equilibrium by keeping the economy moving at peak speed—as if velocity alone will provide stability—but instead aims at reducing the vibrations and muting the effect of the gyrations—even if that means suppressing economic expansion."

That had been the practical implication of Ibrahim's theory, but Abrams wondered whether Ibrahim had a chance to think it through that far. Or whether he'd even had time to think out its implications for risk management.

"What is called risk management in financial circles is just quackery by another name. Investment banks and brokerage firms have wrapped themselves in a mythology that assures them that the tools they possess for managing risk actually do so. But they don't. They fail because they plan only for small imbalances, temporary and minor losses of equilibrium, but not for the crises when they are most needed—and which they never see coming."

Abrams focused on the reddening face of Mitchell Allen Levinson, a Nobel Prize winner for the Efficient Market Theory of Portfolio Allocation. He'd made a billion dollars, and then lost five, as head of ML Capital Partners. Abrams had watched him follow a self-hewn path from theoretical argument toward the cliff edge of practice, and then into a naked freefall through the pages of the *New York Times* and *Business Week* and *Fortune*.

Abrams smiled to himself as he recalled the last of the three-part *Economist* series that had reported that Levinson was now back to teaching Econ 101 at Michigan State, that his private jet was now owned by the CEO of Relative Growth Funds, and that the woman he'd divorced his wife to marry, and who'd once found his bald spot so endearing, had now decided that she only wanted to be friends.

"More fundamentally," Abrams continued, "the theories by which we have managed both the economy and our investment practices are driven not by science, but by . . ."

Ivan Kahn, the mule-teethed 1970s radical, now the

economy writer for *The Nation*, made a fist as if his favorite football team, six points behind with thirty seconds to play, had just made a first down at the one-yard line. Abrams imagined him finishing the sentence in his mind with the word "greed" or "corruption" or "selfishness," the assumed sins of the wealthy.

"But by our having forgotten the real purpose of economic growth, which is to reduce the quantity of human suffering, not to increase the gross national product of gadgets."

Kahn reddened, glanced around, and then slipped his BlackBerry into his shirt pocket.

Abrams felt a certain warmth envelop his body when he said that line and thought back to when he composed it while playing his self-appointed role as an adjunct professor of the New York transit system.

In the weeks after his confirmation by the Senate, Abrams had discovered that a temporary advantage of being a new Federal Reserve chairman was that those who vilify the position still lacked a recognizable face to target. That way it was still possible for him to do his research, not in his Liberty Street office at the New York branch of the Fed, but where it should be done, on the subway. He'd come to view trains not as mere modes of transportation, but as moving classrooms, each stop a mid-term, and the terminus at Pelham Bay or Far Rockaway or Jamaica Center, the final exam.

It was at the Fifty-ninth Street–Columbus Circle Station a week earlier, observing the kids gathered on the platform after their Friday demonstration, clutching their iPods, slipping in their earbuds, texting "c-u-L8-r" on their iPhones, that he'd composed the phrase "gross national product of gadgets," along with another one:

"We look at the world through a microscope of economic analysis or a telescope of political synthesis, when we should be looking in the mirror."

Beautiful. Absolutely beautiful. Abrams wasn't sure that he fully understood the implications of the line yet, but Fed chairmen were allowed to be incomprehensible, even to themselves. After all, it was one of his predecessors who'd said, "I know you believe you understand what you think I said; but what you fail to realize is that what you heard is not what I meant," and who later admitted that he didn't know what he'd meant either.

Abrams glanced at his watch and sniffed at the faint remnants of the tear gas still floating in the air. There would be no time for questions today, and no answers—at least from him—that would move the markets tomorrow.

CHAPTER 13

"T he gross national product of gadgets?" former U.S. president Randall Harris said, as he flicked off the television in his New York office. "The telescope of political synthesis? He makes me miss that nincompoop Greenspan."

Harris looked over at Ronald Minsky, CEO of Relative Growth Funds and former professor of finance at Harvard. "Hasn't he noticed that Relative Growth has solved all of the problems he keeps complaining about?"

Minsky smiled. "Hegel wrote that the owl of Minerva spreads its wings only with the falling of the dusk."

"What the devil does that mean?" Harris finished the question in his mind, *you fucking Jew-boy intellectual.* Abrams. Minsky. Greenspan. They were all the same. But then he remembered that Minsky was a Polish Catholic. *The punk must be a convert.*

"It just means that we only recognize eras once they've passed."

Harris pushed himself up off the couch and walked to his desk. He picked up the Morningstar analyst's report on Relative Growth Funds and waved it at Minsky.

"Hasn't Abrams ever wondered why we've never missed a dividend," Harris said, "never did worse than break even, even during the crashes?"

"He thinks it's just chance or good luck," Minsky said, and then grinned. "And it's not as if we're transparent."

Harris frowned. He didn't like hearing the word. It made him uncomfortable enough just to be on the board of an offshore hedge fund, much less be reminded of the secrecy with which it operated. If it hadn't been for the other two ex-U.S. presidents who'd taken seats on the board before him, he wasn't sure whether he would've done it. And they wouldn't have joined unless George H. W. Bush hadn't already blazed the trail to the Carlyle Group.

Minsky. Everyone had been talking about this genius Minsky. How he'd made his first billions short-selling the franc the year before France adopted the euro. Borrowing and borrowing and borrowing and selling and selling and selling, driving the price down, the international banks and foreign corporations and governments dumping their reserves, forcing the French Central Bank to buy more and more and more to support the currency, then having to cave in at the end and devalue it. The price of bread doubled in a day, the price of gasoline tripled, and the French economy free-fell. Minsky then paid back the expensive francs he'd borrowed with the cheap ones he'd contrived, and Relative Growth pocketed five billion dollars.

Every central banker in Europe knew that sooner or later Minsky would make a move on the euro, they just didn't know when, or how he'd conceal his approach— and neither did Harris.

Harris caught a view of himself in the mirror behind the row of liquor decanters. For a moment he felt more like an oblivious lemming than the Lewis and Clark of the financial frontier. He cringed at the recollection of what his wife had once said about hedge funds: They were like tapeworms living in the intestines of a host, absorbing what they'd made no effort to capture and profiting from what they hadn't earned.

Minsky walked to the bar, poured two bourbons, and handed one to Harris.

"You really want to explain to Abrams how we do what we do just so he'll stop talking about us?" Minsky asked.

Harris's face flushed. "I don't know how we do what we do. It's all gibberish to me. Fractals and scaling and string theory and entanglement." He took a sip of his drink, then held up the glass and smacked his lips. "This is real. You can see it. You can taste it. It can get you drunk and make you act like a fool."

Harris lowered the glass and stared into it. "The problem with financial theory is that you get intoxicated with the idea that you can control the world, and then the world makes a fool of you." He sat down in his desk chair. "What was that punk's name? Levenstein? The guy whose jet you ended up with."

"Levinson, Mitchell Allen Levinson."

"Take a lesson. Look what happened to him."

Minsky smiled at Harris as if at a child. "What makes you think—"

"Don't take that pedantic, patronizing, schoolteacher tone with me."

"I was just—"

"Just what? I'm not sure you even understand the mechanics of this. You've never been able to explain it in plain English."

"It would be like explaining quantum mechanics in words. Can't be done. Unless you can visualize the math and physics in your head, you can't really—"

"And the other thing is that we base all of this on the theories of a traitor. How do I know that Ibrahim wasn't just setting us up? That we haven't walked into some kind of Islamic trap?"

"Because the trillions of dollars held in the Relative Growth Funds are in our hands, not in those of some ayatollah. And not only can't they get to it, not only can't they compete with it, but we make sure we never compete on Islam's home turf. Why do you think we have no investments in oil outside of the United States and have never speculated in oil futures?"

Harris shrugged. "I wouldn't know. I've never seen the books. Hell, I'm not sure anyone on the board has seen the books." He slammed his glass down. Bourbon spilled onto the Morningstar Report. "Hell, I'm not even sure where the goddamn books *are*."

"Tell me what you want to see and you can sit down with our accountants and they'll show it to you."

"Why should I trust them?"

"Who would you trust?"

"People with an incentive to catch each other cheating."

Harris stared down and drummed his fingers on the desk.

"I've got an idea." He looked up at Minsky. "Do we have some kind of petty cash account?"

Minsky nodded. "I guess you could call it that. Usually about fifty million dollars."

"Hire all of the Big Four accounting firms. Have them each audit the fund separately. Everything. Offer a reward of ten million for whoever proves the other three wrong about what's really there."

"Isn't that a little excessive?"

"Look." *You self-important little punk.* "History won't remember you, but it sure as hell will remember me. And I need to control how. I'd sooner blow my brains out than have to stand up there like Richard Nixon trying to convince the world that I'm not a crook—nobody believed him then and nobody would believe me now."

CHAPTER 14

You shouldn't have jumped bail, asshole."

Gage yanked his arm away from the hand that locked on to it. The big man had stepped out of the shadow of the concrete support in the six-level Adirondack Plaza parking structure and grabbed Gage as he was leaving to pick up Elaine Hennessy.

A punch to his kidney from the opposite side stunned Gage. He threw an elbow at where he thought the fist came from, but missed, and the two men spun him down to the pavement. They then twisted his wrist behind his back and knelt on him.

"You . . . got . . . the wrong . . . guy," Gage said. The frozen concrete burned his cheek, and the weight of the men squeezed the air from his lungs. "My name is Graham Gage . . . and I'm not on bail."

"So you say."

While the second man held him, Strubb emptied Gage's pockets, then stood up and laid everything on the trunk of his rental car.

Car doors opened and closed. An elderly couple approached. Strubb flashed a badge at them and said, "I'm a bail agent. This guy skipped out and missed his court date."

They looked away and hurried on.

Strubb flipped open Gage's ID case. "Who'd you steal the California private eye license from?"

"It's mine."

"Yeah, right."

Strubb bent down and compared the picture on the license to Gage's face.

"Good likeness."

He straightened up and opened the envelope that Elaine had given Gage.

"Coupons?" Strubb said. "You're a fucking local boy. No out-of-towner would be carrying coupons."

"Who do you think I am?" Gage asked.

Strubb pulled out a folded piece of paper from the inside pocket of his leather jacket.

"Says here you're David Michaels and you skipped out on a child-molesting case."

The second man punched Gage again, and pain daggered into his side. He leaned in close to Gage's ear and said, "You pervert motherfucker."

Gage held his breath for a few seconds and gritted his teeth, and then asked, "What's Michaels look like?"

"Six-two. Two-ten. White guy. Blue. Brown." Strubb laughed. "I'd say we've got a match."

"Me and a thousand other guys in Albany."

"Hold on to him," Strubb told his partner. "Lemme go make a call."

Strubb walked ten cars away and called Gilbert.

"He's says his name is Graham Gage and that he's a——"

"I know who Gage is. Got a big operation out in San Francisco. Lots of international stuff. This guy must've stolen his ID. What about the envelope?"

"All it had was coupons."

"What?"

"Just what I said. Coupons. Grocery store coupons. Cut out of the Albany newspaper."

"He probably switched out what was in there when he was in his room. Go up there and take a look."

Strubb slipped the envelope into his back pocket, then returned to where Gage lay and said to his partner, "Hook him up. We're going to his room."

After they'd handcuffed Gage and lifted him to his feet, Strubb said, "Just stay cool. If everything checks out, we'll be on our way in a couple of minutes and you can get on to wherever you were going." Strubb grinned. "We'll just call it no harm, no foul."

Gage decided not to fight them. If they intended to kill him, they'd have stuffed him into a trunk and they'd be on their way to the highway by now. He had the feeling they were just puppets and didn't have a clue about the purpose of what they were doing or the meaning of what they'd been directed to look for.

Strubb walked close behind Gage to conceal the handcuffs as they walked through the lobby to the elevator and then again down the tenth floor hallway to his room. Strubb opened the door, then pointed Gage toward one of two fabric-covered chairs near the window facing the backlit stained glass of the gothic Episcopal church and the floodlit state capitol beyond.

Gage sat down on the front edge so he wouldn't be pressing back against his hands and watched them paw through the drawers of the desk and nightstand and then search the closet and his Rollaboard.

Strubb's partner found a second cell phone in an inside compartment and held it up.

"Why do you need a second one?"

"Taxes. One's personal and one's business," Gage said. The man hadn't recognized that it was an encrypted model he used to communicate with his office. "I once got audited by the IRS."

Strubb dropped Gage's wallet and ID case, along with his keys and the other cell phone, on the desk, and picked up Gage's portable printer. He turned it over in his hand and set it down again. He then opened and closed the lid of the laptop, not realizing that the printer was also a scanner and that whatever Gage had collected from Elaine, he might've hidden on his hard drive.

"No paper in this place at all," Strubb spoke into his cell phone. "No other ID or nothing." He fell silent, listening, then pointed back and forth between his partner and Gage.

The partner smirked and then walked between Gage and the window behind him and unlocked the handcuffs.

Gage rose from the chair.

Strubb disconnected the call and slipped the phone into his shirt pocket.

"Sorry man, nothing personal," Strubb said.

"Why don't you send your friend outside for a minute?" Gage said, glancing toward Strubb's partner. "He knows even less than you what this is really about. And it's better if he stays ignorant. I'd hate to see him go down on a kidnapping."

Strubb smiled and shook his head. "We ain't going down on nothing."

The partner reddened and glared at Strubb. "Kidnapping? What you get me into, Strubb? You said—"

"This guy's not gonna call the cops," Strubb said.

"He's right," Gage said. "I won't."

Strubb jerked his thumb toward the door. "Wait in the hallway."

His partner shrugged and then walked out.

Gage stepped over to his Rollaboard and searched through it making sure that nothing had been taken, then went to the desk where Strubb was standing. Gage leaned over as if to inventory his possessions, then spun and slammed his fist into Strubb's side, just below his rib cage. He then faked a jab to the head, and when the man's hands flew up to block it, dropped him to the carpet with an uppercut to his diaphragm.

Strubb groaned as he rolled onto his side and curled up.

Gage bent over and grabbed Strubb's cell phone and wallet, then straightened up and glared down at him.

"You make a move and I'll kick you until I've broken every bone in your face."

"Son of a bitch . . . I'm gonna—shit this hurts . . . I'm gonna be pissing blood . . . for a . . . for a fucking week."

Gage called Alex Z at the office in San Francisco and read off the numbers in the memory of Strubb's phone and the personal data on his driver's license.

"See what you can find out about them," Gage told Alex Z and then disconnected.

Gage looked down at Strubb. "Whose numbers are the last ones you called?"

"Fuck you."

"The only reason I didn't hit you in the eye socket is

that I didn't want to damage my hand," Gage said. "I'm not so concerned about my shoes. Worse that happens, they get a little bloody."

Strubb didn't answer.

"My guy is working on it now," Gage said. "No reason to get yourself kicked in the head for something I'll find out anyway."

"Jesus-fucking-Christ this hurts . . . Gilbert. Tony Gilbert. Works out of New York City."

"How'd you hook up with him?"

"A referral from a PI who hires me to do little jobs once in a while."

"Like kidnapping."

Strubb grunted as he sat up, and then leaned back against the side of the desk.

"It ain't kidnapping when a bail agent does it. He said you was an absconder and that you had some papers somebody wanted. It was supposed to be a two-fer. Double the pay. Anyway, we didn't move you that far. Just up a couple of floors."

"Moving somebody half an inch who doesn't want to go is kidnapping."

Gage paused, trying to think of a gimmick to shake off both Strubb and Gilbert, at least for a while. He then pointed down at Strubb.

"This is what you're going to do," Gage said. "You're going to tell Gilbert and his pals to stay away from me."

"Or what?"

Gage stepped back to his Rollaboard and held up his voice recorder. The red record light was lit. He'd turned it on when he'd reached in earlier. "Or I'll put you and your partner in prison for a very long time."

Strubb winced as he twisted himself onto his knees,

then pushed himself to his feet. He hesitated as though he was thinking he'd make a move to grab the recorder, then his eyes locked on Gage's right fist, and he turned toward the door.

"Not so fast," Gage said, reaching out his other hand. "I want my coupons back."

CHAPTER 15

F aith Gage stood in front of her door and looked over the collapsed warehouse across the narrow street and toward Chengdu in the valley below. Smoke rose in columns from the smoldering remnants of the fires that had been triggered by the earthquake. It then spread like a low fog toward the base of the mountain beneath her, yellow-gray, poisoned by exploding chemical tanks at the factories in the economic development zone. In the near distance she could make out the smoldering shell of the almost completed RAID Technologies microchip plant, the largest building on the western edge of the city.

She recognized that the silent movement of distant things made it hard for her to maintain the images in her mind of the hundreds of thousands of souls entombed in the rubble, the raw hands of searchers, and the roar and grind of earthmoving equipment, and the wail of survivors already gathered in temples, burning incense in honor of the dead.

Shuffling footsteps drew her eyes toward a young man in his mid-twenties carrying a duffel bag over the shoulder of his wool jacket. His dirt- and soot-covered face seemed forlorn against the background of the dusty anarchy of wood, brick, and concrete spilling out into the street. He came to a stop in front of the remains of the wooden shack next to Faith's. He stared at it, then took in a long breath, exhaled, and lowered his head.

Faith walked over. When he looked up she saw that tears had formed, muddying the dirt at the corners of his eyes. She could perceive beyond the tears a somber core, but she couldn't tell whether it was a product of nature or trauma or grief, or of all three.

"Aunt Zhao is fine," she told him in Mandarin, then pointed at her own house. "She's staying with me."

He looked down and sighed, then wiped his eyes with his sleeve, tracking the grime across his face and forehead.

"You are?" Faith asked.

"Her grandson. Jian-jun." He pointed toward Chengdu. "From the city. You must be the anthropologist she told me would be coming."

Faith nodded, then said, "*Chifanle meiyou?*" Have you eaten?

Jian-jun's face relaxed, seeming to find comfort in the familiar greeting, even though spoken by a *gweilo*, a white ghost, in a wasteland.

"*Chifanle*," he answered. I'm fine.

His sunken cheeks told Faith that he wasn't, that he probably hadn't eaten much in days, perhaps even before the earthquake. She led him through the house and into the kitchen where his eighty-five-year-old grandmother sat at the table chopping vegetables for lunch. He walked over and knelt beside her. She reached for him with her thin arms and hugged him against her breast. He pulled back and whispered something to her. She bit her lip and frowned as he again pressed against her.

After pouring him tea, Faith dragged a wooden chair up next to his grandmother. He pulled himself onto it and then warmed his hands on the cup.

"How is it in the city?" Faith asked him.

"Chaos. Fury. Violence." Jian-jun took a sip of tea; he didn't seem surprised or put off balance by Faith's speaking unaccented Mandarin. "Schools and hospitals collapsed everywhere, burying children and sick people."

His hands tightened around the cup and his face flushed.

"The concrete didn't just crack, it crumbled. Disintegrated. Mobs hunted down the builders and the mayor and a couple of party leaders and hung them. They've now surrounded all of the government offices and intend to starve them out and kill them, too."

"Isn't the army—"

Jian-jun shook his head. "The army isn't intervening, and not because they're afraid. They're as sickened by the corruption as everyone else. I think they want to try to contain it to Chengdu and the other cities in the earthquake area, and let it be an object lesson for the rest of the country."

Ayi Zhao stared ahead. Listening.

"And there's no clean water. Chemical runoff from the burned factories flowed into the BoTiao River and the waterworks." He pointed north. "And they can't use the Zi Pingpu Reservoir. It's too polluted by lead and cadmium from the electronic recycling companies up in the hills. People are drinking from their toilets."

Ayi Zhao whispered, "*Tian ming.*" It's the mandate of heaven.

Jian-jun reached over and took her hand.

He and Faith both knew that saying the words was no different than criticizing the party directly. In historical terms, it meant that the government had lost its legitimacy, and withdrawing the mandate was the way heaven authorized an uprising. *Tian ming* had justified every dynastic change for three thousand years and explained every earthquake and flood. Even Communist Party members feared the phrase.

What had always bothered Faith about the concept was that it was circular: The success of an uprising meant that the mandate had truly been withdrawn; the failure, that it hadn't, and millions of lives had been sacrificed over the centuries determining heaven's intentions.

Ayi Zhao raised a finger and said, "All that is solid melts into air, all that is holy is profaned."

Faith cast a questioning look at Jian-jun. It sounded to her as though Ayi Zhao had quoted a lost stanza from Yeats's "Second Coming." She saw, more than spoke, the famous lines in her mind.

> *Things fall apart; the centre cannot hold;*
> *Mere anarchy is loosed upon the world,*
> *The blood-dimmed tide is loosed . . .*

"It's from Karl Marx," Jian-jun said. "From the *Communist Manifesto*. Grandmother was a party member in the 1940s, but Mao purged her for supporting Deng Xiaoping's reforms in the 1970s."

He pointed toward the front door.

"She was sent to a forced labor and reeducation camp outside of Chengdu for five years, but was taken back into the party when Deng took power. Then in the 1980s she was purged again when she protested the Tiananmen Square massacre and Deng's support of the wealthy against the poor."

He held out his arms, as if to encompass the village.

"That's why she's living up here now. But she remains a hero to those living below. The government can't kill her or imprison her without inciting bloodshed. She's like Burma's Aung San Suu Kyi—except that the condition of her freedom and her continued living is silence."

Jian-jun looked at his grandmother, then back at Faith, his gaze seeming to classify her as a Westerner who saw Communism not as a theory, but as a peasant society's delusion.

"For people of my grandmother's generation," Jian-jun said, "Communism wasn't an economic system as much as a philosophy of life and a cry of resistance against foreign occupation, a proclamation of the dignity of labor, even the labor of peasants and farmers."

He pressed his fingers against his chest.

"I'm a Christian," he said, "but does that mean I believe everything in the Bible? Would I turn my cheek if someone harmed my grandmother?"

His voice rose, as though he was repeating an argument he'd already had with himself or with an unseen enemy.

"Do I believe with Jesus that non-Christians are a brood of vipers and that justifies their murder? Do I believe that Christ will return and lead an army that will torment and torture the unbelievers?"

Ayi Zhao looked at her grandson and nodded.

"The people of my grandmother's generation weren't deluded. They knew that China was an agricultural country. They knew that it didn't have the industrial and economic development that Marx said was the precondition of Communism."

Jian-jun spread his arms again.

"What did they know of capitalism? Only British and German and French imperialism and Japanese occupation. The people of her generation weren't stupid, but they, and the generations that followed them, were betrayed."

Jian-jun's words made Faith realize that there were two empty seats at her table.

"What about your parents?" she asked. "Did they follow your grandmother into the party?"

Ayi Zhao and Jian-jun both stiffened.

"I'm sorry," Faith said, "I didn't mean—"

"In China," Jian-jun said, "we still believe in the Confucian virtue of filial piety. We take care of our parents." He locked his eyes on Faith's. "The last thing I did before leaving Chengdu to come here and check on grandmother was hide them from the mob."

ay off this guy. I'm not going back to the joint."
Strubb leaned over the table in a rear booth of the
Jupiter Club on the western edge of downtown
Albany. "I don't know what you got me into, but I don't
like it."

"I didn't know you were so choosy about what you
did." Tony Gilbert smirked. "You did five years in the
joint for a hundred-dollar robbery, this time you made a
grand for ten minutes' work."

Strubb made a fist and slammed it down, rattling the
bowl of pretzels between them.

Two men dressed in black leather body harnesses and
studded wrist gauntlets looked over from the bar. The
bartender, his stomach mounding out between the front
panels of his vest, stared at Strubb and shook his head as
if to say, *If you weren't a regular, I'd kick your ass out of here
right now.*

"Gage knows what he's doing," Strubb said. "He's got
enough on me right now to get my parole violated. No
trial. Just straight back to the pen."

Gilbert snorted, then lowered his voice. "I thought

you liked it in there. You're getting it up the ass anyway." He smiled and tilted his head toward the bar. "The way I hear, it's easier for you guys to get it inside prison than on the outside. They even hand out free condoms."

"Fuck you." Strubb drew back his fist, then winced and rubbed his side in the area of his kidney.

"What? Baby get pushed around a little?"

"Maybe Gage'll do the same to you someday. He knows how to use his hands. Like a pro. He knew how to drop me without breaking any ribs."

"I made calls to some guys in Frisco," Gilbert said. "He did a little boxing when he was a cop. That doesn't make him the Terminator. Anyway, you're out of it."

"You're not listening to me. He's saying I better get you off his back or he's gonna take it out on me. With my record, a kidnapping conviction is life without parole."

Gilbert's cell phone rang. He connected, then asked, "What's up?" and turned the phone toward Strubb so he could hear the answer.

"Gage picked up the woman at her house," the caller said. "We used a three-car rotation to follow him so he couldn't pick us out. They're over at a steakhouse. Angelo's. On Broadway by the Orange Street overpass. I'm parked about a block away."

Gilbert grinned at Strubb and asked the caller, "Anybody left inside the house?"

Strubb clenched his teeth at the words and jabbed a forefinger at Gilbert. "I told you to back off."

Gilbert covered the microphone. "Fuck you." Then back to the caller. "Have somebody keep an eye on the place and see if the kid leaves, too. If she does, go in again and try to find what we missed last time."

Strubb lowered his hands to his lap.

Gilbert disconnected and then looked over at Strubb.

"No way, man," Gilbert said. "I've made a couple of hundred grand on this thing and expect to make a couple of hundred more before it's over. It's every PI's dream. A stack of blank checks. And I'm gonna keep cashing them and cashing them and cashing them."

Strubb reached into his jacket pocket and withdrew a small semiautomatic. He flashed it at Gilbert, then slipped it back under the table.

"You fucking fag coward," Gilbert said. "No way you'll pull the trigger."

One of the men at the bar spun his stool around. "A fucking what?"

"You're right," Strubb said to Gilbert. "Not in here, anyway." He jerked his head toward the door. "Let's take it outside."

"I'm not going anywhere," Gilbert said.

"A fucking what?" Now the man from the bar was on his feet, walking toward the booth, his right fist cocked in front of his chest. He stopped a foot away. The man who'd been drinking with him also walked up.

"Back off, Cinderella," Gilbert said, without looking over. "This ain't about you."

A grating of metal silenced them. They all looked toward the bar. The bartender held a sawed-off shotgun across his chest. His T-shirt read, "My Bar. My Rules."

"You guys have twenty seconds to clear out," the bartender said, "or you're all gonna be wearing buckshot."

"This is the second time you should've listened to me," Strubb said, as he slipped the gun back into his coat pocket and stood up. He then pointed his free hand at Gilbert. "I told you. Let's take it outside."

When Gage returned to the Adirondack Plaza Hotel garage after dropping off Elaine Hennessy, he was ready for whoever would step out of the shadows. If Strubb hadn't succeeded in deflecting Gilbert, he'd have to escalate his efforts to find out what Gage had been doing and what he'd learned—and Gage's ride on the elevator might be replaced by one to the riverbank.

Gage had driven a thirty-mile loop northwest through Schenectady, then back toward the Hudson. On the way, he'd pulled into a truck stop and bought a flashlight. He searched the undercarriage of his car until he located a GPS tracking device that he'd guessed Gilbert had installed. He pulled it free and stomped it with his heel.

As Gage headed back toward the highway, he telephoned his surveillance chief in San Francisco and told him to get on a plane for New York to help him arrange for countermeasures, and then continued down along the river.

Gage drove to the top level of the hotel garage, called

for an elevator, reached inside to press the button for the first floor, then ran to the corner stairs and raced down to meet it. He wanted to come up behind whoever might be waiting for him to come down.

He eased the first floor door open, but found himself behind the elevator shaft. He heard the doors slide open and then close. He tried to stay in the shadows as he snuck between cars and along the walls until he was able to get a view of the front of the elevators.

The area was clear except for a woman staring up at the digital floor readout numbers, shivering despite the heavy hooded coat enveloping her.

Another elevator opened. Two men in trench coats got out. Both gave her sideways glances, then one grinned at the other and they walked past her and toward the lobby. She didn't get into the elevator. She just stood there, rocking back and forth and stamping her feet. It struck Gage that the fidgeting might have been less from cold than from agitation or urgency.

After scanning the floor, Gage came around the van and walked toward her. She turned at the sound of his footsteps.

It was Vicky, her eyes bloodshot and her face raw red.

She took two steps, intercepted him, and then grabbed his upper arm with her gloved hands.

"I need to talk to you," she said, peering up at him. Tears glistened on her checks. "I'm sorry about how I acted today." She leaned her forehead against his chest. "Please. If I don't tell someone, I'll go crazy."

Gage reached for her shoulders and turned her so he could see her face.

"Tell me what?"

"I think I killed my father."

Gage recognized that this was the voice of guilt, not of fact, but that it needed to be heard nonetheless.

"What makes you think so?" Gage asked.

"I told them where he was."

"Who is 'them'?"

Vicky looked down and sighed. "I don't know."

Gage pointed toward the glass double doors leading to the lobby.

"Let's go inside," he said, and then led her into the hotel and toward the coffee shop.

"Can we talk in your room?" she asked, as they passed the reception desk.

Gage shook his head. "I don't want to be seen taking a girl your age up there."

His real reason was that she was too erratic, and maybe too delusional, for him to risk being alone with her. Her self-accusation could easily mutate and turn outward, and he didn't want to become the target.

He guided her to a table along the wall opposite the bank of windows facing the night-lit State Street.

A middle-aged waitress walked up, glancing back and forth between the two of them. Her eyes held for a moment on Vicky's flushed face, then her brows furrowed, as though she'd decided that Gage was responsible for the distress on Vicky's face.

When Vicky looked down at the menu, Gage mouthed the words "boy trouble" to the waitress.

She nodded, then rolled her eyes as if to say she'd been through the same thing with her own kids, then took his order for two teas.

"Tell me what happened," Gage said, after the waitress walked away.

"A year ago an FBI agent stopped me as I was leaving

school. He told me that he was worried about my father, afraid that he might get hurt because of his obsession with Hani Ibrahim, and asked me to spy on him."

Vicky reached for her napkin and smoothed it out on the paper placemat.

"At first I didn't want to do it. But then I watched my father get more and more frantic, so I called the agent and began to pass on to him things I overheard my father say or whatever I found in his office."

Gage saw that the napkin was damp with sweat.

"I only learned about the places my father traveled after he got back." She swallowed hard and crushed the napkin in her hands. "Except Marseilles."

The waitress arrived and set down two pots of hot water and a selection of tea bags. She slipped Vicky a pocket-sized packet of tissues and then turned and walked away.

"And you think the FBI has something to do with his death," Gage said, "by having him killed or badgering him into suicide?"

"That's what I was afraid of, and I'm too terrified to tell my mother what I did." She shrugged and her eyes went blank. "But now I don't know what to think."

"What changed?"

She focused again on Gage. "I started to worry when you showed up and what you might know or tell my mother, so I tried to call the agent earlier tonight, but he didn't answer his cell phone. Then I called the FBI's emergency number." Vicky's eyes again filled with tears. She stifled a sob. "And they told me they'd never heard of him."

"What name had he given you?"

"Anthony Gilbert."

CHAPTER 18

"If you think they're tailing you, then why'd you show up here?" Abrams said to Gage, reaching to close the living room drapes of his Central Park West apartment.

"Don't bother," Gage said. "Enjoy the sunrise. I'm not telling them anything new. They began following me from here. They probably followed us from the airport. Somebody might even have been with me on the plane out here."

Abrams turned back. "Which means?"

"That you're the real target, not me. And it's somehow because of Hennessy." Gage surveyed the room, then walked up next to Abrams and whispered. "How often do you have this place swept for bugs?"

"What?" Abrams said, also in a whisper. "I bought it from a former defense secretary. He would've checked. Anyway, nobody could get in to do it." He pointed downward. "There's a concierge at the door twenty-four hours." He spread his hands. "And there are cameras on every floor."

"Let's go into the kitchen."

"Aren't you being a little paranoid?"

Gage stepped back, pulled up his shirt, and exposed the bruises where Strubb's partner had punched him.

Abrams's eyes widened.

"Paranoia doesn't come in black and blue," Gage said.

Gage led him down the hall to the kitchen, turned on the water, set the nozzle to spray, and tuned to a local television news show to cover their voices.

Over coffee at the table, Gage recounted the previous twenty-four hours.

"If the point was to kill Hennessy before he talked to me," Abrams said, "then why would Gilbert still be interested in what I'm doing?"

"We don't yet know whether Hennessy was murdered, and if he was, whether it was related to you or—"

"Then I'll rephrase it. Once Hennessy was dead for whatever reason."

"Maybe someone is trying to determine whether you're acting on something that Hennessy might've told you ahead of your meeting."

Abrams thought for a moment. "And that would be why they followed you, thinking that I had hired you to follow up on whatever that was."

Gage shrugged. "Maybe. Maybe not. They were interested in what his wife gave me, and that could go either way. It could be that they're only afraid that you asked me to take up Hennessy's search for Ibrahim."

"Or for who or what caused Hennessy to be dead."

"I suspect that they think—or maybe know—that it's the same thing."

Gage's cell phone beeped with an incoming text message. It was from Faith.

I'd like to find a way to stay. Things are calm up here
and the kids are helping the villagers and learning
more about Chinese culture than if they'd actually
done the research project. So am I. Love you.

Gage wrote back.

Love you too. Be careful. Let me know if you need
anything.

Abrams rose and walked to the window and looked
out toward the gray-fogged Central Park West. He took
in a long breath, and then exhaled and turned back.

"I appreciate you coming out here," Abrams said, "but
I think I should just let the thing go. My record in the
world of intrigue isn't so good."

Neither of them had to say what that record was.
Twenty-five years earlier, Abrams had gone on a fact-
finding mission to Chile on behalf of the World Bank
to determine the success of the Milton Friedman– and
Augusto Pinochet–imposed economic upheaval on the
country.

A government economist named Orlando Ferrada
had slipped Abrams secret data showing that the result
of those policies was that forty-five percent of Chilean
families had descended into poverty, seventy percent
of family incomes were being spent on bread alone, and
most of the country's wealth had been transferred to offshore tax havens. Among those funds were ten million
dollars in World Bank loans that had been diverted to a
secret account in Bermuda controlled by Pinochet's wife.

Abrams had passed through Chicago on his way back

to MIT. He showed the documents to an economist at a think tank founded by a Friedman disciple, hoping that the evidence would persuade them that the attempt to impose their economic theories on the people of Chile through shock and terror had been disastrous.

Days later, Ferrada was arrested at his office by Pinochet's National Intelligence Directorate.

"What happened to Hennessy is not your fault," Gage said.

"I feel it in my gut. It's Orlando Ferrada all over again."

"Who did you tell about Hennessy?"

"My assistant, the director of the FBI, and his deputy. Who they later told, I couldn't say. But only my assistant knew I was meeting him in Marseilles."

"If history is repeating itself, then it's Ibrahim we should be worried about, and not because of anything that you did, but because of what Hennessy may have done or learned."

"History is already repeating itself. You got hurt rescuing Ferrada. You got hurt yesterday."

Gage smiled. "The first time was my fault. I was driving too fast."

"Only because they were shooting at you."

Gage had broken Ferrada out of a jungle prison, then had missed a turn on the dirt track leading from Chile into Bolivia. His jeep rolled down a hillside and came to rest in a frigid Andean streambed, fifty yards upstream from a Bolivian customs checkpoint, and they swam across the border.

This morning he'd also driven back roads, from Albany to Manhattan, hoping to determine whether Gilbert or his people were on his tail and whether they were set up around Abrams's apartment house. He'd only hoped that he could use Strubb to shake them off long enough to get a few steps down the trail ahead of them, but listening to Abrams now, he wasn't sure that would happen.

Gage glanced at the television. It was the start of the local weather report. The reporter announced that it was cold outside. The mysteries growing about the fates of Hennessy and Ibrahim made Gage wonder why weather reports always began by telling people what they already knew.

"I have the feeling that you've made the Orlando Ferrada–Michael Hennessy connection before," Gage said.

"I was thinking about that while you were gone, but it's not Chile that worries me. It's the Relative Growth Funds. They're supposed to be based on the work Ibrahim did when he was at MIT—but I don't believe it. For political reasons they don't use Ibrahim's name, but when they refer to fractal analysis, insiders know what they mean."

Abrams sat down and folded his arms on the table.

"I think it's a scam," Abrams said, "at least an intellectual one. Ibrahim being right about the markets tending toward the extremes doesn't mean that you can build an investment model on it. But that's what Relative Growth says is the reason they've beaten the performance of every other hedge fund over the last ten years, even through two economic collapses."

"And you don't see how it's possible to predict the unpredictable."

"Nobody can—and not just as a matter of logic, but of fact. Despite that, they've attracted almost two trillion investment dollars into their funds. Most from the U.S., the rest from Europe."

"How did you find out? I thought Relative Growth was based in the Caymans."

"The CIA director. He was concerned about the foreign entanglements of former U.S. government officials. Their board of directors has three former U.S. presidents, two former defense secretaries, and two former secretaries of state. After *Time* magazine called Relative Growth Funds 'a Republican administration in exile,' he felt he'd better make some inquiries and warn those guys about conflicts of interest."

Abrams glanced at the television screen. A reporter stood in the middle of the Rockefeller Center ice skating rink surrounded by racing, screaming children.

He looked back at Gage.

"There are only three explanations I can think of for Relative Growth's success. The first is simple market manipulation. Shorting a stock like Apple or Microsoft, then planting false stories in the press. But you can't do that too many times before even the most dim-witted reporters figure out they're being used.

"The second is insider trading. Altogether, the Relative Growth members sit on about a hundred corporate boards. No major move happens without them knowing about it." Abrams bit his lip and shook his head. "But I don't think that's what's going on. I know former president Randall Harris well. Very well. He'd blow the whistle, regardless of the personal cost to him."

"There's only one other possibility," Gage said.

Abrams nodded. "It's a Ponzi scheme with an offshore loop. Running new investors through a Cayman Island black hole, then back in to pay off old investors. And something like that could be concealed from the board by a first year accounting student."

"How solid is the two-trillion-dollar number?"

"Only little better than rumor. For the most part, the CIA can only track the money when it moves from place to place. They don't have access to the inner workings of private banks. Relative Growth could have a lot more stashed."

"Or a lot less."

"That, too."

"You think that Hennessy figured it out?" Gage asked.

"Which, the total or the method?"

"The method."

"If so, not in the same way I did. There's no way anyone other than someone with a graduate-level mathematics background could've figured out that you can't build portfolio allocation and risk models based on Ibrahim's theories."

Gage thought of Hennessy's highlightings in the books in his home-office library.

"I think he tried," Gage said. "Maybe he made a kind of intuitive leap and came to the same conclusion you did."

"It's possible, but I didn't ask. I was less interested in Hennessy's financial theories than in what he knew about Ibrahim and where he is. If I could get Ibrahim to cooperate, then I could do something about the Relative Growth Funds."

"And you think they killed Hennessy to keep him from bringing you and Ibrahim together."

Abrams nodded.

"And they've been following you, and then me, to see if we were trying to pick up the scent again."

Gage then realized that it was a mistake to have used Strubb to shake off Gilbert. It would've been smarter to have led Gilbert into a trap. But it wasn't too late. Even if Gilbert had been scared off the case, he still knew what he knew, and while he might not have known why he'd been hired, he knew who hired him.

"You have a phone book handy?" Gage asked.

Abrams reached over and pulled out a drawer of the counter under the television.

The screen showed a view down a commercial alley, and a voiceover said, "New York private investigator Anthony Gilbert was found beaten to death in downtown Albany this morning. Homicide detectives are—"

Gage shook his head, and then said, "Don't bother."

CHAPTER 19

You all right, man?"

Kenyon Arndt blinked up at the personal trainer kneeling over him where he lay twisted on the floor of the 24 Hour Fitness center in Scarsdale.

"Don't move him," someone yelled. "Nobody move him. And turn off the goddamn treadmill."

A second face appeared. "I'm a doctor. Can you bend your arms or legs?"

Arndt looked past the woman toward the television screen hanging from the wall he'd been facing as he jogged. Anthony Gilbert's photo had appeared, followed by a report of the discovery of his frostbitten body in a dumpster behind a market and by a description of his injuries: crushed skull, smashed fingers.

Arndt now remembered the tread belt ripping his legs out from under him, his knee hitting and then his shoulder, and the machine spinning him onto the carpeted floor and bouncing him into the crossbeam of a weight bench.

"I think I can move," Arndt said. He rolled over onto his back. Nausea waved through him and his mouth watered. He swallowed hard and tried to sit up. Dizziness stopped him. He closed his eyes. He let the doctor support the back of his head and ease him back down again.

Arndt felt a towel press against his forehead. He opened his eyes again as the doctor pulled it away. He winced at the splotch of blood.

"Don't worry," she said. "It's not as bad as this makes it look."

"I need to get to my office."

She smiled. "The first sign of a concussion is talking nonsense. And the idea of you driving to your office in your condition is nonsense."

Arndt rolled back onto his side and pushed himself to his knees. She helped him to his feet, steadied him as he found his balance, and then sat him down on the weight bench.

"You'll need to make a stop at the emergency room before you can even think of going into work." She handed him the towel. "Hold this against your head."

The club manager walked up. "We'll have to insist that you get examined," he said to Arndt, then to the trainer, "Rope off the machine until we can determine whether there was a mechanical problem."

Arndt shook his head, then looked up. "It was my fault. I forgot to hook the emergency stop cord onto my shirt."

Someone in the crowd laughed and said, "It's worse than a concussion. It's actual brain damage. Who ever heard of a lawyer passing on a lawsuit."

Maybe he's right, Arndt said to himself. *Maybe I should sue. It may be the only way I'll be able to make money now that my career has gone down the tubes.*

Instead, he said, "I'll telephone my wife. She can take me to the hospital."

"What's her number?" the manager asked, pulling out his cell phone.

Arndt shook his head again. "I'll call her from the locker room."

Five minutes later, Arndt felt strong enough to make his way across the gym. He pretended to call his wife, then got dressed and went out to his car.

His boss answered on the first ring.

"I know," Wycovsky said. "I got a call."

"I quit," Arndt said, staring through his windshield at the gym, imagining Gilbert's face on the television screen. "I want out. I didn't sign up for this."

"You need to have your head examined."

"Craziness is staying involved in this, not in getting out—and I'm getting out."

"Do you have a single shred of evidence that Gilbert's death has anything to do with us?"

Arndt cringed. His mind locked up. He couldn't think of an answer.

"We don't know what else he was working on," Wycovsky said. "He sure as hell didn't work for us full-time. And the guy was a royal asshole. Good at his work, but still an asshole."

By that criterion, Arndt thought, Wycovsky would've been murdered ten times over and a hundred people would still be standing in line to kick his lifeless body.

"Look, kid," Wycovsky said, "every tree that falls in the forest isn't aiming at you."

Arndt knew that Wycovsky was right, logically, but he felt, more than he knew, that the logic was an evasion. Even worse, Wycovsky had once again beaten him back into line with an analogy.

"Anyone who says *capisci*," Wycovsky said, "is just

asking for his head to get kicked in. I'll expect you to be in the office at the usual time."

As Arndt disconnected, he felt a rumble in his stomach, then a sour taste in his mouth. He got the door open just before his half-digested breakfast sprayed out of his throat and onto the slush and snow.

CHAPTER 20

Vice President Cooper Wallace scowled, looking past his wife sitting across from him in front of the inglenook fireplace in their official residence at the Naval Observatory.

"It was what?" Wallace said into his cell phone. "Arson? A billion-dollar arson?"

"That's what the RAID people on the ground in Chengdu are reporting," Chief of Staff Paul Nichols told Wallace. "It withstood the quake, but the story they're hearing is that a mob broke through the perimeter fence. The guards were no match. They were posted there only to prevent thefts from the construction site, not to stop a rebellion."

"What about the Spectrum distribution center?"

"Still standing. Looted, but still standing."

Wallace pushed himself to his feet. "The Chinese government will have to pay RAID and Spectrum back every single dollar—"

"Yuan. And I don't think that's going to happen. You may even want to think twice about asking for it."

"Why the devil not?"

"Because what Tiananmen Square was to political protest, Chengdu will be to economic protest, except worse. The turmoil in the city is starting to spread to other towns and villages in the earthquake zone."

"What about the army?"

"It looks like they learned their lesson in 1989 and are staying out of it—for now."

Nichols found himself once again looking for a way to dissuade Wallace from a course that would make a fool either out of himself or out of the president.

"It only confirms what you've been saying all along," Nichols finally said, suppressing what he was afraid might sound like a patronizing tone. "Neither RAID nor Spectrum should've gone in there. Let them learn their lesson by eating their losses."

Wallace paused and stared down at the morning's *Washington Times* lying on the coffee table. His eyes fell on a profile of the marketing director of the Arizona Camelback mega-church. He then recited, more to himself than to Nichols, *"Moses took the calf they had made and burnt it; he ground it to powder, sprinkled it on water, and made the Israelites drink it."*

"You're right," Wallace said to Nichols. "Let them choke on it. I warned them. If they'd spent as much time reading the Bible as they did spreadsheets and profit projections and financial models, they wouldn't be in this mess."

"I also think we should call the folks at the Baptist Missionary Convention and tell them not to send any kids over there. The mobs haven't turned on foreigners yet, but they will as soon as they connect the dots."

"Connect the dots . . . What do you mean, connect the dots?"

Nichols cringed. Wallace was the leading Republican contender for the presidency, but he sometimes displayed a provincial naïveté.

"Corruption, Mr. Vice President. The RAID facility didn't cost a billion dollars, it cost three-quarters of a billion, the rest was used to pay bribes from Beijing to Chengdu. And one of the things those payments bought was the right to pollute the countryside and poison the people. Right now the mobs are more focused on the corrupt officials who are responsible for the school and hospital collapses and the undrinkable water and the birth defects and rampant cancers, but in the Chinese way, it's only a matter of time before they take revenge against the barbarian invaders."

"If it wasn't the mob, then who burned down RAID? Environmental terrorists? Falun Gong? The ghost of Chiang Kai-shek? Who?"

"We don't know yet, and perhaps we never will. Whoever did it used the chaos that followed the earthquake to disguise who they were, otherwise they would've announced something on the Internet."

"We need to lean on the CIA. What are they for, if not to find out who's attacking American economic interests? If it happened to a Chinese factory in Nigeria you bet your ass the Chinese intelligence service would be on it."

"I'll make a call and see what resources they can put into it," Nichols said, "but I wouldn't count on getting definitive results very soon. They're stretched pretty thin."

"Then maybe what I need to propose as part of my presidential campaign is that we establish a financial security agency, modeled on the NSA."

"Not a bad idea. Just make sure you figure out a way to control it better than anyone has been able to control the CIA."

"Don't worry, that'll be on my agenda. For now, lean on them as hard as you can. If you're not getting anywhere, then send the director to me and I'll take care of it."

CHAPTER 21

F inding out whether Relative Growth is a Ponzi scheme is worth the risk," Gage told Abrams before catching a flight to Boston. "The consequences of not learning the truth could be devastating. If it means locating Hani Ibrahim in order to do it, then let's give it a try."

Gage had decided not to tell Abrams that Tony Gilbert was the person that Strubb claimed had hired him. He'd diverted Abrams's attention away from the television by suggesting that he travel up to Boston to try to retrace Hennessy's steps from when he first began investigating Ibrahim and try to discover what he learned about the professor and his connection to Relative Growth.

Abrams had finally agreed and gave Gage a debit card that drew on a Federal Reserve bank account to cover his expenses. In order to disguise the trail back to Abrams, Gage decided to use his own and replenish it with the Fed card once the work was done.

The storm that had swept through New York confronted Gage as he drove his rental car from Boston's

Logan Airport toward Back Bay. And by the time he'd reached the Harvard Bridge, he was once again in the midst of a blizzard and in the hands of his GPS. It got him to Memorial Drive along the Charles River and to the front of the Sloan School of Management where Hani Ibrahim had his office when he was on the faculty of MIT during the five years before his arrest.

Professor Goldie Goldstein looked up from behind her desk in the Institute for Islamic Finance when Gage's knuckles rapped on her open door. She blinked and smiled, and then made a show of rubbing her eyes.

"I must be dreaming. For a second I thought you were Graham Gage, but he doesn't have that much gray hair."

Gage smiled back. "He does now."

Goldie came from behind her desk. Gage met her halfway and gave her a hug. She glanced toward the hallway as they separated.

"No Faith?"

Goldie knew Faith even better than she did Gage. They'd worked together on the Agunah Project to help Orthodox Jewish women reclaim their right to remarry after having been abandoned by husbands who had refused to divorce them. Faith had raised money to help Goldie's successful attempt to get legislation passed in her home country of Israel.

"She's in China."

"Anywhere near—"

"West of Chengdu. But she's okay. She's waiting until things settle down before she comes home."

Goldie took Gage's coat, then directed him to one of the two chairs facing her desk and then sat in the other.

"You should've called ahead," Goldie said. "My grandson is in town so tonight I'm making noodle kugel with raisins, and tzimmes with potatoes and pineapple."

"I was just passing through, so I—"

She flashed her palms at him. "Don't lie to an old lady. You're up to some kind of cloak-and-dagger and you figured that a busybody like me would know something."

Gage smiled and shrugged.

"And you want to use me as cover or maybe to help you aim the blade."

"Was that a question?" Gage asked.

Goldie nodded.

"Then how about I'll answer with someone's name and you tell me if I've come to the right place."

"Shoot."

"Hani Ibrahim."

Goldie jerked to the side as if dodging a blow. "Sheesh. I didn't see that coming."

"I'm trying to find out what he was up to."

"You and everyone else who worked with him, or even brushed his shoulder. Terrorist financing wasn't something anyone expected would show up on his résumé. No one even thought he had an interest in offshore transactions. His head was always in a dimension of the universe that was invisible to the rest of us."

She reached over to her bookshelf and pulled out an academic journal from her collection and opened it to the table of contents.

"This is that last paper he published."

Gage read the article title, "String Theory and the Structure of Financial Entanglement," and then asked, "And that means . . ."

"It was part of his effort to apply the latest and greatest

from the world of physics to financial modeling. Quantum mechanics and all that. The problem was that he painted himself into a corner." Goldie grinned. "Only portfolio managers had a use for it, but only physicists could understand the math."

She gestured toward the floors above.

"Even the Newtonian Efficient Market Nobel Prize winners upstairs couldn't make much sense out of it, but then again, they had a vested interest in pretending they didn't. The implication of Ibrahim's work was that everything they'd built their careers on was an intellectual fraud."

She lowered her hand and spread her arms.

"There was much joy in the corridors of Sloan Hall when he was led out of here in handcuffs."

She leaned in toward Gage and whispered, "He was right though. What they do up there is *dreck*, complete and utter bullshit. Intellectual compost."

Gage sniffed the air. "I don't smell it."

"That's because hot air rises. You're safe down here. Islamic finance has no need for derivatives, no matter how stringed and entangled. Sharia law requires hard cash."

"I'm thinking that if Ibrahim was an Islamic radical," Gage said, "whatever financial gimmick he used had to be something that Muslims would be comfortable investing in."

"You mean separate from whether or not they knew the money would end up in the hands of terrorists." Goldie frowned. "Unless they knew the whole thing was a sham from the beginning. After all, jihadist ends can be used to justify nonjihadist means."

"Except I don't think that any of the investors were charged with terrorist financing," Gage said. "I suspect they thought that it was a legitimate investment, or at least made a convincing argument to the prosecutor that they thought it was legitimate."

Goldie nodded, and then said, "And you want sly little me to explain to you what the argument was."

Gage smiled to himself. Goldie always seemed to know how to finish his thoughts, the same way Faith did. When they had dinner together, they'd all speak in half sentences.

"I don't know what he did," Goldie said, "if by that you mean the terrorism part—but I have an idea about how he did it." She grinned. "And that's exactly why you came knocking on my door."

"Don't make it look so easy to guess my motives," Gage said. "It'll damage my self-confidence."

"I doubt it."

Goldie clapped her hands, then rubbed them together.

"This is what I think he was up to. Back then, Muslim businesspeople in the U.S. were looking for an offshore tax avoidance structure that was consistent with Sharia law. That means that they're not allowed to make money on interest. It limits the kinds of investments they can make. But—"

Goldie rubbed her hands together again.

"But what if they could surrender ownership of the assets for a while, let those assets earn whatever money they're going to earn—and by any means they're going to earn it—and then have the assets returned to them?"

Gage worked out the implications of the theory himself: It was the perfect way for someone to finance a terrorist organization without being held criminally responsible. The money was out of their legal control while the crime was being committed and then whatever hadn't been spent was returned to them afterward.

"I think that Ibrahim realized that the perfect vehicle is what's called a hybrid company," Goldie said. "It's also called a Manx trust—not after the cat, after the island. The Isle of Man. Since the U.S. taxpayer has no control over the company—none, zip, nada—he's not even a shareholder—he doesn't have to report to the IRS any profits he makes until the company is closed down and the assets are returned to him."

"And if they put the money in the hands of an expert in Sharia law," Gage said, "they could even ensure that the profits won't be tainted."

Goldie smiled and nodded. "Exactly. A Muslim tax dodge."

"And a terrorism financing gimmick."

Goldie shrugged. "Why not? The boss who runs it can be anywhere that has an Internet connection. Pakistan. Saudi Arabia. Sudan. He just e-mails orders to whoever manages the company's money on the Isle of Man." Goldie spread her hands. "So what if the boss gets indicted in the States, the U.S. will never get him."

"And the investors in the U.S. can claim they didn't know what was going on." Gage then realized that the plan came with a built in criminal defense. "And you have two branches of the government working against each other. The IRS saying the American investors don't control the company and the Justice Department claiming they do. No way a jury would convict them. And even if it did, an appeals court would have to overturn the verdict."

Goldie squinted up at the ceiling for a moment, then

asked, "Would that apply to whoever suggested the structure in the first place? Like Ibrahim?"

"As you said, why not? Ibrahim could also claim he didn't know what the structure would really be used for—and I suspect that's why the U.S. Attorney couldn't pursue the case."

Goldie raised her hands as if trying to restrain his movement down a path.

"That's only if I'm right about what he was up to," she said.

"But you think you're right."

"It's a little like reading tea leaves, but I'll tell you why I think I am."

Goldie then leaned toward him as though to pass on some gossip.

"I gave a seminar at the Harvard Law Islamic Finance Project eleven years ago. It was right after I got hired to run our center. I spotted Ibrahim walking in near the tail end of my presentation—have you ever seen him?"

Gage shook his head.

"Very distinctive guy. About five-five, solid build, mustache. Looks like a character out of *Casablanca* or *The Maltese Falcon*." She flashed a smile. "You sort of expect him to appear in black and white and wearing a fez."

Goldie reached again to the bookshelf and withdrew a Sloan School of Management brochure dated ten years earlier. She opened it toward the middle, then turned it toward him and pointed at a portrait.

"That's him," she said.

"Can I keep this?"

Goldie nodded, then said, "I think he must've showed up to meet somebody who was attending the seminar.

He looks at me, or maybe just my name plate on the table, and gives me a funny look. The kind I usually get from Muslim men, like 'What's a Jewish girl doing in a place like this?' Then he sits down in the back row. A couple of minutes later, I'm talking about the problems of control and taxation and how to deal with profits versus capital gains, and I spot him taking notes.

"After he got arrested, the FBI came by and interviewed everybody. The two who talked to me asked questions about Islamic finance and about the prohibition against making money on interest and about offshore structures. They didn't use the phrase 'hybrid company,' but they described the structure and asked about all the different places in the world where one could establish one. I later heard rumors that Ibrahim's gimmick was connected to the Isle of Man. And back in those days, that was the main reason people set up there."

"But not anymore?"

"Nope. After the Ibrahim story broke, the IRS changed the rules. All the U.S. lawyers in the offshore tax planning business were pissed. They'd been making a hundred grand off of every hybrid they set up, tens of millions of dollars a year for a dozen years."

"A cash cow."

"Without the overhead of running a dairy. And there wasn't a one of them who wouldn't have jumped at the chance to put a bullet in Ibrahim's head."

"Or already has?"

Goldie raised her eyebrows. "That crossed my mind. Maybe it wasn't a lawyer who pulled the trigger, but somebody had to have. Ibrahim was a guy who needed, if not to be seen, to be heard. He needed to be recognized as a genius."

"So you don't understand his silence."

She shrugged. "Nobody does, but then again, dead men don't do much talking."

age's encrypted cell phone rang as he drove from the MIT campus toward the western edge of Boston. It was Alex Z calling from San Francisco.

"I checked Ibrahim for friends and associates," Alex Z said. "And there weren't many outside of a Muslim men's group that met at his house. A member has a blog and mentioned Ibrahim's first name and MIT, so it was easy to ID him."

"Find out if the U.S. Attorney up here filed tax fraud cases against any of them. I need to know who was involved. Ibrahim's was the only name I found in the news articles."

Gage heard the rapping of Alex Z's fingers on his keyboard.

"Ibrahim sounds like a real multitasker," Alex Z said, "Terrorist financing, abstract financial theories, and tax evasion."

"I'm starting to think they're all part of the same package," Gage said, "or maybe different passages in the same maze."

."I just entered one of the names in the Federal Case Index," Alex Z said. "Hold on . . . nothing."

"Try the rest and call me back."

The snowfall let up as Gage headed back across the Harvard Bridge and down Massachusetts Avenue. He cut right at Symphony Hall and drove into the multi-story garage, then up the circular floors until he located a dry space between two vans. He climbed out and knelt down next to the car to check for a GPS tracking device. He worked his way around the perimeter and the wheel wells, then checked the engine compartment from below and above.

Nothing.

Whoever had been hired to replace Gilbert hadn't gotten on to him yet. He knew they would, and could, anytime they felt like it. All they had to do was wait for him to show up at the few places connected with Ibrahim, Abrams, or Hennessy—assuming they were following him because he'd met with Abrams, and assuming that they were following Abrams because of Hennessy.

Gage walked the circumference of the garage, scanning the cars parked around the sculpture garden next to the street below and along the front of the Whole Foods Market. His phone rang again as he surveyed the parking places that had a view of the garage exit. If someone was set up to follow him when he left, that's where they would've parked to be ready.

"Bugs everywhere, boss," Viz said.

It was Hector McBride, Gage's surveillance chief. Gage had nicknamed him Viz, for the same reason fat people were named Slim and slim people were named

Fats. Despite being six-four and two hundred and thirty pounds, he was invisible to his targets. Even after a decade of working together, Gage still didn't understand his magic.

"Where are you now?" Gage asked.

"I'm freezing my ass off in Central Park by the reservoir, and Abrams is at his office at the Fed. He doesn't know yet."

"How bad is it?"

"It doesn't get much worse than this. There were multiple devices in every room, but not for fail-safe reasons. I think they were installed by different groups."

"That means that whoever got there second has got to know about whoever got there first, and left the bugs installed."

"That's what I'm thinking. But they may not know who installed them."

"And the second group couldn't disable the original ones without giving themselves away or provoking the first group to come back and reinstall other devices."

Viz laughed. "It's game theory in practice. I should've paid more attention in college."

Gage turned away from the street and walked back toward his car. There were too many possibilities for who'd installed the bugs. Foreign governments. Hedge funds looking for inside information. Those looking for Ibrahim. Maybe even Abrams's estranged wife—and he didn't yet know enough to exclude any of them.

"Interesting thing," Viz said. "One set of devices are modified cell phones. The other set is hooked into his cable system. Both are connected into the electrical system and use lithium ion batteries. That means they're always powered on and can be accessed from anywhere in the world, either by calling into the phones or through the Internet."

"Any way to follow the signals to whoever is listening?"

"I could probably abstract some information out of the SIM cards—at least the numbers that have been called—and maybe Alex Z could backtrack the Internet traffic."

Gage paused next to his rental car and scanned the rest of the vehicles on the floor, then climbed in.

"Call Abrams," Gage said. "Tell him you need him at the apartment. Be cryptic in case they've also got his phones bugged. Meet him out front. Let's assume they've broken into his computer, too. Have him give you access so you can get whatever information you need. DNS. Gateway. IP address. Then go with him to check his office and pass on whatever you learn there to Alex Z. Once he's done with whatever tracing he can do, go back into the apartment and make a show of switching him from cable to satellite and set up something to interfere with cell service in the apartment. Once we figure out who they are, we can switch everything back on and feed them bum leads."

CHAPTER 23

The salesman's smile on Abdul Rahmani's face flamed out when Gage introduced himself as a private investigator. He got up from his desk behind the counter at Ijara Automobiles along Boston's Soldier's Field Road, yanked his pants up an inch, and waddled over.

"Why can't you guys leave me alone?"

"Who is 'you guys'?"

"FBI. IRS. That good-for-nothing Hennessy. And for the last couple of weeks, PIs."

"Like Tony Gilbert?"

Rahmani nodded.

"He won't be coming by anymore."

"You his replacement?"

"Not exactly. We're on different sides." Gage shrugged. "But I'm not quite sure what all the sides are."

Rahmani's smile returned. "Join the club."

"All I know is that the spokes of the wheel revolve around Hani Ibrahim."

Rahmani spread his hands and raised his eyes toward

the ceiling. "May Allah grant my wish that I never hear that name again."

"How about I'll refer to him as Fred," Gage said.

Rahmani looked back at Gage. "And how about you tell me why you're interested in Fred and I'll tell you if I want to talk to you."

"Can I buy you a cup of coffee while I try?"

Rahmani stared at Gage for a few seconds, his head rocking side to side, then said, "Let me get my coat and close up shop. Nobody's car shopping today anyway."

After Rahmani locked the front door behind them, Gage gestured toward the empty lot. "Where are the cars?"

"It's kind of complicated."

Rahmani led Gage past storefront real estate and insurance offices and a liquor store and pawnshop to a Turkish halal café. He waved to the owner as he escorted Gage to a booth at the rear of the empty restaurant. The owner brought over coffee without waiting for their order.

Gage leaned over the table in order to talk without the owner overhearing.

Rahmani shook his head. "No reason for secrecy." He pointed at the owner. "Ilkay got snagged, too."

Gage sat back and said, "From what I've been told, Hennessy—"

"You mean the lunatic."

"Maybe, maybe not. He seemed to believe that Fred was innocent."

"So he told me, but it didn't help me with my tax bill." Rahmani pointed at Gage. "You know what they dinged me for? Sixty thousand dollars in penalties and interest.

And what I spent on lawyers, you wouldn't fucking believe. I had to get a loan to pay for everything."

"For using the hybrid company?"

"And for proving that I wasn't guilty by association with a guy—Fred—who wasn't guilty at all. Terrorist financing? Fred hated those people. Hated—hated—hated. He was barely even a Muslim, much less a radical one. The only reason he participated in the discussion group we had was so that he could tell us every week what hypocrites we were, and he never missed a chance."

"I thought the whole point of the hybrid was Islamic financing."

Rahmani laughed. "Fred meant it as a joke. He only went through with it as an object lesson for us."

Gage shook his head. "You've completely lost me."

"An example." Rahmani laid his forearms on the table, palms up. "You know how Orthodox Jews aren't allowed to turn light switches on or off on the Sabbath?"

Gage nodded.

"The way they get around it is to use a shade that you can rotate so that it blocks the light. They flip the switch on before sundown on Friday and leave it on until sundown on Saturday. By rotating the shade, they get light when they want. Ingenious. They also have elevators that stop on every single floor on Saturdays so nobody has to push a button."

"They invented ways to get around the rules."

"In fact, but not in spirit. It's all bullshit."

Rahmani glanced at Ilkay standing at the counter reading a newspaper, and then lowered his voice.

"Like my business. Muslims aren't supposed to pay interest—*riba*—so instead of the customer financing the car through a bank, I buy it, lease it to them, and at the end of the lease, they give me a little extra and they then own the car." He pointed in the direction of his office. "That's what *ijara* means in my company's name. Lease."

"And your bullshit is calling it profit, instead of interest."

Rahmani raised his cup, took a sip, and then said, "Exactly."

"How does Fred fit—"

"I'll tell you. One evening, Fred explains how a hybrid company works. He says that we're not shareholders. We don't own it. We're what they call guarantors. We're responsible for the debts—"

"Or the profits—"

"—when the company closes down. In the meanwhile it's completely out of our control. Com-pletely. Fred then asks whether it's okay if the hybrid loans out money and earns interest and the value of the company increases, and then pays it all to us as profit when the company closes down."

Rahmani held up a forefinger. "Remember. It's not our company when it's earning the interest. The money is out of our hands and Sharia law doesn't apply."

"And that also means," Gage said, "that the profits at the end could be considered capital gains instead of regular income."

Rahmani grinned. "You're good. Really good. Fifteen percent federal tax rate, instead of thirty or more. And we don't have to take the gains until the company goes out of existence. It's like a 401(k), except offshore and you can put in as much money as you want."

"It should've sounded too good to be true."

Rahmani shrugged. "Nothing ever sounds too good to

be true at the time. At that point we're on our feet dancing, and the idiots that we were, we dance right down the path Fred laid out for us."

"And the rest is history."

"If the terrorist financing allegation hadn't come up, we'd probably still be doing it."

Framed by 9/11, Gage knew that there was no way Hennessy, or any FBI agent or U.S. Attorney, would've found Rahmani and Ibrahim's defense credible. No one sets up a tax fraud as a joke.

But there was still the question of where the money went that these men had put into the hybrid.

"How was the money used for terrorist financing?" Gage asked.

Rahmani shrugged again. "We never learned for sure." He gestured toward Ilkay. "His wife was close to Fred's wife, Ibadat. You know she's a Muslim from China, right?"

Gage nodded. "Xinjiang."

"Ibadat told Ilkay's wife that Hennessy leaned on her about a Muslim separatist group that bombed a U.S.-owned company over there ten years ago. Spectrum. Vice President Wallace's old company. Hennessy implied that money from the hybrid was used to finance the bombing." Rahmani rapped on the tabletop with his knuckle. "But I never saw or heard of a single piece of evidence that proved it."

Gage suspected that pressure to prosecute Ibrahim had come from Wallace and that Ibrahim's deportation must've been a compromise: face saving for the FBI and a way for Ibrahim to protect his wife. And the cover-up of the details served everyone's interest: The FBI prevented the widespread use of the technique and Ibrahim didn't get exposed to the Muslim community around the world as a heretic.

Gage now also understood that Rahmani's "May Allah grant . . ." was an act. The man liked Ibrahim, didn't blame him for anything, not even for the tax bill. And Rahmani had long ago acknowledged to himself that he'd brought that on himself.

"Did you tell all of this to Tony Gilbert when he came by?"

"He didn't seem all that interested. All he wanted was to find Fred. Or so he said."

"You help him?"

Rahmani shook his head. "How could I? I don't know where Fred is or even if he's still alive. And even if I did know, I wouldn't have told him. Gilbert was like a pit bull wagging his tail. You don't know which end to believe, so you keep your hands in your pockets."

Gage smiled. "I thought Muslims weren't supposed to touch dogs at all."

"Religious opinion is divided on the subject." Rahmani smiled back. "It's sort of like tax law."

"But you settled with the government."

"We all decided it would be better for us and for Fred if the story didn't stay in the news—"

"And the details didn't come out."

Rahmani rocked his head side to side, and then nodded and took another sip of his coffee.

"And now you know my story," Rahmani said. "What's yours?"

"Hennessy may have been killed—"

Rahmani flopped a hand toward Gage, cutting him off. "That's his story. I want to know yours."

"Personally, I don't have one. Professionally, someone asked me to locate Fred and find out what really happened."

"Maybe you should go knock on the door of the hedge fund. Rumors in the financial pages say that he's their secret weapon. Maybe they know where he is." Rahmani smiled. "Maybe they have him in an old missile silo, ready to shoot down their competition."

Gage recognized that the maybes were a test to divine his intent.

"It seems a long way around to connect two points," Gage said. "And I'm not sure that whatever he's doing now—or is alleged to be doing now—is relevant to what happened then."

In fact, Gage believed the opposite, but the more narrow the focus, and the more Rahmani believed that exonerating Ibrahim was Gage's aim, the more likely he'd help.

"It seems to me," Rahmani said, "that your real interest is not in Fred, but in what happened to Hennessy."

"Only in the sense that his death provoked my client into wanting to know whether or not Hennessy was right about Fred being framed and whether that had something to do with Hennessy's death."

Rahmani smiled, then looked over at the café owner and called out, "Ilkay, turn on the music. Mr. Gage here seems to want to dance."

Gage shook his head.

"It's true that I wouldn't be here if there wasn't a suspicion that Hennessy had been murdered. And it's true that the person who hired me wants to know whether he's dead because he intended to expose something—

either about the past or about the future." Gage raised his right hand as if to swear an oath. "But at this point, all of the evidence I have points to the past."

When he said the word "evidence," Gage felt a little like Bill Clinton manipulating the word "is" or George Bush redefining the word "torture."

"I can see you're not an idiot, Mr. Gage, so you've no doubt noticed that there are similarities between a hybrid company and a hedge fund. Your money is out of your control for a period of time, you don't know what they're doing with it, and you don't have the right to know."

Gage drew back. "You're not suggesting that the Relative Growth Funds is engaged in terrorist financing?"

"Not with its board dominated by the last three Republican administrations. All I'm saying is that the past may not be all that distinct from the present."

"Only one man knows the answer."

Rahmani nodded. "But if I was that man, I'd want to know who's really asking the question."

Gage leaned forward and rested his chin on his cupped hands, trying to give the appearance of deliberating over whether to reveal the name of his client. There was no way he'd say it was Abrams, but he thought of a partial truth that would satisfy them both.

"You married?" Gage asked.

"Of course."

"You have children?"

Rahmani paused and stared into Gage's eyes, and then said, "I see. This must be very painful for Hennessy's family." He shrugged. "The problem is that Fred agreed to deportation to protect his wife and the group and for that reason broke off contact with us after he left."

They sat in silence for a few moments. Gage didn't think it was safe to pressure him any further.

"I can try to get a message to him," Rahmani finally said, "but I may never know whether it gets delivered or even whether he's still alive to receive it."

Driving away from the café, Gage found that he believed Rahmani, but wasn't convinced of the man's reasoning. It was just as likely that it was Ibrahim who had isolated himself from his past to protect himself as much as to protect his friends.

What worried Gage now was that if Ibrahim had been unjustly prosecuted by his adoptive country, then he'd have a motive to get even, and if he hadn't been the mastermind of a terrorist financing plot before, he might have acquired a reason to become one.

A genius like Ibrahim wouldn't find it hard to divert a few million dollars, maybe tens of millions of dollars, from a two-trillion-dollar hedge fund into a terrorist's hands.

In any case, Gage decided, the answer wouldn't be found in Boston, where the trail had begun, but where it had ended.

He glanced at his watch as he merged onto the highway toward Logan Airport. It was still too early in the Chinese morning to call Faith. The news reports he'd listened to on the way to meet Rahmani had said that the Chengdu uprising was spreading east toward the industrial cities, not west into the mountains, but he was sure it would soon, and he feared she'd get caught up in it, for the largest volume product now being manufactured in China was blame.

on't pretend you know when you don't," Milton Abrams said to Alice Thornton, director of the Fed's Division of International Finance. She'd flown up from Washington to meet him in the local office he maintained at the New York branch. "China is gorging on dollars and euros and we don't have a clue about how many."

"These are just estim—"

"Based on what? The lies they tell us?"

Abrams pushed himself to his feet, yanked off his suit jacket, and then paced behind his oak desk. When he looked back, Thornton was staring down toward her lap, but he didn't think her eyes had yet focused on the report lying open there. He noticed a strand of her brown hair hanging beside her cheek. It had pulled free from the silver butterfly barrette he'd bought her in Marseilles after the meeting as a thank-you for helping him control his fury. The chairman of the Federal Reserve wasn't allowed to appear as a lunatic in public and she'd prevented that from happening.

He walked over and placed a hand on her shoulder.

"I'm sorry. I know you're as worried about this as I am."

Thornton looked up. "And as isolated from the rest of the Barons."

The Barons were the senior civil service staff of the Federal Reserve and the gatekeepers of the information that the board and governors received. Despite the fourteen-year terms of the political appointees, the Barons treated them as visitors passing through their feudal kingdom.

Abrams didn't trust them any more than they respected him, an outsider imposed on them by a president during the lame-duck years of his second term, who only then felt safe in acting on his principles. And one of those was his resolve that plain speaking should replace jargon at the Federal Reserve, and the plainest-speaking economist he knew was Milton Abrams.

The title of the speech that had won the president over was: "Full Employment Is No More Full Than Welch's Grape Juice Is 100% Juice."

It had been an attack on economists' use of the phrase "full employment" to mean a level of employment that wouldn't trigger inflation—which meant that they considered seven percent unemployment to be full employment.

That was followed by an article titled "A Moral Hazard Is Not a Sand Trap" in which he attacked the view that immorality in the world of finance was always likened to a hook or a slice, simply a mistake or an accident that had led corporate officers astray, rather than a willful exploitation of an opportunity to swindle.

Abrams had insisted that the phrase "moral hazard" be replaced by the more accurate "incentive to lie, cheat, and steal."

He did the same thing in other op-ed pieces and speeches for other bits of self-deceiving jargon:

"Price stability objective," which actually meant the rate at which prices rose.

"Core inflation," which excluded the goods that most cut into consumers' budgets: food and heating oil and gasoline.

He then moved on to "balance sheet stress," "favorable supply shocks," "asymmetric policy bias," "capital deepening," and "total factor productivity."

Abrams's first instruction to the staff upon arriving at the Fed was that the language it used in its reports and press releases had to be plain enough for anyone in the country with a high school education to understand.

The *Wall Street Journal* led a protest against the policy, starting off with an editorial titled "Lost in Translation."

CNBC called it "the names game."

The first lesson Abrams learned from the experience was that the war wasn't limited to words and titles. It soon took the form of street battles outside the Fed: police battalions fighting betrayed workers who'd realized that the last four administrations hadn't been trying to eliminate unemployment, but maintain it— and at levels prescribed by academic theories that were as transient as the homeless.

The second lesson Abrams learned, taught to him by Thornton, was that the economic data the government released to the public were no more reliable than the words in which they were framed. And he discovered why: The statisticians in the Labor, Commerce, and Treasury departments had been vetted over the years for their political views, rather than their academic credentials.

Abrams didn't trust any of them. And now he feared

that his demands for clarity in a cloudy world would drive Thornton away.

He returned to his desk and sat down and asked Thornton, "What's the bad news you were about to tell me?"

"The Chinese State Administration of Foreign Exchange announced today that their holdings in dollars have now passed one point one trillion."

"And when you factor in foreign currencies held outside of the central bank, it has to be double that."

Thornton shrugged. "That's my . . . estimate."

Abrams reddened. "Sorry about that."

"I know you weren't angry with me."

"What are the Chinese saying about their foreign debt?"

"A couple of hundred billion, more or less. Chump change."

They both knew that all the figures were unreliable. For more than a decade China had been holding some of its reserves in the names of offshore front companies so that their central bank wouldn't have to report them.

"But here's an interesting thing," Thornton said. "I've been watching a slow rise in the value of Japanese yen and Singapore dollars and Taiwanese NT in the last few months—"

"Which leads you to suspect that the Chinese are using some of their dollars to buy other Asian currencies—"

"In the countries from which they get their imports, especially food."

Thornton handed him a sheet displaying a four-color bar chart showing investment levels throughout Asia for the last two years. She pointed at two side-by-side bars, the previous year on the left and the current year on the right.

Abrams stared at the chart, seeing in the visual presentation what he hadn't seen in the data alone. He felt his body tense. He looked up at Thornton.

"China is turning all of Asia into an economic colony by becoming its central banker and controlling the flows of currency."

Thornton nodded, then pointed toward the flat-screen television on his bookshelf.

"Worse than that," Thornton said. "The last Indian-made Toyota rolled off the factory floor today. I watched it on CNBC this morning. Tomorrow they'll begin dismantling the plant for shipment to China."

Abrams's eyes moved from the blank screen toward the window. He gazed down at the traffic merging at the tip of the sculpture-studded Louise Nevelson Plaza.

"It never crossed my mind," Abrams said, "that someday it would be cheaper to manufacture a car in China than in India. It's absolutely astounding."

He thought of the hundred million Chinese laborers traveling into the cities from the countryside, then from city to city looking for work.

What did Marx call it? Abrams asked himself. *A reserve army of labor.* Surplus, superfluous people who kept wages low not only in China, and not only in India, but throughout the world.

"I'll give you a piece of data about China that's completely reliable," Thornton said.

Abrams blinked himself back to the present and looked at her.

"The CIA is saying that there have been a hundred and fifty thousand labor actions and riots in the last twelve months. There have even been protests at factories owned by the People's Liberation Army, and the military is very unhappy. As if to send a message to the Politburo, older representatives of the PLA have been showing up in full-dress uniforms for meetings, even private ones."

Abrams smiled. "Don't tell me that the CIA has gone back to analyzing leadership photographs like they did in the cold war days?"

Thornton smiled back. "I suspect they even know what you're wearing right now."

"But at least not what I'm saying."

Her smile died and her brows furrowed. "What do you mean?"

He cocked his head toward the reception area where Viz was sitting. Abrams had introduced him only as a friend of a friend.

"We found listening devices in my apartment. Two sets."

The color drained from Thornton's face as she said, "That means that people were listening to us."

She gripped her hands together on her lap and twisted them, her knuckles whitened, and tears seeped into her eyes.

Abrams nodded and came around his desk. He reached an arm around her shoulder.

She looked up at him. "That means they heard every-thing . . . absolutely everything."

"But we did nothing either of us should be ashamed of."

CHAPTER 25

Logan Airport was frozen in time and space. Nothing moved on the runways. Even the deicers sat motionless on the tarmac. In the absence of movement, it seemed to Gage as if history had met its end in a nuclear winter.

Gage turned away from the window and toward the mass of fidgeting passengers inside the terminal waiting for their international flights.

Some glared at the ground crew as though controlling the weather was part of their duties. Others stared up at the television monitors, the story of massive pesticide-induced birth defects in Russia replaced by a breaking news report of flooding in Paris, the Seine River overflowing its banks and transforming the city into a French Venice. The aerial view made the Eiffel Tower look like an islanded lighthouse in a sea of gray.

Gage had intended to fly into de Gaulle and spend a day in Paris visiting bankers, lawyers, and money launderers who were unrelated to Ibrahim or Hennessy, and thereby conceal what he had actually come to France to do. But the floods made that impossible. De Gaulle airport had been shut down.

Instead, he was flying to Nice, east of Marseilles along the Mediterranean, and to mask his intentions by pretending to help a friend from Transparency Watch trace the proceeds of the sale of platinum, allegedly stolen and smuggled out of South Africa by its president.

Gage was certain that whoever replaced Gilbert would catch up with him in Marseilles; he just needed twenty-four hours in the city before that happened.

An elderly Catholic priest standing next to Gage mumbled, and then whispered, "That son of a bitch."

Gage glanced over at him, surprised by the outburst and assuming that his words were meant for the uniformed United Airlines employee standing by the gate. The priest's eyes were focused instead on a wall-mounted monitor showing Vice President Cooper Wallace looking like a celery stalk next to the tomato-shaped Reverend Manton Roberts, red-faced and sweating, with a flop of chin and neck fat oozing over his collar and smothering the knot of his tie.

The priest looked up at Gage.

"Maybe the son of a bitch will eat himself to death like Jerry Falwell. That would be God's justice."

The priest then pointed at the screen as the camera pulled back and displayed a line of suited politicians, evangelicals, and talk radio personalities standing against the background of a two-story American flag with a black cross superimposed on it. It was erected behind a stage centered at the fifty-yard line of the Louisiana Superdome.

"A glutton," the priest said. "A compulsive gambler. A

onetime adulterer. A two-time adulterer. A drug addict. Is there any sin or human corruption that isn't represented on that stage?"

A handful of Korean-American missionaries, white shirts, black ties, and matching backpacks, walked forward as though toward an altar and gathered below the television clutching their Bibles.

"I call on all Americans to come together on Sunday," Roberts said from the podium, "two weeks from tomorrow, at noon Eastern time, all across the country to join in the reciting of the Pledge of Allegiance." Roberts raised his arms as if leading a hymn. "Let everyone driving pull to the side of the road. Let everyone walking pause in their tracks. Let everyone in church stand. Let every checkout clerk's hands fall still. Let every toll taker close his lane."

The camera panned the audience of seventy-five thousand. They had risen to their feet, smiling and clapping.

The priest standing next to Gage spoke again.

"It's a damn national loyalty test, all on one day." He again looked up at Gage. "But loyal to who? The country or their version of Christianity?"

"Let every voice rise up in unison as we celebrate our one nation under God."

The applause morphed into cheering that almost overwhelmed the words, "And let the agents of Satan reveal themselves by their silence."

Faces in the Superdome turned hard and shaking fists shot skyward.

"God's punishment is upon us," Roberts said, his voice now raging and his face engorged with angry blood. "He

speaks to us through the earthquakes and the floods
and the epidemics and the riots. All is in preparation . . .
all . . . is . . . in . . . preparation,

> *for mine eyes have seen the glory of the coming of*
> *the Lord:*

Roberts was speaking the words, not singing them.

> *He is trampling out the vintage where the grapes of*
> *wrath are stored;*
> *He hath loosed the fateful lightning of His terrible*
> *swift sword:*
> *His truth is marching on.*

Then the crowd in a single explosion of song:

> *Glory, glory, hallelujah!*
> *Glory, glory, hallelujah!*
> *Glory, glory, hallelujah!*
> *His truth is marching on.*

The missionaries standing below the television inter-
linked their hands as Roberts spoke again.

> *I have read a fiery gospel writ in burnished rows*
> *of steel:*
> *"As ye deal with my contemners, so with you my*
> *grace shall deal;*
> *Let the Hero, born of woman, crush the serpent*
> *with his heel,*
> *Since God is marching on."*

Gage surveyed the waiting area. A scattering of people stood up. Some of those who were already standing turned toward the monitor.

> *Glory, glory, hallelujah!*
> *Glory, glory, hallelujah!*

Those remaining in their seats glanced at one another. One after another they shrugged and then rose. By the end of the last chorus, nearly half the people in the terminal were singing. The rest sat rigid in their seats, jaws set, eyes locked forward.

> *Glory, glory, hallelujah!*
> *Since God is marching on.*

"We've got massive unemployment," the priest said, "people dying in earthquakes and floods, and their answer is a damn loyalty test." He then shook his head and walked away. "That son of a bitch."

rayed by the swirling low clouds edging the Mediterranean, the hotels and casinos of Monaco and Monte Carlo that Gage observed out of the plane window appeared to have turned in on themselves. The thin breakwaters defining the harbors seemed to lie like broken picture frames on the water and the yachts in their slips seemed like discarded toys.

The cities soon gave way to coast roads and tiled mansions, and then to rocky shores separated by points and peninsulas, until the plane descended over Nice and the tires bucked on the runway.

As Gage emerged from the arrivals hall, Batkoun Benaroun climbed out of his car in the "Kiss and Fly" short-term parking lot across the traffic lane from the terminal. He pointed at the sign over the lot entrance, then held his palm toward Gage.

"Don't take it literally," Benaroun said, his angular North African face rounding into a smile. "My wife wouldn't understand."

"After forty years of marriage," Gage said, smiling back, "I suspect she's done more than her share of understanding." He reached out and shook Benaroun's hand. "Thanks for meeting me."

"No problem. There were a few things I wanted to talk to you about anyway, and I'd been thinking that it would be better that we did it in person."

Benaroun opened the trunk of his Citroën sedan, and Gage slid in his Rollaboard.

"What happened to the little Fiat?" Gage asked.

"My back couldn't take the jolting anymore so I gave it to my nephew."

He pointed at the passenger door, then climbed in on the driver's side.

"His father was no more thrilled with that than with Tabari following me into the Police Nationale. My brother the great rabbi has always found it a little embarrassing that I was a cop. Even becoming an actual detective didn't make up for it. He prefers Maigret and Poirot"—Benaroun flashed another smile—"even Clouseau."

A gendarme vested in fluorescent green walked by the car and glanced inside. His eyes locked on Benaroun's face, and then frowned like he'd sniffed into a wineglass only to discover that it contained vinegar.

Benaroun waited until the guard passed by, then turned the ignition and said in a grim whisper to himself, "Fascist." He glanced at Gage. "His ancestors were still counting on their fingers and toes while mine were inventing calculus, and this idiot makes himself out to be the fortress of French civilization standing against the swarms of brown people." He slapped the steering wheel. "Who else will they get to shovel their shit?"

Benaroun stared ahead for a moment, then shook his head, backed out of his space, and drove toward the exit.

Gage watched him hand the attendant three euros for parking beyond the five-minute limit, and then said, "You sound like you're being squeezed every which way."

He didn't need to articulate which ways they were: An Algerian-Jew. A failing economy that led the white ancestral French to turn on the immigrants, no matter how many generations earlier their families had arrived. And brown-skinned young men, less striking back against a defined target than just flailing with bricks.

"It's like living in a vise," Benaroun said as he waited for the gate arm to rise. "I'm not sure it's been this bad since the German occupation. Just different uniforms. These Muslim kids rioting in Marseilles are burning Jewish businesses, not realizing that the French hate Jews just as much as they hate the kids."

Benaroun glanced over his shoulder at the gendarme watching them drive out of the lot.

"I'll bet his grandfather was a Nazi collaborator," Benaroun said, then he looked over at Gage. "You know the real reason I spent my career in fraud and money laundering investigations?" He didn't wait for an answer. "Because most of the commissioners believe that Jews are good with money. Even Algerian ones. And shrewd and devious enough to understand the financial criminal's mind."

"You seem to be getting bitter in your old age," Gage said.

"It's not bitterness. It's realism. We're internally colonized. All the colored minorities are, whatever their shade." He emitted a sarcastic laugh. "Maybe God should add some bleach to the floodwaters in Paris to decolorize the city."

Benaroun fell silent, then gave Gage a puckish look.

"Sixty-six isn't old," Benaroun said, then he reached for the beginnings of a wattle under his jaw. "Appearances notwithstanding."

As they drove west along the freeway away from the center of Nice and toward Benaroun's foothill home, he pointed toward the storm front that had just crested the bluff.

"God may not want us all white," Benaroun said, "but he sure wants us all wet."

By the time they'd turned north and headed into the suburb of Cagnes-sur-Mer, a curtain of rain had closed against the hillside. It looked to Gage as though they could drive through it and emerge on the other side, but as they traveled the curved roads they found more of the same, the weather seeming as heavy and solid as the brick house in front of which they pulled to a stop.

Benaroun turned off the ignition, but left the wipers on and squinted up through the windshield, trying to see past the splattering rain.

"Let's wait a minute," Benaroun said. "Maybe we'll get a break long enough to run to the door."

Benaroun settled back in his seat and looked at Gage.

"I saw something on the news," Benaroun said. "Is the whole U.S. really going to come to a standstill to recite the Pledge of Allegiance? Manton Roberts sounded like an Islamic imam calling everyone to prayer. Scary as hell."

Gage shrugged. "We'll see, but I suspect that Americans' sense of rugged independence will limit the turnout. The real implication of his filling his mega-church with twenty thousand people every Sunday is that the surrounding ten million didn't show up. I suspect it will be the same with National Pledge Day."

"I don't know," Benaroun said. "Just watching the announcement on the news almost brought the whole of France to a stop. The English word 'hysteria' is what we call a collective noun in French, and it makes us nervous."

A gust of wind drove the rain hard against the side of the car, then there was a moment of quiet. Benaroun raised a finger. He waited for a few seconds after a second gust swept over them, and then said, "Let's go."

By the time they'd grabbed Gage's Rollaboard from the trunk, the rain hit again and they ran through it toward the door thirty feet across the courtyard. It swung open as their shoes hit the slate porch, and Gage followed Benaroun past his nephew and into the foyer.

"Bonjour, Mr. Gage," Tabari said, swinging the door closed and handing Gage a towel. "My uncle suffers from the delusion that he can time the rain."

"He did pretty well," Gage said, drying off his hair. "It's not his fault if I've slowed a step or two."

"Come on," Benaroun said, heading off toward the kitchen. "Let's get a drink. Since he got promoted to detective in the Police Judiciaire he's become a know-it-all."

Tabari grabbed Gage's arm as he turned to follow, then whispered, "Has he told you exactly what he wants to talk to you about?"

Gage shook his head.

"Talk to me before you encourage him to pursue

his theory about the platinum smuggling from South Africa. I think he's going way beyond what Transparency Watch wants or needs. He may have the brain of a thirty-year-old, but he doesn't have the body of one, and I don't want him to get hurt."

CHAPTER

hat do you mean, you don't know where Gage is?"

Edward Wycovsky stood in front of Kenyon Arndt's desk, glaring down, his hands locked on to his suspenders. His vulturelike head was unmoving and his black eyes unblinking.

Arndt knew that a few weeks earlier he would've risen to his feet in fear and then humbled himself as if before a high priest or lesser god. But not now—for he'd discovered that the spreading stain of crime and death had made them equals.

"Didn't you hear what I asked you?" Wycovsky said, his forefinger now aimed down at Arndt like he was a dog who'd soiled the carpet.

No, that wasn't it, Arndt thought. He knew they'd never be equals, for he'd never have the kind of power in the law firm that Wycovsky possessed. Rather it had been their positions relative to the dead body of Tony Gilbert that had established them in a new orbit and would hold them there despite their differing weights and densities. And he had a little red badge of courage on his forehead to prove it.

Arndt fixed his eyes on Wycovsky's rigid face and tight jaw.

"Your people let Gage get away," Arndt said. "And without Gilbert around to tell him how to do it, I'm not sure Davey Hicks—"

"Who?"

"Davey Hicks, his number one helper, can do it alone. He seems to be all thug and no brains."

"What about Abrams?"

Arndt made a dismissive shrug. "Where can he go? He's one of the most watched men in America. All you have to do is call the Federal Reserve press office to find out where he is and where he's going."

"I don't need the sarcasm. Our clients have a lot at stake in this."

"I'll have to trust you on that since I don't have a clue who they are."

And Arndt didn't care. It was merely out-of-focus background to his immediate need.

"And it'll stay that way," Wycovsky said.

"But I do have a thought." Arndt pointed at the computer monitor on his desk. "The local media is saying that police in Albany haven't been able to reconstruct Gilbert's movements on the night of his murder." He paused for a moment of setup. "But we can. And Gage's movements, too."

Wycovsky's eyes narrowed. "And?"

"The link between Gage and Gilbert is a bounty hunter named Strubb."

Arndt reached into his top desk drawer and pulled out

a DVD. He leaned down and inserted it into his computer drive, and then angled the monitor so Wycovsky could see it.

"This is a security camera video of Gage and Strubb and a kid Strubb hired. They're walking from the garage into the lobby of the Adirondack Plaza Hotel a few hours before Gilbert was killed."

A gray-scale image of the reception desk appeared on the screen, along with an expanse of carpet and a semicircle formed by a sofa and two wing chairs. Seconds later, the three came into view.

"That's Gage in the middle," Arndt said. "Strubb is the guy behind him."

"Why are they so close together?"

"They've got Gage in handcuffs. After they searched his room for documents that Hennessy's wife supposedly had given him, Strubb went to meet with Gilbert at a leather bar—"

Wycovsky squinted at Arndt. "Gilbert? Gilbert was a queer?"

"No. Strubb is. Hard-core. Black harnesses, chaps, biker hats, and studs. Gilbert had some kind of fetish that made him want to hire these guys. Sort of a master and slave thing, without the sex."

"How did you—"

"Davey Hicks. He's one, too. He put together the pieces of what happened. He heard that Gage pushed Strubb around and threatened to put him back in prison if he didn't make Gilbert lay off. Strubb leaned on Gilbert. He refused and then Strubb and two other guys took him for a ride, and things got out of hand."

Wycovsky smirked. "I saw the news, they killed him."

"But they did a few things to him first." Arndt jerked his thumb upward. He smiled to himself as Wycovsky winced. He imagined his boss's butt cheeks clenching.

"Hicks is certain that the details of what they did to Gilbert can be deduced from the autopsy report," Arndt said, "but the police haven't released it to the press."

Wycovsky didn't respond for a few moments. He just stood there, frowning.

Arndt suspected that Wycovsky was watching his imagination play out the nightmare of the attack. Arndt wished he had some sort of mental probe so he could determine whether Wycovsky's fantasy of what had happened was a product of his personal terrors or was instead a form of wish fulfillment. It wasn't hard for Arndt to imagine Wycovsky wanting to do physically what he did psychologically to the junior members of the firm.

"I may have underestimated you," Wycovsky finally said.

Arndt smiled as if in satisfaction, but said to himself, *Not in the way you think.*

"Whenever we need to take Gage out of the game," Arndt said, "we'll just finger him for Gilbert's murder. It won't stick in the end." He grinned at his wordplay. "But he'll be out of our client's way for a while."

CHAPTER 28

A persistent, rhythmic thumping and the rattle of the front door against the loose frame drew Faith out of the shadows of sleep into a predawn gray. By the time she'd climbed out of bed and made it into the front room, Jian-jun had opened it. Standing across the threshold from him was a young woman wearing a military surplus coat. A battered scooter was parked behind her on the bare yard, the motor silent, but the headlight glowing into the haze.

The woman whispered two sentences, then fell silent as her eyes widened at the sight of Faith, who wondered whether her surprise was provoked by the fact that this white ghost standing in the darkness hadn't fled like the rest of the Westerners had done in the days after the earthquake.

Jian-jun turned around, following the woman's gaze.

"What is it?" Faith asked.

Jian-jun pointed back over his shoulder.

"She says that a couple of the rebels have found where I hid my parents. But out of respect for my grandmother, they haven't turned them over to the mob."

Jian-jun walked over to where Ayi Zhao was still asleep on a cot and sat down next to her. He touched her on the shoulder. Her eyelids fluttered, then she looked up. He told her what had happened as he helped her to her feet.

Faith gestured for the woman to come inside.

Jian-jun introduced her in Mandarin only as Xiao Mei, Little Mei, and Faith only as "the anthropologist."

Faith knew the unspoken question behind Little Mei's eyes, for she'd heard versions of it throughout her career: for what was an anthropologist, but a spy in plain sight, a psychoanalyst of families and of relationships and of culture using obscure methods to discern the function behind the structure and the living reality behind the camouflage of appearances—at best to objectify people, and at worst, to strip them naked.

Little Mei's blank expression and averted gaze seemed to Faith to be those of a sister or girlfriend who suspected she'd been discussed in therapy and whose secrets had been exposed and dissected—

Except today those secrets were political and the consequence of exposure wasn't shame or embarrassment, but death.

They all understood that there'd be no time to argue filial piety to a mob. Appearances would be everything.

"I'll show myself," Ayi Zhao said, then looked from the woman to her grandson. "That will give the children time to escape."

Jian-jun shook his head. "The army may view your arrival as a provocation. We can't take the chance that they'll use it as an excuse to intervene."

Ayi Zhao raised her palm toward Jian-jun. "They don't need an excuse. Their orders come from Beijing and the issues now are bigger than the symbolism of an old lady." She pointed down toward the city. "Tell them I'm coming."

Faith looked back and forth between Little Mei and Jian-jun, then gestured with her hand through the open door toward the scooter and said, "Go. I'll find a car to bring her down."

Jian-jun grabbed his jacket and then said to Ayi Zhao, "They're in the backup generator room of the burned out Meinhard electronics factory."

He turned to Faith. "It's on the western edge of the city in the economic development zone."

Faith's body jerked sideways as the house jolted in an aftershock. She grabbed a chair back to steady herself. The scooter fell over. A glass next to the sink toppled and shattered.

As Jian-jun reached an arm around Ayi Zhao's shoulders, he and Little Mei stared at each other, trading end-of-the-world looks.

In their anguished gaze, Faith saw that she was a Christian, too. Maybe an evangelical, and this was her secret.

The quake had half the force of the last one, and Faith's internal calculator, calibrated by a lifetime in San Francisco, told her it was either a small aftershock nearby or a huge one far away.

Faith thought of the Three Gorges Dam, fearing that it had given way as the cracking and crumbling schools and hospitals of Chengdu had. But she said nothing, for she knew that they were all thinking the same thing, and they understood that if it had given way, it was too late for fear, or for hope.

"Most of the mob has moved back to the center of the

city," Jian-jun said to Faith. "But be careful. Don't show yourselves until you get to the factory. I'll come out to meet you."

Jian-jun led Little Mei outside and then straightened up the scooter. He sat forward on the elongated seat and she climbed on behind him.

Faith walked to the door and looked past them and toward the valley, wondering what would greet them when they arrived.

The motor rattled, then engaged, shaking the bike. Exhaust belched from the tailpipe as he gunned it to keep it from stalling, then the cloud swirled in the air and grayed the rising sun.

Faith blocked the glare with her hand and squinted at the city. Smoke no longer drifted up from yesterday's smoldering factories in the industrial clusters, but still billowed from the mile-diameter tire pile adjacent to the solid waste incineration plant. She knew that it would burn for months and suspected that the mob, now choking on its fumes, had come to regret having chosen arson as a form of protest. In the pollution that now blanketed the countryside, they had spread the scourge they had fought to contain.

Jian-jun leaned toward the handlebars, pushed the bike off its stand, and accelerated down the dirt street toward the center of town and then beyond it to the highway on the other side.

Ayi Zhao walked up next to Faith and looked up at her.

"You don't need to do this," Ayi Zhao said. "I can find a way down on my own."

"We can protect each other," Faith said. "Because of you, no one will harm me. And because of me, the army and police will see that the world is watching and perhaps will leave you alone."

Faith thought for a moment. It struck her that the best way to shield Ayi Zhao from the army might be to recruit them to help.

"Is there an herbalist up here that you can trust?" Faith asked. "Maybe he can put something together to raise your blood pressure and make you look like you have a fever. Then we can ask the garrison to take you to the People's Hospital. They won't want you to die on their watch."

Ayi Zhao nodded. "I can do it myself. All I need is ephedra, ginseng, and ginger. We can get those at the vegetable market." She paused and then asked, "Do you have any cold pills? They always make my heart beat faster."

"I think so," Faith said, reaching out her hand and gripping Ayi Zhao's shoulder. "Just be careful not to overdo it."

CHAPTER 29

Vice President Cooper Wallace fidgeted with a paperweight on his desk in the West Wing of the White House. He rubbed his thumb across the gold presidential seal, then tossed it onto his blotter. For a moment it seemed turdlike, hard and dried and petrified. He fantasized the president sneaking from office to office, dropping his pants, squatting, and leaving a marker behind, and the thought disgusted him. And the thought that he even had the thought disgusted him more.

Wallace recalled a psychology class he'd taken at the University of Kansas the year after he'd returned from his second tour in Vietnam. The professor was a left-wing freak, a former priest who'd left the Jesuit order to marry the soon-to-be ex-wife of a parishioner. And the class was nothing but a camouflaged attack on religion in general and Christianity in particular, which the professor portrayed as a contradictory mass of outward projections of internal repressions and delusions.

Wallace remembered walking into the lecture hall one morning, seeing quotes from Martin Luther that the professor had written in bold letters on the chalk-board: *I am like ripe shit and the world is a gigantic asshole. I have shit in the pants, and you can hang it around your neck and wipe your mouth with it.*

He'd stopped in the descending aisle as he read the words, the acidic taste of bile rising in his throat. He'd swallowed hard, then dropped in the nearest seat and gritted his teeth and breathed in and out, steeling himself for what was to follow.

Then the professor launched off from the lines into a lecture about Freud and anality and the origins of Protestantism that Wallace didn't hear—couldn't hear—because all his senses had been obliterated by the sight of the words. He even had to feel for his legs after class was over so he could stand up, both his body and soul now too numbed even for rage.

That came later, during a night of wrenching, racing thoughts, at the end of which he resolved that someday, after he'd made his stake in Spectrum with his father, he'd enter politics and find a way to crush those lunatics and cleanse the universities.

But somehow that purpose had morphed over the following decades into something else. What that was, he now wasn't certain, except it led him to the second most powerful office in the world—if he ignored the fact that it had no constitutional power at all. Even as president of the Senate he wasn't his own man, for he had to follow the president's orders.

Wallace glanced around at the blue couch and pale yellow chairs where he'd posed for photographs with the lesser leaders of the world.

Who the hell even knew where Comoros was? Or Burundi? Or Suriname? Or Tuvalu? Or whatever those piss-poor countries were called on the day their leaders came visiting. Collectively they had the gross national product of a Detroit pawnshop. Them coming to beg for money, putting their loyalty up for sale, first to the U.S., then to the Russians, then to the Chinese. Then to all three of the world powers at the same time.

He remembered staring at the wristwatch of one of their prime ministers, a crook who'd graduated from Missouri State, working his way through school handing out towels in the gym, then spending twenty years in his country's civil service, and finally showing up in the White House wearing a hundred-thousand-dollar Rolex.

And the man kept glancing at it as if taunting Wallace, telling him that if the U.S. wanted to buy his country's loyalty, it would have to make the down payment to him first.

But it didn't work because they both knew that as China had done throughout Africa, the resources of his country could be bought for pocket change, just like Sudanese oil, and Zambian copper, and Nigerian natural gas.

A light knock on Wallace's door pulled him from the reveries of the past and onto the obstacle course of the present and toward the president, who was standing by with the starter pistol.

Wallace could see the distant finish line, for it was always in the same place: Tuesday after the first Monday in November—but he hadn't yet figured out how to get there.

President Thomas McCormack was sitting at his desk when Wallace walked into his study next to the Oval

Office. He was alone, reaching for a sheet emerging from his printer. A briefing book lay open before him, the pages both tabbed with blue labels and tagged with yellow Post-it notes. As Wallace sat down on the couch next to the desk, he could see that the writing on the notes was the president's. From that alone Wallace concluded that whatever course the president wanted him to run, he'd designed and constructed it himself, and wanted only two people on the field.

Wallace didn't feel like waiting for the president to meander his way to the issue. Every substantive conversation between them traveled the same route, one that began with their six years serving together, the closeness of their wives, the perfecting of the right and right-center coalition among voters that had won them the White House twice. And ending with self-congratulations on their developing the center coalition in the House and Senate that got more of their own legislation through Congress than any president since Lyndon Johnson.

The president had spent his prepolitical career as a lawyer and never lost the urge or the talent to lay a foundation for the evidence he intended to offer, even if it was obvious.

"Mr. President—"

McCormack shook his head. "This isn't a Mr. President moment. It's personal. Me to you. It's not your political soul that I'm concerned about. It's something else." He tapped the binder with his forefinger. "And I'll shred this thing after we're done."

Wallace felt his body stiffen. He hadn't a clue what was contained in those pages, but he already felt stripped naked, cold and shivering. His mind raced through every misstep and indiscretion in his career, from a fraternity party brawl when he was twenty to his wife's recent second-guessing his appearance with Manton Roberts.

And the president's promise to destroy whatever evidence was in those pages felt less like a guarantee of liberation, and more like a garrote around his balls.

McCormack had issued the most widespread records preservation order in the history of the office. There was no e-mail, no confidential memo, no scrap of paper that he hadn't ordered preserved. The joke at the National Archives was that they still hadn't figured out a method for storing his unarticulated thoughts.

"Is this about National Pledge Day?" Wallace asked. "I didn't know—"

"That's the point. You should've known. You've lent the stature of your office—of this administration—to an event you couldn't control." McCormack threw up his hands. "Jesus Christ, man, you let them turn the 'Battle Hymn of the Republic' into a marching anthem for intolerance."

"I didn't let—"

"Then you consented with your silence. It stands in American history as a symbol, an abolitionist song about liberty for everyone, not the liberty of a few to impose their religious beliefs on everyone else."

McCormack pounded the desktop with his fist.

"Next to the 'Star-Spangled Banner' and 'God Bless America,' it's the most important song in our history. And those sons of bitches have stolen it."

"Mr. President, I think that overstates what happened."

Ignoring Wallace's defensive stab, McCormack

reached for the sheet he'd removed from the printer as Wallace had entered the office.

"Which pledge do you suppose they intend to use," McCormack asked. "This one?"

Wallace took it in his hands. It was marked, "Confidential. From the Desk of Rev. Manton Roberts," and contained a single paragraph.

"Go ahead," McCormack said, "read it."

Wallace read the words to himself.

> I pledge allegiance to the Christian flag, and to the Savior for whose kingdom it stands. One Savior, crucified, risen, and coming again, with life and liberty for all who believe.

"No. Aloud."

Wallace glanced around the room, eyes hesitating on the heat vent and the computer and clock on the desk.

"Don't worry," McCormack said. "The place isn't bugged. Go ahead. Aloud."

Wallace shook his head. "I can't say this."

"I didn't think so, but you put yourself at the front of a crowd of seventy-five thousand people who did before you arrived."

McCormack raised his chin toward a framed American flag on the wall above the printer.

"Have you even read what our party platform says about the flag?"

Wallace shrugged. He was surprised that McCormack had paid attention to the platform. In both elections, he'd neither run on it nor run from it. He'd just ignored it.

McCormack flipped to the front of his binder and turned it toward Wallace.

"This is our position. You don't need to read it aloud."

> Protecting Our National Symbols: The symbol of our unity, to which we all pledge allegiance, is the flag. By whatever legislative method is most feasible, Old Glory should be given legal protection against desecration.

"Do you realize that our party wants people sent to the federal penitentiary for making a necktie out of the thing, and you let these traitors paint a goddamn black cross on it?"

Wallace pushed the binder away.

"That's different," Wallace said. "Desecration means depriving something of its sacred character. This is a Christian nation. Adding the cross confirms it by combining two sacred symbols."

"Don't play word games."

"Anyway it's free speech."

"Wrong again. Not according to the Supreme Court. Flag desecration isn't speech at all. Rehnquist said that it's no more than a grunt or a roar, no more protected by the First Amendment than a fart in an elevator."

Wallace had no answer.

They sat in silence for a few moments, then McCormack leaned back in his chair and said, "I don't understand what's happening to you. If you'd run Spectrum with the lack of insight and consistency you've been displaying, you'd still be selling Bibles and Jesus dashboard ornaments out of your father's garage."

Wallace's face flushed. "I didn't come over here—"

McCormack held up his palm. "Save it. I'm not done." He hunched forward, squared the binder in front of him, and turned toward the middle. "Have you read what Manton Roberts has been writing and preaching for the last twenty years? The guy is a goddamn fascist. Listen to this:

> Our job is to reclaim America for Christ, whatever the cost, as the vice regents of God, we are to exercise godly dominion over every aspect and institution of human society.

"At whatever the cost?" McCormack asked, now glaring at Wallace. "What the devil does that mean? And how many people are supposed to die for the revolution?"

Wallace shook his head. "That's not what they're saying. They're not 1960s Marxist revolutionaries trying to take power by any means necessary."

"Really? How about this:

> Nations are born in revolution, not at the negotiation table. There is no compromise possible for a Christian people. There is only liberty or death. Although a million may fall, the rest shall rise in Glory.

"And who are those million? Remember what he said about 9/11 and Katrina: They were punishments for homosexuality and pornography and for barring prayer from the schools."

Wallace nodded, for he couldn't deny that those were the claims Roberts had made.

"How does that not make Roberts's God a terrorist?

Killing both the innocent and the guilty for the alleged sins of a few. How is Roberts's God any different than a Sunni maniac who plants a bomb in a Baghdad market killing and maiming Sunni and Shia alike?"

McCormack jabbed a finger at another quote. "And this is the hymn he uses to end every rally:

> Seize your armor, gird it on,
> Now the battle will be won.
> Soon, your enemies all slain.
> Crowns of glory you shall gain.

"Is there something about the words 'battle,' 'enemies,' 'slain,' and 'glory' that I'm missing?" McCormack asked, his tone declaring a challenge, rather than posing a question.

"That's just hyperbole," Wallace said. "It's all metaphorical."

"There's not a goddamn thing metaphorical about murder. This is outright treason."

McCormack flipped to another page.

"And as far as the rest of the world is concerned? Open your ears to this one: 'We should invade their countries, kill their leaders and convert them to Christianity.' A goddamn Christian jihad. That's what they want."

The president slammed the binder closed.

"You need to start listening to what these people are saying. This isn't like the fine print in a mortgage, it's right out there. You want to be president in two years, but something could happen to me, and you'd be sitting in this chair tomorrow. And the piper has to be paid. Manton Roberts could just as easily have a hundred million people stopping in their tracks and calling for your impeachment as saying the Pledge of Allegiance."

Wallace felt himself swallow. An embarrassing, involuntary display . . . but of what? Weakness? Doubt? Fear?

"I'm going to leave you in here with this material," McCormack said, rising to his feet. "You may not take what it says literally, but tens of millions do. At least know what he's saying and who he's appealing to. If there's another terrorist attack or if unemployment spikes higher, despair will drive people to him in herds. Unthinking, instinct-driven herds."

McCormack paused and bit his lip. Finally he said, "Have you been following what's been happening in China since the earthquake?"

Wallace nodded.

"We're not immune to that happening here." McCormack looked away, brows furrowed. "And that's what people like Manton Roberts are counting on—he'd even drive the country into the ground if he thought it would bring his Christian revolution closer."

McCormack looked back at Wallace.

"Someone once said that revolutionaries don't seize power, they just pick it up like a fumbled football lying on the field. We need to make sure it doesn't slip out of the hands of the people elected to carry it—and that's you and me."

McCormack turned and headed toward the door.

"Are you going to participate in National Pledge Day?" Wallace asked.

McCormack stopped and glanced back, the sudden change in direction throwing him off balance for a moment. He steadied himself against a bookcase, then said, "You've given me no choice." He then turned toward the door and reached for the knob. "I have to."

A half hour after the president left, Wallace closed the binder and placed it back on the desk.

Nonsense. It was all nonsense. No one took this stuff seriously.

Wallace wondered whether the president had read the Salvation Army's literature when he'd served on their national advisory board.

Does anyone really think that the Salvation Army's War College really intends to train people for armed combat?

Does anyone think their generals are real generals and their colonels are real colonels? That their commissioned officers are commissioned to do anything more than slop mashed potatoes onto metal plates?

Wallace rose and walked to the window and looked through bare tree branches toward the White House lawn. In the thin layer of snow he could make out the footprints of a uniformed Secret Service officer, the steps measured as if by a yardstick or by a metronome or by fifes and drums.

How many times had the president greeted the Salvationists, given them awards, held a July Fourth celebration with them on that patch of grass?

How many times had the president asked him to carry the Salvation Army's luggage up to Capitol Hill? Lobby Congress so the Salvationists wouldn't be forced to hire homosexuals, but nonetheless receive federal funds. Make sure that faith-based didn't really mean goodwill to all.

Apolitical my ass, Wallace thought. *I can do some research on my own.*

Wallace returned to the desk and ran a search for the Salvation Army War College on the president's computer, then navigated to a song titled, "I Am a Soldier in

the Army of My God." He found the words he was looking for and left them on the screen when he walked out:

> *I am a soldier.*
> *Even death cannot destroy me.*
> *For when my Commander calls me from this*
> *battlefield,*
> *He will promote me to a captain*
> *and then bring me back to rule this world with*
> *Him.*

As Wallace made his way down the rustling hallways,
past the ticking keyboards and hushed discussions, he
asked himself a question that he was sure the president
had never asked himself, especially after church on
Sunday with a sermon about the Second Coming still
infusing him with joy and lightening his steps:

What need will the country have for a president, or a
Congress, or a Supreme Court, or even elections when
the Commander returns to govern by the word of God?

And other questions, even more serious ones:

Who is to say when the battle has been won and who
has the right to speak for the winner?

CHAPTER 30

Graham Gage's cell phone rang as he sat in Batkoun Benaroun's kitchen with him and his nephew. He held up his forefinger and thumb spaced an inch apart to keep Benaroun from overfilling his wineglass for a second time, then looked at the number and answered.

"Is everything all right?" Gage asked.

Low engine rumble and the grumbling of tires on a rough road filled the long seconds before Faith answered.

"Can you hear me?" she asked.

Benaroun and Tabari cast him questioning looks from across the table.

"Good enough. Go ahead."

"I left the kids working in the village. I'm in the back of a military ambulance with Ayi Zhao on my way down to Chengdu."

"Is she sick?" he asked Faith, while nodding at Benaroun and Tabari to indicate that at least Faith was okay.

"She's fine. It's just a dodge. Her son and daughter-in-law are being detained by a workers' group. The leaders are willing to meet with her before they do anything. We told the garrison commander that she needed medical attention so they'd drive her down to the city."

"What do the workers want?"

"Specifically, I don't know. Generally, vengeance. Her son was the vice mayor in charge of construction and his wife was the first party secretary. He's ultimately responsible for the collapses of the hospitals and the schools and her for the party failing to protect them from foreign exploitation. And they're rich. Astoundingly rich. But their corrupt money won't buy them out of—"

A blaring truck horn cut off her last words.

"What's that?"

"We're near the edge of town. The other drivers on the road seem to have lost respect either for the military or for ambulances." She emitted a short, nervous laugh. "I'm not sure which. But it's not the China I'm used to."

"Does she have a plan?" Gage asked.

Gage gazed out of the window at the fog blurring the stone-walled patio. It reminded him of an outdoor Chinese court hearing he'd attended in a rural Chongqing village on behalf of Transparency Watch. The defendant had confessed under torture to subversion, a capital crime. Usually these hearings were held in secret, but this one was conducted in public and drawn out over a year to intimidate government opposition in the countryside.

"No plan yet," Faith said, "but I'm thinking that she'll have to persuade the workers that the two are worth more alive than dead. Not financially, but in terms of propaganda—but she first has to convince the mob that they don't have the moral authority to set up a provisional court and start executing people."

"They've already killed—"

More honking, a crash, then a screech of tires.

"What happened?" Gage asked.

"Hold on. Let me look into the cab."

Gage heard rustling as Faith crawled forward and then conversation in Mandarin.

"Some kid by a school gate threw a rock at the windshield. We're moving again."

More rustling as she returned to her seat.

"The problem is that once they believe that the mandate of heaven has been withdrawn, authority is up for grabs. Their view at this point may be that they have as much right as anyone else to run things. The Chinese constitution just becomes a relic of a dead era."

"Do they already believe that it's happened?"

"I don't know, but people are saying the words aloud. One more earthquake. One more riot. One more firestorm. And everything may disintegrate."

"Then don't stay too long."

"I only want to be here long enough to help Ayi Zhao through this, then I'll gather up the kids and get out."

Gage thought again of the trial and the defendant being led head down, wearing a prisoner's blue striped shirt, into the yard day after day to be displayed and humiliated. He also remembered why Faith despised Ringling Brothers, whose bears were forced to dance and whose tigers were forced to leap through rings of fire, kept alive in captivity solely for the purpose of spectacle.

"Maybe she needs to divert them with a circus," Gage said.

"A what?"

"Nobody wants to kill the clown while he's performing under the big top. Like the impromptu trials during the Cultural Revolution, it'll be familiar to everyone. Maybe they'll be seduced by the symmetry or maybe they'll find some comfort in history repeating itself. If she's lucky, maybe she can keep dragging out the interrogations until the rebellion is suppressed."

"Gotcha. I'll pitch it to her." Faith paused for a moment, then said. "I think Ayi Zhao feels horribly guilty, for not saving China from her son and for not saving her son from himself. Now the only hope she has left, and only as his mother, is that maybe she can save his life."

Benaroun was smiling when Gage disconnected. "I thought there was only one crime stopper in the family."

"It's more like applied anthropology," Gage said.

"That's kind of what we all do," Benaroun said. He turned his smile toward Tabari. "You may want to get out your pad and take notes, voices of wisdom are about to speak." Then back at Gage. "I never met a good detective who wasn't part psychologist and part anthropologist, especially in this part of the world."

"And in South Africa," Gage said.

Benaroun's smile faded. He gave Tabari a sour look, a way of saying that he had suspected the kid had betrayed a confidence.

"He didn't warn me off," Gage said. "Just repeated that you wanted to talk to me about something."

"No. It was him wanting you to talk me out of something."

Gage smiled. "Are we going to keep circling, or are we about to land?"

Benaroun cast another glance at Tabari, then said, "I'm starting to suspect that the platinum is being smuggled out of South Africa by air." He pushed his wineglass aside. "The interesting thing is that there are records of the flights arriving in Johannesburg, but no records of them leaving."

"Do you know which planes?"

"My informant promises to tell me when I get there. If Transparency Watch authorizes the onetime payment that I want, I'll deliver it to him in person next week and he'll give me the details."

"That's a hell of a risk to take based on what could be a fantasy or—"

"Or an outright lie," Tabari said.

"Except that he told me a few things that I've been able to verify." Benaroun held up a finger: "First, there's now an artificially induced platinum shortage." He held up another: "Second, buyers are purchasing an enormous volume of futures, placing bets that the price will be rising in the next few months."

Benaroun lowered his hand and leaned forward.

"The contradiction is third: The companies offering the futures contracts are apparently not increasing the reserves of platinum they keep in their bank vaults to secure the paper."

"What do you mean by 'apparently'?"

"My informant is telling me that they're buying on the black market from the stocks stolen by the president—so the reserves are actually there—but they're not reporting them publicly."

"How would he know?"

Benaroun glanced at his nephew, then back at Gage. "He's the deputy director of the South African Secret Service."

Gage thought for a moment. He wasn't sure how someone in South Africa would know what was occurring inside a Swiss vault thousands of miles away.

"There's an alternative," Gage finally said. "Maybe the whole thing is a fraud and the sponsors are simply lying about their reserves."

Benaroun shook his head. "Someone I know who used to be with the Swiss Federal Banking Commission is now the compliance officer at Exchange Traded Metals. He's the one who counts their coins and bars. And he noticed the same anomaly as my informant did."

"Then I think he has an obligation to turn his company in to Swiss authorities instead of in to Transparency Watch and—"

"And get himself killed?"

Gage drew back. "Isn't that a little melodramatic?"

"If there is such a thing as economic war, then there is such a thing as economic terrorism," Benaroun said. "It has to be prevented, and if it's too late to be prevented, people have to be punished." Benaroun gestured toward Tabari. "It isn't just a coincidence that I asked him to come out here from Marseilles to meet you."

Gage looked at Tabari. "Did you work on Hennessy's case?"

Tabari shrugged. "Not directly. There was nothing to work on. It was determined to be a suicide."

"Or someone was determined to make it a suicide," Gage said.

"I wouldn't go that far," Tabari said. "There was no relevant evidence to the contrary."

Gage smiled at Benaroun. "Your nephew may have a career in politics. His every answer is loaded and invites a follow-up question."

Benaroun raised his arm and then rotated his forefinger downward as if telling Tabari to put whatever he knew on the table.

Tabari leaned forward and stared down at the grained wood surface. Gage guessed at the choices he was weighing as he sat motionless except for his flicking eyelashes. They were the existential ones with which second generation immigrants, especially those who have achieved conventional success, are confronted. He was a French Algerian. A Jew. An outsider striving for acceptance. His uncle's asking him to betray official confidences and secrets was more than simply a matter of morality and of integrity, it was a matter of identity.

In Tabari, Gage saw himself thirty years earlier, moving up from Southern Arizona to join the San Francisco Police Department. Everyone in his academy class knew of a local applicant who they'd assumed had been the one pushed aside to make room for Gage, an outsider. The difference was that Gage knew that, unlike Tabari, he wouldn't spend his career as a police officer and the department wouldn't be his world.

Gage also grasped that in this conflict of loyalties, Tabari understood that helping him would be a political act requiring enormous courage. They both knew what Benaroun would have done, but Benaroun accepted his position as a pariah, a near untouchable in French society, and rebelled against it, while Tabari hoped to escape it someday by donning a commandant's uniform.

"I'm not comfortable accessing Police Judiciaire records and releasing the information to you," Tabari finally said, "but out of respect for my uncle, I'll do what I can to help."

Tabari now raised his head and looked at Gage.

"Which means that I'll find a discreet way to get you into the places where evidence was found, and in the order it was found, and put you in a position to see what any observer who happened to be in the right place and at the right time would've seen."

Gage recognized in Tabari's clear-eyed gaze and firm tone that this wasn't a wink and a nod, a game of let's pretend. The young man understood moral limits, and he'd found a line etched in marble that he wouldn't pulverize into sand in order to slide past it.

"And I'll leave it to you to draw your own conclusions."

CHAPTER 31

Former president Randall Harris fanned out on his desk the blue-, red-, black-, and green-covered proposal binders from the four largest accounting firms in the world. Each outlined its strategy for auditing the assets of Relative Growth Funds. He positioned them along the curve as though he was choosing a paint color for his Rockefeller Center office, rather than evaluating the substance of what was contained inside.

Ronald Minsky, CEO of Relative Growth, sat across from him feeling like a messenger from Kinko's delivering on-demand documents to a Rottweiler: a beast who'd be able to absorb them in torn chunks, but not comprehend them word by word—except Minsky knew that this dog had perfect instincts.

"These things weren't written to protect Relative Growth," Harris said, "but to protect the auditors from us if we someday discover that they've screwed up."

Minsky smiled to himself. Harris's nose hadn't failed him.

"Of course they need to protect themselves," Minsky

said. "They can't be held responsible when they rely on others for information."

Harris glared at Minsky.

"Cowards. That's all they are."

He then pointed at Minsky's face.

"I've got a new Golden Rule for you. Forget the old 'Do unto others as you would have them do unto you.' Change it to 'Always act as though you're president of the United States.' He's got no one he can blame when things go wrong. He has to stand up there and take it. If he doesn't, he looks like a goddamn putz and history will judge him to be a weakling."

Minsky felt like pointing out that presidential reputations were matters only of image and had no cash value except in the form of book advances for their memoirs and fees for their memberships on corporate boards. Relative Growth, on the other hand, was about real money: who eats and who doesn't and, as they both knew, who owns the jet.

Instead, Minsky said, "A lawsuit against them would be pointless. None of them have enough errors and omissions or liability insurance to cover even a fraction of the value of the Relative Growth Funds."

Minsky watched Harris absorb the thought, and the implication that the audits would only possess the appearance of accountability. He decided that he'd better pet the dog.

"I assumed that's why you wanted to use the hammer of the ten-million-dollar reward to whoever catches another one's mistakes."

Harris shrugged. "Yeah. Right. Except I don't see much protection in that. My guess is that we'll be paying ten million extra to all of them. I wouldn't be surprised to learn that they're meeting together right now, agreeing on where to leave the bread crumbs."

"You sound pissed off at them and they haven't even begun their work."

Harris pushed himself to his feet.

"You bet your ass I am. These people have never gotten anything right, but I have no choice but to rely on them."

Harris held out his hand, his thumb pressed against his little finger.

"Enron."

He moved his thumb to the next finger. "Adelphia."

Then the next. "Global Crossing."

Then the next. "ImClone."

Then started over. "Sunbeam. Tyco. AIG. Madoff."

He spread his arms. "And how do we value all of these damn credit derivatives and options and swaps? The economy collapses and all of a sudden we're freezing our asses off at two trillion dollars below zero."

"Can't happen," Minsky said, shaking his head. "That's the whole point of the Ibrahim approach. It assumes that a collapse is inevitable and plans for it, profits from it. We're the only real hedge fund that ever existed. The rest of them rode the rising tide, and when the tide fell, they went out to sea with it. But not us."

"Save the advertisement. I don't need to hear the song and dance again. You didn't answer my question."

"Yes, I did. You weren't listening," Minsky said, trying to suppress the annoyance he felt at the former president. "It's not going to happen. It can't. We're the gravity that controls the tide. It rises when we say rise and falls when we say fall."

Minsky thought for a moment.

"Let me put it in concrete terms," Minsky finally said. "You're a commodities guy, right?"

Harris nodded.

"You like gold and silver and oil and rice and wheat."

"All of the above. That's the real economy. That's why I watch the prices."

"Then ask yourself: Why was platinum at twenty-six hundred dollars an ounce a year ago and why it's at seven hundred dollars an ounce today?"

"You and I both know why. A miner's strike and electrical blackout in South Africa."

"And why it will rise to two thousand dollars an ounce three months from now?"

Minsky watched Harris's eyes widen.

"How could you know—"

"Because we rule the market, that's why."

Minsky watched Harris's face flush before he spoke.

"You mean that you manipulate it by putting people out of work," Harris said, "and cutting off the lights by which their kids do their homework when it suits your needs."

"Our needs. Yours. Mine. Ours. The fact is that there's a certain quantity of human suffering in the world, we just move it around so peoples' suffering won't be in vain." He smiled. "At least some peoples' suffering won't be in vain." Then he laughed. "Who would've thought that the invisible hand would have actual fingers."

"You really are a scumbag, aren't you?"

Minsky let his smile harden in place and met Harris's stare and said, "You know what they say. After the tide's gone out, what's left behind is the slime."

They stood in silence, staring at each other. Finally,

Minsky said, "Your State of the Union speeches used to amuse me. 'The state of the economy is strong . . . the genius of capitalism . . . the wealth created by the free market.' You thought it was all real, but it was just ideological poetry."

Harris's face reddened.

"Actually, it wasn't even that. The invisible hand isn't a scientific concept, it's a religious one. It's Calvinism rewrought. It was John Calvin who declared wealth to be a manifestation of the workings of Providence, and transformed greed and accumulation from the devil's work into a sign of God's grace. The words in which he framed it—the invisible hand—are Calvin's, not Adam Smith's. So you see that the very first act of modern science of economics was intellectual theft."

Minsky grinned and spread his hands.

"What am I saying? Economic science, my ass. Smith latched on to the concept in order to define beauty—not the operation of the market—but you wouldn't know that. Would you? Of course not."

Harris's fists clenched by his sides.

"You have no scientific basis for anything you believe. You've simply absorbed the ideas you've lived your life by in the same way a paper towel absorbs a spill."

Minsky watched Harris's fists twitch. He waited for Harris to pull one back, but realized that he'd never swing, for Harris wouldn't want to be remembered in history for a misdemeanor assault and battery.

"The smooth functioning of the market—is there a more stupid phrase ever uttered? Wealth is created when the market breaks down. That's when there are great winners and great losers. Wealth is created not by greasing the wheels of the market, making it more efficient, but by sabotaging it."

"The great computer hardware and software companies are proof that you're wrong. The founders became the richest guys in the world by doing it the old-fashioned way."

"It's proof that I'm right and that you're as deluded as I said you were," Minsky said. "They've all paid out more in civil settlements and fines for monopolistic practices, antitrust violations, market manipulation, and patent violations than the entire net worth of General Motors at its peak. It's called sabotage. And before they became benevolent philanthropists, they were master saboteurs."

CHAPTER 32

Faith spread the curtains that separated the back of the ambulance from the cab and looked through the cracked windshield to determine how close they'd gotten to Chengdu. The open highway that had bisected rice, wheat, and rapeseed fields had now cut into a grid of suburbs composed of silent factories, dark apartment towers, and streets devoid of the cars and trucks and bicycles that had jammed them just days earlier. It seemed as though the city center had become a magnet drawing toward it anything and everyone not anchored in place—

Almost anything and almost everyone.

A quivering speck of color appeared in the distant haze. A vehicle coming toward them on the highway. It seemed to float above the gray pavement. Seconds later, it separated into three, and then resolved from specks into squares, and then from squares into open-bed trucks, their beds crowded, three men standing at the rear of each one, the man in the middle tied to a stake with a painted sign above his head.

A queasy feeling waved through Faith as she read the characters:

人民为敌, Enemy of the People.

捕食者, Predator.

叛徒, Traitor.

And she recognized who the bracketed men were: condemned government officials on their way to the killing fields, the execution grounds to which they or others like them had sent not only fraudsters and murderers, but workers who'd protested working conditions with their bodies and writers who'd fought censorship with their keyboards.

Faith looked down, afraid to see their terrified eyes, afraid their eyes would see hers, and even more afraid that one of them might be the son of Ayi Zhao.

Even the ambulance driver, a rock-faced man hardened by a career among the dying and the dead, looked away and stared down at the white lane lines ticking by.

Faith kept her thoughts to herself and returned to her seat. If it hadn't been Ayi Zhao's son in one of the trucks, by turning back and trying to catch up to find out, they might arrive in Chengdu too late to save him.

Just after the trucks passed, the ambulance cut off the freeway and drove north, heading toward the economic development zone and the incinerated Meinhard plant.

As they neared, the bite of particulate smoke made them tear up and the acridity of burning chemical waste choked their throats.

Ayi Zhao handed Faith a tissue to breathe through, and then covered her own mouth.

Five minutes later, the ambulance slowed to a stop. When the noise of the rumbling motor died, murmuring voices and yelled orders rose up.

The rear doors swung open. Faith tensed as she looked out at a semicircle of faces staring in, men and women bundled against the frozen air in wool coats and down parkas, with gray swirling clouds of moist breath rising in a mass.

The crowd was so transfixed on the impossible presence of a white ghost that at first they didn't notice Ayi Zhao sitting behind her.

Layered behind the first row were hundreds of other peering faces and stretching necks.

Faith's eyes caught a North Face logo on one and Nike shoes on another and Levi's on another, followed by a bitter thought: The new Chinese Revolution will be carried out by an army dressed to kill in tennis shoes and knockoffs.

She leaned forward to make her way out, but Ayi Zhao grabbed her arm.

"Let me go before you," Ayi Zhao said. "Uncertainty is our enemy."

Ayi Zhao pushed herself up from the bench seat and stooped her way past Faith. As two men rushed forward to help her down, those standing behind them bowed one after another as they recognized her. Others murmured her name. The whispered words "Ayi Zhao, Ayi Zhao" swept through the crowd like a rustling breeze.

Bodies shifted like stalks of wheat as someone maneuvered through the mass. The front row held firm, phalanxlike, unwilling to give up their places and surrender the moment. They were transfixed, for none of them had viewed Ayi Zhao since her trial after the Tiananmen Square massacre and the crushing of the revolt.

Hands reached up and grabbed the shoulders of two women standing next to each other in the front row. They lost their balance and cried out. Jian-jun burst through the sudden gap between them. In one motion, the men who'd guided Ayi Zhao down from the ambulance spun back and threw him to the bare ground, and then knelt on his back.

"Stop," Ayi Zhao yelled.

The men jumped to their feet, as if they were soldiers given orders by a commanding officer. They looked from her to Jian-jun and back.

Faith stiffened, stunned by their unthinking obedience and the authority in Ayi Zhao's voice. Faith hadn't seen that kind of personal power exercised since she observed a tribal *jirga* in Balochistan decades earlier, its unelected elders exercising absolute control, the wave of a hand or the nod of a head signifying an unappealable decision.

"He's my grandson," Ayi Zhao said.

The men reached down and helped Jian-jun to his feet and brushed the twigs and soil off his clothes.

But then Faith thought back on the three prisoners driven to slaughter on the killing fields and realized that even the solidity of Ayi Zhao's stature might not be a defense against the force of events.

Jian-jun reached for Faith's hand to help her down, not because she needed it, but because his gesture would be seen as that of a proxy for his grandmother, and Faith would step out of the ambulance and under the umbrella of her protection.

"Are your parents okay?" Faith whispered, as first one foot, then the other touched down on the frozen ground.

"For now."

The front of the crowd separated as though it was fabric being unzipped, and kept opening as Ayi Zhao and Faith and Jian-jun walked toward the generator building. It closed behind them until it had formed again into a single piece by the time they'd reached the entrance to the provisional concrete prison.

Guards with peasant faces and ragged coats lowered their AK–47s, then opened the doors. Jian-jun led them down a hallway, past looted offices and silent turbines, toward a storage room, passing more guards with each step.

The leader stepped forward and removed his wool cap. His skull seemed stark against the soot that masked his fifty-year-old face and etched crevices around his eyes and mouth. He nodded to Ayi Zhao as if they'd once been comrades for whom no spoken greeting was required, and then narrowed his eyes and looked at Faith.

"You're the anthropologist?" he asked in Mandarin.

Faith felt the weight of the question, as if he'd said, *You're the witness. It is you who'll watch and report what we do.*

"I'm not here in the service of science," Faith said, "but of justice."

"Doesn't truth serve both?"

"It hasn't so far," Faith said, "at least in Beijing."

His hard face splintered into a smile.

"Welcome to the revolution," he said, then stepped aside and waved at the man behind him to open the storage room door.

Jian-jun's parents looked up with wide eyes from

where they sat on the linoleum floor, leaning against the wall, their arms around their legs. Their eyes closed and air exploded from their lungs as though they'd received a reprieve in the minutes before their scheduled execution. Together they rolled forward onto one knee, but they didn't rise. Instead, they kowtowed toward Ayi Zhao, lowering their heads, a humbling gesture not seen in China since the Cultural Revolution.

But standing there watching, Faith wondered whether two of the once most powerful people in Sichuan Province were begging for forgiveness from someone who couldn't give it—at least not alone—or simply playacting a traditional role to save their lives.

The revulsion in her stomach told her it was the latter.

Then she remembered what her Mandarin teacher had once warned her: The true survivor in China wasn't the tiger, but the chameleon.

CHAPTER 33

Sunlight infused the blue-hued palette of the Mediterranean cove and warmed the backs of Gage and Tabari Benaroun as they hiked the juniper-bordered trail along a cliff edge east of Marseilles. In the previous hour, shadows had descended the limestone walls and the distant sea had lightened below the wide sky and merged with the southern horizon.

They'd driven from Nice the evening before, mostly in silence. Gage had decided to let Tabari control the conversation and not to press him to violate the oath he'd made to himself and reveal more than he intended. In Gage's mind, Tabari, like his uncle, was not a rag to be used to wipe away grime and then thrown away. He was certain that the young detective would find a way to lead him to discover the facts on his own.

They were a slow mile in from the trailhead parking lot near the fishing village of Cassis. As they started out, Tabari had pointed out where a stolen car had been discovered on the day after Hennessy's body was found. Tabari hadn't commented about it beyond showing where it was parked and the condition it was in, and then had led Gage down a dirt road to the trail.

Tabari stopped and then braced himself against an oak tree and kicked at a granite boulder, knocking off the mud that had built up around the soles of his boots.

"How far?" Gage asked as he did the same.

Tabari pointed across the inlet toward a columnar outcropping that looked like the hoodoos Gage had seen in Zion and Bryce canyons in the American Southwest, but instead of glowing red or orange or yellow, it stood chalk white against the mazy green hillside and the cut brown trail and the azure sky.

"Just to the right," Tabari said, "where the path nears the rim." He lowered his hand until his finger settled on a spot just above where the incoming tide lapped against the rocks. "Hennessy's body was found on that ledge."

Gage imagined Hennessy walking their same route. Despite the cold, but wearing no jacket or overcoat, at least according to what Milton Abrams had learned, and passing three other inlets along the way and dozens of other places where he could have jumped.

Why, Gage asked himself, did Hennessy suffer the shivering and the frozen feet and the wind biting at his face and hands and piercing his clothing and needling his skin? Why not just get it over with? Put to an end both his psychological and physical suffering.

And if Hennessy had been murdered, why not do it in the parking lot, or along the road at the first outcropping above the shoreline rocks?

It didn't make sense.

Gage pulled a map out of his jeans pocket and unfolded it. He traced a path from Cassis where he and

Tabari had started the hike all the way along the coast to Marseilles, twenty miles to the west. If Hennessy had begun at the trailhead closest to Marseilles, it wouldn't have been an hour walk, but a ten-hour walk, with tough ascents and treacherous descents on slippery stones and mud.

But say he really did start at Cassis? A mile or so of indecision, or of confusion, or of anguish—

"Exactly," Tabari said, after watching Gage's eyes scan the map. "From either direction it's a long way to go to commit suicide."

"Maybe not," Gage said, picturing San Francisco's Golden Gate, almost two miles in length. "Most people walk to the middle of a bridge before jumping, maybe looking for a certain kind of symmetry, maybe one that confirms their place at the center of the universe at the pivotal moment."

"Or as distant as they can get from solid ground," Tabari said. "I assume that people imagine they'll enjoy a pristine death, as if the water below would simply absorb them whole and unbroken."

"Either way," Gage said, gesturing toward the rocky trail before them, "they can walk a long way before they kill themselves, sometimes a very long way."

Tabari took the lead as they headed toward the deepest part of the cove. The area seemed to Gage to be a counterpoint image of the Utah Badlands, with fractured white chasm walls in place of red rock cliffs, with a pale sea in place of shadowed valleys, and with mesquite and sage and piñon pines in place of Aleppo and myrtle and ferns, but just as desolate.

After Gage and Tabari made the turn back toward the

water, they stopped in the shadow of an oak tree. Through binoculars Gage scanned the path they'd traveled, checking whether they'd been followed. He then inspected the ridges above. He didn't expect to see anyone, or at least anyone shrewd, since a person assigned to track them and who'd seen where they'd started could've guessed where they were headed. In any case, a fishing boat would have been a better choice for surveillance.

Gage suspected that if he'd been followed to the trailhead and the follower knew their destination and what they would find, he might've settled on taking some photos of Tabari and then headed back to Marseilles to try to identify him—

Unless that someone wanted to follow them not just long enough to identify Tabari or even just to the spot where Hennessy went over, but also to make sure that he and Tabari followed Hennessy all the way down to the rocks below.

"You tell anyone that you were coming out here?" Gage asked, lowering the binoculars.

"You see something?"

"No."

"I didn't even tell my father."

Gage raised them again and turned the lenses toward the Mediterranean, starting at the pale blue water at the head of the inlet, then back and forth along the shoreline and finally following the darkening channel toward the open sea. A sailboat slid into view from the direction of Cassis, forty feet of white fiberglass and chrome reflecting the risen sun, sails down, motoring, its engine a distant murmur, its wake foaming the still surface.

A flash of glass told Gage that binoculars had been

raised toward them, but had passed on. Gage figured that either they'd just been spotted or they weren't the person's target.

Gage focused on a woman standing alone on the bow. The binoculars flashed again and she raised her arm and pointed, not at them, but at the hill rising up behind them. Gage looked over his shoulder, for a half second expecting to spot a sniper poised on the hill-crest. Instead, it was a peregrine falcon swooping down from a pine top, its nearly two-foot wings first wide and flapping, then folded as it rocketed toward the water. A seagull shrieked and took flight from a yellow buoy at the mouth of the cove. The falcon swept down below the bird, and then slammed up into it, sending it tumbling and flailing, finally catching it by the back of the neck and carrying it to a ledge halfway up the cliff.

The woman on the boat turned as a man ran toward her. She raised her palm in a high five. He slapped hers with his, then they both jumped in place like delirious football fans after a winning touchdown.

"I've never understood how anyone can celebrate death," Tabari said. "Any death."

Tabari ran his fingers along a rosemary branch, then raised them to his nose. He breathed in the scented resin and said, "This, not death, is worth celebrating."

"You sound like your uncle," Gage said.

Tabari smiled. "And every day he sounds more like my father than he lets on." His smiled faded. "Except angrier. A kind of Old Testament, Moses anger."

"I noticed that at the airport," Gage said. "Why the change?"

"His world has gotten larger since he retired, or at

least he's being confronted by more of it. The narrow, focused gaze that he moved from case to case when he was a detective is now like a searchlight that moves from country to country, from disaster to disaster, from crime to crime, illuminating one evil after another that he feels helpless to stop." Tabari stared down at the boat, then looked over at Gage and said, "That's what his platinum smuggling investigation is really about."

"You mean it's not as serious as he makes it out to be?"

"No. I suspect that he's right about that. But it'll continue whether he gets killed trying to stop it or not."

"Why are you convinced it's that dangerous?"

"Not because I have inside information, but because the breadth of the thing, the size of the organization, the length of the chain and the amount of money involved. It doesn't make sense for whoever these people are to engage in this wide of a conspiracy unless there are not just millions, but billions at stake. Whoever is behind it has developed the means to control mines and power plants and banks. They can make airplanes appear before the world's eyes like fireflies in the night and then disappear again. They can make tons of precious metals jump from place to place like they're subatomic particles—"

"And you don't think your uncle gets it."

"Worse. To them, he's just a piece of lint to be flicked off their lapels."

Gage understood conceptually why Tabari was worried, but he didn't have enough facts to know whether they supported the theory. After all, Tabari's fear could be just the mirror image of his uncle's misunderstanding of what had been going on, but he'd need time to figure it out.

"If you want," Gage said, "I can talk to the people at Transparency Watch. Ask them to pull him off of it or assign him to something else for a while."

Tabari shook his head. "That would just humiliate him. He might become even more reckless and try to pursue it on his own."

They stood in silence for a few moments, then Gage said, "Let me think about it. I'll come up with something."

"Just don't get sucked into it, too. You don't show it, but I know you scan the darkness of the world using the same searchlight as my uncle does. That's why you and he are friends."

Gage didn't respond. It wasn't the same searchlight, or if it was, it had never left him feeling helpless. Would it someday? He didn't know. His father, who'd run his family medical practice into his late eighties, had never felt helpless, perhaps because he'd come to accept the contingencies of life and didn't fear death. But Batkoun Benaroun seemed to accept neither.

Gage turned and led the way along the trail. Soon they were midway through the section they'd seen from the opposite side.

Emerging from a tunnel formed of dense juniper and overhanging oak trees, Gage again spotted the outcropping from which Hennessy had gone down. They walked another hundred yards, then Tabari stopped and pointed down.

"This is it," Tabari said.

Gage held on to a pine trunk and leaned out. Tabari braced himself against the tree, then grabbed the back of Gage's jacket as insurance against him falling.

Looking down, Gage imagined Hennessy's body tumbling and flailing like the seagull, thudding into the first ledge fifteen feet down before tumbling down onto the two ledges below, each one angled out like stair steps, each ten feet tall, until a final, hundred-foot drop to the rocks along the water's edge.

Gage reached for his binoculars again and inspected the porous limestone below for blood spatter that might've been absorbed into the rock, and therefore might not have been washed away during the storms that passed through on the days following Hennessy's death.

"Looking for blood?" Tabari asked.

Gage nodded.

"There was some, but not much. I suspect that he died on impact."

Gage straightened up and Tabari released his grip.

It didn't make sense. A suicide wants it to be over in an instant, a straight drop into oblivion, not a bouncing journey down a flesh and bone grater.

Except maybe as self-punishment for sins Gage couldn't yet imagine.

When Gage looked over, he saw that Tabari was staring at him, a smile on his face. Gage knew that Tabari had guessed what he was thinking.

"He went over at night," Tabari said. "He couldn't have seen that it wasn't a freefall to the bottom. He might've done what you just did. Found an outcropping. Found the place closest to the edge, held on to the tree to position himself, and then pushed off."

Gage shook his head. "His eyes would've adjusted to the darkness. Even on a cloudy night—"

"Which it was."

"The ledges down there would've glowed."

Tabari knelt down and picked at specks in the dirt that looked like mica. He wet his finger, pressed it against one of them, and held it up toward Gage.

"Water white glass," Tabari said, "with an antireflective coating." He wiped it off against his pants. "Flashlight glass."

"And you recovered the flashlight?"

Tabari nodded. "The officers who searched the area. Not me personally."

"That's all the more reason why he wouldn't have jumped here."

"The detective who handled the case theorized that Hennessy did what you did, but lost his balance and committed suicide a little sooner than he planned and in a less advisable place than he would've wanted."

"In which case it's an accident and not a suicide since he still could've changed his mind."

Tabari shrugged. "But nonetheless, not a crime."

Gage thought back on the suicides that he'd investigated when he was a homicide detective and on the training he'd received. He couldn't think of an instance in which a suicide released his grip on whatever was in his hand. A Bible. A cross. A love letter. The instinct was to hold on. He couldn't imagine Hennessy dropping the flashlight as he jumped or tossing it behind him.

But Tabari could still be right. It could've been an accidental suicide.

"Of course," Tabari said, raising his eyebrows, "this is all conjecture."

Gage flashed on an image of the trailhead and the

stolen car. "And whether it's correct depends on the means of transportation he used to travel out here."

"And maybe also on what we know about what he couldn't have used to travel out here."

"And when will I get that answer?" Gage asked.

"Tomorrow. I think tomorrow."

CHAPTER 34

The tyranny of history and the force of its contradictions weighed on Faith as she sat in a corner watching Ayi Zhao, her son, her daughter-in-law, and Jian-jun confronting one another at the metal table in the center of the storage room.

In the previous days, in sitting with Ayi Zhao at dinner in the house and around the stove they'd used for cooking and heating, fragments of times past had emerged and the roles her family members had played in recent years had become clear.

Ayi Zhao: once a fifteen-year-old Communist revolutionary whose parents died in the Long March in the 1930s, herself marching toward Beijing in January 1949, studying philosophy at the Sorbonne in Paris, purged by the party when it turned totalitarian, rehabilitated when it liberalized under Deng Xiaoping, then banished to the countryside by Deng in 1989 after the Tiananmen uprising.

To her right, her son, Zhao Wo-li: vice mayor of

Chengdu, a city with a population of eleven million. An engineering Ph.D. and owner of secret offshore bank accounts funded with bribes from foreign corporations.

To her left, her daughter-in-law, Zheng Mu-rong: Communist Party Secretary, enforcer of ideological discipline in Chengdu from the top floor of a two-hundred-million-dollar government complex. Owner of mansions on the Italian Riviera and in San Francisco that were held in the names of Hong Kong front companies.

Across from Ayi Zhao, her grandson, Jian-jun. A Christian pacifist and rebel against both Communists and capitalists.

And all sitting in the ruins of a German-owned factory built by penal slave labor in the early 1980s.

Wo-li straightened in his chair, removed his hands from his overcoat pockets, and laid them on the table in a let-us-begin gesture as though he was leading a meeting of government officials.

He doesn't get it, Faith said to herself as she watched him. *He's deluded. He thinks he's still in charge because he's under the protection of his mother, but he's actually drifting in a purgatory of his own making between a past he created and a future that he can't control.*

Faith glanced at the closed door and noticed the rumbling voices in the hallway outside. At any moment, it could be yanked open and men could rush in and drag Wo-li and his wife out to waiting pickup trucks destined for the killing fields. She was certain that the signs had already been painted. Maybe they'd even wipe off the blood of the executed and reuse the old ones:

人民为敌, Enemy of the People.

捕食者, Predator.

叛徒, Traitor.

Ayi Zhao raised a forefinger and wagged it at him.

"Don't deceive yourself," she said. "The conditions outside this room may be temporary, but death is permanent."

Wo-li's face flushed and his flat hands tightened into fists.

Ayi Zhao spread her arms. "What is happening here is happening all over Sichuan Province. The people have no prisons in which to house the corrupt, nor have they the certainty that they'll have power long enough for the sentences they might want to impose to be completed."

Wo-li's widening eyes showed that he understood the implication even before she finished her thought.

"This means," Ayi Zhao said, "that the only punishments available for them to inflict are beatings or executions."

Faith knew, and was certain they all knew, that since some of those serving below Wo-li and Mu-rong had already been killed, the rough parity observed by the provisional people's courts would require death for the two of them.

Wo-li looked across the table toward Mu-rong; something unspoken passed between them. Faith couldn't determine what it was, but she was certain it wasn't surrender.

Like so many of their caste whom Faith had met over the years, she knew them as Nietzschean Supermen, founders of a new but impermanent world in which the strong prevailed and in which they perceived themselves as self-sufficient gods of right and wrong.

And why shouldn't they?

Faith had answered that question countless times in lecture halls at Berkeley: They'd grown up in a country that had spent thirty years without a criminal code and in which justice was truly in the hands of the beholder. And they'd been raised in the absurd contradiction of a Communist-capitalist society in which careers were made or destroyed, lives were taken or given back at a whim, sometimes ideological, sometimes political, sometimes personal.

It was a world in which nothing was certain and fixed except the inevitability of death, and it was clear to Faith that Wo-li, unlike his mother and his son, believed in nothing beyond his own instincts for money and power.

Faith heard an echo in her mind, the last description wasn't her own, it was Graham's. It was how he'd described an American hedge fund manager whose firm had been bailed out by the Federal Reserve in the late 1990s.

"What do they want?" Wo-li asked.

"Justice," Ayi Zhao said.

Wo-li forced a laugh. "You mean money."

"When workers haven't been paid in months, they're the same," Ayi Zhao said. "But that's not what brought them here."

Ayi Zhao paused and stared at her son, then she lowered her head and closed her eyes. After a few moments she looked up and asked, "Do you know what the death toll was when the Number Two Hospital collapsed?"

Wo-li glanced at his wife, then shrugged.

"Or at the girls' school?" Ayi Zhao pointed over her shoulder toward the door. "The people outside of this room do."

Wo-li said again, "What do they want?"

"You already know," Ayi Zhao said. "But we have to give them a reason not to do it. A reason to keep you alive."

Wo-li pulled back and threw up his arms. "What? Play the part of puppets in their new Cultural Revolution? Turn us into political clowns and march us through the streets and then stand us up on chairs with signs hanging around our necks announcing our alleged crimes?"

Jian-jun stared at his father in the silence that followed, and then said, "That's the problem. They aren't merely alleged. It's all an open secret. They know you have accounts, they just don't know where. And they know that you filled them with payoffs from construction companies and foreign corporations, they just don't know how and who helped you."

"And it's better that they hang you in effigy," Ayi Zhao said, "than for real, especially"—she spread her hands again—"since this will not likely last and they know they must act before the rebellion is crushed."

Ayi Zhao glanced over at Faith, then back and forth between her son and daughter-in-law.

"They want names."

CHAPTER 35

Gage's cell phone rang as he checked his e-mails at the desk in his hotel room in Marseilles. The window next to him overlooked the Old Port from high above the night-jeweled Quai de Rive Neuve that formed its southern border.

He looked at the number and the time. It was Faith and it was 3:30 A.M. in China. As he reached for the phone, he felt the force of the contrasting images of the devastation in Chengdu and the starlit perfection of sailboats rocking in their slips and the purring Mercedes limousines sliding by below.

"I need some help," Faith said.

"Is everything—"

"I'm fine, really. The government shut down the Internet and I need to check something."

"Hold on." Gage closed his e-mail program and opened a Web browser.

"What are you trying to find out?" he asked, as it loaded.

"Do you know who Donald Whitson is?"

"The CEO of RAID Technologies. He was on the

news the other day, talking about the destruction of their plant in Chengdu."

"I need to know whether he was once head of their East Asian operations."

Gage navigated to the RAID Web site, the officers' tab, and then to Whitson's résumé page.

"From 1988 through 1991," Gage told her, then heard her repeat the information in Mandarin. "Who are you with?"

"A workers' committee in the economic development zone east of the city. They want evidence that Whitson was in a position to have arranged payoffs to Ayi Zhao's son."

"Let me call Alex Z and I'll conference you in."

Gage put her on hold and punched in Alex Z's number in San Francisco, then connected him to her and explained the issue.

"We need something fast," Gage said, "so they won't think Faith made it up. But she's got no e-mail access."

"No problem, boss," Alex Z said. "I'll get Whitson's résumé on my monitor. I'll bypass the Internet by sending a photograph to her cell phone. A screen shot. I'll magnify it so it's readable and she can zoom in even closer."

Gage heard the ticking of Alex Z's keyboard in the background, then "It's on its way."

"Keep sending whatever you can find about Whitson," Gage said. "Then find out where he lived in China, who he worked with, and who the RAID bankers in Asia were at the time."

"I'm on it," Alex Z said, then disconnected.

"Do you need to get out of there?" Gage asked. "I can send Mark Fong over."

"Let me go into another room," Faith said.

Gage listened as a door was opened and closed, then murmuring voices, then another door opening and closing, then the tap of her shoes, and finally silence.

"I'm not sure that it'll be necessary to smuggle us out," Faith said. "Anyway, a snakehead's background may be a little too shady for the circumstances."

"Which are?"

"What's going on here is one of the most astounding things I've ever seen. The farmers and workers have formed themselves into an investigative body, kind of like a French inquisitorial court. Some of these people can barely read and they're questioning and deliberating like the best judges I've ever seen. If only——" Faith's voice broke. She paused, then sighed. "If only the mobs hadn't killed so many before they got to this point."

"I know it's small comfort," Gage said. "But it could've been worse. China usually kills in the millions, not in the hundreds."

"You have a better perspective than I do since you've been in the middle of this kind of thing before. I've always been the note taker that comes by afterward, when things are settled and new institutions are in place."

Faith fell silent. Gage didn't interrupt her thoughts.

"There have been some amazing things," she finally said. "You should've seen Ayi Zhao's grandson. A sweetheart of a boy. He took the leader aside before the meeting began in which his parents were first questioned. They call him Lao Mao, Old Cat. Not because of his appearance—he's tall and long and lean—but because of his silent pantherlike grace and because of the look he has in his eyes, how he takes things in and sees inside of people. He seems severe until you look at him closely, then you can make out how weary he is. Just beat. These people haven't slept much for days and days and you can see it in his face. He's in his mid-fifties, but right now he looks mid-sixties.

"They stopped a few feet away from me, just outside of the door to the provisional court. Jian-jun looked up at Old Cat and told him the story of Moses and how God wouldn't let him enter the Promised Land because his hands were bloody from fighting his way across the desert. He was trying to explain to Old Cat that legitimacy requires clean hands."

"I'm not sure whether that's courageous," Gage said, "or just crazy."

Faith exhaled. "I was holding my breath. Old Cat gave him a puzzled look, then walked inside and whispered to a man already seated at the judge's table. I was sure he'd just given the order to have Jian-jun hauled away. The man nodded and Old Cat turned back, and then walked past Jian-jun and out the door. Just like that. It was stunning."

"And that's the difference between tyranny and rebellion," Gage said. "I hope it lasts."

"I'm afraid that tyranny will return pretty soon, but from another direction, when the government decides that things have gone far enough and sends in People's Liberation Army troops to take control—hold on."

Ten seconds later, Faith said, "The photo just arrived from Alex Z."

"There should be more coming in a few minutes."

Gage heard a door open in the background, and a voice calling to Faith in Mandarin.

"I need to go," she said.

"Call me the instant you need to get out. I'll find a way."

After Faith disconnected, Gage checked his contact list and called a number in Taiwan.

The phone rang four times before a man said, "*Wei,*" then yawned.

"Mark, it's Graham."

"Ah, *Da-li Shi-fu.*" Marble Buddha was Mark Fong's nickname for Gage, given to him when they'd last worked together. "What do you need?"

"Faith is in Chengdu."

"And you need to get her out?"

"When she's ready. Her and students. Six altogether, one with a leg in a cast. And not by air since the airport may still be shut down."

"Why not just have someone drive them over to Chongqing. My cousin can meet them and help them get tickets and they can fly out from there. They won't even need to change planes in China. They can go straight to Bangkok, then back to the States."

Gage stepped to his window and looked toward downtown Marseilles at the east end of the port, and at the cars streaming out of the city center.

"I have a feeling that the country may cave in toward the middle," Gage said, "and they'd be trapped. They may need to take a land route, maybe across a few borders, and I need someone who knows how to get that done."

Fong laughed and said, "You mean someone who can slither like a snake?"

"Exactly."

ou don't need to stay with me," Milton Abrams said to Viz McBride, sitting on his couch. "It's not like I'm in any personal danger."

"I'm not the guy you have to convince," Viz said. "Graham is."

"And if I asked you to leave?"

"I'd tell you that you'd have to call 911 and have me arrested. Graham wants me with you until he gets back and can figure out who killed Tony Gilbert, and why."

"Then maybe your time would be better spent doing that."

Viz rose from the couch. He hoped that his six-foot-four height, supplemented by his cowboy boots, might help accomplish what he hadn't through argument: put an end to the discussion.

"I do two things," Viz said, looking over at Abrams sitting at the dining table. "And two things only. I protect people and I do electronic surveillance and countersurveillance. That's my role in Graham's firm. He may send someone out here to look into the murder or he may not. There's a reason why he hasn't and I'm not going to second-guess him."

Viz walked past Abrams and into the kitchen and poured himself a cup of coffee.

"What about my privacy?" Abrams asked when Viz returned.

Glancing over at the DVD player in which Abrams had watched him locate a bugging device, Viz said, "You haven't had any privacy for a long time."

Abrams reddened. "You know what I mean."

Viz caught on to what the real issue was for Abrams.

"You want to get laid, get laid," Viz said. "It's not like I'll be sitting in your bedroom." He sat down on the couch again. "You sleep with her before?"

Abrams nodded.

"Then it ain't no secret." Viz pointed at the table. A couple of legal pads lay in front of Abrams, along with a stack of Federal Reserve research papers. "Don't you have testimony to prepare?"

Abrams opened his mouth to speak, as if to keep argu-ing the point, but closed it again in surrender. He then nodded and said, "I think it's more of a public suicide."

"Graham says you're a straight shooter," Viz said. "Makes it more likely that you'll catch a ricochet. You want to try it out on a civilian?"

"You follow the markets?" Abrams asked.

Viz shrugged. "Not really. I look at my retirement ac-count statements, but Graham and his people make all of the decisions."

"That bother you?"

"No. We've ridden out all of the . . ." Viz grinned. "What do you all call them? Corrections? I'm not sure what was being corrected, they all seemed like collapses to me."

"And I think there's going to be another one."

Viz's grin died. He didn't like to hear from a Federal Reserve chairman that his retirement account was going to tank. He leaned forward on the couch.

Abrams turned fully toward him, resting his arm on the back of the chair.

"You know what an equity bubble is."

Viz nodded. "Like the stock market in the late 1990s and the real estate market in the 2000s."

"We now have a government debt bubble. We have about ten trillion dollars of treasury bonds and treasury bills out there, but they're not worth that much. Not even close, because we can't pay back all of the money. The only way we'd ever be able to is to turn over chunks of the country to the holders of the bonds."

Viz pointed toward the window. "You mean hand over Central Park to the Chinese in exchange for the paper?"

"And Yosemite and Yellowstone and Ellis Island and Alcatraz."

"What's gonna happen when people figure that out?"

Abrams smiled. "We'll have what we used to call a correction."

Viz thought for a moment. "But if you come out and admit that, then the whole thing—"

"Collapses."

Abrams rose and walked toward Viz, stopping in the middle of the room.

"The year before the Berlin Wall fell," Abrams said, "Graham told me a story he heard in Dresden." He pointed upward. "A kid watching a circus asks his father, 'What's the man on the tightrope doing with that pole?' The father answers, 'He's using it to balance himself.' The kid then asks, 'What if it gets away from him?' And the father answers, 'It won't. He's keeping it steady.'"

"Sounds like at least some people recognized that the Soviet Union was on the verge of falling," Viz said.

"But not the CIA, not Reagan, not Bush, not Kissinger, not Rice, not Rumsfeld, not Cheney, not the State Department. Nobody. They all got it wrong. They were completely, even ideologically, oblivious."

"But they all took credit for it when it happened."

Abrams locked his hands on his waist. "This time around it will all be about blame."

CHAPTER 37

Just before dawn, Gage walked from his hotel, past the sailboats tied up at their slips and east along Quai de Rive Neuve toward the head of the box canyon port. He bought a cup of café Americano at a boulangerie, then walked across the boulevard and stopped next to a small boathouse. From there he looked over the water toward the wall of stone and stucco buildings, extending from the thirteenth-century Fort Saint-Jean at the entrance to the harbor, up past the seventeenth-century city hall, and then past twentieth-century marble-faced apartment houses. He didn't look over his shoulder, but felt the granite gaze of the Basilique Notre Dame de la Garde from atop a distant limestone hill.

As he sipped his coffee and watched the steam swirling above the cup, Gage wondered whether Tabari Benaroun was already at his desk in the Hotel de Police a few blocks beyond the façades of civilian life across the water, and what he was thinking, and whether his supervisors had pressed him about where he'd spent the last two days and who he had been with.

Gage was annoyed at where Tabari had decided to draw the line; his leaving unanswered how Hennessy had gotten to the coast trail and his showing-but-not-telling-draw-your-own-conclusions method.

At the same time, Gage recognized that he hadn't been forthright with Tabari either. He hadn't told the young detective, and had asked Benaroun not to tell him, about how Hennessy had arranged the meeting with Abrams, about how Abrams had given the signal that it would take place, and about the reason that they were meeting.

Anyone watching him and Tabari on the trail the previous day would've assumed they were hikers, perhaps concluding from their clothing that one was a local who was guiding a foreigner. Two men out early, before the boaters and rock climbers, when the air was still and the path untrodden and the shadows on the inlet walls were still waning and falling toward the sea—

That is, almost anyone.

Gage thought of Faith. She could recognize a rite of passage where a tourist would see only a native dance.

And Batkoun Benaroun. He could recognize money laundering where a bank clerk would see only a wire transfer.

And Viz. He could recognize countersurveillance where a pedestrian walking on Madison Avenue would see only a man reading a New York transit map.

Connected dots sometimes made not just a route, but a picture.

Gage wondered who was watching him and how, and what they were recognizing in the places and things that he could still only perceive as pieces of a puzzle scattered on a floor.

A church bell rang in the distance. The faint D-G-B notes were soon lost in the rush and rumble of the early morning traffic, but they repeated themselves in his mind with a vague familiarity that merged with his imaginings of Hennessy.

In the ringing bells Gage heard the first three notes of "Amazing Grace." And they led him to thoughts of Hennessy's blindness, and of his coming to see, and of what must have been a struggle for redemption, and of his wife and his daughter and the trail of tears that had led them into the emotional wilderness in which they now wandered.

Gage felt a heaviness in his chest as he rested his forearms on the wooden railing next to the boathouse. He stared down at the blue water, at the rocking boats and the reflections of the lightening sky and the buildings on the other side of the port.

Maybe he wasn't so wrong when he implied to Ibrahim's old friend in Boston that Hennessy's family was his client. After all, for Abrams, Hennessy's death was merely an episode in his life, while for Hennessy's wife and daughter, it was the event that now gave their lives its meaning.

The hymnal notes sounded again and Gage remembered walking from his Saturday job at the local newspaper when he was fifteen years old to his father's medical office in Nogales, Arizona, stopping on the sidewalk to listen to choir practice at the storefront Papago Baptist Church, the hymn sung in a low guttural Spanish. Then he thought of Hennessy's wandering in a desert of his inadvertent design, one that was pooled with mirages and whose horizon receded as he had advanced.

Gage let the song fade to silence in his mind, then

pushed off from the railing and continued along Quai de Rive Neuve. Soon he was enveloped by the diesel exhaust of buses and the salty-slimy stench of the fishmongers' stands lined up along the dock. He heard a yelp and glanced over to see a fisherman holding up a squirming octopus, waving it like a wet mop, and two old women giggling and backing away and then him slamming it down like pizza dough on a marble slab. Next to him a sea urchin vendor waved a sample and yelled at passersby, "*Treize a la douzaine, Treize a la douzaine*," thirteen for twelve, a baker's dozen.

As Gage passed three fishermen mending their nets near the corner, he spotted the grass meridian that split into halves the boulevard that bordered the east end of the port. Beyond it was central Marseilles: the financial district, museums, mosques, cathedrals, Arab markets, and elite chain stores.

Gage continued until he reached the spot where the broad La Canebiere, the city's Champs-Elysées, dead-ended at the port. From there he could make out the front of the Bourse et Chambre de Commerce, the old Stock Exchange and Chamber of Commerce, where Abrams had met with the other central bankers before his planned meeting with Hennessy.

But instead of seeing the delivery trucks and commuters that were driving toward him, Gage imagined a line of limousines making a turn south.

Except one.

Abrams's car had spun off the other way and had escaped into the Basket, a maze of streets and alleys that might have served the needs of the city a thousand years earlier, but now left it choked with traffic, and might have done so on that night. If the limousine had broken through to the other side, it would have then worked its way toward Belsunce, the North African section of the city, an area of old cafés, bars, and couscousaries where Abrams would have climbed out and entered a restaurant and found a back table at which to wait for Hennessy.

Perhaps it was as simple as that, Gage said to himself as he looked from intersection to intersection, from café to café, from storefront to storefront, scanning for the place where Hennessy might have stationed himself.

Maybe Hennessy missed the signal, or worse, maybe he caught it but got stuck in traffic, his one chance lost—and he just gave up, broken under the strain of failure and of events he couldn't control.

Gage's eyes drifted higher toward the rooftops of surrounding office and apartment buildings and church bell towers, all places from which Hennessy could've watched—

Or could have been watched.

Had Hennessy been followed? And by someone who grasped the meaning in his motions and understood what he was trying to accomplish? Maybe just a hired hand like Gilbert and Strubb. Go. Hunt. Fetch. Don't think. Just do.

And what steps had Hennessy taken to lose them? Abandon his car, grab a taxi, then ditch it and grab another—steal another? Each moment the clock ticking down.

Gage's ringing cell phone crashed into his thoughts. He recognized the number. He stared at the bright screen as he forced Hennessy's confusion from his mind, and then answered.

"*Bonjour*," Tabari said. "How are the legs?"

While Tabari had driven back to Marseilles, Gage had taken the trail a few miles farther before he returned to Cassis, searching for evidence of Hennessy's activities before his death. Gage wasn't convinced that the stolen car found at the trailhead was connected to Hennessy. Suicides don't wipe away their fingerprints, but car thieves do.

He hoped that Tabari could get time away from work, for today's trip was supposed to take them to where Hennessy's rental car had been discovered by the police three days after his body.

"I'm ready for more," Gage said. "When——"

"It won't be me. The transport workers have a strike scheduled for this morning. Days off have been canceled and everyone has been assigned to riot duty."

Gage remembered reading about the last one, a month earlier. Young North African and Arab teenagers had used the pretext of a battle between the strikers and the police as an excuse to ransack and torch a hundred shops.

"My uncle is on his way to pick you up. He had a couple of errands to run beforehand, but he should be near you in a minute or two."

And that would mean that the inspection would be all show with no chance at all of tell.

Gage scanned the storefronts, then started walking toward a canopied restaurant on the bottom floor of a triangular-shaped building at the terminus of Rue de Republic.

"Have him pick me up in front of Café la Samaritaine," Gage said.

"No problem," Tabari said. "I'm sorry I can't help you more, but I hope today you'll find the answers you're looking for."

Gage crossed the quay and sheltered himself under the café awning against the rising sun. From there he watched buses offloading office workers and listened to the distant wail of sirens. Two car honks from La Canebiere caught Gage's attention a few minutes later. He looked over and spotted Benaroun waving from the driver's window of his Citroën as he rolled to a stop along the near curb. Gage climbed in and Benaroun looped around the meridian and headed south, away from the chaos of the city and once again toward the turmoil that had been Hennessy's last days.

CHAPTER 38

Ayi Zhao stared down at her rice bowl, too tired after thirty-six hours without sleep to lift her hands and manipulate her chopsticks. She closed her eyes and sighed.

"My son is nothing but a criminal," she said, then looked up at Faith. "Do you have children?"

Faith shook her head.

"It's better that way."

Faith reached out and held Ayi Zhao's hand. "But then you wouldn't have such a wonderful grandson."

"I know, and it's a shame that he's been so humiliated by his parents. I hope he's finding comfort in his faith." She shrugged. "I don't understand it. Christianity seems so odd. I try to imagine heaven and hell, but I can't see them except as distorted reflections of what is around me. And I can't imagine Jesus as a god, only as a foreigner's benevolent ancestor."

Ayi Zhao paused for a moment and her eyes went vacant, then she shook her head as if to say that she'd somehow gone off course.

Faith released Ayi Zhao's hand and pointed at her bowl. "You need to eat."

Ayi Zhao reached for her chopsticks and managed them well enough to capture a sliver of green bean lying on top of her rice. Instead of eating it, she said, "It bothered me that Wo-li traveled so much and that he'd never tell me where he was going or where he went. It bothers me even more now that I know what he was doing."

Knocking on the open storeroom door drew their attention to Old Cat, who walked in.

"We need to know whether Wo-li will do it," Old Cat said, looking back and forth between them. He spread his arms. "People's courts have now sprung up in Chongqing and across the border into Qinghai and into the Muslim areas of Xinjiang."

Old Cat reached into his pocket and pulled out a cell phone, and then held it in his hand by the edges, as though it represented an unfamiliar form of magic.

Faith guessed from his manner that he'd never handled one before this day.

"They're looking at us for guidance," Old Cat said.

Ayi Zhao and Faith understood exactly what he meant by guidance: If Chengdu could find a nonviolent form of justice, the others might follow.

"Your grandson was persuasive," Old Cat said, "and for that reason I was willing to let a judicial process take place, but we've reached a stalemate with Wo-li, and the army can attack at any moment—it's time to act."

Faith was certain that Old Cat didn't expect Ayi Zhao to plead for the life of her son and daughter-in-law, and she didn't.

"If you spare their lives," Ayi Zhao said, "Wo-li will tell you everything."

Old Cat cocked his head toward the door and pointed at his ear. Only then did they notice the background murmur of voices in the hallway and the chanting from outside of the building.

As the chanting rose into cheering, Old Cat said, "We've liberated a forced labor camp north of the city—"

Ayi Zhao pulled back, as if jolted by Old Cat's words.

"Does that mean that you freed Xing Ming and Wang Bai?"

Faith recognized the names: Xing and Wang were eighty-year-old women whose sentencing to hard labor for planning a protest at the Beijing Olympics had engendered worldwide condemnation.

Old Cat nodded. "The criminals imprisoned there have fled into the hills, but the political dissidents have joined us here. And having suffered the way they did, they have their own ideas of what should happen to Wo-li and his wife. Especially his wife." Old Cat looked at Faith. "The party runs the slave labor system and she's the highest party representative in Chengdu." Old Cat shrugged. "So you see, their lives are not entirely in my hands."

"Of course they are," Ayi Zhao said. "You can let them escape after they cooperate."

Old Cat squinted toward the ceiling, then looked back at her and shook his head.

"They're too well-known and they don't have false papers. Even if they could get to a foreign border, there's no way they could cross."

Faith raised her hand as a prelude to speaking, but then lowered it. The only immunity she possessed arose out of her position as "the anthropologist," the nameless professional witness. She looked at Ayi Zhao and understood a mother's duty, and then asked herself where her own duty lay—and she was neither a mother, nor a revolutionary, nor even Chinese.

But then an image came to her mind of a wire service photographer that she'd once seen in a newspaper. His laying down his camera and diving into a Rwandan river to rescue a Tutsi baby who'd been thrown in to drown by a Hutu militia man—except that Wo-li and his wife weren't innocent children. They were despicable adults, but they had a mother who didn't deserve to suffer.

"I can get them out," Faith said.

CHAPTER 39

Where are we going?" Gage asked Batkoun Benaroun as he gunned the six cylinders of his Citroën around the rising curves of the Marseilles hills. He sped through the oncoming flow of commuter traffic like a salmon swimming upstream, and with the same driven instinct.

"I'm not allowed to say until we get there," Benaroun said.

"Isn't this a little silly?"

"Of course, it's like dancing the rumba without music or watching *The Man in the Iron Mask* without sound." Benaroun glanced over and smiled. "In any case, we've come to the point in the program where we'll have to supply our own lyrics." He pointed ahead to where the road rose between banks of apartment buildings. "All they found up here was the car Hennessy had rented. Nothing else."

Benaroun reached into his glove compartment and handed Gage a map. Looking at it, it wasn't difficult for Gage to guess their location. The port was to the north behind them. The Mediterranean to the west. And the

Basilique Notre Dame de la Garde, overlooking the city, was high in front of them and now coming into view atop a limestone cliff.

They worked their way through the winding streets west of the church until the road forked, one prong heading toward the entrance, the other around the back. They then made a final ascent, and Benaroun drove to the base of the hill on the west side of the church, where it bordered a residential area composed of one-story bungalows and multistory apartments.

Just after he turned onto a narrow dead end street, Benaroun gestured toward the backs of the wall-to-wall hillside homes whose balconies on their far sides faced the sea a mile away.

"He parked just by that yellow one with the green shutters," Benaroun said. "In front of the door."

"You mean his car was discovered there," Gage said.

Benaroun's face reddened. "Sorry. I went a little beyond the evidence."

He then made a three-point U-turn and pulled to the curb across from a spreading stand of aloe cactus and olive trees and bushes growing from patches of earth and from cracks in the hillside rock.

The sun that met them as they stepped from the car seemed to Gage to cast pure white light, hard and stark, that made the pastels of the houses and reds and blacks and blues of the cars on the street seem less like overlaid coloring and more like the things themselves.

Gage walked twenty-five yards to the end of the street. He stopped and looked west through a gap between the houses toward the Frioul archipelago a mile offshore. He could just make out the Chateau d'If, France's Alcatraz, on the smallest of the four islands. It was where the French government once imprisoned political and religious dissenters. Despite the actual suffering inflicted there that Gage had read about in school, the castle-shaped structure now existed in the public imagination only as the setting for the fictional *Count of Monte Cristo*. He wondered whether Hennessy, too, had hesitated at this spot and saw Ibrahim and himself in the fictional mirror of a wrongful prosecution and a struggle for justice and redemption.

Gage continued a little farther, past the end of the pavement and onto a dirt trail. He walked another thirty yards to where he could overlook the port—and realized that Benaroun had not at all gone beyond the evidence.

Standing in this place with the city glowing gemlike below, even without binoculars Hennessy could've made out the north end of the grass meridian at the head of the port and the backdrop of buildings that framed it. With binoculars, the limousine procession would have passed before him like a line of ants under a magnifying glass.

Gage heard Benaroun's footsteps come to a stop next to him.

"Is this where he was watching from?" Benaroun asked.

"No," Gage said, staring down at the city.

Benaroun turned toward Gage and squinted up at him. "I don't understand."

Gage directed his thumb over his shoulder. "Hennessy wouldn't have parked back there and then walked all this way. There was no reason to. He'd have parked where the pavement ended." He thought of Hennessy's wife and her smile when she mentioned her husband's investigative techniques. "His FBI training would've insisted on it. He would've parked as close as he could to where he was headed and then faced the car in the direction he wanted to go when he left." He smiled at Benaroun. "Just like you did."

Gage turned and pointed up at the basilica, then drew a line with his finger from the gleaming golden statue of the Madonna and Child at the top and down to where Hennessy's car had been parked and then back up again.

"He must've been a mountain goat," Benaroun said. "Even if he wanted to park down here for some reason, there are stairs close by." Benaroun made a curving motion to the right with his hand, indicating the far side of the hill. "Those would've been easier. Or he could've walked back down the main road until he reached the fork and then back up again to the front of the church."

"It's likely that he did just that," Gage said, enacting in his mind what Hennessy might have been thinking. "I suspect that he was concerned about surveillance. He'd do some evasive driving through town to get here, then pretend to be a tourist. Take the stairs and mix in with the crowd. And if he became convinced that they'd caught up with him, he could slip into the shadows and work his way down the hillside."

Gage pointed up at the church. "How about drive me up to the top and I'll make my way back down. You come back here and search a strip along the bottom of the hill, maybe ten meters wide. See if you can find anything."

Gage's cell phone rang as they walked back to the car.

"I need the snakehead after all," Faith said.

Gage didn't express the relief he felt.

"You ready to come out?"

"I need to stay a little longer. It's for the students and Ayi Zhao's son and daughter-in-law."

Benaroun cast him a puzzled look, and Gage mouthed Faith's name.

"How soon?"

"Two days. Assuming Wo-li agrees to it."

"You mean the rebels are trading exile for information?"

"And Wo-li is deciding how much to give them. For him it looks like a long-term solution to what may be a short-term problem. If he spills everything and the rebellion fails, he'll have torpedoed his future. The government will have to arrest him and will probably have to execute him as an example."

"At least this way," Gage said, "he saves his life, and once he's out of the country he can find a way to catch up with wherever his offshore cash is hidden."

"As much as she hates to do it, that's the pitch his mother is giving him."

"I'll call Mark Fong and give him your number."

"Won't he want some money?"

"I'll take care of it," Gage said, then thought for a moment. "Make sure you gather up whatever identity documents Wo-li and his wife have and any extra passport pictures. Mark may need to fudge up some papers to get them across the borders."

Gage called Fong after he and Benaroun had gotten back into the car.

"We'll settle up afterward," Fong said.

"How soon—"

"My cousin in Chongqing will rent a big van and arrive there tomorrow, me the day after. We'll collect the students first"—Fong laughed—"and then the criminals."

Gage then understood why Fong wasn't worried about payment. Either Wo-li and his wife would direct their offshore banker to wire the fee into Fong's account, or he'd make sure that they'd never make it out of China.

"If you have to leave them somewhere along the road," Gage said, "then leave them, but make sure the kids get out."

"Of course."

Gage disconnected and slipped his phone back into his pocket.

Benaroun grinned at Gage as he turned the ignition.

"Exile?" Benaroun said. "Like the Dalai Lama?"

"Not exactly."

"And you trust this snakehead? The name certainly doesn't inspire it." Benaroun smiled. "I think I'd have more confidence in something a little more marsupial."

"The situation calls for someone cold-blooded," Gage said, "and I know of no one colder."

CHAPTER **40**

A s Gage climbed the steps from the east parking lot to the entrance of the Basilique Notre Dame de la Garde, he was certain that Hennessy had ascended them with a stronger feeling of expectation than he did. Gage even suspected that he might be wasting his time, for he recognized that he was following a chain of possibilities and probabilities, no stronger than its weakest hypothetical link.

Even more, Gage wasn't sure that he'd come to understand Hennessy any better for having retraced his route. But he had to do it. And he knew Benaroun had to do it. Despite his claims that his relegation to financial investigations was an anti-Semitic gesture by the commissioner, his compulsive, methodical persistence made him a perfect choice for that kind of work, and for this kind, too.

Without articulating the need, they both understood that neither one of them was willing to suffer the lingering thought that the Marseilles police had missed something. And Gage was already certain that the detectives had misunderstood why Hennessy had parked on the street below.

Gage attached himself to the trailing end of a German tour group as he passed through the wrought-iron front gates and ascended the zigzagging steps to the terrace. He stayed with them as they walked the low-walled perimeter. The angle of view toward the port was now more extreme and the entire meridian was visible.

Gage followed the group up another level, checked the perspective, and then walked back down and out through the gate.

A footpath to his left led away from the concrete walkway. He followed it along the arched walls at the base of the church, his view of the city curtained and shadowed by oaks, pines, and brush. He soon emerged into daylight and worked his way over a limestone bluff until he could see the yellow house next to which Hennessy had parked his car.

Gage glanced up at the golden Madonna statue, concluding it would've been the most visible landmark at night, then picked his way farther, in between aloe and evergreen bushes, until he was in a direct line between it and the car. But a few steps down showed him that a direct line didn't mean a direct route.

The shortest distance between where Gage stood and the car was a long drop off a slick boulder. He worked his way first down to its right, then back to the top and down to its left, looking for some sign that Hennessy had passed on either side: a pen, a scrap of paper—anything.

But he found nothing.

From there, Gage headed down through a tunnel of brush and trees until he emerged into a clearing. He looked up at the Madonna and found that he was off course by thirty feet. He imagined that Hennessy, descending in the darkness down the angled slope, had drifted in the same direction.

Gage heard rocks tumble, a landslide of dirt and stones, Benaroun yelping, and then, *"Merde. Merde. Merde."* Shit. Shit. Shit.

"You okay?" Gage yelled down.

"I got a damn aloe thorn in my ass. How do you think I am?"

"You need help?"

"I'll survive."

Gage worked his way back toward the direct line, sidestepping down the incline until the hill flattened just behind the trees and the plants that lined the street. He searched back and forth along them, inspecting between the rocks and along the rough ground, then gave up and stepped into the street.

Benaroun was grinning and leaning back against his car wearing a wrinkled, mud-smeared overcoat, arms folded over his chest.

"I like your new wardrobe," Gage said, as he walked up.

"It's not mine exactly," Benaroun said. "But since I punctured my butt getting it, I could make a claim. Anyway, the man who owned it is not coming back to get it."

"How do you figure?"

"I figure because you were right." Benaroun pointed up the hill, seeming to enjoy the clowning. "It was jammed into a bush about twenty feet up."

"What does that have to do with us?"

"Hennessy must've taken it off trying to change his appearance."

"What?" Gage's eyes narrowed at the coat. "Are you sure—"

"It's got an American mobile phone and a little leather notebook with the initials MH on it."

Benaroun unfolded his arms and reached out to hand the items to Gage.

As Gage accepted them, his mind jumped back past Benaroun's conclusion to Hennessy falling coatless over the cliff, then jumped forward to the present.

"He only would've changed his appearance," Gage said, "if he thought someone had spotted him."

Gage scanned the street and rooftops and the hillside looking for surveillance. He found none. Or at least nothing obvious. He pointed at the car.

"Let's get out of here," Gage said.

Benaroun cast him a puzzled look. "You don't want to look for more?"

"Not now." Gage pointed at the driver's seat. "Let's go. I don't want to get trapped."

Benaroun started the engine even before his door was closed. A black Mercedes squealed around the corner. Its momentum and the driver's overcompensating yank on the steering wheel carried it in a sweeping curve from one side of the street to the other. Benaroun punched the accelerator and shot through the gap, then hung a hard right and rocketed down the hill.

Benaroun glanced over as he cut through an alley toward a boulevard leading to the center of the city, and asked, "How did you know?"

"I didn't." Gage pointed at the overcoat. "That thing told me that whoever killed Hennessy wasn't done with him yet."

s that everything?" Old Cat asked, standing next
to the table in the Meinhard storage room, hands
locked on his waist.

Neither Wo-li nor Mu-rong looked up from where
they sat across from each other. They just nodded.

Between them lay bank records, spreadsheets, and
notes that Jian-jun had retrieved from a safe anchored
to the foundation in the basement of their mansion.
Down the hallway and in the remaining buildings on
the Meinhard property, workers were questioning other
government officials and party members and factory
managers—each now confessing who paid them, how
much money, by what routes—not pleading for their
lives, but truth-telling for them.

Faith glanced up from her notes. She didn't believe
that Wo-li and Mu-rong had disclosed everything, and
the expression on Old Cat's face told her that he didn't
believe they had either.

But she did believe something else: If what they had
admitted to so far was confirmed by their records, every

U.S. corporation that had invested in Sichuan Province could be convicted of violations of the Foreign Corrupt Practices Act in the U.S. and their officers convicted of bribery in China. She imagined the business elite of the Western world, men and women dressed in suits and handcuffs, lined up in front of courthouses in London, New York, Paris, Bonn, and Beijing and taken in bus caravans to prisons.

She flipped back through the pages, the mass of names and amounts. Two hundred million from RAID Technologies. A hundred million from Spectrum. A hundred million from Meinhard. Payments made to officials from Beijing to Chengdu and into accounts and shell companies from Hong Kong to the Bahamas to Zurich, to front companies in every world capital and in every offshore haven.

A shudder of dread shook through her. In the intensity of the last hours, her mind hadn't broken free from the immediacy to realize that thousands of officials and company officers would kill to suppress what lay on the table and what was contained in her notes. Like the odor of the stale food on the table and the old sweat stained into their clothes and the generator oil soaked into the concrete floor, she'd been too enveloped in it. Now she could see that the trails starting from these records would eventually implicate the entire Chinese government and its corporate elite.

Her eyes fell on her notes about RAID and she knew what Graham would've done next: followed the RAID money back to its Hong Kong account, then out to all the other Chinese officials they'd kicked money up and down to.

A fist rapped on the door.

Old Cat grabbed the documents, dropped them into a cardboard box at his feet, and folded the lid closed.

The man he'd whispered to before the start of the people's court hearing entered. He fixed his eyes first on Wo-li, then on Mu-rong. Finally he looked up at Old Cat.

"Have they cooperated?" the man asked.

Old Cat nodded. "But we'll need another forty-eight hours to examine their documents to verify what they've told us."

Wo-li and Mu-rong both slumped as though to say they couldn't endure another two days of questioning.

Unless it was an act, Faith thought, they didn't seem to realize that Old Cat had just told them that he'd decided to let them escape.

"Tell the people to return to their homes," Old Cat said. "There's nothing for them to do until we call them back for the trial."

Mu-rong's hands flew to her face. Moments later, sobs emerged from behind them.

Old Cat's arm shot out and he backhanded her. Her head snapped to the side.

"Shut up," Old Cat said. "The time to cry was when the hospital collapsed."

Faith pushed herself to her feet. Old Cat turned toward her, facing away from the man, a slight shake of the head telling her that though the violence was real, it was a performance to convince the audience of one standing at the door that justice would be done.

Mu-rong's sobbing stopped.

Faith sat down and lowered her head, acting as though she'd been reprimanded and as though she feared that he'd slap her next.

Old Cat looked back at the man, then said, "Go."

The man nodded and turned away.

"Wait," Old Cat said, "let me have your gun."

The man turned back and handed Old Cat the semi-automatic that was stuck between his belt and pants.

"One more outburst like that," Old Cat said, "and I may finish her off myself."

Faith tensed. The words hadn't sounded at all like a performance.

CHAPTER 42

What the devil is the Chinese army doing?" Vice President Cooper Wallace asked the CIA director. "Are they going to stand by while those criminals destroy every American asset in Central China?"

Wallace's coffee had turned cold in the study of his Naval Observatory home as he'd inspected dozens of satellite images of the burned-out Spectrum distribution center in Chengdu, and farther south in Chongqing and Guiyang, and even farther south in Kunming. Other photos showed incinerated Meinhard plants and RAID factories and branches of German and French and Taiwanese companies, the smoke from the ruins hovering like patches of fog over the crosshatch of roads and buildings in the special economic zones.

CIA Director John Casher slid a DVD across the desk and pointed at the vice president's laptop. Wallace pressed it into the drive.

Casher waited until the video activated, then said, "These shots were taken outside of a meeting of the Politburo Standing Committee of the Communist Party."

Wallace's eyes jerked from the screen to Casher.

"How did you—"

The director waved his hand. "It's not important. What is, is that you see three old guard PLA generals walking inside. The last of the true believers."

"What does it mean?"

"We think it means that the army, or at least part of it, is taking the position that the rebellion in Central China should be allowed to run its course." Casher pointed at the computer. "During the 1950s, when these men were young, Mao staged what was called the Hundred Flowers Campaign."

Wallace nodded. "I read about it in college. Let a hundred flowers bloom—and then Mao snipped them off one after another."

"Exactly. What's happening now is that workers, laborers, and farmers are identifying and rounding up corrupt officials. And it seems as though the army wants those flowers to bloom."

"Are the flowers the rebels or the officials?"

"Both. But our intelligence is telling us that the army is most focused on making an example of some of the officials and on having it happen in the outlying provinces where it can be contained. When the time comes, they'll crush the rebellion before it spreads to Beijing or Shanghai or Guangzhou where it might spin out of control."

Wallace remembered something else from his Asian history course.

"It could just as easily spread like a wildfire and we'd have another Cultural Revolution that would bring their economy to a halt." Wallace pointed toward the window. "And ours too. Eighty percent of our suppliers are in China. Store shelves will be empty in a matter of days. Car assembly lines will stop moving. A million empty containers will stack up at our ports with nowhere to go."

Wallace looked down at the satellite images lying on his desk.

"Isn't there something you can do about stopping the destruction?"

Casher spread his hands and shrugged.

"For the most part," Casher said, "all we can do is monitor what is going on with the few agents we have in those areas and by monitoring telephone traffic."

"What about the Internet?"

"The Chinese have suspended it out there. They've left it up along the industrial coast since international commercial order processing requires it."

"Which means you have to listen to a billion phone calls to figure out what's going on?"

"Sort of."

Wallace stared at the director. He had a sense that Casher had slipped something by him, maybe because Casher didn't fully trust him with the entire truth, but wanted to shift the burden onto him for not asking the right questions in case there were recriminations later.

Then it hit him. "What did you mean by 'for the most part' all you can do is monitor with a few agents?"

Wallace watched Casher stiffen. He smiled to himself. *These bureaucrats, maybe even the president, think I'm some kind of bumbler, but they forget that I'm the one that made Spectrum the biggest multilevel marketing company in the world.* Maybe he hadn't adjusted to the political game as early as he should have, and as quickly as he should have, but he knew how to listen.

Casher took in a breath, then stretched his neck and adjusted his tie.

"We're . . . uh . . . sharing information with the PLA."

Wallace fixed his own expression in place. He knew that Casher expected him to redden and pound the desk, furious at the thought of making an alliance with the second most powerful army in the world that was also the force behind the economic machine aimed at crushing the West.

Instead, Wallace asked, "Is it a two-way street?"

Casher nodded.

"And what have we gotten for what we've given them?"

Wallace watched Casher lean forward, not quite like a dam breaking, but close.

"Most of our attention is focused on Chengdu because that's where the rebellion began—"

"Because of all of the deaths in the earthquake."

Casher nodded. "The surrounding provinces are watching the rebels there. A leader has emerged, a quiet guy, but charismatic. Over the last few days he's stopped the killing and burning and organized the mob into a militia of sorts. He's even set up people's courts and detention centers for corrupt officials."

Wallace's face betrayed him with a smirk. "Some kind of a Sichuan-flavored George Washington?"

"Not as different as you might think. And that's why the PLA takes him seriously."

Wallace felt the pressure of Casher's stare.

"You ever put your life on the line for something?" Casher asked. "Knowing that you were going to lose it?"

They both knew the answer. Wallace's two tours in Vietnam were spent working in the embassy. Never once in his life had Wallace doubted but that he'd die in his sleep when old age had depleted his body. Even the occasional death threats he'd received from fringe lunatics hadn't driven him toward thoughts of mortality and the shuddering terror of a violent death.

"Old Cat is a dead man and he knows it," Casher said. "He's shouldering the guilt for the lynchings and the bullet-in-the-back-of-the-head-executions even though it was just mob violence and he didn't order any of it."

"You sound like you have a lot of respect for the guy."

Casher sighed. "I wish he was on our side. I'd trade for him in a heartbeat. I'd trade away all of our wannabe Pinochets and Afghan tribal leaders and Mubaraks and the whole lot of Saudi princes for just one like—"

Wallace raised his hand. "This isn't the time or place to get into those issues. The question on the table is what we can learn from him."

Wallace watched Casher flush, and he knew he was wrong. He grasped that now was exactly the time and place, and that the failure to address those kinds of issues at the right time and in the right place had led to one U.S. foreign policy disaster after another, from Vietnam to Iraq.

"Let me rephrase that," Wallace said. "Let's start with what's going on now, then you can have as much time as you need to tell me what you think all of this means."

Wallace picked up his telephone from its cradle and punched in the intercom numbers for his secretary. He waited for her to answer, then said, "Cancel all of my appointments for the rest of the day . . . all of them."

He hung up and looked at Casher and nodded.

"The PLA has made sure that there is uninterrupted cell service in the areas in which Old Cat operates," Casher said. "His people have taken over the government complex in central Chengdu and they're operating a court at the Meinhard plant in the special economic zone."

"Does he realize that he's being intercepted?"

Casher shook his head. "I don't think so. He's a farmer. He'd probably never even touched a mobile phone until a few days ago. But he's using one now and the people around him are using them, too. And one of those is an anthropologist from Berkeley, Faith Gage."

Wallace did a little head shake. "You mean an American has joined the revolution. Or worse, is leading it?"

"Not quite. She's there with her students doing research. Her husband is Graham Gage, the private investigator."

"From San Francisco. I know who he is. Spectrum hired him years ago when a triad tried to extort our people in Taipei. He made the gangsters go away, but I never found out how."

"His wife has been feeding information about payoffs—names, dates, and bank account numbers—to the staff in his office. And then they're using it to do a huge amount of data mining to put it all together in what will in the end probably look like a mass criminal indictment."

Wallace cocked his head as he looked over at Casher. "Are we allowed to intercept domestic Internet traffic without a warrant?"

"We're not doing it. The PLA is and then they're passing the information on to us."

Wallace bit his lower lip for a moment, and then said, "I don't know much about criminal law, but that sounds like illegally obtained evidence."

"It's only evidence if we use it to prosecute people,

which is not our intention. But Old Cat is. They're debriefing officials and company owners and executives and then trying to verify what the crooks say before they act on it."

"You mean line people up against the wall."

Casher nodded. "Probably."

Wallace thought back to the exasperated expression on his chief of staff's face as he explained to Wallace the facts of Chinese corruption and the hundreds of millions of dollars in bribes that RAID had paid over the years, and by implication what Spectrum and other U.S. companies had paid.

"How bad will it be for us if this information gets out?" Wallace asked.

"Devastating. We'd be forced to indict the elite of our corporate leadership or lose whatever moral authority we have left in the world."

The words hung in the silence that followed, sharing space with the implication that disclosure was unavoidable.

"Is Graham Gage connected to what his wife is doing?" Wallace asked.

"Indirectly. He's only done two things: He set up the connection between her and his staff to do the research, and he sent in a human trafficker to smuggle out a couple of people in exchange for their cooperation with the rebels."

"A human trafficker? He's made a career of fighting those gangsters."

"He does what he needs to do." Casher said the words in a tone that implied what they both knew to be true: that Casher had done the same and would do it again. "His only motive is to save lives. He's doing his part long distance, from Marseilles, where he's working on something else—or at least we think it's something else. But we're not sure since most of the calls he's made to his office have been encrypted and the only nonencrypted call was too vague for us to draw any conclusions from."

Wallace paused, realizing that things were moving too fast and as part of a game that seemed to be without rules. He knew that he needed to slow down. He took a step back.

"Will the PLA really let these people get away? They must know it's going to happen."

"We assume they do, but we don't know whether they'll allow it. If they charge into the Meinhard facility within the next twenty-four hours and execute everyone, then we'll have our answer."

"And what do we want them to do?"

Casher pointed over his shoulder toward the door. "That's up to the man in the Oval Office, not me."

CHAPTER 43

Batkoun Benaroun filled two shot glasses with bourbon. They were sitting in the back room of a North African bar owned by a childhood friend of Benaroun's fifteen minutes after they'd broken free from the Mercedes. It was a space of chipped paint and ground-in dirt, of a floor that was swept, but seldom washed, and of hand-smudged entrance and exit doors with deadbolts, but no doorknobs.

"Great driving," Gage said, reaching for a glass and raising it toward Benaroun, who raised his in turn. "I owe you."

Gage took a sip.

Benaroun tossed his drink into his mouth, and then swallowed with a grimace.

"It's kind of hard to calculate the balance of debt," Benaroun said. "If you hadn't said let's get out of here, we never would've made it." Benaroun poured himself another shot and then took a sip. "But if you hadn't made me go there, we wouldn't have had to escape."

Gage smiled. "So you're saying we're even?"

Benaroun smiled back. "Not exactly. Any new thoughts about who they were?"

Gage shook his head, then pointed at Hennessy's cell phone and his small water-soaked notebook lying on the table.

"The answer is probably in there," Gage said, "but it'll be a while before we find out."

"You want me to see if someone at the Police Scientific Laboratory can help us?"

"Can't take the risk. It might put Tabari in a compromising position."

Gage picked up the cell phone, opened the back, and removed the battery and the SIM and memory cards and set them on a napkin. All three sheened with water that soaked into the paper. He moved them to another. He laid out more napkins, then spread the leather covers of the notebook as supports and stood it on end.

Benaroun rose. "I'll see if Mashaal has a space heater. Maybe that will speed things up."

After he left, Gage brushed the corners of the pages with his thumb, trying to get a sense whether they were soaked through to the middle. None of them separated. They were a mass of pulp. It would take hours of slow heat to find out whether they were pulped all the way through.

Gage closed his eyes, trying to re-create in his mind the moment when the Mercedes had made the corner and had faced them head on. He had only a cloudy image of the faces of the two men inside. Mid-thirties. Dark-skinned. Sunglasses. Suit or sports jackets, but no ties.

No question but that like Gilbert and Strubb, they were hired help. But by whom and for what reason?

Benaroun returned with a small radiant heater. He set

it on the table and plugged it in. Gage positioned it so that just a breath of heat touched Hennessy's notebook; he didn't want to warm it too fast and cook the pulp into a hard mass.

"I once had a stack of bank records we recovered from a money launderer found floating in the sea," Benaroun said. "He'd only been out there for a short time, but the plastic bag they were in had leaked a little. I used a razor to cut off the edges and was able to spread the pages."

Gage thought back to when he had skimmed through Hennessy's books in his office and had noticed the high-lightings and handwritten notes.

"Can't take a chance," Gage said. "Bank records have margins, notepaper doesn't. And Hennessy was a scrib-bler who wouldn't have respected them anyway."

Benaroun smiled. "So we just sit here and watch the water evaporate."

"And think." Gage leaned back in his chair and folded his arm across his chest. "Who sent those guys and what were they up to? People hunting for Ibrahim?"

"Or maybe people protecting him."

"I suspect that it was someone trying to find out what Hennessy had learned."

A knock on the door drew their eyes away from the drying notebook.

Mashaal walked in carrying beers they hadn't ordered and set them down.

Gage watched Benaroun's face harden and his jaw clench as Mashaal spoke to him in Arabic. Benaroun nodded and Mashaal walked back out to the bar.

"He says that the people who chased us now know who I am," Benaroun said. "And they're looking for me."

Gage sat forward. "How did they figure it out?"

Benaroun shrugged. "Maybe they recognized me. Maybe they got my license plate number. Their story is that I fled from the scene of an accident."

Gage thought of Benaroun's Citroën parked in the alley two blocks away. "But your car isn't damaged."

Benaroun sighed. "It is now."

Gage tilted his head in the direction of the car. "How'd they find it?"

"I don't know. I used to use this room to meet with witnesses who were afraid to come to the Hotel de Police. Mashaal and I grew up together in Algiers. They must've gotten someone in the department to—"

Benaroun's cell phone rang. He looked at the screen and said, "It's Tabari." He answered, listened for thirty seconds, and then nodded.

"Where were you when they called?" Benaroun asked. He listened again for a few seconds and shook his head at Tabari's response.

"And your partner doesn't know who they were?" Benaroun asked.

Gage held his palm up toward Benaroun, who told Tabari to stand by.

"We may need some help getting out of here," Gage said, then pointed back and forth between the bar and alley. "I'm sure they've got the place covered."

Benaroun passed on the information to Tabari, listened again, then disconnected and said to Gage, "He's on his way from the strike with a couple of cars of uniformed police. They'll be here in a few minutes."

As Benaroun reached down and withdrew a small Beretta from an ankle holster, Gage pointed at a spot to the left of the door from the bar. Benaroun walked over and braced himself against the wall with the gun aimed waist-high so anyone in the frame would get hit in the gut.

Gage unplugged the heater and surveyed the room looking for a place to hide Hennessy's phone and notebook. He dragged a chair over to the opposite wall, climbed up, and pulled off the cover of an air duct and placed the items inside. He then positioned himself next to the back exit. As he listened for sound from the alley, he caught a whiff of garbage seeping between the door and the loose frame and saw that the concrete abutting the metal threshold was slick with grease and blackened with mildew.

"Mashaal pretended that he hadn't seen us," Benaroun said.

"Let's not put him in a bad spot. Call Tabari. Have them first scare away whoever is in the alley and we'll go out that way."

Benaroun made the call, then disconnected and said, "They'll be here in—"

The back door exploded inward, the lock shattering the frame and shooting wood fragments into the room as it slammed against Gage's shoulder. He pushed it away, then kicked it, swinging it back. A gun discharged. A man grunted. The door swung back at Gage again. He stepped around and reached for the leather jacket of the gunman crouched in the doorway and pulled him facedown to the floor. The gun bounced out of the shooter's hand when it hit and slid across the linoleum toward Benaroun. Gage dived, sliding along behind it. As he grabbed for it, he heard pounding at the door from the bar, then the thud of a shoulder or a boot smashing against it. He looked up. Benaroun was slumped against the door, his body jerking with each impact. Gage leveled the barrel at a chest-high spot on the door—then heard whooping sirens, their scream rising in the alley. He rolled over and sat up and turned the gun toward the alley door. But the man was gone.

Gage climbed onto the chair again and slid the gun inside the vent next to the phone and notebook, then jumped down and ran to Benaroun. Blood oozed from a hole in his jacket, just below his ribs.

"I didn't feel the shot . . . until now." Benaroun grimaced. "But the pounding . . . it hurt like hell."

Benaroun slid his hand into the inside chest pocket of his coat, pulled an envelope partway out, and said, "Personal . . . hospital . . . shouldn't see . . . hide."

Then his eyelids fluttered and he lost consciousness.

Gage heard Tabari calling from the other side of the door.

"Wait," Gage yelled back, then took the gun from Benaroun's hand, laid him down, and pulled him away from the threshold. Holding the gun by his side, Gage opened the door.

Tabari looked down at his uncle and raised his radio to his lips.

Gage reached for his cell phone.

CHAPTER 44

After he disconnected from Gage, Alex Z set his encrypted cell phone down on his desk and made intercom calls to the senior staff of the firm. He then picked up a binder and a folded flowchart and walked up two flights to the conference room next to Gage's office.

Derrell Williams, Gage's investigations director, was waiting. Two others entered after Alex Z and sat on either side of Williams.

They all felt the unusual dynamic.

Alex Z, running the meeting. A tattooed computer genius whose authority derived from the trust Gage invested in him.

Williams, in the opposite chair, whose authority derived from his judgment and mastery of investigative technique honed during twenty years with the FBI, the last four as special agent in charge in San Francisco.

Alex Z slid the binder across the rosewood table. Williams flipped it open. The woman on Williams's right and the man on his left leaned in and scanned the first ten pages as Williams turned them.

Williams pushed the binder toward the woman, then looked up and asked, "How much of this have you verified?"

"I've been going at it from another direction," Alex Z said. "The problem is that we don't have access to the underlying bank records of the corporations that made the bribes to determine whether they match those that Faith has seen. The result is that I've had to focus on what I could prove is false, the kind of data that would show that these officials are lying and that their documents are forgeries."

Williams nodded. "You mean trying to determine whether or not those who allegedly paid the bribes were in a position to do it—"

"And whether the offshore companies existed and the banks had branches in the relevant places at the relevant time. If we can prove they lied about one thing, we have to doubt the rest of what they're saying."

"And have you proved anything false?"

Alex Z shook his head, then unfolded the three-foot-by-three-foot flowchart and turned it toward them.

"This is what it looks like. The boxes on the left are the corporations who paid the most in bribes to officials in Chengdu. The middle boxes are the intermediaries that handled the money. The boxes on the right are the recipients." Alex Z pointed at the RAID box. "Follow that one."

Williams traced the alleged money trail from RAID to a company named Tai Hing Consulting in Hong Kong to the bank accounts of Zhao Wo-li in the Cayman Islands and of Zheng Mu-rong in France, and to the accounts of a dozen other Chinese officials.

"Why is there just a dotted line from Tai Hing to Wo-li?" Williams asked. "The rest of the lines are solid."

"Because the money didn't travel directly and Wo-li, and his wife didn't know that part of the route. The RAID money went into the Tai Hing account in Hong Kong, but came out of a numbered account in the Bahamas. Wo-li assumes they're related entities, maybe two branches of the same company, but he's not certain."

Williams nodded.

"Wo-li has now signed an affidavit saying that he negotiated the payment directly with Donald Whitson when he was head of RAID's Asian operations."

"That makes both him and RAID guilty of a violation of the Foreign Corrupt Practices Act."

"Violations, plural. These bribes were renegotiated and paid every year." Alex Z pointed at the corporate names on the left side of the flowchart. "And they were all doing it. And if Wo-li is telling the whole truth, and the Justice Department chooses to act on it, the boards of RAID, Spectrum, and the rest will be holding their semiannual meetings in Leavenworth for the next ten years."

"And you're bringing this to us now . . ."

"Graham. Things have turned a little rough in the thing he's working on in Marseilles and he's worried about Faith and about us."

Williams narrowed his eyes at Alex Z. "Us?"

"As leverage against him and to keep what we've put together from becoming public."

"At this point it's all unverified."

"But what will happen to the markets if they fear that the Chinese might act on their own and seize the assets of the largest U.S. and European corporations over there? It'll start a run on the companies' stock and the stocks of all of the banks that they borrowed money from to build those factories."

Williams leaned back in his chair and closed his eyes. When he'd been the FBI's legal attaché in Hong Kong eight years earlier, the Economic and Political Section had estimated that China was underreporting foreign investment by at least fifty percent. It was a hundred and fifty billion dollars a year in the manufacturing part of the economy, not seventy-five billion, and of that, twenty-five percent had been paid out in bribes and kickbacks. He opened his eyes and stared down at the flowchart and saw that the method by which the bribes were paid was lying on the table before him.

The investigators to the left and right of Williams stirred in their seats. They'd seen the implication, too.

Williams looked back at Alex Z and said, "And Graham thinks he may have inadvertently set us up."

"And Faith, too. He's pretty sure his calls to her have been intercepted, either at his end or hers, and he's trying to get her out of there."

Williams spread his hands, pointing at the two sitting next to him. "Let's lock the place down and guard the perimeter."

Both got up and left the room.

Then to Alex Z. "Shut down the network. Internet access. E-mails. Everything."

Alex Z pointed down toward the two floors of investigators below. "What about them?"

"Wipe the hard drives on a couple laptops for them to share for e-mails."

The conference phone in the middle of the table beeped. Williams pressed the speaker button.

"What?"

"It's Ray Kaplan downstairs. Is something going on? I'm watching a rising curve of attacks on our system. It started last night and it's moving exponentially for the last few hours."

"Have they gotten in?" Williams asked.

"Not yet."

"Disconnect us."

Kaplan's voice rose. "You mean—"

"Unplug anything that connects our computers to the outside world."

CHAPTER 45

The smoke from Old Cat's unfiltered cigarette merged with the fog as he walked across the parking lot and away from the generator building. The whispering and snoring and soft lullabies he heard through the thin cloth of the makeshift tents intermingled with memories of the communal life on the collective farm of his youth.

He continued for a hundred yards beyond the last tent and the last guard, until there was only silence, except for his slow drag of air through the tobacco and his long exhale. The low mist separated and he could see stars against the blackness and high clouds side-lit by the moon. He shivered as the mist closed over him again.

His mind drifted back to nights listening to the elderly veterans of the Long March who'd fled the advance of the Nationalists, the long, circling retreat, and he wondered whether a long march of defeat awaited him, too, or whether it would be a short walk with his hands tied behind him that would end with a bullet in the back of his—

"Don't move."

The voice was low and harsh.

Old Cat grabbed for the semiautomatic in his coat pocket. Arms locked on to his.

Warm breath wafted toward him from faces inches away. Cold metal dug into his ear.

"Make a sound," the voice said, "and I'll shoot."

Handcuffs snapped around his wrists. Tape slapped against his mouth. Hands clamped onto his elbows and turned him ninety degrees and forced him forward. He stumbled two steps, then his feet caught up with him. A car motor started. A door opened, but the inside light stayed dark.

From fifteen feet away, he recognized that it was a PLA Brave Warrior combat vehicle. He'd seen them on the roads around Chengdu and often wondered who was the enemy.

Now he knew. And it was him.

Soldiers bracketed him in the rear seat as the SUV crept across the parking lot and toward the road leading out of the special economic zone. As they drove toward the gate, Old Cat glanced back at the lamp-lit tents, imagining the comforting sounds he'd heard just minutes earlier, and the nostalgic moments that followed, and became aware that while he regretted dying, he wasn't afraid.

The headlights came on and illuminated the near highway, but faded into a distant darkness—

And that was it. That was the source of his regret: a future he couldn't imagine.

Perhaps if he'd gone to college, maybe even as far as high school, he might've been able to devise a destination for himself and for the rebellion.

Instead, all he knew, all any of them knew, was what they were fleeing from:

Confucianism had been death.

Nationalism had been death.

Communism had been death.

And now capitalism had become death.

They had all believed that a rebellion would come someday—all the starving farmers and the sick children and the slaves and the wage-slave workers and the land-less laborers.

No, that wasn't it.

They had all merely hoped. And since it had been mere hope, they hadn't prepared, and not just with arms, but with ideas.

Old Cat watched the lights of the Chengdu Military Air Base rise up in the distance, a razor-edged jewel stark-lit in the surrounding dark countryside.

And he wondered how they would kill him.

Preparation. How does one prepare? Maybe that had been the Chinese problem all along, the legacy of Buddhism. One endures. One suffers. One burns incense for ancestors who suffered before. If life is suffering, then death is no more than a flame gone out and memory is no more than dissipating smoke, and the future can be no different than the past.

An image of the innocent face of the Christian kid came to him. What was his name? Jian-jun? Yes. Jian-jun. He had a good story to tell, but his religion had no answer either.

The man on the cross, would he build a car or dam a river or spray pesticides? If not, what work would he do?

Old Cat then remembered a cartoon he'd seen years earlier: a textile worker looking up from where he was sewing a "What Would Jesus Do?" baseball cap and saying, "I'm not sure what Jesus would do, but I'm sure he wouldn't be doing this."

Old Cat thought of the anthropologist sleeping in the storage room. She must have answers to these questions. She'd spent her life watching, listening, thinking. Maybe she had seen a society where people didn't poison each other, where all was not suffering and exploitation.

The Brave Warrior came to a stop.

A gate slid open.

Soldiers saluted. Their arms sleeved in sharp-creased jackets. Their heads encased in matte-black helmets. Their machine gun barrels glinting in the headlights.

If only there'd been time to ask.

CHAPTER 46

"T he hearing will come to order."

Senator Geoff Prescott struck his gavel a second time and the news reporters and photographers spread into streams moving from the front of the room and circling toward their seats. He then looked at Milton Abrams.

"I apologize for the delay due to the archaic nature of the Senate's roll call procedures, Mr. Chairman." Prescott smiled, a smile that Abrams assumed he was not alone in recognizing communicated the opposite of the sincerity that Prescott intended. Abrams suspected that Prescott enjoyed as much as the others hearing his name called in the Senate chamber. "It's not just the economy that needs modernizing."

Prescott looked over the notes lying before him. "Where were we?" An aide stepped forward and then pointed down. "Ah, yes. I see. We'd just gotten to the issue of inflation and the theory under which your predecessor operated, in effect, claiming that price stability requires less than a hundred percent employment."

Abrams nodded.

"But let's clarify our terms," Abrams said. "Until I was confirmed as Federal Reserve chairman, the phrase 'full employment' meant up to seven percent unemployment, and price stability meant inflation at a rate that didn't threaten what was called full employment. What I did was to simply—"

"You made your ideas clear at your confirmation hearing and we all know you executed it." Prescott glanced at his watch. "Can't you advance the ball here a little bit?"

Abrams thought of Viz McBride sitting in the back row of the hearing room and remembered the size of his hand when he'd picked up a water glass in the kitchen. It was so large that his fingers met the base of his palm— and Abrams imagined it wrapped around Prescott's throat.

"The point I intended to make, Senator, was that the figures that we've relied on for the last four administrations have underestimated inflation by at least fifty percent, perhaps more, and the same is true of unemployment."

Abrams pointed his finger over his shoulder at the business press.

"The markets need not panic," Abrams said. "Indeed, anyone who trades in the next few hours based on those comments is a fool. The world is what it is. The economy is what it is. None of that has changed in the last thirty seconds."

Abrams noticed that three of the twelve senators smiled, seven frowned, and two were looking at their BlackBerrys and had missed the exchange altogether.

Prescott's face flushed.

"You're saying that the last four presidents have been

lying to the American people about the true rates of inflation and unemployment?"

Abrams ground his right knuckles into his left palm under the table. He wanted to answer by saying that they couldn't have been lying because none of them understood enough about the economy to know what the truth really was. They lied no more than his brother-in-law's myna bird did when it proclaimed to anyone entering the living room that the sky was falling.

"No, Senator. I think that they were misled by certain conceptual issues of measurement and definition."

"And the point is?"

"That we need to be realistic about inflation, about real inflation. The world is watching. The fact that we lie to ourselves doesn't mean that foreign governments on whom we rely to buy our debt aren't telling themselves the truth." Abrams raised his finger. "The only reason—the only reason—that the U.S. bond market hasn't collapsed in recent years is that foreign purchasers of our debt—based on their own, independent calculations and based on readily available data—still believe that despite the true rates of inflation and unemployment we're still a good risk."

Abrams let them absorb that thought, then said, "In addition to inflation as normally defined, there is also what I call functional inflation. Eighteen percent interest on credit card debt and the decline in real wages during the last thirty-five years, both have the same effect as inflation, but it has not been recognized as such."

"Say our real inflation rate is seven percent," Prescott said, "say our real unemployment rate is fourteen percent—I'm not conceding that it is—but just say. What does that mean for our bond markets?"

"It means that if there's a spike in worldwide commodity prices, for example, for tin, copper, and platinum, inflation will skyrocket. We won't be able to pay our debts and the usual buyers of our treasury bonds will back away."

"To say nothing of what would happen if oil prices increase again."

Abrams nodded.

"And if that happens all at once?"

Abrams heard the rustle of the business reporters leaning forward in their seats to make sure that they got the quote right.

"The economy won't recover for a generation."

Abrams thought for a moment, then decided to put the problem in the kind of concrete terms the public would understand.

"Let's put it this way. To the holders of treasury bonds alone, we owe an amount equal to the gross domestic product of the U.S. for a single year. That is, all of the goods and services produced for consumption inside of the country—and there are a couple of ways at looking at how to pay it off."

Abrams spread his hands.

"Just for purposes of perspective, here's a hypothetical. Imagine paying it off in one year. Every penny that anyone earns goes to pay the debt. That means that no one in the U.S. eats anything, burns any fuel, drives anywhere, buys anything."

Abrams watched a smirk appear on Prescott's face. Apparently the only hypotheticals he appreciated were the ones he himself offered.

"Imagine on the other hand that we pay it off in ten years," Abrams continued. "In that case, American lives will be limited to three things. Working, eating, and sleeping. And every penny that isn't needed to pay for housing or for food, won't go into movie tickers or cell phone bills or iPods, but will travel offshore to pay off the debt."

Abrams watched the senators swallow and reach for their collars and dress necklines as if the truth was suffocating them.

Senator Prescott's face flushed again.

"That's science fiction, Mr. Chairman. Not economics. You can take any scenario and stretch it and expand it and turn it into a nightmare."

Prescott's pounding finger thunked against the oak dais, reverberating through the microphone in time with his sentences like a creeping monster.

"And I see no benefit in playing out in this hearing a fantasy of zombies and the world coming to an end."

CHAPTER 47

CIA Director John Casher's eyes surveyed the flow-chart displayed on the wall-sized monitor at the opposite end of the conference table. He then glanced over at Glenn Pollock, the head of the Analysis and Liaison Division of the Financial Crimes Information Network.

"Does Gage have any idea of what he's stumbled into?" Casher asked.

"About as much as we do." Pollock pointed at the flow-chart. "We believe that Tai Hing Consulting handled a little over a billion dollars in bribes and kickbacks, mostly for business done by U.S. and EU companies in Sichuan Province."

"And they weren't the only ones."

Pollock shook his head. "They took five percent of whatever passed through their accounts, then trans-ferred—"

"Five? I thought money launderers were still getting seven."

"That was only step one. Another five percent was

taken as the money went through accounts in the Bahamas—but there are some troublesome crossovers." Pollock paused for a moment. "Really troublesome. For one, Tai Hing operates out of the same address as the front company that paid for the Muslim bombing in Xinjiang nine years ago that led to the arrest of Hani Ibrahim."

Casher squinted over at Pollock. "Why pick that one to mention?"

"Because we think that Gage is on the prowl for Ibrahim."

"His idea or someone else's?"

Pollock shrugged.

"What do you mean by 'same address'?" Casher asked. "Street number, suite number, what?"

"All of the above. It's a shell company that's managed by a British law firm in Hong Kong."

Casher didn't break his gaze, but felt himself cringe. The Muslim separatists had made the CIA look like idiots. The wire transfer order that paid for the bomb-making materials used by the terrorists stated on its face that it was in payment for explosives, but to be used in seismic studies to find natural gas deposits. It was like hiding in plain sight.

Casher looked back at the flowchart. "Any of the other companies on that thing operate out of the same place?"

Pollock nodded. "Two we've identified so far. Altogether the firm manages the affairs of about a thousand clients."

"You mean they move money around for about a thousand clients without asking questions."

"That goes without saying. Lawyers in the firm have come up on a hundred different money laundering investigations. Italian prime ministers. Colombian drug traffickers. Offshore gambling. The French accused them of handling some of the bribes that Halliburton and KBR paid the Nigerians during the 1990s."

Casher rose and walked to the monitor, then pointed at three empty boxes and asked, "How long will it take you to fill these in?"

"That's a problem. Gage's office has dropped off the Internet grid and the last information that his wife called in was coded somehow."

"You mean they caught on that we and the Chinese are watching and listening in?"

"It looks like it, but we don't know what alerted them."

"Let me get this right," Casher said, and then held up his right arm high and to the right. "Over here we have some Muslim businesspeople in Boston who sent money to an offshore island, supposedly as a tax dodge." He raised his left arm. "And over here we have a Hong Kong company that the money passed through and ended up in—"

"That's not quite right. The account wasn't in Hong Kong, but in the Caribbean, same as for the Boston people that Ibrahim set up the trust for."

Casher lowered his arms.

"This bribery scheme isn't really a Hong Kong operation," Pollock said. "Except to the extent that the formalities are run out of there. The RAID bribe was drawn from the proceeds of sales of Asian-made memory chips that they negotiated in Dubai—"

"For tax reasons?"

"They deposited the money into accounts in the Caymans because there's no corporate or income tax. From there, chunks went into Tai Hing and out again to pay the bribes."

Casher glanced at a stack of binders on the conference table. "Do you have spreadsheets of all of this?"

Pollock walked over, selected one, opened it, and then returned to show it to Casher.

"The first section sorts the transfers first by company," Pollock said, "then by date, by account, and by amount. The second section sorts first by date."

Casher knew what he was looking for so he flipped to the date-sorted spreadsheets. He ran his finger down the amount column on the first page, then the second and third, until he got to the end.

"Just what I suspected," Casher finally said. "The amounts fall as time passes."

Pollock shook his head. "Can't be. Investment into China has gone up every year, so kickbacks had to have gone up also." He turned the spreadsheet pages back and forth from the first to the last, then looked up at Casher. "You're right. What does it mean?"

"It means that they moved from paying the bribes in dollars to other currencies. It's the Patriot Act kicking us in the ass. We made it so hard to launder money in dollars that they moved into euros, and dropped off our radar."

CHAPTER 48

Old Cat found himself examining in mechanical terms the method of his execution: who, what, where, when, and how, at the end, they'd dispose of his remains.

Left on the roadside as an example for others?

Maybe separated into reusable and unusable body parts. Liver, kidney, bladder, and leg bones in one pile. Head and skin and intestines in another.

Runway lights came into view in the distance and he had his answer: dropped from the sky like a propaganda leaflet.

When he was young, he'd heard about the CIA doing that in Vietnam and the military doing it in Chile. The tales had been passed around by little boys like himself who thrilled to scary and violent stories. Later, in school, he'd watched a film about the Vietnamese War of Liberation that showed a body falling from an American Chinook helicopter, but by that time he'd learned not to believe anything he was taught. Once they'd tried to teach him that in the nineteenth century one of every three people in the American South had been a slave. He realized that the number would be equivalent to four hundred million slaves in China. An impossibility. He knew it couldn't be true and wondered which of its own crimes the government had been concealing under the lie.

As the Brave Warrior drove past the barracks, armories, and hangars of the Chengdu Military Air Base, Old Cat felt the connection snap apart that had linked him and the farmers and workers in the fields around the Meinhard plant. He could see them in his mind's eye, but couldn't feel them. He knew there was a phrase for the thing his brain was doing to him. He thought of *jing shen fen lie zheng*, the mind-split disease, but he knew he wasn't crazy. He felt an internal shrug and wondered if that was also something the anthropologist might understand.

The officer in the passenger seat pointed toward an unmarked airplane parked on the tarmac between two facing rows of fighters. The SUV made a hard right and pulled to a stop. A hand reached over and pulled at the edge of the tape covering Old Cat's mouth, then stripped it away. Old Cat thought that it had been duct tape and had imagined the awful pain of its being ripped off, tearing at his face and his five days' beard. He was surprised to see that it was just the thin paper type used for painting.

The soldiers guided Old Cat out of the backseat and onto his feet, then removed the handcuffs. He felt like rubbing the feeling back into his wrists and hands like he'd seen criminals do on the television shows, but decided not to. Let them think he wasn't afraid of pain, then maybe they'd pass on any thoughts of torture and just get it over with.

As he was escorted toward the tail of the plane, Old Cat looked up at the side door. He'd seen that on television, too. How skydivers jumped out. He imagined himself one of them, in freefall. Arms and legs spread, falconlike. Not flailing. After all, what would be the point? But then his body tensed as he saw himself hitting the ground—except it seemed like someone else's body, for imagining the impact was like imagining himself dead.

Old Cat glanced over his shoulder, trying to look past the floodlights to find an escape between the buildings, or even out onto the runway, but it was like trying to look through fire. The soldiers on either side of him spotted the motion and tightened their grips.

A jet swooped down onto the runway sounding like a giant vacuum. Its tires chirped as they struck the concrete. Old Cat felt air getting sucked by and then dust swirled around him and pecked at his eyes.

They were now steering him like his body was a wheelchair. Now turning left and stopping at the bottom step and looking up into the dark interior of the plane. The soldiers slid in behind him. A slight pull upward on his arms and he took the first step. Then another and another. Ten more and he was standing in a kitchen. Narrow. Tiny. They'd always seemed bigger in the movies. It smelled of black beans and chili paste and *chow fun.*

Whoever it is that wants to watch me freefall, Old Cat thought, *has simple tastes, like a farmer.*

A door opened in front of him. He felt the brief pressure of a hand against his back and then he walked on his own into the cabin. A lone man in an officer's uniform sat in a leather chair fifteen feet away. His pressed green jacket bore no insignias. He could be any rank from a *lie bin*, private, to a *yi ji shang jiang*, first-class senior general, except his age—seventy or seventy-five—meant he had to be high up, very high up.

Old Cat was certain that it couldn't be a *yi ji shang jiang*; few had claimed to have seen one in person. Some farmers thought they were mythological figures like the ancient warlords in the Three Kingdoms legend since they'd only seen images of them in the news, but never in real life.

The officer rose, then stepped around the desk and approached Old Cat. He reached out an arthritic knotted hand and said, "I'm Shi Rong-bang."

Old Cat extended his hand in return, but only as he'd test the handle of an iron teapot to see how hot it was.

"I apologize for the means I used to bring you here," Shi said, then gestured toward the chair across the table from where he'd been sitting.

Only then did Old Cat recognize the soldier from a generation ago within the uniform that seemed to sheath, rather than clothe, his thinned body, and beneath the corroded patina of old age: the liver spots and wisped hair and sagging skin and drooping eyelids.

The recognition immobilized Old Cat, gripped by a Confucian tradition that he recognized and despised, but couldn't resist. No one sat in the presence of men like First-Class Senior General Shi. He lowered his gaze.

Shi took Old Cat's arm. And like a lever, it moved his

feet and walked him forward until he reached the chair and sat down.

Old Cat's body felt like it was floating on the soft leather. He pulled his hands off the armrests for fear of soiling them or scratching them with his calluses. Imprints of palm sweat gleamed under the fluorescent light. He felt his face flush as he wiped them off with his sleeves.

The plane shuddered as a jet fighter powered up off the runway next to them, then stilled as the engine scream faded into the distance.

"They tell me you're a farmer," Shi said. "Alone in the world. No wife. No children. No parents still alive. And a very exceptional man."

Old Cat swallowed. "What do you intend to do with me?"

"I didn't bring you here to harm you."

"Then . . ."

"I thought I'd better meet the most important man in Central China."

Old Cat squinted at General Shi and asked, "What are you talking about?"

"Don't you understand that the whole world is watching you?" Shi opened the laptop on the table and turned it toward Old Cat. The screen displayed the front page of Taiwan's *China Times*. On the left was a photograph of Old Cat standing before a throng outside the Meinhard plant, and above it were printed the characters: 老猫麻痹北京, Old Cat Paralyzes Beijing.

Old Cat felt his stomach turn. The headline was a death sentence, if not at the hands of the man sitting across from him, at the hands of those in the capital.

"How—"

"We thought it was important that the outside know what was happening in Chengdu," Shi said.

Old Cat stared at the screen, his mind trying to link the words on the page with Shi's statement and with where he'd just come from.

"What *is* happening in Chengdu?" Old Cat finally said, looking up. "Maybe you can explain it to me."

Shi smiled. "They were right about you. You are an insightful man. I should've said that we wanted the outside world to know that *something* was happening in Chengdu."

Old Cat didn't smile back. "I'm not an educated man—"

Shi cut him off with a wave of his hand. "We've had too many educated men in China." His voice rose. "The educated class in China has become a criminal organization, a cancer that replicates itself and spreads until"—Shi pointed high and away—"until even the high streams of Mount Emei Shan are polluted."

They fixed their eyes on each other. Old Cat's home village sat on a flank of the Buddhist holy mountain, just below its snow and fog, but within its sacred forests.

Old Cat didn't trust Shi enough to dismiss from his mind the fear that beneath the general's observation was a threat: Cooperate with us, for we know where your friends live and where your ancestors are buried.

Shi's softening eyes suggested that he realized that his gesture of common cause had backfired.

"I, too," Shi said, "have climbed to the Golden Summit. It was years ago, to visit my son." He smiled again. "Now I take the tram."

The air around Old Cat thickened with meaning. Shi's son must be a monk who lived on the mountain.

"What do you want from me?" Old Cat asked.

"Only what China needs from you."

"China? There is no China in the way you mean," Old Cat said, his voice strengthening. "There are only people pursuing money. China is merely the land on which they do it."

Shi shook his head. "The Chengdu rebellion is evidence that you're wrong."

Old Cat wasn't so sure.

"How do you know that the people aren't motivated by greed," Old Cat finally said. "To take from the rich and distribute it among themselves?"

"Is that your aim?"

"I don't know what my aim is. I can't imagine a future that's any different from the past." Old Cat looked hard at General Shi. "Can you?"

Shi shrugged. "We Chinese have never been good at political theory. We replicate. We pirate. Sometimes well. Sometimes badly. We are masters, not of invention, but of improvisation, of living without a past or a future, with neither a history nor a script to guide us."

Old Cat felt rage blossom in his chest. He now understood Shi's intentions.

"For you Chengdu is merely an experiment, like grafting a shoot onto a persimmon tree or a new heart into a dying man. If it takes, fine. If not, you'll rip it out."

Shi shook his head again. "It's more than that." He leaned forward and rested his forearms on the table. "Look what you've done with your courts. Look at how you've controlled the violence. You've created fair institutions in the place of corrupt ones. And did it in just days. We want to see what grows in the time it has."

"And then?"

"We'll find out together."

Shi paused and gazed into Old Cat's eyes and realized that he owed the farmer not just part of the truth, but all of it.

"But don't think that you'll come out of this alive," Shi said. "I don't see how that can happen."

CHAPTER 49

Gage nodded at Tabari, then slipped out of the hospital after Batkoun Benaroun was moved from surgery to the recovery room in Hospital St. Joseph. A platoon of retired police officers guarded the hallway. Gage wasn't sure that any of them believed the mistaken-identity story that Tabari and the bar owner had told the detectives, but Gage knew that they were all men and women who'd spent careers suspending disbelief in the hope of eventually learning the truth. If they had any doubts, they left them unspoken.

But Gage had to ask himself whether Benaroun was the target, not himself.

Once seated at the bar of an empty café, Gage removed Benaroun's blood-smeared envelope. In it was a business card–sized piece of paper with three numbers on it: B–3001, B–3020, and B–3134. The envelope itself was unmarked.

It didn't make sense to him that these numbers could

provide a motive for murder, for Benaroun could've passed them on to another person in a five-second telephone call or memorized them and put it into an e-mail or text message.

The waiter came out of the kitchen wiping his hands on a towel and took Gage's order for a cappuccino and a water.

Gage reached for his encrypted cell phone and called Alex Z.

"You set up again?" Gage asked.

"We're running things through a series of proxy servers," Alex Z said. "What do you need?"

"Benaroun had been trying to find out the identification numbers of the planes that have been smuggling platinum out of South Africa. I think I have them."

Gage read them off. He heard Alex Z's keyboard click.

"If they're really aircraft registration numbers," Alex Z said, "and not model or part numbers for something, then they're all Boeing 737s owned by North China Cargo Airlines."

"For how long?"

"A year. The first was originally owned by China Eastern . . . and the second . . . and the third by China Southern. That's assuming the Air Registration Database is accurate."

"I may have more information later," Gage said. "I'll call you back."

Gage disconnected, now wondering whether the planes were involved in the smuggling of platinum from South Africa or were somehow connected to Hennessy and Ibrahim, or even whether they were plane registration numbers at all.

As the waiter delivered the order, Tabari walked in

and climbed onto the stool next to Gage, who slid the cappuccino over to him.

"My father is with my uncle," Tabari said. "He'll call as soon as he wakes up."

"When will his wife arrive? I'd like to see her."

Tabari glanced at his watch. "Another couple of hours."

"But I don't want to be in the room when Batkoun comes to. In his drugged state, he may look at me and say something he shouldn't within the hearing of people who shouldn't hear it."

"I thought of suggesting that," Tabari said as he stirred a spoonful of sugar into the cappuccino, "but I was afraid I'd be misunderstood and you'd think I was blaming you for what happened."

"One way or another," Gage said, "I suspect that I am to blame. Either because in my preoccupation with Hennessy, I made us too easy for people watching him to follow us, or because the people who were following me in the States had caught up with me here and I hadn't spotted them."

They ceased speaking as the waiter passed behind them to greet two customers at the door, then Tabari said, "You want us to move around Marseilles for an hour and leave a wide scent to see if anyone follows?"

Gage thought for a moment. He didn't like the feel of it. "I don't want there to be two Benarouns in the ICU."

Tabari reached up and squeezed Gage's shoulder.

"Look on the bright side," Tabari said, now smiling, "there could be a Gage and a Benaroun up there instead. You and my uncle could even share a room."

Gage shook his head and smiled back. "No way. I learned when we worked together in Milan that he snores."

"How about this," Tabari said. "You need to get your stuff out of your hotel room anyway and—"

"And I need to go back to the bar and collect something."

Tabari drew back. "What thing?"

"A gun that the shooter dropped. I hid it and in the rush to get your uncle to the hospital, forgot to retrieve it. Maybe you can trace it to someone or to some other crime and figure out who shot your uncle."

Tabari narrowed his eyes at Gage. "Anything else?"

Gage changed the subject by removing Benaroun's envelope from his pocket and handing it to Tabari.

"This may have been what they were after. I think they're airplane registration numbers."

Tabari's jaw clenched and his face reddened as he looked at the numbers inside.

"I knew this would happen." He turned and glared at Gage. "Did you—"

Gage held up his hands. "We hadn't even talked about South Africa since we were at your uncle's house the day before yesterday." He lowered his arms. "I had no idea that one of his errands this morning before he picked me up had anything to do with this—and I still don't know for certain." He pointed at the envelope. "And he didn't say anything about it until after he was shot."

Tabari fell silent, then shook his head.

"Sorry," Tabari said. "I think I've taken to seeing him as an irresponsible child, and that makes you the adult who failed to supervise him."

"He's come to understand that his useful days are counting down," Gage said, "at least those that would allow him to do the work he's always done. And I don't see that he's ready to remake himself."

"If the doctors' fears are realized, he'll have no choice." Tabari paused. His eyes moistened and he tried to blink away tears, then wiped them with the back of his sleeve. "He won't be able to do the work he wants to do from a wheelchair."

CHAPTER 50

F aith Gage awoke on her cot in the Meinhard storage room to the squeak of a hinge and the scrape of shoe leather. She squinted toward the doorway and made out a charcoal silhouette against the shadowed hallway. It was in the shape of a tall, thin man with the angular bulge of a semiautomatic on his hip. Four others stood semicircled behind him, two men and two women.

She felt her body tense and her heart jump in her chest. She gripped the bed frame and sat up. She wouldn't let herself be shot lying down.

The man's hand rose. His forefinger paused in front of his lips, and then he gestured for her to follow him by a quick turn of his head.

By the profile she recognized Old Cat.

Faith turned toward the sleeping Ayi Zhao as she stood.

"*Bu yao*," Old Cat whispered. Don't.

Faith pulled on her coat, then followed Old Cat down the hall and outside. The tents were dark and still except for faint snoring and a baby's soft crying that sounded less like a child in discomfort than an adult's grief-stricken sobs. The guards passed by and waited to the east of them. She could see a red-gray hint of dawn on the horizon.

"It's time for you to leave," Old Cat said. "There's nothing more you can do. You need to go with the others when the van arrives."

Faith looked up at Old Cat. "How did you know?"

"The army has been listening to your calls and those of your husband and now those of the man coming to get you."

"But I hadn't decided—"

"I've decided for you." Old Cat pointed toward the four. "And they will carry out my orders."

Old Cat looked away, then back at her. She could tell by the distance in his eyes that he was about to speak to her as a professional witness.

"This will all be over in a few days," Old Cat said. "Soon the army will have learned what it wanted to learn from our efforts and will have no further use for us. And we can't defeat them." He spread his arms toward the tents. "I'm not willing to sacrifice these people in a lost cause. Our rebellion will not become a revolution."

"But what about this?" Faith pulled out her cell phone and scanned through the images, and then turned the screen toward Old Cat. It was an image of part of the front page of the *New York Times* online edition. "My husband's office sent me this."

Old Cat took it in his hands and peered at the words, then shrugged. "I can't read English."

Speaking together in Mandarin all during these days had seemed so natural that she'd forgotten the language gap between them.

Faith felt her face flush. "I'm sorry. I didn't mean . . . I only wanted to show you proof that . . ."

Old Cat smiled. "It's okay. What does it say?"

"That there's a mass movement of transient laborers toward Beijing. Ten million of them."

"They'll fail, too," he said, shaking his head. "The army is the one who got them moving and is prepared to stop them."

Gage's words came back to her: Uprisings in China take lives in the millions, not in the hundreds.

"You mean—"

"No, not with guns this time, but with rice from the military's storehouses."

"And you think that they can be bought off?"

Old Cat's voice hardened. "They're betraying no one, least of all themselves. For them, from the beginning, for all of us from the beginning, this uprising has been about the basics of life, and for them that's food."

In the rising gray light Faith watched Old Cat's breath condense in front of his face and float there for a moment and then dissipate.

"In the end, that's all we've been able to offer them," Old Cat said. "I have no ideas about how our lives could be different. I think it would've been better if I'd been born as a silkworm and could've secreted my world around me like a cocoon, instead of a man who had to create it with his mind."

He looked down at Faith. "You've traveled the world. You know politics and economics. You've seen how different cultures have organized themselves. Tell me. Tell me how we can build a different society, one without oppression and exploitation. Show me the model. We'll copy it." Old Cat spread his arms. "That's what we do here. Copy. No people are better at it. We . . ."

Old Cat's voice trailed away, and in that silence Faith recognized that neither he nor she knew who that "we" was who would take charge and remake the world.

"What about you?" Faith asked. "What will happen to you?"

Old Cat shrugged. "The army has seen to that, too."

Faith reached for his arm. "Then come with us."

"And leave others to be sacrificed in my place?"

"If the army has planned this as well as you say, then they've already decided on their victims. What you do is irrelevant to them."

Even as she said the words, she felt the bad faith of not believing what she was saying. The army would scour the countryside looking for him. She released her grip and lowered her hand.

"What I do is not irrelevant to them," Old Cat said.

"Then go on your own Long March." Faith pointed at the tents. "Take them all with you."

"And come back to what?" Old Cat again smiled at her. "See? We've gone in a circle." His smiled faded. "And I'm trapped inside of it."

Faith searched inside herself for an argument that would dissuade him, but found none. Now she felt foolish in bringing students to China. She didn't understand it. Didn't understand the man standing in front of her. And had nothing to offer him.

But as she looked up at him, there was something that seemed even worse. He was a man without a family, and now no chance to have one, a man who would have no descendants to burn incense and to close their eyes and to bow and to remember him on the anniversary of his death.

Old Cat furrowed his brows, then raised a forefinger and said, "Jian-jun told me that the other name for the one that Christians call the Devil is the Prince of This World." He lowered his hand. "I think now we both can see why."

Faith looked past him and through the thin dark smoke at the fading orange moon above the city and felt the whole of the world's evil shudder through her. She wanted to reach out to him again, this precious man, but she knew he'd withdraw from any gesture of comfort.

Old Cat pointed at the generator building. "Go. Wake Ayi Zhao and Jian-jun and collect your things. The van will be here in fifteen minutes. Your students are already inside."

"What about Wo-li and his wife?"

Old Cat lowered his voice and leaned down toward her.

"They have escaped."

He then cocked his head toward the south.

"Perhaps you will encounter them along the road as you drive toward Chongqing."

CHAPTER 51

L isten to me." Former United States president Randall Harris pounded the podium with his fist. "Relative Growth isn't a Ponzi scheme."

Despite the grainy picture of the old television and the tinny sound, Gage sensed that Harris didn't believe what he was saying. Maybe because it echoed in tone Richard Nixon's "I'm not a crook" proclamation during the Watergate scandal.

Gage was watching from the dining table of a vacation cottage in La Ciotat, east of Marseilles, belonging to the parents of a colleague of Tabari's. The house was anchored to an oak-treed hillside high above a narrow fishing port lined with tiny night-lit restaurants and slowly rocking trawlers. Lying before him was Hennessy's cell phone, along with the SIM and memory cards and his notebook. All were drying by the warmth of a space heater.

Gage hoped CNN International would stay with the press conference until the end.

Harris gestured toward the two ex-presidents standing behind him to his left, then said, "We . . . are . . .

not . . . crooks." And then toward the heads of the Big Four accounting firms to his right. "And these men and women aren't Arthur Andersen and they are in no way willing to betray their clients and shareholders and the public in pursuit of fees."

The camera drew back in time to catch the hand of *The Nation*'s Ivan Kahn shooting up from the crowd of reporters seated in the room. His body followed it upward and he began speaking.

"Then there really are assets of two trillion dollars held by Relative Growth?"

Harris ignored the questioner, but answered the question from his prepared remarks.

"We've spent over fifty million dollars to obtain four independent audits of the holdings of the funds."

Kahn cut him off. "That just means you kept moving money around so it would be counted over and over."

Harris now acknowledged him.

"What paper are you with?" Harris asked, his face flushing. "The *Socialist Workers Gazette*?" He paused, then jabbed a forefinger at Kahn. "I told you, the assets are there."

"Then open your books."

"So everyone in the world can imitate us? So every day trader in the world gets the results of hundreds of millions of dollars' worth of research for free?" Harris raised his forefinger. "Our advantage over others—our only advantage—in the world of finance is our ability to identify opportunities and capitalize on them before anyone else even figures out they exist. Opening our books is the same thing as revealing our trade secrets."

Harris glanced back at Lucille Nonini, head of AccountCorp Worldwide. "You want to take this?"

Nonini stepped up next to Harris.

"We've looked at the books," Nonini said. "And we did a lot more than that, more than any accounting firm or group of accounting firms ever has. In a matter of a week, we fielded five thousand accountants throughout the world who took simultaneous snapshots of all of the funds' holdings. There was no opportunity to move money around or transfer assets from one account to another."

Harris leaned over the podium and pointed at Kahn.

"The kind of false accusations that you and others have made triggered redemption demands by our clients and the only way to dissuade them was to disclose more about our investment strategy than even our investors have the right to know."

A couple of reporters laughed. Others shook their heads.

Harris's face flushed and he pounded the top of the podium. "Investors have a right to a share of our profits, not to our methods."

"What about off-balance-sheet liabilities like Citibank hid in structured investment vehicles?"

Harris shook his head and glared down as though he was about to throw aside the podium and jump Kahn.

"Read . . . my . . . lips. There's nothing—nothing—that's not included on our balance sheet."

Harris thinks he's telling the truth, Gage thought, but it couldn't be true. There was no way they could've kept paying out dividends unless they were doing it with other investors' money. Not throughout the massive economic upheavals of the last decade. And calling them chaos funds, as Harris and Minsky usually did, wasn't an explanation, it was just a label, a marketing gimmick.

The camera operator seemed to anticipate that the next question would come from Kahn and framed his face.

Kahn glanced at the camera, the attention seeming to act as an invitation.

"What about liabilities?" Kahn asked.

Harris rolled his eyes and said, "What do you think the bottom line of an audit is composed of? It's assets minus liabilities."

"That's not what I meant and you know it. I'm asking about liabilities arising out of complex derivatives. If no one has developed a method of pricing them, then how can anyone estimate the liabilities that arise out of holding them?"

Minsky walked forward. Harris stepped to the side.

"We're a hedge fund," Minsky said, "and hedging means, among other things—and without giving away our trade secrets and intellectual property—that we take countervailing positions. One part of the economy goes down, another goes up. One currency depreciates, another appreciates."

Minsky smiled as though he was dismissing a waiter who'd splashed the water onto the tablecloth as he poured it from a pitcher.

"In any case," Minsky said, "they're not all that complex and therefore not that hard to value."

A camera again focused on Kahn's face, but he remained silent. Gage didn't think he was alone in seeing in Kahn's eyes not the aggression he'd displayed before, but a kind of dread. Minsky's answer had been too simple, his manner had been too slick, and if he was lying, Relative Growth would someday collapse and take the world economy with it. The camera drew back, displaying Kahn standing alone, like a man at the sea-shore watching an approaching tsunami.

Gage looked from them to the drying notebook and the SIM and memory cards and suspected that the answers about Relative Growth that those at the press conference were searching for might lie concealed before him on the table. He looked at his watch. In another twelve hours he'd know what was in there, Faith would be out of China, and he'd be on his way back to New York and to the beginning of another trailhead.

CNN cut away to the floods in Paris.

Gage turned down the sound, but left the picture on in case coverage continued. He then went into the bathroom and retrieved an electric hair dryer and then returned and focused the streaming heat on the back of the notebook.

The television screen flashed red and white with breaking news: "Mine Collapse in China."

Gage reached for the remote and increased the volume. An earthquake aftershock in Sichuan Province had triggered the cave-in. Three hundred miners were trapped and feared crushed or asphyxiated. The satellite image on the monitor behind the announcer disappeared, replaced by a grainy and jumpy cell phone video, wives and mothers screaming and weeping on either side of the mine entrance, PLA troops using plastic shields to create barriers to hold them back. The area was gray with mist and low clouds.

It cut to young men rocking a black Land Rover, the bodies of the suited men inside jerking around, shoulders and heads smashing into the windows and against one another. Soldiers stood at the perimeter, not intervening. The SUV went up on two wheels, then back down. Up on two wheels again, then back down, bouncing and rocking when it hit the ground. Then up again on two wheels, hesitating, balancing, then slamming onto its side and mud splattering and men climbing up and stomping on the glass—

The image was replaced with another. An old woman, tears flowing, staring at the camera as though she knew the world was watching. The voice-over translation failing to capture the fury in her words and tone.

"They all knew . . . everyone knew it would collapse." She jabbed her hand at an unseen enemy. "They forced the men to work. Work or starve. Work or die."

Gage knew from growing up in Southern Arizona that what she really meant was: work *and* die. The trapped and dead were no different than the Mexican zinc and copper miners in the 1950s, paid cheap wages to keep the white workers' wages depressed, forced to work unprotected in the dust, their union leaders beaten and murdered, those who chronicled their struggle in print and film arrested—

Gage reached for his cell phone.

Faith answered his question before he had a chance to ask it. "The van is on its way now."

"And you?"

"Yes. I'm going, too."

Gage stifled a sigh. She didn't need to carry the burden of his worry with her as she fled.

"We'll be traveling out by way of—"

"Stop," Gage said, "I think my calls are being intercepted."

Faith didn't respond right away. Gage grasped that she was trying to think of a way to communicate something indirectly.

Finally she said, "Maybe mine are, too, but that's just an amateur's opinion."

That was the expression they would use when one of them came up with an idea that would help the other in his work.

"Gotcha," Gage said. "E-mail me when you get to an area where there's Internet access. Use the same encryption code that we use to send our financial information."

After Faith disconnected, Gage noticed a slight corner separation midway through Hennessy's notebook. He walked into the kitchen and retrieved a fillet knife, then laid the book on its spine. He eased the thin blade in the opening and rocked it back and forth, separating the pages, taking care not to slice into them as he slid along the top edge. As he made the turn, he noticed the sharp-edged corner of what seemed to be a thicker square of paper inside. But as he moved the knife farther, it hit a patch of paper that had disintegrated into pulp, a border at least a quarter of an inch deep. He resisted the urge to push on and force the blade edge through it. He couldn't take a chance that it would rip away salvageable writing. And for all he knew, it was just a baggage claim check or a train ticket.

He withdrew the point and set the knife down on the table, then once again propped the notebook up, directing the heater toward the inside and hair dryer toward the outside.

Staring at it, he was certain there was something inside that would lead him to Hani Ibrahim and to whatever it was that Hennessy wanted to tell Milton Abrams, but it wasn't yet ready to reveal itself.

He looked down at Hennessy's SIM and memory cards. He had less hope for them, for the circuits of both might've blown when the rain that soaked through Hennessy's trench coat had shorted out his phone. And that wasn't all. Hennessy would've encrypted whatever he had stored on the memory card and it might take Alex Z days to break in.

Gage wedged the hair dryer between two serving bowls, then rose and walked to the window. The last of the fishing boats were powering into the harbor, invisible except for their running lights and the winking of glass and chrome against the shore lights and flashing buoys.

Encrypted. The word echoed in his mind. *Encrypt. Decrypt. Crypt. Cryptic.*

He turned back and stared at the table. If the files on the memory card were encrypted, the notes on those pages would be vague and veiled, their substance concealed in a form that Hennessy would think that only he could understand. And if he had been mentally unstable, or even distraught, they'd be incomprehensible, or worse, misleading and they'd send Gage searching down a trail with no end.

atching water evaporate," Gage answered Milton Abrams. His call had come in as Gage was washing his dinner dishes.

"You're being a little cryptic," Abrams said.

Gage crooked the phone between his neck and shoulder and dried his hands.

"I have to be for a while," Gage said. "Is Viz around?"

"He's in the kitchen cooking chili for lunch. You want to talk to him?"

"Just tell him I'll call him in half a minute."

Gage disconnected, then retrieved his encrypted cell phone from his jacket pocket.

Viz answered the first ring.

"How's Abrams behaving?" Gage asked.

"His sex life seems to be suffering, but otherwise he's okay."

"Anybody show up to take Anthony Gilbert's place?"

"Seems so. One of his gofers has taken over. Davey Hicks. He has a New York PI license, but only subcontracts for others. I learned from a guy I worked with in the DEA who's now gone private that Hicks is a nose-to-the-ground grunt. Cash up front. No questions asked. Fired from NYPD three years ago for shooting a suspect in the back."

"How good is he at surveillance?"

"I don't know yet. We've only been going to public places so I haven't needed to try to evade him."

"With Gilbert out of the way, this is probably his big break." Gage thought for a moment. "But that may depend on who hired him. It's likely that it was Gilbert, but we don't know for certain. He could've been hired by Abrams's wife, trying to find out who he was sleeping with. The fact that she's not talking to him doesn't mean that she's not watching him."

Gage heard Abrams's voice in the background.

"Let me talk to him," Gage said.

"Here," Viz said to Abrams.

"Why the Dick Tracy phone?" Abrams asked.

"My calls are being intercepted. It could be at this end or as they pass through switching stations in the States. And Faith's are being intercepted at her end by the PLA. She's been helping the leader of the Chengdu uprising expose corruption in the area."

"The one the press is calling Old Cat?"

"The PLA is using him to let a hundred thorns bloom."

"Now it makes sense," Abrams said. "I get it."

"Now what makes sense?"

"I got a call from CIA Director Casher yesterday. He'd also called the vice president and the secretary of state saying we may want to respond to the big Chinese media blitz at the Davos World Economic Forum this week, accusing the U.S. of trying to undermine their economy. He's calling it their Whine, with a 'wh,' and Dine Strategy."

Gage now wondered whether it was the CIA that was intercepting Faith's calls and if they'd gotten on to her because they'd been listening in on him. He stared out of the kitchen window at telephone and power lines illuminated by a streetlight and swaying in the breeze, and imagined the air around him crisscrossed with signals, some intersecting, some dodging and bending and fighting off attacks.

"I don't think it's entirely whine," Gage said. "We've gathered almost enough information to get the CEOs of RAID and Spectrum and a dozen others indicted for violations of the Foreign Corrupt Practices Act and I suspect the CIA has filled in the empty boxes on our flowchart."

"With the underlying threat that we better make some trade concessions or they'll start painting bull's-eyes on all of the corporate heads in the U.S."

"And Europe."

"If they start naming names and banks and accounts and amounts," Abrams said, "the Hong Kong stock market will crash the next morning, followed by the rest of the exchanges one time zone at a time."

"I take it that Casher didn't mention that part."

"No. He just said to stand by for an update."

"Why was he talking to Wallace instead of the president?"

"I wondered the same thing, then I saw on the news that today is the president's annual physical. After that he'll be exercising with schoolkids and then giving a speech announcing a new commission on obesity." Abrams snorted. "If I was him I'd worry more about our gorging on debt rather than our gorging on fried chicken."

Gage didn't respond. He wasn't in the mood for either an economic tirade or sarcasm, not with Batkoun Benaroun lying in a Marseilles hospital with a bullet lodged next to his spine, the latest in a trail of casualties that might lead to Abrams's doorstep.

Might lead.

Now Gage wasn't so certain. He looked through the kitchen door at the dining room table. Only then did he hear the hum of the heater and the hair dryer.

"Let me call you back," Gage said. "I'm in the middle of something."

"Are you any closer to finding Ibrahim?" Abrams asked.

"That's what I'm in the middle of."

"You're being cryptic again."

"Let's keep it that way, at least until I've found him."

Gage disconnected and walked over and inspected Hennessy's notebook. The narrow opening had widened as the surrounding sheets had dried. He retrieved tweezers from the bathroom and tilted the top edge of the notebook toward the lamp next to the table and reached into the space and tugged at the square of paper. He felt it pull free from the opposite side, then he worked it back and forth up the gap. First a white glossy border appeared, the gray of concrete, then the black of leather shoes and laces, then the brown of socks and cuffs, the slacks splotched with water or—

The photograph slipped free of its sheath. It was blood.

Gage stared at the mutilated body. Its arms bound with wire that cut into the skin. Its shirt torn exposing a chest pocked with burns. The slacks pulled down to its knees. But the face was untouched, eyes dulled with death, mouth open as if he'd died with a last gasp.

Gage opened the MIT brochure that he'd gotten from

Goldie Goldstein and matched the portrait of Ibrahim to the face in the photo.

It was him. There could be no doubt.

A newspaper lay next to the body. The *International Herald Tribune*. The photo on the cover showed the French president greeting the world's central bankers in Marseilles on the day before Abrams was to meet Hennessy.

The message was clear. Hennessy couldn't have missed it. There was no need for words, for an explanation, or an accusation, or a threat.

In his pursuit of Ibrahim, Hennessy had forced someone's hand, and they'd used it to torture Ibrahim to death and then aimed the photograph like a sickle to slash at the fragile membrane that had shielded Hennessy from the abyss.

CHAPTER 53

Tabari waited in the hallway of Hospital St. Joseph's ICU with his uncle's retired colleagues while Gage entered the room alone. Even in the semidarkness, the sterility shocked him, offended him. The unforgiving stainless steel. The disposable plastics. The starched sheets. The cool air. The caustic stink of disinfectant. The mechanical clicks and beeps—each of them—all of them—belied not only the broken body of a man who'd tried to do good in an evil world, but the tragedy of a wife's grief and the distress of a rabbi sitting outside, head in hands, whose God had failed him.

Benaroun's hands lay folded on his chest. His legs, unmoving. His head turned and his eyes blinked at the sound of Gage setting down a chair close to the bed. Benaroun glanced at the remote to raise the bed and Gage eased him up from a flat to an angled position. Benaroun then raised a forefinger and pointed it toward his feet. Gage leaned over and followed its trajectory.

Benaroun's big toe moved.

Gage felt his chest fill and moisture come to his eyes. He grabbed Benaroun's shoulder and squeezed.

"First a toe," Benaroun whispered, "then someday a foot . . . and then someday a leg."

Gage's eyes closed and the tension of the last twenty-four hours seemed to sigh out of him.

A slight smile met his gaze when he opened them again.

"You shouldn't worry so much," Benaroun said, his voice now a little stronger. "Bad for the heart."

"It was as much guilt as worry," Gage said.

"You have nothing to feel guilty about." Benaroun licked his lips. Gage dipped an oral swab in a cup of water and then wet them. "They were after me, not you."

Gage pulled the airplane registration numbers out of his jacket pocket and held them up for Benaroun to see.

Benaroun nodded.

"They're owned by a Chinese company," Gage said. "But I don't know what that means."

"I do. The Chinese got mining concessions from the South Africa president—"

"For smuggling out the platinum for him."

Benaroun nodded. "And gold, manganese, and vanadium. He kept the Russians out and gave it all to China."

"And no money trail back to him."

"He plans to leave the platinum in Swiss vaults until the Chinese drive up the price."

"How did you—"

"The promise of the money was enough and my informant in the"—Benaroun glanced toward the closed door—"in the South African Secret Service. He called me and then sent the numbers."

"You sure it was the money that persuaded him?"

Benaroun stared past Gage for a few seconds, then looked back and said, "I don't know." He yawned and his eyes closed. He shook his head and opened them again. "Maybe patriotism. The last flight in brought Chinese saboteurs to shut down the mines."

Gage turned at the sound of a light knock on the door. A nurse entered, followed by Tabari.

"I think that's enough for now," she said, coming to a stop next to Gage. "There will be time later to catch up with friends."

Benaroun's face flushed. "But I need—"

"Rest. You need rest." She adjusted Benaroun's pillow, then looked at Gage and asked, "Can you return later?"

Gage rose to his feet and glanced at his watch as though he intended to suggest a time. But he knew that he wouldn't be coming back. His flight to New York was leaving in two hours.

A siren wailed outside, its blare muted by the double-paned windows and heavy drapes.

When Gage looked back at Benaroun, he found that the exertion of his protest had drained him and he'd fallen asleep.

Gage noticed that he'd been holding his breath. He released it. At least now he wouldn't have to lie to his friend.

here is he?" Gage asked as he stepped into Viz's rented SUV next to the curb at John F. Kennedy Airport.

"He should be on his way back to a Fed Governors meeting in D.C. I recruited a retired FBI friend who does executive security to stay with him."

Viz handed Gage a new cell phone. "This will probably be good for a day or two until the bad guys catch on to it." He then pointed at the leather attaché case on Gage's lap. "That have the stuff?"

Gage nodded. "I didn't try the SIM or memory cards. I was afraid there might still be moisture inside."

"No problem. I'll take care of it."

Viz turned the ignition. His headlights reflected off the limousine in front of them and enveloped it in swirling snow as if in a globe.

"What about the rest?" Viz asked as he merged into the passing traffic.

"A lot of his notebook was pulped by soaking in water, so I wasn't able to recover much, and what I did find is so cryptic that I don't know what to make of it. Parts of it read like the stream-of-consciousness rambling of those homeless guys who hang out in public libraries scribbling in spiral notebooks. And flowcharts, or at least pieces of them."

Gage turned on an overhead light, and then opened the briefcase and removed a sheet of paper.

"I tried to piece them together, but there was only one box common to all." Gage tapped it with his finger. "RGF."

"Relative Growth Funds."

"I assume so."

Viz glanced over as Gage held up one of the flowcharts he'd recovered.

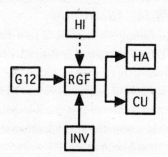

"And HI is Hani Ibrahim?"

"It was always in the biggest letters and always framed by an input box as though he was the mastermind behind Relative Growth Funds. But if Abrams is right, that Ibrahim's theories were just beautiful nonsense, it can't be true. No one could build an investment strategy on them."

Viz smiled. "He gave me that speech a few times. Hell, I didn't know what the uncertainty principle was, or entanglement, or fractals. I'm not sure Abrams even noticed that I didn't have a clue what he was talking about." Viz laughed. "I understood what he said about it being impossible to predict the unpredictable only because I learned what a tautology was when I took sociology."

"I take it he got a little excited."

"How'd you guess?"

"Because Abrams knows that Ibrahim's argument wasn't just a word game, playing with definitions. Ibrahim's argument was that what people have always considered to be unpredictable isn't."

"You mean that it's predictable that I'll get a raise once we get back to San Francisco."

It was Gage's turn to smile. "That depends on whether you can lead me to Davey Hicks."

Viz looked at his watch. "That's easy. In a couple of minutes, right after Abrams climbs out of his limousine in front of his apartment building, Hicks will drive into Central Park, pull off the road, and hide his car in a thicket. After that, he'll layer-up like an Eskimo and sneak in among some evergreens and relieve the lookout he's had sitting there all day---does that mean I get my raise?"

"Probably."

"Why's he so important?"

"I found his name in Hennessy's notebook. Along with Anthony Gilbert's."

Viz's head snapped toward Gage. "You mean Hennessy knew they were on to him?"

"But I don't know whether he acted on the knowledge."

Viz pointed at the flowchart. "What about the rest of the acronyms?"

"I can't even guess what HA, CU and G12 are," Gage

said. "I think INV stands for investors and the lines are transfers of money, but I can't be sure of that."

Gage reached into his attaché for another sheet.

"The words and phrases I found scattered among the pages, like bond derivative and strike date, were intermingled with nonsense telephone numbers and ramblings and self-accusations like 'I'm an idiot' or 'I had it backward' or 'financial Armageddon,' as if every time he learned something it made him doubt himself. And some were just crazy. There was half a page devoted to the sound of a motorcycle engine: *buffeta-buffeta-buffeta.*"

"Sounds like he's a Honda man," Viz said. "A Harley-Davidson guy would've written *potato-potato-potato.*"

"We'll never find out."

Gage turned off the overhead lamp and stared past the slow sweeping windshield wipers and through wisping snowfall at the New York skyline advancing toward them, the city lights haloed by moisture and reflecting off low clouds. He then took out his laptop to check his e-mail. The one he had been waiting for had finally arrived. He decrypted it and then read it to himself.

We're in Chongqing. Things are calm. Mark Fong is holding on to Wo-li and Mu-rong. He said you wouldn't mind if he made them pay their own way. I thought a snakehead would look more gangsterlike, but he made me think of Bartleby the Scrivener. He has the face of a nineteenth-century bookkeeper. I sent all of the kids home except the one with the broken leg. He suffered some swelling on the drive down and I didn't want to risk making it worse. A doctor will give him a blood thinner for the trip. We'll catch a flight within the next 48 hours. Love.

A new message arrived in his office e-mail folder. It was from Alex Z.

I was able to decode some of Hennessy's telephone numbers. The first was once assigned to the University of Hydraulic & Electric Engineering in Yichang City in Hubei Province. The line is disconnected.

The university was merged with a couple of others in 2002 and is now called Three Gorges University. We checked their Web site and no one with the name Ibadat Ibrahim is on the faculty there.

The second number is a disconnected cell phone in the Xinjiang Uyghur Autonomous Region.

The third number is an unlisted fax machine in Beijing.

"I don't get it," Gage said. "The only telephone numbers I found in Hennessy's notebook are either disconnected or a fax number." Gage stared at the numbers. "Unless they were coded a second time. But by only one or two digits. Something Hennessy could figure out in his head."

Gage sent an encrypted e-mail back:

Alex: See what happens if you keep increasing the last digit of each telephone number by one. Call Annie Ng and ask her to come up with a Chinese name that sounds a little like Ibadat. Maybe something like Yei bao-dai, then have her call. It may provoke Ibadat to say her name if we get a hit. It's 8 A.M. over there now.

He then did a search on the Three Gorges University Web site, then sent an e-mail back to Faith.

Hennessy was convinced that Hani Ibrahim was murdered, and the evidence is strong, but the road leading to the answers I need will pass by his body, whether he's dead or alive. Any chance you could fly up to Yichang and check at the Three Gorges University for his wife? Alex Z is working on some leads. Press reports are saying that things are calm there. They have a Culture Research Center in the College of Arts. Maybe you know someone from an anthropology conference.

Gage closed his laptop, then pointed his thumb over his shoulder.

"What do you think? Anyone behind us?"

Viz shook his head. "Can't tell, but it doesn't make any difference. I'll lose them once I get into Manhattan." He looked over. "That's where you want to go, right? After Hicks?"

"I'm thinking, maybe not. If we corner Hicks and then he runs to whoever hired him, they'll be ready for us. I'm thinking we go after somebody who's got nobody to run to."

"And that means?"

"Shake whoever may be tailing us, and head north."

hy isn't Strubb hiding out?" Viz wondered aloud as he pulled to the curb across the street and half a block away from the Jupiter Club at the edge of downtown Albany.

"Because if the police could've made him for the murder of Gilbert," Gage said, "they would've already."

Viz looked over at Gage. "I hope his apartment manager didn't drop a dime on us and tell him we came looking for him."

Gage stared ahead at the broken neon sign tacked to the brick façade of the bar, the J burned out and "upiter" flashing in red.

"He probably didn't," Gage said. "There's too many people coming by looking for Strubb—probation officers and parole agents and cops—that he doesn't bother anymore."

Two leather-chapped men walked into the recessed entrance. Muted light flooded the shadow as they opened the door and was eclipsed as it swung closed behind them.

Opening the SUV door, Gage said, "I'll go around

to the back of the building just in case he tries to slip out that way." He stepped down in the slush mounding up from the street and over the curb and then looked back into the cab. "On second thought, if you're getting a raise, maybe you should be the one to chill your bones out here instead of me."

"That's fine with me. I'd rather do that than what you have in mind for me." Viz smiled. "If he doesn't come out of there in the next half hour, you're gonna want me to go inside and dance with somebody."

"Shoot," Gage said, smiling back. "I was going to make that a surprise."

Viz reached into his jacket and pulled out Hennessy's SIM and memory card, then said, "I'll try to do some work on these while we're waiting."

Gage closed the door, made his way down the side-walk, turned left at a corner store, and then looped around to the alley. The far streetlight backlit two men smoking next to a dumpster by the rear door to the Jupiter Club. They stamped their feet as they smoked, their wool-capped heads clouded in gray swirls. Even in puff jackets they seemed too thin to be Strubb, and although wearing motorcycle boots, they seemed too short. One after the other, they flicked their cigarettes in high arcs like single streams of fireworks that exploded when they hit the rear wall of the building across the alley.

Just after the men reentered the bar, Gage angled to the other side, then worked his way along the trash cans and delivery trucks until he obtained a straight-on view of the back door through the muck-splattered passenger and driver's windows of a cargo van.

A man came out alone, lit up, and then reached for his cell phone and made a call.

"Hey. It's me . . . I'm out in the back. It's dead as dead can be except for Eddie." The man laughed. "He thinks he's gonna hook up with Strubb and Pike, but there's no fucking way that's gonna happen . . . That's what I told him." The man laughed again. "Three-way Eddie will be going it alone tonight . . . No, his phone got turned off. You want to talk to him? . . . I'll get him."

The man opened the back door and yelled inside.

"Strubb. My buddy wants to talk to you."

Strubb filled the doorway ten seconds later. He held a beer bottle in one hand and a pool cue in the other. He traded the cue for the phone and stepped outside.

"Who's this?" Strubb asked, then listened for a few seconds. "Yeah, I'm kinda between jobs. The last one went sour so I'm not working with Davey no more. Guy's an asshole. Stiffed me. He shows up here again, I'm gonna kick his butt back to NYC . . . Sure. What's the gig? . . . Yeah. I can do that . . . I'm good. Only had one beer. Pick me up out front in ten minutes."

Gage reached for his cell phone as soon as the door closed behind Strubb.

"He'll be coming out in a couple of minutes," Gage told Viz. "Waiting for someone to pick him up. Blue jacket. Jeans. Work boots. The voice recorder is cued up to the right spot. Come up on him from the east. Soon as you reach him, I'll head in from the west."

Gage worked his way back to the corner market and waited until Strubb appeared. He watched Viz step out of the SUV, and then stroll up the block and stop next to Strubb. Viz set himself so that Strubb's back would be facing Gage as he walked up.

Ten feet away, Gage heard his own voice on the recorder:

322 • STEVEN GORE

No reason to get yourself kicked in the head for something I'll find out anyway.

Then Strubb's.

Gilbert. Tony Gilbert. Works out of New York City.

Strubb backed away from Viz.

Then Gage's voice again.

This is what you're going to do. You're going to tell Gilbert and his pals to stay away from me.

Strubb spun and took a step. He jerked to a stop when he spotted Gage, who grabbed his jacket front and took him down to the sidewalk. Viz locked down Strubb's legs before he could start kicking, then Gage froze him with a wrist lock and they pulled him to his feet.

"Say anything and I'll break your arm," Gage said to Strubb, and then looked at his watch and said to Viz, "His pal will be here in a minute or two."

Gage and Viz marched Strubb across the street and down the block to the SUV. Viz frisked him, then they waited in its shadow as a pickup truck pulled to a stop in front of the bar. It waited a minute, then the driver honked twice, then leaned on the horn for a long one. Finally the driver walked inside the bar. He came out thirty seconds later.

Gage pulled up on Strubb's arm, a reminder.

The driver looked up and down the street, braced his hands on his waist, then kicked at the slush and climbed back into the cab of the truck and drove off.

Gage watched him fishtail around the corner, then pushed Strubb against a storefront.

Gage wasn't too worried about traffic passing by. The storefronts along the blocks heading toward downtown were empty except for yellowing "Going Out of Business" signs and dusty counters. And the bungalows and apartments in the opposite direction were more boards than windows, more bare wood than paint, and more cracks than concrete covering the driveways. It was a neighborhood that commuters sped through during the day and in which night drivers feared stoplights that set them up for carjackers. It was also one in which curious residents had learned not to stay curious for long.

"Remember what you said to me last time?" Gage asked.

"Fucking asshole," Strubb answered over his shoulder, his cheek pressed against the glass. "What did I say to you?"

"You said just stay cool. If everything checks out, we'll be on our way in a couple of minutes. We'll just call it no harm, no foul."

"And I was pissing blood for a week."

Gage pressed against Strubb's ribs. Strubb winced.

"Good," Gage said. "It'll be easy to hit the same spot again."

"Just tell me what you want."

"I want to know who hired Anthony Gilbert."

"How the fuck should I know? I told him what you said and he paid me off and we went our separate ways."

"You went your separate ways all right, but you left Gilbert laying dead in a dumpster."

Strubb rocked his face against the glass, trying to shake his head. "It wasn't me. It was some guys from the bar. He was calling us fags and stuff and they went after him."

Gage looked over toward Viz and asked, "You think this and the recording is good enough for a murder conspiracy conviction?"

"People have gotten themselves into a bunk on death row for less," Viz said. "But then again, I'm not a lawyer."

Gage heard a car slow down in the slush behind them. Viz crossed the sidewalk to the curb and flashed his old DEA ID. The car sped away.

"Let me paint a picture," Gage said. "You don't need to say anything until I get to the end, and then you can fill in the blank."

Strubb shrugged.

"You and some guys took Gilbert somewhere," Gage said. "Gilbert has no way to fight back except by trying to threaten you. But what's he got to threaten you with?"

Strubb turned his head toward Gage. "That's not—"

Gage pushed his head back. "I told you it's fill-in-the-blank, not question-and-answer."

Strubb nodded.

"All Gilbert's got to threaten you with is somebody bigger than him. Somebody he'd be terrified of if he was you."

Strubb nodded again.

"So Gilbert says: You lay a hand on me and my boss is gonna hunt you down and blow your head off. And you ask: Who's your boss? And Gilbert says . . ."

Gage twisted Strubb's wrist and yanked up on his arm.

"Wycovsky. Shit, man. Ease up. He said the guy's name was Wycovsky."

Strubb pushed himself up on his toes to relieve the pressure on his wrist and elbow.

"I didn't know who that was and I didn't stay around to ask him neither. I swear."

Gage eased up in the arm, then said. "Did you find out later?"

"Yeah. I went through Gilbert's cell phone. Wycovsky's at a law firm in the city. Him and another guy named Arndt."

"That's it?" Gage said. "He just threatened you with a lawyer?" Gage forced a laugh. "Like he was going to sue you?"

"Not Wycovsky, dumb ass. Whoever hired him. Gilbert said they had a lot of reach. World-fucking-wide. And no, he didn't say who that was. I don't think he even knew. People say shit when they're scared."

"Like you?"

"I've met tougher guys than you."

"I'm not surprised," Gage said. "Where's the phone now?"

"After I found out what those guys did to Gilbert, I tossed it in the Hudson."

Gage released Strubb's wrist and turned him around.

"I tell you what I'm going to do," Gage said. "I'm releasing you on your good behavior. Kind of like on parole." Gage smiled. "You know how that works. You behave and we've got no problem. You misbehave, and I'll yank the leash and deliver you and the recording to Albany homicide."

"What good behavior?"

"Keeping your mouth shut." Gage looked hard at Strubb. "Can you do that?"

Strubb shrugged.

Gage glanced at Viz. "I've got to get back to New York. Can you take him down to the police sta—"

"Okay. I'll keep my damn mouth shut."

Gage stepped aside and pointed toward the Jupiter Club. "Why don't you go back inside and play with your friends."

CHAPTER 56

V ice President Cooper Wallace rose from his chair at his kitchen table as CIA Director Casher entered, then shook his hand and directed him to sit across from him.

"I hope you don't mind," Wallace said. "I've always found it easier to do my hard thinking in here."

Casher had often seen print and television advertisements of the iconic black-and-white photograph of Wallace and his father talking over Spectrum business at their kitchen table in Topeka in the 1970s, but until this moment he thought it had been only a marketing gimmick.

Casher set his briefcase on the floor and sat down.

"What can I get you?" Wallace asked.

Casher pointed at a half-full pot of coffee on the granite counter next to the sink. "That's fine."

Wallace poured him a cup and took his seat.

"Before we start," Wallace said, "I want to thank you for our discussion last week. It's rare that anyone in Washington wants to talk about what events mean, except in a narrow partisan sense of which party gains and which party loses."

Casher watched Wallace's eyes go blank for a moment. He recognized that in recent days Wallace had put himself on trial and found himself guilty of the same offense. His role in both presidential campaigns had been to engage the enemy party in sniping skirmishes away from the central fronts of health care, terrorism, and economic uncertainty.

Wallace blinked, then looked at Casher and said, "We talk policy and implementation, then end up finding ourselves in a political or military or economic wilderness and don't know how we got there."

He needs a confessor, Casher thought, *someone to guide him through the psychological rebirth he seems to be undergoing.* The problem was that Casher could see only two possible outcomes from the experience, and both were nightmares. The first was that Wallace would be paralyzed like a college freshman by the glare of a sudden confrontation with too many questions and possibilities. The second was that he'd choose Reverend Manton Roberts as his midwife.

Wallace half smiled. "I know you didn't come here to listen to me ramble. You came to talk about financial issues, but I need to ask why you came alone. I expected that someone from the Treasury Department or maybe Milton Abrams would be with you."

Casher had anticipated the question and so had the president. He leaned forward, rested his forearms on either side of his cup, then said, "The president has been undergoing some medical tests in the last few weeks."

"I haven't noticed him leaving for—"

"They were done in the facility in the basement of the White House."

"What have they found?"

"A brain tumor—"

"Dear God."

Casher saw in Wallace's eyes what he and the president feared he'd see: wide-eyed bewilderment. Casher waited until it seemed to pass, then said, "It's not malignant, but it's growing and has to be removed."

"When did he find out?" Wallace asked.

"About two weeks ago he began to suspect that there was something wrong. Vision and balance problems. Headaches. Numbness in his hand. They first thought that he had suffered a minor stroke, but an MRI found the tumor."

Wallace reached into his pants pocket and pulled out his cell phone.

Casher raised his palm. "This isn't a good time to call. He knew you would want to and asked me to thank you in advance. He's explaining to his wife and kids what the treatment will be."

Wallace set his phone down on the table.

"And that is?"

"Surgery. Preceded by an induced coma." Casher pushed on before Wallace could react. "He's less worried about surviving the surgery than about post-operative side effects."

The president was also worried that in his single-minded pursuit of the office he'd made a bad choice for vice president. But Casher suspected that Wallace already knew that.

"He's concerned about emotional instability, loss of memory, and impaired judgment, and that he won't be capable of assessing whether he's competent to reassume the duties of the office."

Casher watched Wallace bite his lip. Wallace now understood that soon he would be the acting president of the United States.

"The president recognizes that it will fall to you and the Cabinet to determine whether he's competent."

Casher withdrew an index card from his suit jacket pocket and slid it across the table to Wallace.

"This is a list of neurologists and psychiatrists that he's asked to stand by in the days and weeks after the operation to help you make that determination."

Wallace fumbled as he tried to pick up the card, squeezed the edges until it buckled up off the table, then gripped it with both hands. Staring at it, he said, "I think he's the most courageous man I've ever met. Who else has the mental toughness to think things through like this?"

"The president would like to meet with you at 8 A.M. tomorrow. That will be followed by a National Security briefing in the situation room and after that a Cabinet meeting at 2 P.M. He'll make the announcement, then carry on with his schedule in what he suspects will be an unsuccessful attempt to minimize the impact. At 8 P.M., he'll meet with you, the speaker of the House, and the president pro-tem of the Senate and submit a letter saying that as of six o'clock the following morning he'll be unable to discharge the powers and duties of his office."

Casher watched Wallace's face work its way through a kaleidoscope of scenarios: a frown, upper teeth scraping across his lower lip, a squint into the distance, a hand through his hair.

Finally Wallace asked, "Why you? Why didn't his chief of staff come here to tell me?"

"Because the president knows that I'll never speak or write about what we say and do here tonight and because he doesn't want his thoughts and warnings and wishes to be filtered through the mind of a political animal."

Wallace drew back. "What warnings?"

"Manton Roberts and National Pledge Day."

Casher watched Wallace flush. He wasn't sure whether it was from anger or from embarrassment. He hoped it was the latter.

"The president knows that he's leaving you in a difficult position, but he's not willing to risk his life by delaying the operation in order to defuse what he considers a temporary political stunt."

"It's not—"

Casher raised a forefinger to cut him off.

"At the same time . . . at the same time, people all over the world are nervous about it. They see it as a kind of mass hysteria, especially combined with Roberts's ranting about the coming apocalypse and end times. They doubt his motives and suspect that he wants to see the world collapse into anarchy and is trying to push it in that direction."

Wallace locked his hands on the end of the table. "That's just hyperbole. No one embraces that kind of terror."

"If somebody yells fire in a theater, then everybody runs. They don't sit back and look around and ponder the person's intentions—but I'm not here to argue. My role is only to communicate the president's thoughts, and fill you in on some intelligence matters."

Wallace peered at Casher. "What intelligence matters?"

"Ones relating to China. We think that there are only a few days left in the rebellion, but long enough to do us a lot of economic damage. The president doesn't know whether it will land in the Oval Office while you're sitting there, but he wants you to understand the situation."

Wallace hunched forward.

"The PLA now has dossiers on at least ten U.S. business leaders," Casher continued, "and on a group of Chinese government and party officials that they've paid bribes to in the last ten years. More than enough evidence they'd need to charge them in Chinese courts."

Wallace nodded. "Or to force us to charge them in U.S. courts."

"The Chinese are focusing on these specific ones—including the CEOs of RAID and Spectrum—because of the impact the allegations would have on world markets. Our estimate, and it's only an estimate, is that the Dow will drop about a third in the first hours of trading after they make the announcement and display their proof to the world."

"Have they disclosed their evidence to you?"

Casher shook his head. "But we suspect that they've been able to fill in more boxes on their flowchart than we have on ours."

Wallace thought for a moment, furrowing his brow, then asked, "Is Graham Gage still helping them? And, maybe more importantly, should he be helping a foreign government?"

"To answer your second question first, it's more complex than that. And as to the first, not that we know of. But let me come back to him."

"How do you know the threat of exposure is real?"

Casher opened his briefcase and withdrew a DVD. "You have something we can watch this on?"

Wallace took it and then rose and opened a pocket door, revealing a small television and DVD player. He turned them on and slipped in the disc. Seconds after he pressed the play button, a dim video activated. It showed a wood-paneled room. Men in Chinese military uniforms sat on one side of a conference table. Men in suits on the other.

Casher stood next to Wallace and pointed at the left side of the screen.

"The uniformed man in the middle is Shi Rong-bang, First-class Senior General. We thought he was fully retired, but it looks like we may have been wrong. Even in retirement, he's been the conscience of the PLA. He lives like a monk in a place called Heng Shan, Balancing Mountain, in Hunan Province. He hasn't shown his face in public for a decade."

Casher moved his finger to the right side.

"His face is blocked by the man next to him, but sitting in the middle on the other side is the Chinese president. He may turn out to be a problem for us since he doesn't like you any more than you like him."

Wallace locked his hands on his hips as he stared at the screen.

"The general is doing most of the talking," Casher said. "The given—what both sides accept as true and is the foundation for what they're talking about—is the data on the flowchart. Who got what from whom and where the money went."

"Then what's the issue?"

"Shi is laying out the conditions for the army's suppression of the rebellion. They both know the police and internal security forces can't do it. They couldn't even control Beijing if they had to. Not now. Not with millions of laborers in tent camps on the outskirts of the city."

"But the military is as corrupt as the rest."

"The ideologues in the PLA are ready to clean their own house, too."

"Then what's the condition?"

"The main one is they want the Group of Twelve—"

"The what?"

"The Group of Twelve. It's the nickname for the People's Foreign Investment Fund managers. They're the most powerful corporate leaders in the country. Ten years ago they were tasked with coordinating China's use of foreign currency reserves. It was modeled on Japan's Ministry of International Trade and Industry, but has even more power."

"And Shi wants them reined in?"

Casher nodded.

"What are they suspected of?"

Casher reached for the recorder, punched the off and eject buttons, and removed the DVD.

"That's one of the things that's assumed by everyone participating in the conversation, but not actually discussed."

Casher gestured with his head toward the table and they both sat down again.

"And that brings us back to Gage," Casher said. "Milton Abrams hired him to find out what happened to an ex-FBI agent named Michael Hennessy."

Wallace nodded. "I know who he is. I was briefed on him years ago after that Muslim professor—"

"Hani Ibrahim."

"—was nailed for funding the bombing of the Spectrum distribution center in China."

Casher raised his hands. "We're now not so sure about that."

"What?" Wallace's face flushed. "I'm the one who leaned on the FBI to bury that guy." He thumped the table with his forefinger. "And now you're telling me he didn't do it?"

Casher shrugged. "Not yet. We're pursuing a lead, but we don't know."

Wallace lowered his gaze and shook his head. "This is absurd." Then he sighed and looked up again. "What *do* we know?"

"We know that Gage is trying to follow a trail through Hennessy to Ibrahim and from Ibrahim to Relative Growth, which Abrams thinks is a multitrillion-dollar fraud."

"Why don't you go after Ibrahim yourself?"

"Two reasons. First, we don't know whether he's still alive—some things happened to him that it's better you don't know about."

Casher watched Wallace's eyes widen. He pushed on before Wallace had a chance to form his fears into a question.

"And second, if he's still alive, we know we'll spook him. Gage won't. He's been able to get the guy who was Ibrahim's closest friend—Rahmani, a car dealer of sorts—to talk to him when he hasn't been willing to talk to anyone else. Same thing with Hennessy's wife and daughter."

When Wallace looked away and stared at the dark window, opaque but for the reflection of the kitchen against it, Casher feared that he'd dumped too much on him at once, and had provoked the paralysis he had feared.

Casher now felt sorry for the man, wondering what it must feel like to know with certainty that in a matter of hours he would be transformed by events out of his control from a mere appendix to the presidency, to the body and mind of a nation.

And Casher also thought of himself and felt a shudder of self-revelation: He'd always understood himself as a man who'd never been afraid to pull the trigger, as a marine, as a field operative, as deputy director of the CIA, and as director—but now he grasped that someone else had always loaded the gun and either ordered him, or gave him permission, to fire.

Casher found that he was staring at Wallace, wondering who would emerge from Wallace's reverie: the corporate executive who built an international corporation, the vice president who seemed to become less and less effective over the two terms, or a man cowering in the shadow of responsibility.

"I don't want to tell you how to do your work," Wallace finally said, now looking back at Casher. "But have you considered bringing Gage in and grilling him about what he knows?"

Casher nodded.

"We thought about it, but he's not the kind of guy who'd give in to grilling and we're not the only ones who are tracking him. Not only are the Chinese intercepting his calls, but somebody—we don't know who— has added physical surveillance. It would be tricky to haul him in without being noticed."

"Doesn't all that suggest that we're not the only ones trying to use him to find out what's going on?"

Casher thought for a moment, then said, "The problem for us and for them is that Gage travels fastest on the tiniest of trails. And we've lost him. Maybe the other side has, too. We don't know."

"Does that mean you have to sit on your hands?"

"No, we're pursuing our own leads, but because we don't know everything Gage knows, they may take us into a minefield."

ou want to go after Wycovsky?" Viz asked as they drove south along the Hudson River toward Manhattan.

"I'm not sure yet," Gage said. "I'm trying to think through the dynamics. Gilbert threatens Strubb with Wycovsky, the guy who Gilbert is afraid of. But it looks like Gilbert was also reporting to Arndt. That means that he's probably the underling. The gofer."

Gage withdrew his laptop from his attaché case and located the law firm's Web site. He found Wycovsky's photo among the partners. Sitting at the far end of a conference table, the five other partners semicircled behind him, Wycovsky looking like a wolf among hounds and terriers. Gage navigated to his personal page. A ten-year gap between when he graduated from Brooklyn College and when he completed Flatbush Evening Law School.

Arndt's page showed him to be a second-year associate with a Yale Law School degree, wireless glasses, and a haircut like a Chihuahua.

"How does an Ivy Leaguer end up taking orders from a guy like Wycovsky?" Gage asked.

"Maybe bottom of his class and lots of student loans to pay off."

Gage returned to the home page and looked for a tab for notable cases or firm achievements or recent cases or trial wins. There was none.

Whatever kind of work they did, they didn't want to advertise it.

"Don't close it up," Viz said, then reached into the console and pulled out a memory card reader. He handed it to Gage along with Hennessy's cards. "The SIM is shot. The other one is okay. It has only one file on it, but I couldn't open it."

Gage plugged in the reader and copied the file onto his computer. He tried a few different programs, but none would activate the file.

"I better let the genius give it a try," Gage said, then forwarded it to Alex Z.

Three hours later, Viz dropped Gage off two blocks away from Milton Abrams's apartment, then drove over to Shadden Phillips & Wycovsky to watch for Arndt.

Gage had just finished filling Abrams in and going over Hennessy's notebook, when Viz called.

"I spotted Arndt leaving work early. I called his office pretending to be a friend from Yale. His secretary said he had an appointment near his home in Scarsdale, then was going to work out at his club."

"Did you get the name?"

"I played dumb and she spilled it," Viz said. "I'll come by and pick you up."

Thirty minutes later, Gage was riding with Viz toward Scarsdale, and sixty minutes after that they were looking in through the storefront windows of a 24 Hour Fitness center.

Gage found it easy to spot Kenyon Arndt wiping his face with a towel as he ran on a treadmill in the middle of a line of others.

"I don't think anyone's face is supposed to be that red," Viz said.

Gage nodded as he cracked a window to keep the windshield from fogging. "He's getting into heart attack territory."

Arndt reached up and punched at the display. A few seconds later his legs accelerated.

"Should I go in there and stop him before he kills himself?" Viz asked.

"It looks like that's the point. With debts like Alex Z says he's got, money from his life insurance may be the only way out for his family."

A personal trainer wearing a club jersey and shorts walked up to Arndt and pointed at what looked to Gage to be a bruise on Arndt's forehead, then down at the display.

Arndt stared forward, shaking his head.

She made a football referee's timeout signal with the fingers of one hand T'd against the palm of the other and held it in front of Arndt's face.

Arndt shook his head again, and she yanked the safety cord. Arndt's legs slowed to a stop. He threw his towel against her chest, then turned and marched away.

"Kind of a punk," Viz said.

"I suspect there's a lot going on in his head that we don't know about," Gage said, then pointed at Arndt's Volvo parked two spaces away, between two BMWs. "Why don't you head on over there. When he comes out, pretend you dropped your keys in the slush."

Viz looked over. "I guess it's my turn for the cold job."

"Only because he might've seen a photo of me, either from Davey Hicks or somewhere else, and I don't want him to bolt. I'd rather not have to tackle him in the snow."

Gage's encrypted cell phone rang as Viz walked away.

"That file was a pain in the ass," Alex Z said, "but I got it, boss. I just e-mailed it back."

Just then, Arndt walked from the entrance toward his car.

"I'll look for it. Thanks. I've got to go."

By the time Arndt arrived at his driver's side door, Viz was bent down sifting through the slush.

Through the gap in the window Gage heard Arndt challenge Viz, "What are you doing next to my car?"

Viz angled his head upward. "Looking for my keys."

Gage got out of the SUV.

"Do it after I'm gone," Arndt said.

Viz straightened up. Gage came to a stop behind Arndt, who looked back. The flush of exercise and anger faded from Arndt's face.

Arndt turned his body sideways in the narrow space between the cars and spread himself flat against the BMW. His head swiveled back and forth between Gage and Viz. Gage had four inches on him. Viz had even more. Arndt's gaze settled on Viz, a seeming effort to convince them that he hadn't recognized Gage.

"What do you want?" Arndt said, his voice sounding forced, as though trying to use the words not as a question, but as an accusation.

Gage answered. "Let's not play games. You know who I am and what I want: the name of your client and why he wanted me followed."

"You're asking the wrong guy," Arndt said, now looking up at Gage. "My name's not at the top of the letter-head, only in the small print along the side with the rest of the grunts."

"I'm not sure why it's on the letterhead at all," Gage said. "You commit a sin in a past life?"

"It pays the bills."

"No it doesn't. I've seen your credit report."

Arndt folded his arms across his chest. "And I've seen a hotel surveillance video of you and Strubb taken just before Gilbert's murder."

"Is that supposed to worry me?"

Arndt opened his mouth to speak, but then closed it again.

Gage could tell that Arndt had realized that the role the video had been acting in the theater of his mind didn't match reality.

"I also want to know why you were having Hennessy followed," Gage said, "and whether you had anything to do with him going over the cliff."

Arndt's palm shot out toward Gage. "Wait a second. I didn't get involved until just before he . . . he . . ." His arm now hung there without purpose, the meaning having been drained from the gesture by his inadvertent admission. He lowered it, followed by his head, and then clenched his fists by his side. "I knew it would come to this. I knew it—I knew it—I knew it."

Gage pushed past the little-boy rant. It was too early to allow Arndt to see himself as the victim.

"Why did Wycovsky want you to manage the surveillance?" Gage asked.

"It sure as hell wasn't because he thought I was competent," Arndt said, shaking his head. He still hadn't looked up. The slushing of club members' feet as they shuffled from their cars to the entrance was now lost to him. "He just wants everybody's hands as dirty as his."

Gage turned and leaned back against Arndt's Volvo, trying to make Arndt's position seem less claustrophobic.

"I don't know all of the details," Gage said, "but I think your hands may be dirtier even than what you imagine when you're lying in bed at night—and I'm not talking about Gilbert's murder. I know why that happened and it had nothing to do with you."

Arndt looked up at Gage. "Nobody said anything about killing Hennessy. They were just supposed to follow him."

"Who are they?"

"I don't know. They were different than the local people. I took over the Albany end when Wycovsky left for Marseilles."

"What were they trying to find out?"

Arndt shrugged. "I still don't know. But I think they were playing defense, not offense. Trying to find out how much Hennessy knew about something and how much he'd shared with others."

Gage thought of Elaine Hennessy's empty DVD cases. "And I take it that was the reason for the burglary at his house."

Arndt's eyes widened at Gage. "How did you—"

"Putting two and two together," Gage said, "and that addition puts you in the middle of a conspiracy—but I'm not telling you something you don't already know. You realized it when Wycovsky came back from France, but by then you had no way out."

Arndt lowered his head again. The silence that followed was flat and hard. There was no deep meaning to be probed. It had all come to the surface.

Gage looked past Arndt toward Viz, whose frown and set jaw suggested that he'd seen in Arndt what Gage had: one of those men they'd too often found at domestic crime scenes whose sleepwalk through life had ended with the sound of a gunshot and gunpowder residue on their hands.

"I need you to help me with something late tonight," Gage said. "Do it, and I'll make sure you never see the inside of a prison. Don't do it, and you'll never get out."

CHAPTER 58

The gasp of opening elevator doors blew down the silent hallway of Shadden Phillips & Wycovsky and past the closed door to Wycovsky's office.

Gage felt himself tense. He glanced at his watch: 3 A.M. They'd completed their search of the lawyer's computer and his file cabinets and were just seconds from slipping away. He pointed at Arndt and gestured for him to hide behind Wycovsky's desk. Then at Viz and toward the wall to the right of the door. He then switched off his penlight and crouched on the left side.

Shadows of legs in the hallway crossed the gap between the bottom edge of the door and the carpet.

A whispering voice said, "We missed it. It's back there."

Shadows again barred the gap, followed by the scrape and click of the bolt sliding and coming free of the latch plate.

As the door opened, a sliver of light expanded into a beam and then into a flood that was blocked by two man-shaped shadows. A head turned and nodded. The face silhouetted on the carpet appeared jagged and angular.

Gage guessed they were wearing night vision goggles. He had only seconds to surprise them before they spotted him. He waited until the first stepped inside, then sprang between them and punched an elbow into the gut of the trailing man and a fist into the kidney of the leader.

Gage lowered his shoulder into the stomach of the one in the hallway and drove the flailing man into the opposite wall. He then felt a massive weight pound into his side, tumbling him down the hallway. He came to a stop facedown.

"Freeze. Police."

A cocking weapon above his head froze him in place.

Gage heard the words repeated behind him, then glanced over his shoulder and spotted two men in black tactical jumpsuits holding semiautomatic pistols, one pointing down at him, one aimed through the office doorway. The man he'd tackled lay slumped and groaning between them.

"Put the gun down." It was Viz's voice. "Or I'll drop you where you stand."

Gage guessed that Viz had wrested a gun away from his man and was using him as a shield. Gage used the stalemate to push himself up to one knee, and then onto his feet. He raised his hands, and turned around.

"Stay cool until we find out who these guys are," Gage yelled to Viz, and then said to the man in front of him. "Show me a badge and some ID."

The man reached into his pocket, but instead of retrieving a badge case, pulled out a cell phone, pressed one button, then put it to his ear.

"This is Madison," the man said into the phone, then listened for a few seconds and asked, "You Gage?"

Gage nodded.

Madison holstered his gun, looked behind him down the hallway, and said, "Lower your weapons," and then handed his cell phone to Gage.

Gage held it down by his side and asked, "You have a search warrant?"

Madison pointed down at the phone. "Ask him."

"I'm asking you."

"I'm not a lawyer."

"Then I've got my answer."

Gage raised the cell phone and asked, "Who is this?"

A male voice answered, "I'm a friend who'd like you to ease on out of there and let us do our work."

"I'm not interested in playing games. Tell me who you are."

"I'm not authorized to do that."

Gage disconnected and pulled out his own cell phone. He yelled down the hallway, "Viz, these guys are either CIA or something close to it," and watched Madison stiffen.

Madison's phone vibrated. Gage answered with, "You've got five seconds to identify your agency, or I'll make a call on my phone and whoever is on the other side of this thing will know where I am and what I came for."

"Don't." This time it was a female voice. "Stand by. I need to go up the chain of command."

Gage pointed at Madison, then past him toward the lobby. "Collect all your people down there."

Madison didn't move.

"Look, pal," Gage said, "the war is over. It's only a

question of the terms of surrender." He pushed a couple of the phone's buttons, and then said to the woman, "You're on loudspeaker. Tell him."

She spoke again, now issuing an order. "Stand down."

Madison kept his dignity by saying, "No problem," then turned away.

"How far up the chain are you ready to go?" Gage asked her.

"That depends on what you found."

"I found most of the answers I was looking for. And they're probably the same ones you came after."

"Hold on."

The phone line went silent.

Gage watched the agent lying on the floor use the wall to leverage himself onto his feet. Moments after that, another agent limped out of the office, grimacing and holding his side.

The office lights came on and Viz appeared at the door.

"How bad is the damage inside?" Gage asked.

"Things got knocked around, but nothing broken."

Gage pulled out his digital camera, with which he'd taken photos of the office before they disturbed it, and then walked down the hallway and handed it to Viz.

"Put everything back the way it was."

Gage glanced into the office. Arndt was standing behind the desk, his arms wrapped around his chest, biting his lower lip.

"It's okay," Gage said to him. "Things are under control."

The phone came alive with a rush of static.

"Would you be willing to come to Washington?"

Gage looked at his watch. He wanted Arndt present at

whatever meetings took place to reassure him that he'd done the right thing in throwing in with Gage and to give him confidence that he'd be protected when Wycovsky realized what he'd done.

"No," Gage said. "I've got someone to protect. We'll have to do it here."

s there any way the CIA hasn't screwed this up?"
Gage asked John Casher, as they faced each other
in the living room of a midtown hotel suite. Scattered about the room were Arndt, Viz, Madison, and a
CIA deputy director. "A false accusation. Delivering up
Ibrahim to be tortured. Hennessy driven to suicide, or
set up to be murdered."

Gage pointed at Arndt sitting on the couch with his
shoulders slumped, forearms on his knees. "A fifty-
billion-dollar intelligence budget, and it falls on this kid
to do your work for you?"

"I'm not going to argue," Casher said, "but I don't have
evidence in front of me that'll let me believe you."

Gage could feel a lump pressing up against his sole:
the memory card on which he'd saved images of documents and downloads of Wycovsky's files. He had no
reason to think that the CIA would do any better with
that information than it had with everything else—

Except that Casher hadn't been appointed director
until years after Ibrahim's indictment, and the fact that
he came to meet Gage himself might mean—might

mean—that he was trying to find a way to set things right.

"I don't have to show you anything," Gage said. "But I'll tell you what I believe."

"That's a start."

"I think Wycovsky gave the orders to transfer the money from Ibrahim's Manx trust to the Hong Kong law firm and then to the terrorists who bombed the Spectrum facility in Xinjiang."

Casher's gaze drifted toward the deputy director sitting at the dining table. Her eyes fixed on his. Her face didn't change expression.

"But I guess you knew that," Gage said.

Casher shook his head. "We only suspected. That's what we went in tonight to try to find out. But it still doesn't get Ibrahim off the hook."

Gage felt a slow rage begin to build. He pointed at Viz leaning against the wall by the kitchen, then at Arndt, and said, "Let's go."

Arndt rose to his feet. Viz pushed off and started toward the door. Gage turned to follow behind them.

"You're not going anywhere," Casher said, gesturing to Madison to block their way.

Gage spun back and glared at Casher.

"What are you going to do? Bind and gag us and send us off to Saudi Arabia, too?" Gage hardened his voice. "Don't try to play cards you don't have in your hand. If I want out of here, there's nothing you can do to stop me."

Casher opened his mouth to argue, then closed it and looked from face to face, everyone staring back at him, and then said, "You all go into the bedroom."

Everyone moved except for the deputy director.

"You too," he told her. "I'll fill you in later."

As soon as the door closed behind them, Casher said, "I don't know who Wycovsky's client is, so I can't clear Ibrahim. It's as simple as that." Casher pointed at the dining table. "Let's sit down. I'm beat. There's a lot going on."

They sat down across from each other.

Casher folded his forearms on the table and leaned forward.

"We know from UK phone records that the director of the Manx trust made back-to-back calls to Wycovsky and Ibrahim many times in the months before the trust was set up and then again just before the bombing."

"But no calls directly between Ibrahim and Wycovsky."

Casher shook his head. "But we wouldn't expect there to be. It would make it too easy for someone to connect the dots."

"You did anyway," Gage said, "or at least thought you did."

"Then who was Wycovsky's client?" Casher asked.

"I don't know yet," Gage said. "It was coded in their records, or maybe it was an acronym, and"—he tilted his head toward the hallway to the bedroom—"and Arndt doesn't have any idea."

Casher narrowed his eyes at Gage. "How was it coded?"

Gage shrugged. "All it said was G12."

Casher drew back and shook his head. "It's not coded. It's been on our radar for the last few years. It's the People's Foreign Investment Fund. They're known to Chinese insiders as the Group of Twelve."

Gage pushed himself to his feet, then slammed his fist into his palm. "Son of a—"

"What?" Casher asked, squinting up at Gage.

"Ibrahim was working for the Chinese."

Casher blinked as though stunned by a camera flash. "How do you get from—"

"And when Hennessy began to suspect it and went hunting for Ibrahim, they killed the guy."

Gage hesitated. He closed his eyes and locked his hands on top of his head. That couldn't be right. If Ibrahim was dead, then there'd be no reason for Wycovsky to put Gilbert and Strubb and Hicks on his tail—

"Unless the Chinese are looking for Ibrahim, too," Gage said aloud. "And that means they believe he's still alive."

"Have you gone nuts?" Casher asked.

Gage sat down and reached for the deputy director's legal pad. Casher's hand snaked out and grabbed Gage's wrist, thinking that Gage was trying to read her notes. Gage yanked it free.

"Don't be an idiot," Gage said. "I just need a blank sheet of paper." He flipped to the middle and tore out a piece and drew part of the flowchart that Alex Z recovered from Hennessy's memory card.

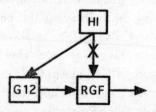

"We found this in Hennessy's records," Gage said, then pointed at the HI and G12 boxes. "I think he figured out that Ibrahim was working for the Chinese, not Relative Growth."

"Or both," Casher said.

Gage shook his head. "I don't think so." He looked over at Casher. "Where'd you send Ibrahim after you deported him?"

Casher flushed. "I didn't send him anywhere. It was before my time." He shrugged. "Anyway, you know the answer."

"And you—collectively—created an economic terrorist."

"We don't know that."

"You suspect it strongly enough to commit a burglary on U.S. soil."

Casher shrugged. "But what could the Chinese possibly need Ibrahim for?"

Gage was now beginning to understand Abrams's preoccupation with Ibrahim, or at least part of it. And the Chinese were focused on the same thing: If the old theories had proved themselves false, then maybe Ibrahim's could prove themselves right—with huge Chinese foreign currency reserves behind them.

"Capitalism needed a new god," Gage said, "a new master of the universe."

"And they chose Ibrahim?"

Gage shook his head again. "You *gave* them Ibrahim."

CHAPTER 60

There's a chance Ibrahim is still alive and I don't want to get him killed," Gage told Milton Abrams after recounting the previous night's events. "But we need to find him and figure out what the Chinese are up to."

"And you're afraid you'll be bird-dogging him for the Chinese who may be worried he'll spill the beans, whatever they may be."

Gage picked up his cup from the kitchen table and took a sip.

"Exactly."

Gage's cell phone rang. He'd left it on the kitchen counter the previous night so those who were tracking him would think that he'd remained in Abrams's apartment. He didn't recognize the number, but it had a Boston area code. He could think of only two people who could be calling: Goldie Goldstein or Abdul Rahmani. He didn't answer it, but watched to see if the caller left a message. He or she didn't. He retrieved his encrypted phone and called Alex Z in San Francisco.

"Sorry to wake you up," Gage told him when he answered. "I need you to call a number and see who it is and what they want. I don't want people listening in on me."

Alex Z yawned. "No problem, boss."

Gage gave him the number and disconnected.

Alex Z called back a minute later.

"He wouldn't ID himself," Alex Z said. "But he was pissed and he said that he'd heard from someone you two called Fred."

Gage's hand tightened around the phone. Ibrahim was alive. "What did he say?"

"That Fred is also pissed, homicidal, something about his wife having to go into hiding. The guy said you'll know where to find him at 1 P.M. today."

As Gage disconnected, Abrams's cell phone rang. Moments after he answered it, his eyes widened, and he said, "I'm on my way," and then flipped it closed and rose from his chair.

"I've got to get down to Washington," Abrams said. "Rumors are flying about the president's health, and the markets have no confidence in Wallace. They want me and the treasury secretary standing in front of the cameras when the New York Stock Exchange opens."

Gage thought of the surveillance outside Abrams's apartment house and of his need to dodge them on the way out.

"How are you getting there?" Gage asked.

"A limo from here in five minutes, then a helicopter from a pad downtown."

Gage pointed his thumb upward. "Can I hitch a ride partway?"

"Why not? I suspect that the taxpayers are going to owe you a lot more than a helicopter ride."

Gage called Viz, who'd taken Arndt home and then had checked the layout of the surveillance in Central Park.

"It's practically a convention out here," Viz said. "It's hard to tell who's who. Hicks is in his usual spot along with two others spread out on either side. And there are two vans stationed at either end of the block that are using as much bandwidth as T–1 lines, but I have no way of knowing whether they're aware of each other."

"I need you to come back inside and turn all of the bugs back on as soon as Abrams and I leave."

Gage disconnected, then called out to Abrams, who was in his bedroom changing into his suit, "You have a large briefcase I can use? I need to take a lot with me, but I don't want to be seen with my Rollaboard and clue them in that I'm on the move."

"In my study. There's an old-style leather catalogue case in the closet."

Gage retrieved his nonencrypted cell phone to make a call so that those intercepting him would believe that they knew where he was going and called Alex Z.

"Abrams and I are on our way down to Washington," Gage said. "By helicopter. We'll stop along the way to pick up one of his underlings."

Abrams came back into the living room, tying his tie, as Gage turned the phone off again.

"Should you be telling our plans to the other side?" Abrams asked.

"When they hear on the news that you've been called to Washington, they'll assume the rest is true, too. Except I'll be getting off where they think someone is getting on."

Abrams smiled. "I like my job better than yours. It's a lot simpler."

Gage collected Abrams's briefcase, stuffed it with his own attaché case, along with a change of clothes, and then pointed toward the door.

Abrams's limo took them first to the helipad, then to Newark Airport where Gage got off. To disguise his trail, Gage rented a car with the unused Federal Reserve card that Abrams had given him the previous week, and then headed north toward Boston. Three and a half hours later, he pulled up in front of the Turkish halal café down the block from Ijara Automobiles.

The owner, sitting by the cash register, lowered his paper and cast dead eyes at Gage as he entered.

Abdul Rahmani, the only customer in the café, neither looked up nor rose from his seat.

Gage pulled up a chair across from him.

"You're as much of a bungler as Hennessy," Rahmani said, shaking his head. "I should've known."

"Ibrahim could've picked up his phone at any time since I first came knocking on your door."

"Why should he have? There've been dozens of people looking for him over the years. Investigators. Intelligence agencies. Business reporters. Professors. Graduate students. Hedge fund managers—why should he bless you of all people with a call?"

"Because I know the truth about what happened to him."

"That only means that you know what he knows. Bravo."

"Thinks he knows—and he's wrong. Maybe dead wrong."

Rahmani spread his hands. "So? Let's hear it."

"I'll tell it only to him, and only in person. I'll also explain to him why some of the people he thought were his friends are now on the hunt for him."

"It doesn't make a difference, they won't find him. No one will ever find him, unless he wants to be found. I don't even know where he is."

Gage inspected Rahmani's face, trying to discern a connection between his aggression and door-slamming protection of Ibrahim and the fact of his calling to get Gage to come to Boston. He then surveyed the café, wondering whether it was bugged.

"How long would it take for you to get in contact with him?" Gage asked.

Rahmani shrugged.

Gage walked over to the counter and grabbed a take-out menu and a matchbook and brought them back to the table. He drew out the flowchart that he'd drawn for Casher, showing Ibrahim's connection to the Group of Twelve. He then spun it around so Rahmani could see it.

"Can you describe this to him?" Gage asked.

Rahmani reached for it. Gage pulled it away. Rahmani's face reddened.

"It's not complicated," Gage said. "Just memorize it."

Gage let Rahmani stare at it a little longer, and tore it up. He then removed Rahmani's saucer from under his coffee cup, piled up the pieces, and set them on fire.

Gage held his open hands over the flame and then rubbed them together.

"Let's see whether this generates a little heat where Ibrahim is, too," Gage said. "And then maybe a little light."

CHAPTER 61

Vice President Cooper Wallace sat alone in his office in the Executive Office Building after the security briefing. He flicked on the television and then changed the channel from CNN to CNBC. He wasn't interested in the political pundits' speculations, but in the numbers that reflected the financial mind of the country. The header rotated from the prices of gold, silver, and oil to the Dow and NASDAQ. They'd both dropped four percent on the news of the transition, then gained three back. The same in London and Berlin.

At first, he felt relief. The markets had time to absorb the news about the president's health, to weigh it, to allocate their resources, and decided that the world wasn't coming to an end. Maybe those economics textbooks were right after all. It really was a self-adjusting mechanism, a collective mind that takes in data and prices itself accordingly.

But then a shudder of self-doubt waved through him.

Maybe it wasn't confidence in him that the market was showing, but a belief that the president would soon resume his place as the captain of the ship of state and that Wallace's assignment was merely to hold the rudder steady in the meantime.

He, too, had watched the surgeons' press conference. He, too, had felt no doubt that the surgery would be routine and successful. He, too, saw the confidence in the wire-rimmed Harvard Medical School faces of the white coats. He, too—

But then his mind twisted back down the tunnel of the past, to the president calling him into his study, warning him to think and to listen.

You want to be president in two years, but something could happen to me, and you'd be sitting in this chair tomorrow.

Now the white coats seemed like costumes and the wire rims like props and their words spoken from a script written by the president.

Tomorrow had arrived.

Chief of Staff Paul Nichols knocked on his door, then entered.

"This is the list," Nichols said, handing Wallace a sheet bearing five names. He then pointed his thumb over his shoulder. "Russian and Chinese interpreters are standing by. The French, German, and Japanese presidents will speak to you in English. The British prime minister will go first."

Wallace skimmed down the page. He didn't mind the others, but was disgusted by the thought of having to call the Chinese president to reassure him that the pull on the American oars would remain steady. He could see the man's soft, round face, beaming like the owner of a company store—

No, that wasn't it. It was the self-satisfied smirk of a colonial master. They owned the debt and therefore had the U.S. by the pocketbook.

Americans could still feed themselves, but they had to cook on Chinese stoves and in Chinese pots and pans and pay tribute in the form of interest on a trillion dollars of treasury bonds. *If Casher is right*, Wallace thought, *they have us not only by our hearts, minds, and consumer cravings, but by the balls.*

Wallace reached for the remote to turn off the television. He hesitated as an inset box appeared showing Manton Roberts standing before a microphone. The business reporter's voice was replaced by Roberts announcing that National Pledge Day would include prayers for the president's recovery.

"Smart move," Nichols said to Wallace. "He never misses a trick. He'll quadruple the participation. Even the crippled will stand to say the pledge and even the deaf will hear the prayer."

Wallace didn't rise to the sarcasm. He might not believe in the event, but he believed in the power of prayer.

"Is Casher still out there?" Wallace asked, punching the mute button.

Nichols nodded, then walked back out to the reception area. Casher entered a moment later carrying his briefcase.

"Was it your decision or the president's not to mention in the Cabinet meeting that the Chinese are putting together criminal cases against us?"

"The president's. He didn't want to chance a leak."

Wallace wanted to say, *You mean he doesn't trust his own people?* but he left the thought unspoken for fear of appearing to have forgotten the fundamental lesson of politics: The political animal is first of all an animal, and while some might doubt the theory of evolution, everyone accepted the truth that the first law of nature was survival. And loyalty, like betrayal, was just a weapon.

"But he did ask me to meet with the attorney general," Casher said, "and in a fill-in-the-blank-later fashion outline the bribery evidence against the corporate officers the Chinese appear to be targeting."

"You mean to take to a grand jury?"

"Only in case you, or the president, decide to get ahead of the Chinese and charge them with violations of the Foreign Corrupt Practices Act. The U.S. Attorney can simply code all of the targets' names, the companies' names, and the offshore accounts that he presents in evidence. Once the grand jurors accept that crimes have been committed, it will take all of ten minutes to fill in the blanks and issue an indictment."

Wallace didn't like the path laid out before him. He felt like the Chinese were leading the U.S. into a trap.

"I don't like the idea," Wallace finally said. "The Chinese set the terms for doing business over there. If their officials weren't corrupt, we wouldn't be paying bribes. Isn't that what the Mexicans tell us: Stop using drugs and we'll stop shipping them?"

"You're right, but it may be out of our hands."

Casher laid his briefcase on the desk, then opened it and handed Wallace a draft indictment.

"This is it," Casher said, "with all of the blanks filled in."

Wallace flipped through the twenty pages. "It seems short, given how massive the scheme was."

"The indictment doesn't have to outline our entire theory of the case and every act in the conspiracy," Casher said, "only enough to prove a single count for each defendant. We picked the most provable."

"You've also named some French and German defendants."

"We don't want to take the whole blame."

"But what's our jurisdiction? They're not U.S. citizens."

"But they paid some of the bribes in U.S. dollars. Our currency, our jurisdiction. That's good enough for the Supreme Court."

Casher took it back and opened to the overt acts alleged against RAID, then turned it toward Wallace.

"You'll see that we've tracked a single payment from a RAID account in Singapore to a Hong Kong law firm, and then to the offshore account of a coconspirator we've identified only as 'Chinese Official One.'"

Wallace read down the page. "Who is it?"

"The vice mayor of Chengdu, Zhao Wo-li."

"Why didn't you name him?"

"It would make things too messy. He's escaped the PLA encirclement of the city. We don't want the story to become one about a massive manhunt—"

"Unless we later want to shift the blame onto the Chinese."

Casher nodded. "We can also lessen the damage to us by orchestrating the announcement of the indictment and the replacement of the officers so they happen simultaneously."

"I still don't like it," Wallace said. "I don't like us taking the blame for other countries' problems." Wallace flipped the indictment closed. "But if it happens, let it not be during the few days of my watch."

e're here," Gage said to Rahmani, sitting in the driver's seat of his car. They were parked under an overhanging oak tree along the edge of Chestnut Hill Reservoir north of Brookline. "Now what?"

The angled parking places on either side of them were empty, save for a pickup truck idling seven spaces away, its occupant talking on his phone and turning pages in what looked to Gage to be a map book.

"We wait." Rahmani waved his finger back and forth as though to mark the extremes of the area. "My friends are watching to make sure you weren't followed."

Gage withdrew his cell phone. "How do you know someone isn't tracking me through this?"

Rahmani smiled. "I asked around. You wouldn't let that happen."

"Then why the bungler crack when I walked into the café?"

"That was Hani's word," Rahmani said. "It didn't sound quite right when I repeated it."

Two Indian men in their mid-sixties came into view walking along the wet concrete path between the car and windswept water. They squinted for a long moment at the windshield as they passed, but didn't interrupt their conversation.

Rahmani pointed at their backs.

"Indians are much healthier than us Muslims. They walk and walk. We sit and sit." He patted his stomach mounding up under his seat belt. "Fat as a pig without the benefit of pork."

The buzz of his cell phone drew Rahmani's eyes away from the men. He answered in Arabic, listened, and then hung up and said, "Let's go."

Rahmani started the engine, backed up, and merged onto Chestnut Hill Road. Ten minutes later, they looped through the circular driveway of the redbrick Newton City Hall, then headed north up a tree-lined street and pulled into the driveway of a gambrel-roofed Dutch Colonial.

Gage recognized the address. It was Rahmani's house. The countersurveillance effort now seemed amateurish and idiotic: Anyone who'd been watching Rahmani and had lost him would've sent people to his home and office to wait for him to show up.

"I have a communications system in the basement," Rahmani said as they walked inside. "Let's see if we can get Hani to respond."

Rahmani led Gage into the kitchen and opened the door to the basement. He reached around the doorjamb, flipped the light switch, and said, "You first."

Gage shook his head.

"It's not like I'm planning to take you prisoner," Rahmani said. "You're not so interesting to me."

Gage pointed at the descending wooden stairs.

Rahmani shrugged, took a couple of steps, ducked under the single lightbulb hanging from the ceiling, and continued down. Gage's shadow caught up to him at the bottom where Rahmani was waiting. It revealed light emerging from under another door. Rahmani opened it, but didn't invite Gage to walk in first.

Gage stepped in behind him.

Hani Ibrahim looked over from a wheelchair parked in front of a desk at the far end of the room.

Anger mushroomed within Gage's feeling of surprise at the unexpected discovery, and at the childish smirk with which Ibrahim greeted Gage.

"Aren't you supposed to yell tag?" Ibrahim said.

"I didn't think it was a game."

"Of course it is. Money is nothing but a game." Ibrahim pointed toward a chair at the side of his desk. "Have a seat."

Gage shook his head. He wanted to stay positioned between Rahmani and the door.

"You'll sit," Rahmani said, his tone sounding less like an order and more like a declaration of a future state of affairs.

Gage looked over. Rahmani was pointing a small revolver at his chest.

"Let me have your cell phone," Rahmani said. Gage handed it to him, then Rahmani gestured with the gun barrel toward the chair.

"Suddenly you're looking a whole lot less like a victim," Gage said to Ibrahim as he walked the ten feet and sat down.

Gage found himself facing a hospital bed across the room, canopied by an electric-powered patient lift. At its foot stood a small chest of drawers. A door opposite the entrance led to a bathroom.

"I was once a victim," Ibrahim said, "but now I'm the judge and the executioner." He looked over at Rahmani and then cocked his head toward the door. Rahmani stepped through it and locked it from the other side. "But not of people."

Gage surveyed the blank walls and concrete floor. It was as bare and hollow as a monk's cell.

"You a prisoner in here, too?" Gage asked, looking over at Ibrahim.

"I've been deprived of my liberty, as you can see, but that has little to do with my living conditions."

"And what I've been trying to find out is why," Gage said.

Ibrahim flushed. "Don't pretend to be naïve." He pointed at the computer monitor centered on his desk. "I've had quite a bit of time to research you. You're not a naïve man."

Ibrahim reached over, touched his mouse, and then pressed the page-down key. The monitor flashed with a series of news articles about Gage, many of them the same ones that Hennessy's daughter had printed out for her mother. Following those were excerpts of transcripts of old court testimony. The last image on the screen was a twenty-year-old photograph of Orlando Ferrada, the imprisoned and tortured Chilean economist that Gage had rescued on behalf of Milton Abrams.

"I'm certain that you know who put me in this condition," Ibrahim said, "and I'm certain that you know why."

Gage shook his head. "I don't know why. That's one of the things I've been trying to find out."

"It's simple. Hennessy framed me to make himself the

hero of post–9/11 America and to advance his career."

"For me," Gage said, "that's still a question, not an answer I'm ready to accept. What makes you think he's the one that framed you?"

Ibrahim didn't answer at once. Gage watched him rock his head side to side, as though deciding whether it was worth the effort. He straightened in his wheelchair and adopted what seemed to Gage to be an air of professorial distance.

"The interesting thing about a frame," Ibrahim finally said, drawing a square with his forefingers in front of Gage's face, "is that there's nothing within the four corners. It's like a skeleton without flesh."

Ibrahim lowered his hands. "Did you read my indictment?"

"What there was of it."

"See. A frame. A skeleton without flesh. Overt Act One: Ibrahim conspired with Unindicted Coconspirator A to establish a Manx trust. Overt Act Two: Ibrahim conspired with Unindicted Coconspirator B to wire transfer funds from the Manx trust to the bank account controlled by a Hong Kong law firm. Overt Act Three: Ibrahim conspired with Unindicted Coconspirator C to wire funds from the account controlled by the Hong Kong law firm to a U.S. State Department–listed foreign terrorist organization."

Gage shrugged. "I'm sure you've done the research and know as well as I do that indictments don't—"

"Inform someone what they're being charged with?"

"—detail every fact. That's not their function," Gage said, annoyed both by Ibrahim's childish evasion and by his pedantic sneer.

"Don't play dumb," Gage said. "They told you exactly

what you were charged with." He looked hard at Ibrahim. "How long did it take you to figure out who the unindicted coconspirators were?"

Ibrahim tapped the side of his head. "I knew as soon as I looked at the indictment."

"And the Hong Kong law firm?"

"The same."

"And the terrorist organization?"

Ibrahim waved Gage off. "This is silly. I'm not an idiot."

"Didn't it cross your mind to wonder why you were even aware of the names of the Hong Kong law firm and the terrorist organization?"

Ibrahim didn't respond.

"And to wonder about who told them to you? And about why they told you? And about what they did to connect you to them?"

Ibrahim's brows furrowed and his eyes darted around the room, but he didn't answer.

Gage pushed on. "It's not the guy who finds the evidence who does the framing, it's the guy who plants it."

Ibrahim's eyes flickered upward. It seemed an unconscious gesture on Ibrahim's part, but Gage got a piece of the answer he was looking for.

Ibrahim clenched his jaw and shook his head.

"It was Hennessy." Ibrahim jabbed his finger at Gage as though he was Hennessy's stand-in or proxy. "It was Hennessy who was out to get me. And when the criminal case collapsed under the weight of his idiocy, he put me on a chartered flight to London." Ibrahim's voice rose. His finger now thumping the desktop. "And then onto a military flight to Saudi Arabia so his helpers could rip off my flesh in order to put some meat on the skeleton."

Gage reached into his jacket pocket and pulled out the photo he had discovered inside Hennessy's notebook and slid it on the desktop toward Ibrahim.

Ibrahim's eyes narrowed as he focused on it, then he said, "It's a fake."

"Not all of it," Gage said. "And I think Hennessy understood which part was real."

Ibrahim nodded as he stared at the photo.

"I don't remember this being taken," Ibrahim said. "I'd probably passed out. But I know where and approximately when they took it." He rubbed his finger over the area of the photo showing where the rope bound his ankles. "You can see they still needed to restrain my feet, so my spine hadn't been broken yet."

Gage winced and for a moment regretted the aggression he'd displayed.

"I don't understand how one human being could do that to another," Gage said, shaking his head and looking down at the picture. He looked up again. "What were they trying to do to you when that happened?"

Ibrahim shrugged. "It's not important. Let's just say that torture isn't an exact science and they ended up accomplishing more than they intended."

"Which was what?"

Ibrahim's face flushed again. "I told you. A confession. But once they'd broken me in two, I was no good to them. Testimony from a man whose body they destroyed wouldn't be convincing." He pounded the arm of the wheelchair. "A witness they have to roll into court is useless."

Gage pointed at the newspaper lying next to Ibrahim's body in the photograph.

"Who do you think superimposed this?" Gage asked.

"Where'd you get this photo?"

"It was among Hennessy's things. Someone forged it and gave to him in the hours before he died."

Ibrahim shrugged. "How should I know?"

"Maybe you should think about it."

Gage watched Ibrahim's eyes make their darting motions again.

"And about who could've gotten hold of the original."

Ibrahim's eyes fixed on the blank far wall above his bed, then went vacant.

"And about why those people wanted to convince not only Hennessy that you were dead, but those who were tracking him or who later took up his search."

Ibrahim blinked and looked back at Gage.

"If Hennessy wasn't behind what was done to me," Ibrahim said, "what did he have to feel guilty about?"

Gage shook his head. "Your question contains its own answer. He figured out that he'd been used to frame you. That's why he started searching. But he discovered something along the way, something he was desperate to tell Abrams about."

Ibrahim swallowed. Gage sensed that he was trying to control his tone, but his voice rose anyway as he asked, "And did he?"

"Sort of."

Gage reached for a piece of paper and drew out his version of Hennessy's flowchart, showing the line from the HI box to the G12 box.

Ibrahim nodded. "Rahmani told me about it."

"HI is you. G12 is the Group of Twelve, the People's Foreign Investment Fund. RGF is the Relative Growth Funds." Gage looked up again. "Hennessy figured out that you were working for the Chinese."

Ibrahim smirked. "So what. Why shouldn't I have worked for them?"

Gage pointed at the wheelchair. "Because they're responsible for you being stuck in that thing and they've been on the hunt to finish you off before you found out the truth—or at least before you could act on it."

Ibrahim's eyes widened.

Gage pointed upward and said, "My guess is that Rahmani sold you out nine years ago and he's about to do it for a second time."

Ibrahim's eyes darted. Gage watched his fingers rubbing against each other and his brows furrowing as if a fragment of an idea in his mind linked with what Gage was claiming.

"Even if what you're saying is true—if—it couldn't have been Rahmani. He's not the one who put me in contact with that lawyer in New York. Wycovsky."

"Who did?"

"A Turkish guy in our discussion group. Ilkay. A halal café owner. His brother is an accountant who knew the people on the Isle of Man—" Ibrahim shut his eyes and shook his head. "No. Stop. You're just trying to confuse me."

Gage thumped his fist on the desktop. "Who made the connection between you and the Uyghur terrorists who bombed Spectrum?"

Ibrahim kept shaking his head. "There was no connection. My wife asked . . ." Ibrahim opened his eyes and glared at Gage. "Now you're saying my wife set me up?"

"What did your wife ask you to do?"

"Talk to other Muslim professors about writing an open letter for a Xinjiang Web site to protest the bombings." Ibrahim furrowed his brows and bit his lip for a moment. "I did some research about the Uyghur Jihad on the Internet and about how the Chinese government was moving in millions of Han Chinese in order to make the Uyghurs a minority in their own land. The FBI found it."

"And who planted the idea in your wife's mind that you should do it?"

Ibrahim's hands flew up as if trying to block the implications of Gage's question, his rising cuffs exposing red scars etched into his skin by the wire that had been used to bind his wrists. He then interlaced his fingers on top of his head and rocked back and forth in his chair like an autistic child, trying to hold on to his sense of reality.

Gage watched his eyes fluttering, his mind disassociating, and his hands gripping the wheelchair arms as though he was anchoring his body against a cyclone that was ripping away the landmarks that defined his world—

And in Ibrahim's terror, Gage saw that this wasn't the first time it had happened.

But then Ibrahim stopped rocking and he whispered to himself, "How could I have missed it? How could I have missed it?"

He looked at Gage and said, "It's Ilkay. It has to be."

Ibrahim lowered his arms and tapped the flowchart.

"If I'd flowcharted the last ten years," Ibrahim said, "all of the arrows would've pointed at Ilkay. He was even the one who arranged for me to be released to the Turkish embassy in Riyadh. He helped get me on a flight to Istanbul and then to Beijing."

"Does he know you're here?"

Ibrahim shook his head. "I had a breakdown while I was working for the G12. They put me into an institution, and when my head cleared I got permission to travel to Canada. I needed to think things through. After I decided not to go back, Rahmani met me there and smuggled me across the border. I'd done what I wanted to do to get even for what America had done to me and just wanted to be left alone."

"Get even how?"

Ibrahim didn't answer. He just stared at the flowchart. Finally, he said, "It doesn't make a difference. Even if the Chinese framed me, it was the Americans who had me tortured."

"All Americans?"

"Have any of them been punished for what was done to me?" Ibrahim's voice rose, almost to a scream. "Anyone at all?"

Gage paused before he answered. The answer was obvious, but maybe not to a man tortured into hating everything American.

"Yes," Gage said. "Three weeks ago in Marseilles."

CHAPTER 63

anton Roberts is calling." Cooper Wallace's secretary spoke over the intercom. "He wants to know whether there's anything you'd like him to do."

Wallace knew that what he wanted Roberts to do was to cancel National Pledge Day. He'd woken up twice the night before: the first time in a hot sweat, his mind pounding out, *Mine eyes have seen the glory of the coming of the Lord,* and the second time in a cold sweat, the words of "For What it's Worth" coming at him again. He knew that something was happening, and that what it was wasn't at all clear.

"I'll talk to him."

I have read a fiery gospel writ in burnished rows of steel.

Wallace heard the click of the connecting line, then said, "Thanks for calling, Manton."

"Is there anything—"

"I wish that you'd consider postponing National Pledge Day," Wallace said. "There's uneasiness in the country and I wouldn't want to exacerbate it."

"I think everyone pausing together will have the opposite effect," Roberts said. "It will bring us together."

Wallace felt Roberts's heavy, evangelical tone seeping into him.

"It will be like a moment of silence at a football game," Roberts said, "like for fallen soldiers or for police officers."

"At least keep it short," Wallace said, "and try to mute the apocalyptic tone that seems to have dominated your recent Sunday services and rallies."

"I don't think it's something that I'm imposing. It feels to me like a welling up of the Holy Spirit."

Wallace winced. The least attractive aspect of Roberts's personality was his view of himself not as a self-motivated actor in the world, but as a vehicle of a higher power.

Roberts continued before Wallace had a chance to respond. "Maybe it's just another way of expressing what you call uneasiness."

"You could be right." Wallace felt a sort of relief as he said the words. He did believe in a higher power, and not an impotent one. One that intervened in the world, not observed it like it was a cosmic experiment. But still—

"Would you consider coming to the White House and leading it from here?" Wallace asked, wondering whether Roberts would rather have the long-term prestige of the place than the immediate thrill of standing before a filled stadium.

"I'd be honored," Roberts said. "Maybe you could lead the pledge and I'll say the prayer for President McCormack."

"We'll work that out between now and then."

Wallace's intercom beeped. "I have a meeting that's about to start," he said to Roberts. "I'll talk to you soon."

Wallace punched the flashing button and said, "I'll come out." He then walked from his office and into the reception area. Former president Randall Harris rose from the couch. They shook hands.

"Thanks for seeing me," Harris said.

Wallace led him back inside and shut the door.

"I expected you'd be dropping by," Wallace said, directing Harris to one of two wing chairs, then sitting down in the one next to it. "Or someone like you. The president has always had an indirect way of communicating with me."

In Harris's stiffening face Wallace saw that Harris knew that was not entirely true, that Harris knew about the private meeting in which President McCormack himself had warned him about Manton Roberts.

Wallace ignored it and asked, "What did he want you to pass on?"

"That you should be prepared to finish out his presidency."

Wallace drew back. "That's not what—"

"He doesn't think he'll make it."

"Of course he's worried," Wallace said, "but I—"

"It's not that. He's had his doctors minimize the seriousness in order to give you breathing space, to reduce the pressure on you by making the public see you as a caretaker for as long as possible."

Harris leaned forward in his chair. "He realizes that he made a mistake in how he's treated you over the last few years. Isolating you. I think, and this is just my opinion, that increasingly powerful vice presidents over the years have created an unnecessary imbalance. And in righting it, he's afraid he overcompensated."

Wallace used a nod of understanding for his response. It wasn't an I-told-you-so moment.

"He now realizes that you'll need time to get your own team together," Harris said. "Usually new presidents have months for a transition, not days."

"Is he asking you to help me?" Wallace asked.

Harris shook his head. "I think part of the reason he picked me to meet with you is because he knows I'm in no position to help, or interfere for that matter."

"Because of Relative Growth?"

Harris nodded. "It's a mess. I made a serious mistake in getting involved with those people. And as soon as this flurry dies down, I'm getting out."

brahim had remained silent all through Gage's recounting of how he'd spent the days after he'd been called to New York by Milton Abrams.

"Abrams is driven by questions not only about Hennessy," Gage said, "but about Relative Growth Funds. He thinks it's a fraud and that they're using your academic work as a kind of camouflage."

Gage expected a protest. Instead, Ibrahim nodded.

"He's right. It was all nonsense. I was doing what everyone else in academia and Wall Street was doing back then, descending into the occult. There's no objective reality that matches phrases like 'two-step binomial trees,' any more than you can take a stroll down the block into the seventh dimension to buy a pack of cigarettes."

"Then what did Minsky and Relative Growth want from you?"

Gage guessed the answer before he'd finished the question, and suspected that Abrams would've guessed it, too.

"Magic," Ibrahim said. "You have all of those quantitative analysts on Wall Street and in hedge funds who pray to a mathematical god that speaks in equations. They needed one of their own. More even than money, they needed the magic and the mystery and the miracle. Minsky isn't an economist. He's barely a mathematician. But he's a master psychologist. Untrained, but innate. Like a professional gambler or a mega-church evangelical minister. Newton said that he could 'calculate the motions of heavenly bodies, but not the madness of people.' Minsky can do both, but only some of the time."

"Which means you set him up."

"Of course. And very personally. It's his own fault that he began to believe in his own magic. He deserves what's coming to him."

"And what's that?"

"Humiliation."

Gage shook his head. "Hennessy wasn't worried about Minsky's possible humiliation. It was something else."

Ibrahim pointed at Gage's flowchart. "It's right there."

"You've got better vision than I do."

"Are there more boxes than you've shown me?"

Gage drew the rest from memory.

Ibrahim reached over and tore it up.

"Hennessy was close, but didn't get it quite right." Ibrahim then drew a new one.

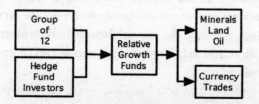

Gage looked it over and said, "I take it that the arrowed lines are investors' money going into Relative Growth?"

Ibrahim shook his head. "Not only money. The G12 put in something else. And that something else is the foundation for almost everything Relative Growth did."

"China only has one other asset: U.S. treasury bonds."

"Bingo. We have a winner. And they dumped every single one into Relative Growth."

Gage inspected Ibrahim's face, looking for a sign that the claim was hyperbole or exaggeration. There was no way China could've unloaded a trillion dollars' worth of U.S. debt without anyone in the financial community realizing it.

"When you were in Marseilles," Ibrahim asked, "did you notice the China-NexCo Towers?"

Gage nodded. The twin structures, slick glass and matte gray, had just risen fifty stories tall next to the container port. Like the Great Wall, they were large enough to be visible from space.

"The construction financing was provided by Relative Growth Funds," Ibrahim said.

"It was in the news," Gage said. "No one was hiding it. The money came from investors in the hedge fund."

Ibrahim leaned toward Gage. "But what secures Relative Growth's loan to NexCo for the construction?"

"What always secures loans, the land and the building. If NexCo defaults, Relative Growth forecloses and takes the property. No different than a home mortgage."

Ibrahim shook his head, then grinned with owner's pride and said, "The loans are secured by U.S. treasury bonds."

Ibrahim paused to let Gage repeat the phrase in his

mind. Only on the second time through did the reality of it hit him: The loan wasn't secured by the hard asset, but by soft paper, by no more than a promissory note.

"And that's not the only one," Ibrahim said. "It's the same thing with the tens of millions of acres they've bought in Africa for bio-fuel production to free them selves from their dependence on Middle East and Russian oil. Same for mines and platinum futures and currency speculation. If NexCo or any other Group of Twelve investment defaults on a loan, the Group of Twelve simply surrenders the treasury bonds to Relative Growth."

Gage felt the vertigo of free-falling off a cliff. "And when the financial community discovers that China has dumped all of its bonds—"

"The bond value plummets and Relative Growth is left having to make good on the loans, but they won't have the cash to do it. Their investors will lose trillions of dollars and the banks that Relative Growth borrowed money from will lose trillions more. The entire U.S. economy will collapse and take Western Europe with it."

The assumption that China needed a strong U.S. economy and needed to support the dollar and the prices of treasury bonds had disintegrated.

Even worse. Gage remembered once listening to Warren Buffett on the radio as he was driving to an appointment in San Francisco. Buffett saying that it was impossible for the Chinese to dump their bonds because they'd just have to exchange them for dollars and if they didn't, the bond prices would collapse faster than they could sell them since there would be a rush to sell by all of the world's bondholders.

If Ibrahim was right, Buffett was wrong. Fatally wrong.

Buffeta-buffeta-buffeta. The secret had been in the ramblings of Hennessy's deteriorating mind. It wasn't the sound of a motorcycle, but the sound of wrenching chaos.

"It doesn't make sense," Gage said. "Why would they do something like that? The U.S. is their biggest customer."

"For how long? The Chinese government came to the conclusion that the U.S. economy would eventually collapse under the weight of its debt—not just the mortgage-driven debt and the government debt, but the money Americans spent on junk. iPods, plasma TVs, and SUVs."

"That's a long way—"

"No it isn't. Within ten years, the people of the U.S. will be spending ninety percent of their GNP on two things: debt servicing and food."

"So they're grabbing everything they can now and are turning the U.S. into a colony," Gage said.

"Don't be an idiot," Ibrahim said. "It's already a colony. Eighty percent of the goods in American stores comes from China now. And they'll still come from there because the U.S. won't have the money to rebuild its industries."

"They're insane," Gage said.

Ibrahim looked away. Gage saw a flutter of uncertainty in his eyes, as if he himself was drowning in the meaning of the events. He then looked back at Gage, and said, "The Chinese have a concept, *tian ming*—"

"The mandate of heaven."

Ibrahim nodded. "They watched the growth of religious and political millennial movements in the U.S. The fantastical self-deceptions and delusions of economists and hedge fund managers, the contradiction between building up companies and then cutting them up to sell off the pieces for a short-term profit—and realized that when the going got tough, Americans would turn on each other. American history may be invisible to Americans, but it's not to the Chinese. They saw that if a civil war happened once, it can happen again. They remember the genocidal violence committed against the native people, and believe that it can be—will be—turned on immigrants and homosexuals and Jews and Muslims."

Ibrahim's eyes went blank for a moment, then he blinked.

"I used to watch CNN with my Chinese colleagues. They were fascinated by Manton Roberts and his movement and by people like him, and amazed that Americans couldn't see him for the revolutionary that he is. To Chinese ears, he's been saying for a decade that the U.S. was founded as a Christian nation, as the City on the Hill, but that Christ's mandate has been withdrawn. In his mind, that's all he needs to justify a revolution."

"I'm less interested in their theories of politics," Gage said, annoyed that Ibrahim was drifting into a political justification for his participation in the conspiracy, "than in how the Chinese government pulled off this scam."

"Easy. It discounted the value of the bonds and put them into the hands of the Group of Twelve. All of them were educated in U.S. business schools and each of them was a bearer of the amorality taught there. They then cut a deal with Relative Growth Funds, with Minsky himself."

Gage could see the dominoes lined up and realized

that there was no way to stop the first one from falling, even if it could be located and exposed.

"I know what you're thinking," Ibrahim said. "But if you expose it, it will create a panic that'll trigger it."

Gage nodded. "Relative Growth is resting on nothing but air."

"Worse than that," Ibrahim said. "What keeps it hovering is its investors' money and the loans they get to leverage their currency transactions and commodity speculations. The loans are short-term, but massive. Bank after bank will collapse as they discover that Relative Growth can't pay them back."

Gage thought of Batkoun Benaroun and the platinum flown out of South Africa on the Chinese planes, and imagined the same thing happening throughout the world.

"They were so powerful," Ibrahim continued, "that Minsky, with the help of the Chinese, could move the price of almost any currency or commodity or precious metal at will."

"Including platinum," Gage said.

"Of course."

Ibrahim reached for his mouse, searched his document directory, and opened a platinum price chart.

"Virtually every price movement," Ibrahim said, pointing at the dips and spikes, "was controlled by Minsky. They didn't gamble on the future price of platinum, they controlled it and leveraged everything they did with it. For every hundred million dollars of their own money they'd use, they'd borrow ten times more. If they forced the price of platinum up a hundred dollars, they'd make a thousand. If they laid out a hundred million, they'd make a billion."

Gage heard in his mind Abrams's accusations and former president Harris's defense.

"Then Relative Growth isn't a Ponzi scheme," Gage said.

"Of course not. It was foolish to think it was. But it all rests on one thing, the bonds."

"But how did they conceal that the Chinese were dumping them?"

"They set up Chinese-sounding front companies as nominal owners, as middlemen for the transfer. It's just a computer entry for the Treasury Department. There was no paper involved. It looked as though the bonds were simply moved from one Chinese hand into another. It was probably unnecessary, since no accountant would ever check." Ibrahim shook his head. "The accounting firms that Relative Growth hired certainly didn't. And they found what they expected to find: two trillion dollars of assets. What Relative Growth hid from the auditors was that their assets were somewhere in the neighborhood of three trillion, not two."

Gage thought for a moment, then it came together. "And by concealing assets that they were using as security for some of their borrowing, they concealed both their methods and their liabilities."

"Exactly. It's not that different from someone applying for a mortgage to buy a house and failing to disclose that he owns a dozen other houses, all with big mortgages."

Ibrahim spread his right hand open on the desk. "Over here we have what Relative Growth is willing to allow the world to see." He spread his left hand. "Over here, we have the secret manipulations of an offshore hedge fund." He brought them together. "In the middle is Minsky."

"Why the devil did he go along with this?"

"Because he doesn't understand it, or if he does, he thinks that Relative Growth is powerful enough to control the world—but it isn't."

"Can it be stopped?"

Ibrahim glanced at a calendar standing on the far corner of his desk, and then shook his head.

"Right now, Relative Growth needs cash to pay the dividends to its investors that are coming due. And forcing the collapse of a major currency is the fastest way to get it. Just like Soros did in England in 1992 by betting against the pound and breaking the Bank of England—except Relative Growth is wagering not just ten billion like Soros did, but a hundred billion."

"You haven't answered my question," Gage said.

Ibrahim looked again at the calendar.

"The problem is that Relative Growth uses a currency trading system that's decentralized in a thousand trading desks around the world. When they attack a currency or a commodity, no one can trace the move to them. It just looks like the whole world is moving at once and all in the same direction. And they use an algorithm that's triggered by a set of events they stage and then it operates on its own."

"What events?" Gage asked.

Ibrahim shrugged. "Only Minsky knows, but it will happen soon. The Group of Twelve has decided that it's time to kill off Relative Growth and are arranging it so that Minsky pulls the trigger himself."

"And you know this because ..."

"I designed it," Ibrahim said, then spread his arms to encompass his cell. "And have been managing it from here since I came to the States."

Ibrahim lowered his hands and gripped them together on his lap.

Gage had the sense that Ibrahim had preserved his sanity during the last few years by losing himself in the mechanics of the scheme or maybe in the aesthetics of it.

Ibrahim sighed. "It seemed so perfect, so beautiful." He looked at Gage. "Isn't that what we all expect from justice? A certain perfection? A certain cut-diamond symmetry?" He fell silent, then shook his head, and said, "People forget—I forgot—that in order to create a brilliant diamond you first have to rip apart the earth that sustains us."

Gage watched Ibrahim hunch over and seem to close in on himself, trying to shut out of his mind the chaos and violence and starvation that would follow a worldwide collapse. But Ibrahim's darting eyes and clenching fists told Gage that the man had failed.

"God help me now."

need to see you," Ibrahim spoke into the telephone. "Now. Right now. We have a problem."

Gage watched his face mutate, as if it was the expression of a slow-developing chemical reaction.

Frown.

"Tomorrow will be too late."

Jaw tightened.

"Not on the phone."

Bit lip.

"You know where."

Nod.

Ibrahim hung up. "Minsky says he'll be here in an hour."

Gage reached into his pocket for his encrypted cell phone and called Alex Z.

"I'm not sure this phone is still safe," Gage said, "so I'll e-mail you some information in a minute. Do what it says, then e-mail me back."

Gage disconnected, then used Ibrahim's computer to send Alex Z Casher's cell number and Rahmani's address.

They turned at the sound of a light knock on the door and Rahmani entered with a tray bearing two plates of lamb couscous and stuffed grape leaves.

"I take it I'm not a prisoner anymore," Gage said.

Rahmani set the tray down on the dresser, carried the plates over to the desk, and set them down.

"You knew I wasn't going to shoot you," Rahmani said. "Anyway, the truth is that one way or another, we're all prisoners. Here, everywhere." He gestured toward Ibrahim. "He calls it human gravity. We're all subject to it, but no one knows how it operates."

Gage looked at Ibrahim. "That sounds like something Milton Abrams might've said."

Ibrahim nodded. "He did, back when we were friends."

Gage pointed at the outline of the revolver in Rahmani's front pants pocket. "You really need that?"

Rahmani's face flushed.

"I got it because I handle a lot of cash at the dealership." Rahmani pulled it out and rested it in his palm. "But the thought of shooting someone makes me nauseous." He pursed his lips and shook his head. "The whole idea seems absurd, like death itself."

Gage thought of Kenyon Arndt and the fantasy role he'd planned for the videotape in the theater of his mind, and then of Rahmani, standing behind the counter in the gun store, who'd now admitted to doing the same thing.

But an armed man in the midst of that kind of existential confusion was as dangerous as a sleepwalker wielding an ax.

Gage held out his hand. Rahmani glanced at Ibrahim, who nodded. He then passed it over, more like he was abandoning it rather than surrendering it. Gage swung out the cylinder, slid out the bullets to check their condition, replaced them, snapped the gun shut, and slipped it into his jacket pocket. He then noticed that the two had been watching him as though they were spectators at a military exercise.

Rahmani sat with them as they ate, then collected their plates.

Gage's encrypted cell phone rang as Rahmani closed the door behind him. He glanced at the screen, and then said, "It's my office calling."

"It's about Faith," Alex Z said. "She's been detained by the PLA in Xinjiang, along with Ibrahim's wife. As soon as she walked into Ibadat's apartment, soldiers closed in."

Gage felt his body tense, but only nodded, as if the call was the confirmation that Alex Z had passed on the message to Casher.

"Anything else going on?" Gage asked.

"Boss, didn't you hear what I said? Oh. I get it. Somebody's listening."

"Exactly."

"They let her make some calls. She doesn't understand why, but for some reason they wanted you to know. She tried your regular cell, but it was turned off and your encrypted phone blocked her call, so she tried here. They're flying her and Ibadat from Xinjiang to Beijing right now."

"Did they say why?"

"No. But the BBC is saying that the PLA has arrested about a thousand government officials and have given the rebels a deadline to turn over the ones they hold, along with company officers."

"Give me a call if anything changes," Gage said, then disconnected.

Gage took a sip of tea, afraid to display his worry to Ibrahim, afraid that Ibrahim's loyalties would reverse again if he learned that his wife had been captured by the Chinese.

"If you don't mind my asking," Gage said, trying to anticipate Ibrahim's reaction when he found out, "why aren't you and your wife together?"

"She is a religious person and I committed the sin of theological sarcasm with the offshore tax scheme."

Gage pointed upward and said, "Rahmani told me that the whole thing started as a joke."

"It's more complicated than that," Ibrahim said.

The words echoed in Gage's mind. They were the ones he'd said to Hennessy's wife, the ones she'd quoted back to him, her husband's refusal to explain.

"I'll admit that the Manx trust was a stunt, but it was directed at the people involved, not the principle. If the West had followed Sharia finance, which prohibits making money from other money, there wouldn't have been a dot.com collapse or a mortgage crisis. There would've been investment in real production, rather than in gambling on financial derivatives."

Ibrahim cocked his head and looked away as though he was rethinking his last thought. Finally, he shook his head and said, "It's not even gambling, because in gambling you can estimate odds. You know how many spots there are on dice. You know how many suits there are in a deck of cards. These idiots risk trillions on dice whose spots keep disappearing and on cards whose face value keeps changing."

"I'm not sure that answers my question."

"From my wife's perspective, my sin was unforgivable every which way. I sinned against the faith. I made it possible for Muslim separatists to blow up innocent people. And I worked for a Chinese government that is repressing her people."

Ibrahim sighed. "I should've spent the last few years inventing a time machine, that way I could now go back and do things differently."

Gage looked toward the door as it opened. He rose as Ronald Minsky strode in. Minsky glared at Gage, and then at Ibrahim. It seemed to Gage as though in an intuitive leap Minsky grasped the meaning of the three points in the triangle they formed in the rectangular world of the room.

"So you've gone over to Abrams's side," Minsky said, his face flushing. "And sold out Relative Growth."

"But from which side did I move?" Ibrahim asked.

Minsky's eyes narrowed as he stared down at Ibrahim, but he was looking for an answer that lay somewhere in the past.

"Who do you think I've been working for?" Ibrahim asked.

Gage pointed at the chair next to the desk that he'd vacated. Minsky glanced at Gage and seemed to grasp that it was an order. He walked over and sat down.

"Tell him how you set him up," Gage said to Ibrahim.

Ibrahim looked across the corner of the desk at Minsky, his lips tight, overcoming internal resistance like a surgeon saving the life of a man who'd killed his wife.

"Let me guess what happened in the last few weeks," Ibrahim said. "They forced you to restructure Relative Growth so you could pass the audit and, more importantly, so you could conceal from the auditors how you manipulate the markets." Ibrahim lowered his head and raised his eyebrows. "Yes?"

Minsky didn't answer.

"But that left you sitting on a lot of cash that wasn't earning you anything. The Chinese then suggested that it was time to make a move on the euro. Do the same as what you did to the franc in the old days, except on a huge scale, in the scores of billions. A shock and awe attack that no one would see coming."

Gage watched Minsky half smile, unable to suppress his owner's pride.

Ibrahim grabbed his mouse and navigated to a spreadsheet, but the entries on it weren't financial. They were a list of business and financial media. The *Financial Times*, Bloomberg, CNBC, the *Wall Street Journal*, India Market Watch, and Reuters UK, and next to them falsehoods, half-truth headlines, and fact-sounding rumors and the times they'd be planted in the press:

**"STRIKE TO SHUT DOWN SOUTH AFRICAN
PLATINUM MINES"
"TERRORIST ATTACK ON RUSSIAN
GAS PIPELINE THWARTED"
"FRENCH FLOODS CAUSE LOSSES
IN THE BILLIONS,
MASSIVE SPIKE IN UNEMPLOYMENT"
"EU REVEALS $500B TRADE DEFICIT
WITH CHINA"
"GERMANY FALLS BEHIND CHINA IN EXPORTS"
"MAD COW DISEASE FOUND ON DUTCH FARM,
CATTLE INDUSTRY THREATENED"**

Gage imagined Minsky's currency trading network then engaging, starting to dump euros from a thousand different trading desks around the world, and speculators watching their monitors, then panicking and rushing to trade their euros for dollars ahead of the collapse, each sale driving the euro lower and lower.

"You think the Group of Twelve are on your side," Ibrahim said. "A strong dollar means high bond prices. You win, they win. But the truth is that they'll win, and you'll lose. The Group of Twelve will be buying the cheap euros you create."

Minsky smirked. "You don't really think that I'm going to fall into a trap and reverse our bets. It'll break Relative Growth."

Ibrahim ignored the protest.

"In a matter of hours after you begin your attack, NexCo and others will announce that they're defaulting on their loan payments. Which triggers what?"

Minsky didn't respond, but his now-fidgeting hands told Gage that he knew the answer.

"The Group of Twelve will surrender to you the treasury bonds that are securing the NexCo property and all of the rest of their assets around the world, and the loans will be paid off."

Ibrahim looked over at Gage. "See how the setup comes together? The loans on the assets were secured by the bonds, not by the land or buildings or mines. The Group of Twelve will walk away with all Relative Growth's investors' money and leave the bonds behind."

He looked back at Minsky. "But you'll say to yourself, 'That's okay, investors' rush into dollars makes the bonds worth even more than before,' but then the Group of Twelve goes public and the world learns that China has shed them all—and then there's worldwide panic. A rush to sell as bond prices collapse. Then the dollar collapses and Relative Growth is wiped out."

In Minsky's wide eyes and licking lips, Gage saw that Ibrahim was telling the truth.

"You think the Group is conspiring with you against the euro," Ibrahim said, thumping the desk, "but they're aiming to collapse the dollar you intend to stand on."

Minsky rose, wobbled, and then steadied himself against the desk. "I've got to stop—"

Thudding shoes sounded on the stairs.

Rahmani threw the door open. "The house is surrounded."

The crack of shattering wood and fracturing glass racketed down the stairwell. Minsky ran toward Rahmani, elbowed him aside, and turned up the steps as if he believed that those breaking in had come to rescue him.

Gunshots exploded.

Gage ran to the door, yanked Rahmani back into the room, then grabbed Minsky's jacket collar and pulled him backward and down to the floor. He pulled out Rahmani's gun, reached around the doorjamb, and fired up toward the kitchen. He heard a grunt, then thudding as a body tumbled down the stairs.

Gage slammed the door just before the body fell against it and then he looked back into the room.

Rahmani was kneeling over Minsky, staring at the almost bloodless hole in his chest. Minsky was dead before he'd hit the floor.

Gage glanced over at Ibrahim hunched over in his wheelchair, sobbing, his body trembling, hands covering his eyes; his mind fleeing from the invading chaos of the world.

Footsteps pounded on the floor of the kitchen and dining room above, followed by snapped orders: Freeze—On your knees—Under arrest. Followed by pleas of surrender.

In the silence that followed, a rough voice rumbled from the top of the stairs: "Gage?"

It was Mark Madison, the CIA unit leader.

Gage grabbed Rahmani's arm, pulled him to his feet, and pushed him away from the line of fire and toward Ibrahim. He then pressed himself against the wall near the door.

Gage turned the knob, pointed the revolver downward, and opened the door a few inches. He backed away as the dead man slumped backward over the threshold and to the floor.

"I'm coming down. The director is on his way."

Ten seconds later, Madison stepped into the room and over the body, then glanced down at Minsky. His eyes widened as he recognized Ibrahim, but he didn't say anything. He turned away and knelt down and searched the man lying in the doorway. He pulled out an ID case and opened it.

"You ever hear the name David J. Hicks?" Madison asked.

Gage nodded. "Davey Hicks. He's a private investigator who'd been tracking Michael Hennessy. He switched to Milton Abrams and then to me."

Madison rose. "Why's that?"

Gage pointed his shoulder at Ibrahim. "To find him before he found out the truth and to keep him from talking."

Madison reached for his radio. Gage slipped the gun into his jacket pocket.

"We're gonna need some bodies hauled out of here," Madison said. "And go around to the neighbors and cool them out." He cocked his head at the sound of rising sirens. "And the local cops, too. Make sure they understand that they don't want any part of this."

Gage pointed at Rahmani, then at the door. "Why don't you head back upstairs."

Casher appeared at the threshold ninety seconds after Rahmani left, and surveyed the room. His eyes settled on Ibrahim, now sitting numbed and mute, then he looked at Gage.

"He's not our only problem," Gage said, pointing down at Minsky.

Gage recounted to Casher what had led Minsky to grasping that he'd been set up by the Group of Twelve and to Gage realizing that only Minsky knew how to stop the automated currency attack.

"But the solution died with him," Gage said.

Casher looked upward. "I think that was the idea. We caught Wycovsky driving away. Minsky thought Wycovsky had been sent to protect him, but it was just the opposite. The Group of Twelve guessed that once you got to Ibrahim, you'd find out the truth of what they were up to, and they didn't want it to leave this room."

CHAPTER 66

V ice President Wallace sat at the head of the conference table in the situation room thinking that the two men whose judgment had guided him throughout his political career might as well be dead: President McCormack was in a coma and former president Harris would likely be implicated in a crime.

Looking across at Abrams and Casher, Wallace realized that the president trusting them more than the secretaries of treasury and state, maybe said more about him than about them, but it was irrelevant. The treasury secretary was already in Davos for the World Economic Forum and the secretary of state was in the midst of global warming treaty negotiations in Japan.

Wallace didn't want Graham Gage in the room at all, didn't understand his motives, except maybe the pressure he felt to get his wife out of China. And it made Wallace suspicious, that the route Gage had traveled to discover the scheme had taken him through one twisted mind after another: Hennessy, Ibrahim, Minsky.

In the end, he had to agree with Casher: Everyone who knew what the country was facing must stay together until a decision had been made. It was the only way to ensure that there wouldn't be a leak that would trigger the collapse. Even the Secret Service agents assigned to Wallace had been sent to the perimeters so nothing could be overheard.

Except that Gage's gaze from where he stood leaning against the paneled wall gave Wallace a chill, like a frozen wind against his bare skin, like being exposed to the elements. Gage had been deferential toward the office of the vice president only in manner, not in substance, as though he could see through the constitutional form and into the heart of Wallace's personal weaknesses and uncertainties, and as though Gage already knew how this would all end.

Wallace felt his body move toward the table, an unthinking, almost gravitational force sliding his chair closer and rolling his shoulders forward. The movement gave him a sense of having closed a circle with Casher and Abrams, but then he felt a moment of vertigo, for he knew that soon he'd have to push back again and sit up and make a decision.

"Try to make it simple," Wallace said, looking back and forth between Abrams and Casher. "And in English." He pointed across the room toward the blank wall-sized monitor, and then looked at Gage, arms folded over his chest. "We need to make sure that there will be no misunderstandings when your wife translates what we say into Mandarin for the general."

Abrams rose from his chair and walked to a whiteboard.

"I'll smooth the edges of this thing by using round numbers," Abrams said. "And go step by step."

Heads nodded.

"First, the Chinese Central Committee decided that debt levels in the U.S. had passed the point at which the principal amount of the treasury bonds they held could be paid back. In fact, they estimated that in five years the U.S. would even default on the interest payments— I'm not saying they were right or wrong. It's irrelevant at this point."

Wallace caught Abrams's eye and said, "That's where the Group of Twelve came in."

Abrams nodded. "The idea was for the Group of Twelve to use the bonds as collateral for loans they needed to buy hard assets: land, buildings, mines, forests, oil leases. The Central Committee fronted the bonds to the Group of Twelve, which used them to secure loans from Relative Growth. In effect, a trillion dollars of bonds was turned into a trillion-dollar loan, turning what they considered dead paper into live assets."

Abrams paused and looked around the room.

"Remember, it appeared in the Treasury Department records that we were still paying interest on these bonds to the Chinese government."

Abrams waited until he was certain Wallace understood, then said, "The Group paid interest on the loans as the years went along, with a balloon payment at the end, like an interest-only mortgage. When that date arrived they could either pay back the principal in cash or simply transfer the bonds over."

Wallace raised a finger to get Abrams to pause.

"Which means that if the bonds had gone up in value," Wallace said, "the Group would keep them and repay the loans to Relative Growth in cash. But if the bonds had gone down, they'd repay Relative Growth with the bonds."

"That's what Minsky thought and that's why he was willing to make the bet. But the Group had no intention of paying a trillion dollars back in cash. Their plan from the start was to surrender the bonds to Relative Growth, but only after they forced what we estimate will be an eighty percent collapse in their value."

"I don't get it," Wallace said. "What difference does it make to the Group what the bonds were worth? They're giving them up anyway."

"You've just hit on the genius of the plan," Abrams said. "The Central Committee was so focused on ridding themselves of the bonds that they agreed to be paid back in cash based on the bonds' value on the repayment date."

"And that's on Monday at 9 A.M., Hong Kong time," Casher said, "based on the evidence we've collected from Ibrahim's computer."

Wallace looked back and forth between Casher and Gage. He wished Casher had used the word "facts" instead of "evidence," for evidence only suggests, while facts tell. But that thought was swept away as Wallace's mind caught up with the implications of what Abrams was saying.

"If I understand you," Wallace said, "an eighty percent collapse means that the Group plans to pay the Chinese government only two hundred billion dollars for what was once a trillion dollars' worth of bonds?"

"Exactly.

Wallace slammed the table. "You mean these crooks are going to rip off the Chinese people for eight hundred million dollars and Relative Growth for another eight hundred million?"

Abrams nodded.

"It's worse than that. We estimate that the total losses to Relative Growth, its investors, the Chinese government, the banks, and the other hedge funds that lent money to Relative Growth will be closer to five trillion. And when it becomes clear that Relative Growth doesn't have even a fraction of what they need to pay everyone back, the entire international banking system will collapse."

"In a matter of a week," Casher said, "grocery store shelves will be empty, service stations will run out of gas, pharmacies and hospitals will run out of medicines, people will be arming themselves to protect what they have."

"What kind of monster created this thing?" Wallace asked, and then saw Gage push off from the wall. Wallace knew it was coming, for Gage had stood there like the number twelve on a clock, waiting for the second hand to arrive.

"Ibrahim," Gage said. "And we created him. Just like we created Minsky and the Group of Twelve and your pal Harris who gave them cover while they—"

Wallace threw his hands up. "Don't bring Harris into—"

"You don't think he suspected what they were up to? He didn't believe that audit for a second. He was just too much of a coward to ask the right questions and demand the truth. He just wanted to find a way to get out, leaving his reputation intact."

Wallace lowered his hands and exhaled. Gage was right. That had been Harris's message, and the real reason he wanted to extricate himself from the board of Relative Growth. And Wallace knew that he wouldn't be able to save him.

Wallace looked over at the videoconferencing monitor.

"Why don't we admit our part in this," Wallace said, "and then ask the Chinese government to arrest the Group of Twelve and seize their assets. That way no one loses anything."

"Seize their assets where?" Gage asked. "The money they stole is invested outside of China, in thousands of places. It could take a decade. And they have no control over Relative Growth or over Minsky's currency attack. Ibrahim decentralized it so that only Minsky would have a single switch to turn it off."

"If we had another twenty-four or forty-eight hours," Casher said, "time to break into Relative Growth's Cayman Island headquarters, then we could stop it." He then shrugged and shook his head. "But we don't."

r. President—"

Cooper Wallace shook his head, cutting off Reverend Manton Roberts. He leaned back on the couch in the president's study and looked over at Roberts balanced on the cushion edge.

"Please don't call me that. As long as Tom McCormack has a chance to recover, he's still the president of the United States."

Roberts raised his stubby, fat-creased hands. Wallace wasn't sure whether it was in defense or in surrender. Roberts stretched them higher, palms up, and then looked heavenward. "And I pray every moment for his recovery."

"What I need, and the reason I asked you here, is that I need you to pray with me and to give me guidance."

Roberts lowered his arms. "I'm honored."

Wallace felt the presence of Billy Graham in the room. A dozen presidents had sat where he sat now, bowing their heads as the evangelist spoke, but none of them faced the decision that he would have to make.

"But to do that will require that I disclose some matters that demand not just discretion on your part, but absolute confidentiality."

"Of course I—"

"Not so fast. At some point it may mean going to jail."

Roberts's brows furrowed. "You haven't committed a crime, have you?"

Wallace shook his head. "Not yet. It's more in the realm of state secrets, but eventually there may be—there will be—hearings about my conduct. What I knew. When I knew it. Who stood to gain. Who stood to lose."

"Maybe you should go to Congress now. Isn't there some procedure—"

"There'd be too much danger of triggering precisely what I'm trying to avoid."

Roberts shifted his body more toward Wallace, who felt the couch sag and rebound under his weight. "You're being a little too cryptic."

Wallace nodded. "According to Milton Abrams..." He watched Roberts struggle to repress a display of disgust. "We are on the verge of an attack on our economy."

"Why should you believe Abrams?"

The distain in Roberts's words made it sound to Wallace as if Roberts had asked, *Why should you believe the Jew?* For all his biblical wisdom, Wallace recognized that one of Roberts's failings was that he loved Jews only in the abstract, in the way one pities stray dogs awaiting euthanasia at the pound: precious, but doomed to the terrors of the Apocalypse. In the concrete present, in the flesh and blood and black hair and dark eyes and Semitic noses, they were unredeemed Christ killers.

"We've confirmed most of what he's saying."

"Most?"

"Most. If I knew for certain, I'd have already found a way out of this and acted on it."

"I see."

Roberts pointed at the carpet under Wallace's feet and they slid down to their knees.

"Dear Lord, please guide your servant Cooper Wallace as he faces the challenges of his office. Thou has created the great United States and it has grown according to Thy will and Thou has sent this good and courageous man to lead it. May he be as confident as a sleepwalker led by Thee through a minefield toward the Promised Land. Thou has always granted victory to those most worthy. Though we see but through the glass darkly, Thou sees all."

Roberts paused for a long moment, and then said, "Amen."

Wallace eased himself back onto the couch. Roberts pushed his hand down onto the edge of the cushion, struggling to jack his body up from the floor. He grunted as he pulled one knee up. Wallace stood and reached down a hand. Roberts accepted it and then rocked forward, leveraging himself high enough to slide onto the cushion. He leaned back and straightened his suit jacket. Wallace unbuttoned his.

"In . . . the end," Roberts said, his breathing heavy from the exertion, "all . . . we can do . . . is let the invisible hand of God . . . work through us."

Wallace gazed at the bulbous red face—one not of a holy man, but of a glutton—and felt a natal rage rising within him and an inarticulate thrashing: at himself for not listening to President McCormack, and at the sudden meaninglessness of the world, his faith, and the faith of his father, now seeming more like fog, than light.

"And if we're wrong," Wallace said, "He forces us to walk into hell on a road we've paved with our good intentions."

Roberts smiled his Sunday-morning-let-us-read-from-Scripture smile. "That's what our faith is for, to bear us forward in the face of our doubts." He raised a finger. "Yea, though I walk through the valley of the shadow of death, I will fear no evil: For thou art with me."

Wallace stared and stared and stared at Roberts until his beatific smile faded into one of awkward uncertainty, and then asked, "The question is not whether God is with me, Manton. But whether you are."

CHAPTER 68

Gage held his breath as the teleconference monitor in the situation room flashed. He had no reason to trust General Shi Rong-bang, now appearing on the screen with Faith sitting to his left. He'd already guessed what General Shi planned to do with Old Cat once he'd served his purposes, but was terrified of what Shi would do with Faith once she'd served hers.

Standing against the wall behind Wallace, Casher, and Abrams, Gage could see two sheets of paper lying on the table in front of General Shi. It was clear that he intended for them to be seen, and they all knew that the discussion would end with them.

For a moment Gage felt grateful that Ibrahim had broken down, and hoped that the catatonic world of nothingness he now occupied felt safer than the reality that would've confronted him here.

Gage watched Faith translate the introductions, her eyes staring back at him. He could feel his heart beating, and knew it was doing so in time with hers.

The official PLA translator on the opposite side of

General Shi nodded as Faith reached the end of each sentence.

General Shi sat without expression, monklike in his impassivity, his unadorned uniform sagging on his body.

Gage had listened in on the earlier discussion between Abrams on one side and the head of the Chinese Central Bank on the other and knew what both sides had come to understand about the origins of the crisis.

Except that Abrams hadn't disclosed that Minsky was dead and that his secrets about what would trigger the collapse, and how to stop it, had died with him.

"Mr. Vice President," General Shi began, "we both know that to a large extent, the resolution to this crisis rests with you." He waited for Faith to translate, and then continued. "All we have to offer is our cooperation, but there is a condition."

Wallace didn't respond.

"My single concern," Shi continued, "is with the stability of the People's Republic of China. And there is only one way to end the current troubles, short of violent suppression: punishment of those responsible for the crimes committed against the people of China. I have a much freer hand in the matter than you, for China is not a nation of laws. As long as I have the power, I'll decide what a crime is and how it will be punished. I'll decide what a contract is. I'll decide who owns what. You don't have that power. Your wrists are bound by legal handcuffs."

Shi paused, but not as though he was waiting for an answer, then said, "I used to be jealous of the American legal system, but now I see that when law and justice diverge, you are helpless to act."

Gage suspected that Shi was only jealous in the abstract. In the concrete, he'd always wanted—needed—the power.

"Assuming we come to an agreement," Shi said, "I'll use my authority to abrogate the contract between the Central Committee and the Group of Twelve. The bonds will remain in the hands of the Chinese government. That way, they will maintain their value. That act, however, will leave the Relative Growth Funds naked, with no security to back up its trillions of dollars of obligations."

Gage saw Abrams's body tense, and knew what he was thinking. The Chinese could walk away with both the bonds *and* all the assets purchased with the Relative Growth money.

Abrams cast a glance at Wallace, as if to ask whether the vice president understood the implications.

Wallace nodded without looking over.

"I think it's time for you to tell us what you want," Wallace said.

Shi held up one piece of paper in his left hand. "This is a list of our Group of Twelve." He held up the other sheet in his right hand. "This is your group of twelve, including the CEOs of your old company, Spectrum, along with that of RAID and ten others who've paid the largest bribes in China and poisoned our people."

Shi lowered his left hand and turned the sheet facedown on the table.

Gage saw Faith swallow and her eyes widen.

Shi looked over at her. "No," he said, "they haven't been executed." He looked back at Wallace. "But at the proper moment they'll be arrested. I want you to do the same with yours. And I want the Japanese and the British and the Germans and the Taiwanese to arrest the ones on the lists I've made up for them."

Shi looked at Casher and said, "I suspect that your lists and mine contain the same names."

"You're asking me to eliminate the cream of world-wide corporate leadership," Wallace said.

Shi lowered the second sheet and stared at Wallace.

"You mean the scum." Shi rose. "I'll need your answer in two hours."

The screen went dark.

Gage glanced down at his watch, but his mind still saw Faith's frightened, weary eyes.

Wallace bit his lip as he stared at Abrams, then said, "He doesn't know that without Minsky we have no hope at all of turning this thing off."

"And that if even a hint of any of this gets out," Abrams said, "currencies will begin gyrating, Minsky's algorithmic trading program will activate, and we'll go into a black hole."

Wallace raised his palm toward Abrams. "And we don't even know if all of this is real."

Gage felt a flash of rage. Backtracking and pretending it wasn't real was the way Wallace had chosen to excuse his inaction and to escape responsibility. Abrams looked back and caught Gage's eye and shook his head as if to say: *Give him time.*

Wallace stood, and said, "I need to meet with someone for a few minutes." He then walked out of the room.

"Who?" Gage asked Abrams.

"I think Manton Roberts is waiting in his office."

Gage rolled his eyes. "Not only is Wallace a coward, but he's delusional. He thinks Billy Graham is sitting in there, but it's just a lunatic."

CHAPTER 69

allace tried to focus on Manton Roberts's face as he came to the end of the story, wanting to read something in the tea leaves of the minister's eyes. But his focus kept drifting toward Roberts's fidgeting legs, his thighs squeezing together like a little boy who needed to pee.

"If what they are telling me is true," Wallace said, "the economy will contract into a black hole, a nuclear winter in which nothing will move on the streets of America."

But then he noticed Roberts's widening eyes and scissoring legs moving in tandem and realized that the thought of the world collapsing gave him a kind of sexual excitement.

Wallace watched Roberts's fists clench, like a child in the instant before fate would decide whether a wish would come true.

And Wallace grasped that Roberts wanted it. Wanted a financial earthquake, an economic Armageddon. He was already imagining himself living in the prophesy, standing on top of the biblically ordained Mount Megiddo, looking beyond a mere seizing of power, of taking control of Congress and the courts and the presidency, but of watching the final battle between the armies of Christ and the Antichrist—and reveling in it.

Roberts pushed himself to his feet. He paced the carpet, his fists pulsing. He turned back toward Wallace.

"Let it happen. You have to let it happen." Roberts stopped and closed his eyes and held his fingers to his temples. "I see it. This is the Book of Revelations come true." He opened his eyes again. "Who says that the end times have to begin only with floods and earthquakes and pestilence and disease? Why can't it begin with a crime we commit against ourselves?"

Wallace felt his body tense. "You mean let the world financial system collapse and let people starve?"

Roberts nodded. "It's God's will."

It was Wallace's turn to rise, and for the first time he felt like he was truly the president of the United States. He faced Roberts, planting himself like a statue in his path, then jabbed a forefinger into his chest.

"No, Manton. It's your will, and your will alone."

Roberts shook his head. His sagging chin and wattle swung, painting the knot of his tie with sweat. He pushed away Wallace's hand and glared into Wallace's eyes.

"Don't trivialize the Word of God into mere opinion," Roberts said. "He speaks to me. He's always spoken to me, and this is His Word."

Roberts pushed by him and mumbled as he strode toward the door.

Wallace could only make out a fragment.

"What about hands?" he asked. "What are you saying about hands?"

Roberts glanced back and said, "I said, it's now out

of your hands." He then drew his cell phone out of his jacket pocket and reached for the door handle. "In thirty seconds, the whole world will know."

Wallace ran forward, grabbed the back of Roberts's jacket, and yanked. Roberts fell back into Wallace. He tried to hold Roberts up, but his body was too heavy to control. Wallace ducked aside as Roberts lost his balance and stumbled toward the center of the room. Wallace covered his eyes as Roberts's forehead slammed against the edge of the desk, and then opened them in time to see Roberts slump to the carpet.

The door opened. Gage and Casher ran in.

Gage knelt down next to Roberts, feeling for a pulse at his wrist.

Casher's eyes darted back and forth between Wallace and Roberts, and then fixed on Wallace.

"What happened?"

"I had to—"

Gage threw his hand up toward Wallace. "Stop. Don't say anything."

"I have to tell—"

Gage reached up and grabbed Wallace's shirtfront and yanked him down onto the couch, and then pushed himself to his feet and leaned down against him.

"I told you to shut up."

Gage glanced over his shoulder and said to Casher, "Roberts has a pulse." Then back to Wallace, "If the Secret Service finds out what happened, they'll have to arrest you. And we don't have time to swear in the next in succession." Then back to Casher, "When the medics get here we'll say that Roberts fainted from the stress."

Casher nodded.

Wallace struggled under Gage's weight. "What if—"

Gage shook Wallace, glaring down at him. "Not . . . another . . . word." He looked over at Roberts, then at Casher. "Where can we put him?"

Casher pointed downward. "There's a medical facility in the subbasement."

"Once we get a doctor in here," Gage said, "lock down the White House. Nobody in. Nobody out." He looked back at Wallace. "That's what you were trying to do, right? Keep him from telling the world?"

Wallace nodded.

"Then let's get him down there before he comes to," Gage said.

Casher called the operator to send for medical help, and then ran from the room and down the hallway until he spotted a Secret Service agent and ordered him to retrieve a gurney.

Gage had guided Wallace to his desk chair by the time Casher had returned.

Gage glanced at his watch. "Everybody's waiting." He pointed at Casher. "You take him with you. I'll wait here and tell a fable."

Wallace took in a breath as if preparing to protest. Casher shook his head, then signaled for Wallace to follow him.

When Gage arrived back at the situation room, Wallace was asking Casher, "Do you have the indictments?"

Casher nodded. "And the provisional arrest warrants. You give the order and they'll be served on Swiss authorities in Davos. Their police are standing by, but they don't know why yet."

Abrams gestured toward the chair next to him and Gage sat down. Wallace looked back and forth between them. "Ibrahim?"

Gage shook his head. "Even if we could bring him out of his catatonic state, I'm not sure he knows where any of these traders are located."

"What can we do?" Wallace asked.

Bodies stirred in their seats, and pairs of hands fidgeted on the table.

"I mean, what can I do?" Wallace said. "I don't even know if all of this is true. I mean . . ."

Gage pushed himself to his feet, feeling a revulsion he'd never felt before.

Ibrahim had been broken. Hennessy was dead. Batkoun Benaroun was paralyzed. Gage had seen the look in Minsky's eyes moments before he died. And Old Cat would be getting a bullet in the back of the head. It was true. Every bit of it was true—and Faith was in the hands of General Shi.

Gage glared down at Wallace, his disgust rising like lava in his throat.

"There is only one thing you can do."

Wallace stiffened. "And what exactly is that?"

Gage pointed at the monitor as if General Shi were still visible on the screen and holding up the lists.

"Do what he wants and then stop the world."

"What . . . what do you mean, stop the world?"

Gage looked at Abrams. "You explain it to him. I'm going to get my wife."

CHAPTER 70

"This is the captain speaking."

Bodies stirred in the shadowed airplane cabin. Gage squinted at his watch. They were still four hours from Beijing, too early for the breakfast wake-up announcement.

"I need to advise you that while we will land at Beijing as scheduled, your credit and ATM cards will not function. The entire international financial network has been shut down."

Hands reached up to turn on reading lights as if they would illuminate what had been said.

"Those of you who have cash with you should have no problem. We've been advised that the crisis will soon pass and everything will return to normal within thirty-six hours."

Gage found his palms pressing against his pants pockets, filled with fifty thousand dollars' worth of yuan, euros, and dollars that Casher had delivered to him at Dulles Airport.

"The travel advisory issued by the State Department has been withdrawn as far as Beijing is concerned. The city is calm and the revolt in the Western Provinces is nearly over."

A click seemed to end the captain's communication, but then he came back on.

"We'll be routing BBC News through video channel eleven."

Gage pressed the remote, but didn't put on the headphones. He knew what the pictures and video would mean; he didn't need it explained to him. The screen showed a Forex trading monitor with the currency values unchanging. The camera drew back. Farther and farther, until it encompassed a silent trading floor. Hundreds of dealers sitting in silence.

The image switched to a video of downtown Chicago, wool-coated pedestrians staring at a television in a department store window, then to the streets of New York and San Francisco and a pub in London and a café in Paris.

Everyone was looking up at monitors showing the vice president sitting at a desk, not standing to lead the Pledge of Allegiance, their faces bearing the expressions of people just told that nuclear war had begun.

A digital clock appeared in the lower right corner, its red numbers counting the seconds toward noon.

Gage heard gasps from those sitting around him, as though the captain's announcement had been part of a dream and they'd woken up to find it matched reality, as though they were experiencing *jamais vu*: their minds still trying to deny what they knew to be true.

The camera zoomed in on Wallace's face. He glanced to his left, toward someone not visible on the screen, and nodded as 12:00 showed on the clock.

That was the moment when the world had stopped.

The screen divided as Wallace spoke. His face on the left side, a list of the world's stock and commodity exchanges on the other, the word "closed" appearing next to each name.

The image of the right side changed. A video of PLA troop carriers rolling into Chengdu and laborers and farmers walking, or riding in open-bed trucks, out of the city, returning home.

Then to Davos. The Swiss police herding dozens of suited and handcuffed men and women into buses for the ride to the airport and delivery to the Schloss Thorberg prison in Bern and later extradition to their home countries for trial. A breaking news alert flashed at the bottom of the screen: "Trading on world's stock markets and futures exchanges suspended for forty-eight hours as corporate boards replace arrested officers."

Now both images faded. Replaced by a head shot of Manton Roberts and the headlines: "Massive brain hemorrhage. Fainted at the White House during prayer." Followed by his dates of birth and death.

And Gage knew that the truth would be buried with him.

When Gage walked from the gate into the terminal, he was met by a funereal silence. The duty-free shops were open, but empty. The Starbucks was crowded with huddled Americans and Europeans. Lines extended from the windows of the currency exchanges, but the clerks just stared forward, unmoving, as if waiting for someone to tell them what yuan or dollars or euros were now worth.

Passing by a row of chairs, Gage spotted the front page of the English language *China Daily* lying on the floor.

He stopped and looked down at it. A man gazed back at him from the bed of a troop carrier, tied to a stake. Even before Gage spotted the headline bearing the man's name, he guessed it was Old Cat. Chinese characters were painted on the sign above his head. Gage didn't know what they said, but he knew what they meant: Old Cat's heroism had been reduced to mere criminality and he'd been taken to the killing fields.

A broom reached past him and swept the newspaper into a long-handled dustpan that then lifted it into a wheeled trash barrel. As Gage watched the forlorn image of Old Cat drop into the garbage, he felt like grabbing the oblivious janitor by the front of his shirt and tossing him in, too.

But he needed to save himself for another fight that would soon begin.

Gage heard thumping footsteps behind him, maybe passengers running to make a connection. Then he felt stiff cloth brush his shoulder and found himself bracketed by PLA soldiers. Without glancing over his shoulder, he knew that at least one more was behind him.

"Start walking," one of them said in English. "General Shi is waiting."

Gage saw two others poised at the opening to the long hallway leading to immigration and passport control.

With his free hand, Gage touched his pants pocket holding part of the money Casher had given him. He now understood the director's generosity: It was part of a setup to deliver him into the hands of General Shi.

But why?

Because only one person other than Casher and Wallace knew the truth about how Roberts had died and the

New York Times was just one phone call from a headline reading: "Acting U.S. President Murders Evangelical Leader."

And it wasn't that Casher had any interest in protecting Wallace. His motive was entirely patriotic, and it had made him bedfellows with General Shi.

The two soldiers opened a side door, and the five marched Gage down outdoor stairs to a jeep that then sped them across the tarmac to the rear stairs of a waiting jet. They held him in the kitchen long enough to strip him of his money, his cell phones, and his identification, and then opened the door to the main cabin.

Faith turned toward him as he stepped inside. They met halfway down the aisle. They were still in a silent embrace when a door opened and General Shi shuffled toward them from the cockpit. They separated. Shi reached out an arthritic hand. Gage left it untouched.

"The blood is too fresh," Gage said. "I saw the photo of Old Cat."

Shi lowered it and said, "I didn't expect to hear that from you." Gage was surprised to find that Shi spoke English. "From your calls that we intercepted, I imagined that you were a man who understood historical necessities. Old Cat understood and went willingly."

"That's a lie," Faith said.

Gage now looked at her full-on and saw that her eyes were bloodshot and the skin around them raw.

"He didn't resist because he didn't want others murdered in his place." Faith lowered her head. "I tried to convince him to flee, but he refused."

"His death was a condition of the Central Committee's cooperation. They couldn't risk him becoming a rallying point for further uprisings." Shi spread his hands and then looked at Gage. "People die all the time in order to preserve order."

"How can you be sure that they won't decide to make your death a condition of their future cooperation," Gage said, "or a means to withdraw it?"

Shi smiled. "Because I'm more mythological than real. Some people even doubt that I exist, and one doesn't kill a myth so easily."

"Then why didn't you try to save him?"

"There wasn't time. It was only a matter of hours before the army fragmented," Shi said. "Part of it siding with the rebels and part siding with the government. There would've been a civil war."

He then gestured toward two of the four seats around the table.

"Maybe it would've become a revolution," Gage said, after they all sat down. "Isn't that what you wanted?"

"When I was young, but now I know that it isn't possible." Shi shrugged. "I've learned that the concept itself is meaningless. Even your own revolution left everything the same for most of your people, the destitute, the slaves, and the Indians. And a revolution here would do the same, except for the million or two who would die in the process."

The plane's jet engines engaged with a low rumble and then a wail.

Shi gazed toward the airport lights, then sighed and said, "In any case, no one in China will miss a simple farmer."

Gage stared at the profile of the old man, his face paled by fluorescent lights, its lines etched deep, his withered body shelled by a uniform that no longer fit, and saw in his wet eyes that Shi would miss Old Cat as much as Faith.

Their bodies jerked as the plane began to roll toward the runway.

"Where are we going?" Gage asked, pointing toward the now whining engines.

"To complete fulfilling promises I made to your wife and to Old Cat. To your wife, I promised to send Ibadat Ibrahim to the States to care for her husband, and to send Ayi Zhao back to her home in the mountains. The garrison will protect her."

"And to Old Cat?"

"I promised to allow your wife to burn incense for him on Mount Emei Shan, near his home, for he has no family left to do it."

In a single sweeping move, the plane swung onto the runway and accelerated, and thirty seconds later it rose from the tarmac. Gage watched the lights of Beijing spread out beneath them, then contract as they turned west, toward Chengdu. When he looked back, General Shi had fallen asleep.

"The two of them weren't that different," Faith whispered. "Neither one of them had a vision for the future. They both felt helpless, as if they'd somehow lost traction in the world."

"Except that one of them had his finger on the trigger of the largest army in the world," Gage said, looking at Shi, "and history didn't pull it, he did."

Faith stared at Shi for a moment, then nodded and removed her cell phone from her pocket and held it in front of her.

"Old Cat once showed me the phone they'd given him.

He'd never touched one before the rebellion began. He told me that some children had explained to him that it had a GPS. He stared at it and said that it could tell him on what street corner he was standing, but couldn't tell him his place in the universe."

She pressed a key and the screen lit up.

"The kids also showed him how he could get news from all over the world . . ." Tears came to her eyes and her body curled forward. Gage reached his arm around her shoulders. "And he wondered aloud how anyone could bear to witness that much suffering."

They remained silent for a few moments, then she returned the phone to her pocket and said, "I think that at the end, all of existence seemed to him to be absurd and strange and alien."

"Does that mean he'd resigned himself to dying?"

Faith's eyes narrowed in thought, and then she said, "Only in the sense that wisdom teaches people to accept the inevitable."

Two hours later, Shi awoke as the plane landed at the military base northwest of Chengdu. He pointed toward the back of the plane and told them that a guide and a driver were waiting, then rose and walked into the cockpit. Seconds later, the rear door opened into daylight and the staircase ratcheted down. A soldier returned Gage's phones, money, and identification at the top of the stairs. As they arrived at the bottom, a young man climbed out of a jeep.

Faith reached for him, and they held each other's hands as she introduced Jian-jun to Gage.

They rode in silence as they skirted the western edge of the occupied city, past the ruins in the special economic zones, and then into the foothills, the road narrowing from the four lanes that had passed through crosshatched suburbs, down to two lanes, and then from pavement to dirt tracks through hillside villages.

It was clear to Gage that Jian-jun didn't trust the driver, perhaps viewing him as General Shi's spy, perhaps assuming that if he knew where Old Cat's body lay, he'd been one of those who'd buried him—and did so in a place too remote to become a shrine for the masses.

Faith shrugged when Gage cast her a questioning look.

Jian-jun sensed the movement, and then looked back from the front passenger seat and said, "Old Cat's ancestors made pilgrimages to a little monastery on the western flank." He pointed toward the driver. "He knows where it is."

Gage caught glimpses of the Emei Shan mountain range from different angles. They seemed to be circling the mountain rather than aiming toward its foot, where Buddhist pilgrims usually began their climb.

Two hours later, they ascended into mist, then through it into low clouds. The green of the pine trees faded to gray against the charcoal of the deep forest. And an hour after that, they made a long, curving turn and the road funneled into a path. The driver parked and they got out of the jeep. The cold thin air told Gage that they had ascended eight or nine thousand feet since leaving Chengdu.

The driver pointed down the path and spoke to Jian-jun in Mandarin.

"It's about a forty-minute walk," Faith told Gage, as they began the hike, Jian-jun in the lead and the soldier at the rear.

After just a few steps, the mist and shadow closed the

trail behind them, and a few steps after that monkeys revealed themselves, shrieking at the invaders and leaping from branch to branch above them. Others chattered in the distance, as though warning the rest of the troop hiding in the forest.

As they approached a wooden bridge, the crash of a waterfall drowned out the monkeys' screams, and a couple of hundred yards after they crossed the stream, the trail came to a rocky overlook. They could see an open-walled, six-sided pinewood temple, no bigger than a living room, on the opposite side of the valley. Its sweeping roof tiles were covered in moss and lichen and their upturned corners seemed to reach into the canopy of trees. And beyond it in the distance, the steep peaks of karstic mountains emerged above the mist.

It reminded Gage of looking across the Mediterranean inlet at the limestone pillar near where Michael Hennessy had come to rest, and he realized with an ache in his chest that the only kind of incense Elaine would ever burn for her husband would be in the form of suffering and rage and guilt that would continue to smolder. He felt he understood her well enough to know that convicting Wycovsky and his Chinese accomplices for his murder wouldn't extinguish her pain.

The temple was no more than a hundred yards away, but the valley cut deep into the mountain. They didn't see it again until they took a turn a half hour later and the mist and fog separated in front of them. They stopped ten yards away and through a blur of swirling incense smoke watched two monks, bundled in dark robes against the cold, meditating before the altar inside.

Beyond the temple and nestled higher up on the hillside, Gage could make out the monks' quarters, raw wood on a rough stone foundation, appearing no more substantial than a migrant shack.

The soldier waved them forward and then turned back. They waited until the thudding of his boots died away and walked to the temple steps.

The monks turned at their approach. The younger one rose and helped the older one to his feet. Both were tiny men with bald heads and soft eyes. Neither seemed surprised by the arrival of the two *gweilo*, the two white ghosts.

The old man waved Faith forward. She slipped off her shoes and into a pair of slippers and stepped inside. The younger monk handed her the last incense stick from a bamboo tube below the altar and she lit it from a candle. After fanning away the flame, she held it between her palms for a few moments, and then pressed its bare end into the sand next to the rest.

Gage removed his shoes and stepped forward and took her hand as she stared down at it, the monks now chanting, the stream of sandalwood smoke rising, interlacing and merging with those around it. He'd heard the same rumbling Sanskrit and the dark flat-toned rhythms before, meditations on dying and acceptance and nothingness, and wondered how many pilgrims had come to this place over the centuries and whether they'd received the comfort they'd sought.

The door to the monk's house scraped open. They turned toward it and looked past the trees and through the rolling mist. They expected to see a novice monk bringing more incense to the temple or a line of older monks coming toward them to pray or perhaps a pilgrim come to honor an ancestor.

Instead, a tall, unshaven man appeared in the shadowed doorway, dressed not like a monk, but in a long wool coat and cap and heavy boots, standing straight, his arms hanging by his sides. Gage heard Faith draw in a breath and felt her hand tighten around his as the man's face came into view. After gazing at her for a long moment with his deep and unblinking eyes, Old Cat nodded, and then turned away, and slipped back into the darkness.

Acknowledgments

I n addition to my wife, Liz, my first and best reader, friends made enormous efforts to try to keep me from making an idiot of myself. Denise Fleming gave the manuscript the sort of close reading only a genius could give and improved the book in ways only an artist can. Davie Sue Litov asked all the questions a writer needs to hear. Seth Norman helped me say what I meant (and thanks to his mother, Enid, for her encouragement and enthusiasm). Chris Cannon, friend and lawyer, participated as a coconspirator in crafting parts of the fictional crime. Ernie Baumgarten took walks with me that rambled in more ways than one, and during which Lulu Fleming-Baumgarten always took the lead.

In the spirit of sometimes learning the most from the worst people, this book has benefited from conversations with certain government officials, military officers, and business executives in China who provided insights into the practices of corruption that are reflected in the book, with money launderers in Hong Kong and elsewhere, with environmental polluters in the Americas and in Asia, and with snakeheads in San Francisco,

Bangkok, and Taipei who described the craft of human smuggling.

Thanks also go to my agent, Helen Zimmermann, to my editor, Carl Lennertz, and to the other publishing professionals, Pamela Spengler-Jaffee, Wendy Ho, Eileen DeWald, Barbara Peters, Shawn Nichols, Marcus Opsal and Eleanor M. Mikucki, who have been so dedicated to the success of my novels.

The quote, "Our job is to reclaim America for Christ . . ." is from Dr. James Kennedy, pastor of the Coral Ridge Presbyterian Church in Florida, and was part of a statement distributed at his "Reclaim America" Conference, in February 2005. "Seize your armor, gird it on . . ." is from the hymn "Soldiers of the Cross, Arise." "We should invade their countries . . ." is from Ann Coulter in a *National Review* article, "This is War" (September 13, 2001). "I pledge allegiance to the Christian flag . . ." is from "Theocratic Dreams" in the *National Catholic Reporter* of January 26, 2007. "We obviously are viewing an economy . . ." is a condensed version of a comment by Alan Greenspan, cited in *A Term at the Fed* by Laurence H. Meyer (Harper Business 2004, p. 47). "There was a flaw in the model . . ." is abbreviated from an Alan Greenspan interview with ABC News (http://abcnews.go.com/Business/wireStory?id=6095195). "I am a soldier . . ." can be found at the Salvation Army War College Web site. The Martin Luther quotes are from *Young Man Luther: A Study in Psychoanalysis and History* by Erik Erikson (W. W. Norton & Company, 1993, pp. 204 and 244).

The story about the balancing pole that Gage hears in Dresden is one I heard in Central Europe. Various versions were passed around the latter years of the Soviet

Union. The original author may have been Kurt Koffka in *The Principles of Gestalt Psychology* (first published in 1935, Routledge, 1999, p. 86). Another version appears in *The Language of the Third Reich: LTI—Lingua Tertii Imperii: A Philologist's Notebook* by Victor Klemperer (Continuum, 2006, p. 8).